FOLLOW
THE RIVER

FOLLOW THE RIVER

Albert Mayer

DOUBLEDAY & COMPANY, INC.
Garden City, New York
1969

Library of Congress Catalog Card Number 68–10579
Copyright © 1969 by Albert Mayer

To
Oliver L. Bardes

"Between 1787, when the Ohio Associates' contract was closed, and 1795 when 'Mad' Anthony Wayne induced the Indians of the Wabash to sign a quittance to the lands along the Ohio River, a new colony was planted in the West."

History of the American Frontier
1763–1893, by Frederic L. Paxson

BOOK ONE

---◆---

THE MOUNTAINS

Comfortable Philadelphia . . .

Of the Red City, in his *New Travels in the United States of America, Performed in 1788*, Jacques Pierre de Warville wrote:

> Philadelphia may be considered as the metropolis of the United States. It is certainly the finest town, and the best built, it is the most wealthy, though not the most luxurious. You find here more men of information, more political and literary knowledge, and more learned societies. Many towns in America are more ancient, but Philadelphia has surpassed her elders . . .

If I remember correctly, the eminent Frenchman spent a full forty-eight hours in the city of my birth in order to reach these conclusions. His well-received book became purchasable in Philadelphia during early 1790, which is when I read it. This was some fifty years ago when I, Thomas A. Morrow, was twenty-nine years old.

I have quoted the de Warville appraisal not because I consider it accurate, but because the people inhabiting the part of Philadelphia in which I moved about were convinced, with becoming modesty, that the Frenchman was a most astute observer.

It is possible to be precise and say that I read de Warville's book on May 2nd, for this was two days before I left Philadelphia on my second sabbatical. It is odd, is it not, how certain bits of trivia can remain fixed so vividly in one's mind while, over the years, more important matters have a way of becoming dim almost beyond recognition. Yet I can still see old, ever-grumbling Mr. Crocker at the Loganian Library on the day I read de Warville's book. He was tacking a statement on the entrance door announcing that, since it was now summertime, the library would be open evenings so long as there was light enough for people to read. I can still see the bench upon which I sat while reading the book and I recall how incensed I became while wondering if the Frenchman, in reaching his conclusions, had taken the time and trouble to visit Philadelphia's fish market.

At this time I was still a teacher of rhetoric, logic, and *belle lettres* at the William Penn Charter School. Being of reasonably sound mind I was fully aware how greatly a Philadelphia schoolmaster's academic reputation became enhanced if, during his sabbatical, he matriculated in a well-known European university, even if while abroad he didn't so much as look at a book. Nonetheless, after much thought, I had reached what I considered the most important decision made so far in my life. I would spend the coming year teaching at Losantiville, a settlement located almost five hundred miles down the Ohio River from Pittsburgh, one of three settlements comprising the Miami Purchase, a newly established real estate venture brought into being by Judge John Cleves Symmes of Trenton.

To this day I am not certain what actually prompted my decision. I might say that when I learned that township lots number sixteen of the recently created Territory Northwest of the River Ohio were being set aside for educational purposes, something inside of me seemed to explode. "This is a great thing!" I said to myself. "It is a wonderful thing!"

I might say also that for some time now it had been occurring to me that I was fast turning into an academic fool and that unless I removed myself temporarily from the company of people whose brains were addled as my own—there would be no hope. I might mention, too, that I wished to write a book about the Ohio Country. Yet, when I add all this to other random possible reasons—the sum total does not seem to produce an adequate explanation . . .

On the morning of my departure I was awakened by a knock on the door of my living quarters at the Indian King Inn, which is where Benjamin Franklin's Junto meetings were held, a respectable inn located on Market Street near Third. "It's time to get up, Mr. Morrow," one of the inn's lackeys called out.

Scarcely moving a muscle, I didn't open my eyes. Streaks of pain rushed through my forehead. Although I overindulged seldom, whenever I did I usually went at it whole-hog and always paid such a price. Yet on this morning, I felt contented and grateful. The previous night's *bon voyage* symposium had come as a complete surprise. Tendered by many friends as well as fellow schoolmasters, it was a rousing and most enjoyable occasion.

"It's time to get up, Mr. Morrow!"

Sighing deeply, my eyelids still feeling as if composed of tar, I nodded, then suddenly realized that the voice was feminine and that it had not come from outside the door.

"Wake up, you old sleepyhead!"

A warm, naked body snuggled up against me. "Susan!" I said. "In heaven's name, are you still here?"

"No," Susan said. "I ain't still here, it's your great-grandmother. Now I ask you! Ain't that a brilliant question to be asking?"

"I fully deserved that reply, Susan."

"You fully deserve me too," Susan said and, kicking off the covers, rolled her superbly formed body on top of me.

"Please, Susan," I said, "you're smothering me."

"My but you're grouchy this morning."

"I'm not wide awake yet to know," I said. "I'm trying to breathe. It's most difficult with your breasts clamped around my nostrils."

"Oh, all right!" Susan said. Perversely, though, she remained astride me, moving only enough to permit me to breathe normally.

"Thank you," I said.

"And I thought this would be such a nice way to say good-bye," Susan said and began pouting. Barely turned nineteen, she could still do this without the faintest suggestion of a grimace. Red haired, Susan was very pretty and knew it. Even if she weren't, her saucy smile and natural exuberance would have made her seem so. And she was quick as a whip mentally. Within two months, under my tutelage, she'd learned to read and write better than passably well.

"It would be," I said. "Unhappily, I have to board the seven o'clock coach."

The Christ Church chimes began bonging. "Count!" Susan said. "See! We've got plenty of time."

"Five o'clock . . ." I said. "I asked to be called just before six."

"I had it earlied up!"

"Susan," I said, "if there is such a thing as incarnation, you will return to this earth as a minx."

"Then you ain't mad?"

"I probably am, Susan," I said, "but not the way you mean."

II

Although it was not a secret, I had never asked Susan her last name and Susan had never gotten around to mentioning it. Yet from general conversation I knew that Susan had come to Philadelphia from Camden where, presumably, she was born. She had a younger brother who'd been hanged, in Trenton, for horse stealing. Apparently her mother, who did household chores, still resided in Camden. There was no animosity between Susan and her mother. The two simply went their own separate ways, no questions asked. The father, a blacksmith, had been killed during the War of the Rebellion, at Brandywine Springs.

I had met Susan, or rather inherited her, some six months before, around eleven o'clock at night. This was exactly two years since the death of my wife, Mary Livingston Morrow, following a miscarriage. During the afternoon I had gone with Dr. and Mrs. Livingston to the Valley Forge Cemetery to place flowers on Mary's grave. There'd been dinner afterward at the Livingstons'. This was a dreary affair and Mother Livingston had again brought up the inscription on Mary's tombstone which presently read: MARY LIVINGSTON MORROW, BORN 1764–DIED 1788.

Originally Mother Livingston had wanted a poem on the tombstone, preferably a Shakespearean ode. She had expressed this desire soon after Mary was pronounced dead, before *rigor mortis* had set in, and I had said, no, under no circumstances would there be a poem on Mary's tombstone. Mother Livingston was a short, dumpy woman who had asthma and wheezed constantly. Giving up easily was not one of her shortcomings. For a good year she hammered away on the poem and some praise, I believe, is due me for being able to hold steadfast against this determined assault. By now though Mother Livingston was prepared to settle for: "A beautiful and devoted daughter and wife, called to Heaven so early in life, sorely missed and never-to-be-forgotten by her loving parents and husband."

"Surely you don't call that a poem," Mother Livingston said.

"You are quite right," I said. "I don't."

"It is a simple and dignified statement," Mother Livingston said.

When Mother Livingston said that Dr. Livingston, who was playing solitaire in the far end of the room, cleared his throat. This represented the sum total of protest which that meek man dared elicit. Yet Dr. Livingston possessed a good mind and was well thought of in our profession. At home, he had simply given up. Occasionally I wondered what sort of a person he'd be were he not headmaster of Philadelphia's School for Boys Desirous of Attaining Excellence in the Fine Arts and Sciences, an institution of learning in which Mother Livingston's family owned a controlling financial interest.

"The tombstone looks so bare," Mother Livingston went on to say. "People will think I did not love my only child."

"We've been over and over it all many times," I said. "The matter must be considered settled."

I could see the pupils of Mother Livingston's tiny gray eyes revolving as she schemed. She would never give up and neither would I. At this time I had not yet definitely decided upon going to the Ohio Country, but if I did so decide and if, during my absence, Mother Livingston had any further material carved on Mary's tombstone, I vowed silently that I would knock down the damned tombstone and put up another.

A favorable phase of the evening was that time was on my side. At ten o'clock, exactly, the Livingstons always prepared to retire. This ritual, violated only on holidays, had been begun by Mother Livingston's great-great-grandfather and it was why, Mother Livingston believed, everybody on her side of the family lived to such ripe old ages. Thus at ten o'clock Mother Livingston stood up and so did Dr. Livingston, although he had not completed his game of solitaire.

"There is no moon. I think you should stay here overnight, in Mary's room," Mother Livingston said and felt the need to explain in complete detail a state of affairs well-known to everybody in Philadelphia: footpads abounded on the city's notoriously inadequately lighted streets.

"Thank you, no," I said. "I still have themes to grade."

Taking my leave, I walked to the Crooked Billet Inn on Wharf Street above Chestnut, hoping that my friend John Buchanan was still there, but John had just left. Ordering a mug of ale, I derived no pleasure from drinking it. A visit with the Livingstons always put me in a morose mood and this time it was worse than usual. While conversing, I had noted all too many of Mother Livingston's facial expressions and general mannerisms which strongly reminded me of Mary.

Without finishing my ale, I returned to the Indian King Inn. Thinking about my marriage, the Ohio Country, and the unsatisfactory way my life seemed to be progressing had made me nervously wide awake. Aware that sleep would be impossible unless I made myself physically weary, I began circling the block bounded by Arch, Fifth, Market, and Fourth streets, which is where as an undergraduate at the College of Philadelphia I'd taken part in student footraces.

Rounding Fourth onto Arch, I heard a woman scream, then men's laughter. "Provost's constables!" I shouted out and although it was too dark to be able to see, the sound of feet scampering over cobblestones told me the men were in full retreat.

The woman who'd screamed was Susan. Her dress was cut to shreds and when I reached her she went after me with both fists, also kicking me on the shins. "Please restrain yourself, madam," I said. "I'm the one who rescued you."

It was necessary to repeat this statement a number of times before Susan chose to believe me. "You're quite all right now, madam," I said. "I'm not certain I can say the same for myself."

"Who were those bastards?" Susan wanted to know.

"College students. Actually they weren't going to harm you," I said and explained that in the spirit of good fun certain students of the College of Philadelphia, sons of the town's best families, slept during the day at a well-known tavern on Fourth and Chestnut streets. In the evening they prowled the streets, sought out unaccompanied women, slashed their dresses with razors, and sent them on their way, unharmed, but frightened out of their wits.

"Well, I'll be damned," Susan said. "My dress and petticoats! They're ruined."

"Where are you going?" I asked. "It might be well if I accompanied you."

"I don't mind," Susan said, "if you don't mind walking all night."

"I'm afraid I don't understand."

"They need scalers at the fish market. That's where I'm going, to look for work, in the morning."

"Does that mean you have no place to go until then?"

"That's what it means, mister."

"I see . . . In that case—"

"No, you don't see, mister," Susan said, "because right now I'm not in the mood."

"You misunderstood me," I said. "I'm trying to be helpful. Are you able to wait on tables?"

"Anybody can do that."

"Apparently the proprietor of the Indian King Inn, where I live, doesn't think so. Only this morning I heard him say that he'd give his right arm for a good barmaid."

"Well, aren't you the sly one! So that's where I'm supposed to go with you!"

"Only if you feel perfectly safe in my company," I said, quite annoyed and sorry I'd assumed the role of a good Samaritan. "But I am going to the Indian King Inn. If you decide to come with me, I will introduce you to the proprietor."

"I'll come," Susan said.

On Market Street we passed a lamppost. "You're not old!" Susan exclaimed.

"May I ask what prompted that statement?"

"You talk like an old man. I thought you were fifty years old."

"How charmingly you put things," I said.

She walked with long strides, I could now see, and her hips swayed noticeably. She was quite young, I realized, shapely and surprisingly pretty.

Susan indicated her dress. "The proprietor won't hire me, looking like this."

"I'm certain he'll understand."

"Mister, you never get excited about anything, do you?"

"I do," I said, "if I have something to get excited about."

"You sure are a funny one . . ."

Six o'clock the next morning, while still in bed but marshaling the energy to arise, I heard the rattle of my door key. Within seconds Susan entered my room. In a plain housemaid's dress, her hair neatly combed, she looked demure as the smiling Mona Lisa. Her slightly freckled cheeks glowing, she held up the house key to show me how she'd gained access to my room. "Good morning, Mr. Morrow," she said.

"Good morning," I said. I still did not know her name.

Making a devilish movement with her lips, Susan removed her dress, then all other garments except her petticoats. These she began dropping to the floor, one after the other. Stark naked, her soft, slenderly made body was exquisitely formed and possessed that subtle grace one sees in statues of ancient Greek girl athletes. Stepping daintily out of the heap of petticoats: "You didn't think I looked this nice without my clothes on, did you?" she said when she reached my bed.

"No, I didn't," I said, at least part of my amazement stemming from the fact that it had never before entered my mind that an undertaking of this nature might also be pleasurable in broad daylight and before breakfast.

III

———◄◆►———

I know that if I had suggested such a pastime to Mary before our usual hearty breakfast, she would have been horrified and mortified as well. Although we were legally married I was never permitted to see Mary naked any more than, so Mary said, her father had ever seen Mother Livingston in the nude. In fact Dr. Livingston wasn't even allowed to tighten Mother Livingston's corset stays, a task which Mary let me carry out for her.

Mary had been taught that bedroom activity was a cross which women must bear, something which was necessary to produce children, who were needed to make for a full family life, and also to keep the earth from becoming a place where there were no human beings, only animals. Since Mary considered it sinful not to have children, we carried out our obligation to society with considerable frequency. Yet, I must confess, during the four years of our marriage I never quite got over the notion that I was taking advantage of my wife.

Since other young men of my acquaintance didn't seem to have such misgivings, this worried me and for some time I thought possibly it was my imagination or that something was wrong with me. I recall my surprise when John Buchanan told me he felt the same way and how, after his first performance as a husband, he was amazed to discover that his wife didn't look different.

Back in college I had always considered John as a leader when it came to conquests with the opposite sex. In our frequent discussions of the subject, it was he who spoke eloquently of his actual exploits. Like our other friends, I thought John was exaggerating, but one evening someone suggested we visit a house of ill-repute and everyone was afraid to say no. The naked hags paraded before us in that dirty tavern off Wharf Street, it seemed to me, would have made any sane man seriously consider a life of celibacy and everybody but John had cold feet. "All women are alike in the dark," John announced jauntily and went upstairs, thereby stifling all doubts as to the veracity of his earlier statements. Eventually John confessed to me that he had paid the lady double for permitting him to sit in the room with her long enough to make the rest of us think he was a hale fellow, well met.

I know that Benjamin Franklin sired many illegitimate offspring and my reading tells me that the era when I was a youth was a period during which many men of Philadelphia did not behave as if residing in the Vatican. I am, however, convinced there was a sizable group, to which I belonged, whose members were late in following the crowd, if they ever did.

I am exaggerating only slightly when I say my kind had virtually been led to believe that our parents reproduced by immaculate conception. Enlightened as my own father was, he adhered to this point of view. How I was conceived was a subject studiously avoided. Yet, somehow, I knew that young ladies must be treated with the greatest respect. At the age of twelve, I was given a sort of preliminary schooling. "Thomas," my father said, "you will spend the afternoon in the Reverend Reed's company."

There was a peculiar air of mystery about my father's manner of speaking and shortly I found out why. The Reverend Reed took me to the city morgue. "Thomas," he said, "I believe you are old enough to know that it is women who, like bitches and female cats, give birth to babies?"

"Yes, sir," I said, "I know that."

"And I assume you know something about how children are brought into this world."

"Well, no, sir," I said.

"You have not heard older boys talk?"

"Yes, sir," I said, "I have."

"You must not believe everything older boys say, Thomas, for they are prone to exaggerate."

In the morgue Reverend Reed first showed me a red dress and said young ladies would do well to be most careful about wearing seductive colors, but it had to be recognized that they frequently did. The red dress he was showing me, he said, had played its part in the tragedy whose aftermath I was about to witness.

We walked into a large room which stank of dead people. On a table lay the naked body of a young lady who, even in death, I could see was heavy with child. "She was unwed, has taken her own life, and her soul in now in Hell," Reverend Reed told me. "Thomas, I want you to look at her closely. Women are sometimes weak and very foolish. It is the duty of gentlemen to protect them from consequences such as this."

My father never, even indirectly, referred to my visit to the city morgue. It was, though, an awesome experience and surely must have influenced my thinking.

IV

Only the other day I was reading the work of a relatively unknown German philosopher, Albine Kauffmann, who made the point that the way parents bring up a child has a great deal to do with what the child will eventually become. One hardly, it seems to me, needs to be a philosopher to know this and also to know that the premise may be interpreted to explain any way the child finally turns out. However, what Kauffmann wrote reminded me that Mary, without benefit of philosophical reading, frequently said the reason I was a poor husband is because I might as well have been brought up in a pest house. "The trouble with you intellectual people," I recall her saying and on this occasion she meant her father as well as me, "is that you haven't got any sense."

While I think I would have preferred a workhouse to being reared by Mother Livingston, that is merely my opinion, and I can understand how Mary felt. The point Mary was making is that being a motherless boy, reared by an impractical father fifty years his senior, living in the Indian King Inn where no chores were required—I knew nothing about the management of a household.

My mother, whom I scarcely remember, had died when I was eight, during one of the smallpox epidemics which were the scourge of Philadelphia. My father was Robert A. Morrow, the well-known pamphleteer whose name was usually mentioned along with Anthony Benezet's as a Philadelphia pioneer in the education of young ladies and Negroes.

My parents, second cousins, were born in Edinburgh, my mother being some thirty years younger than my father. I, their only child, was born prematurely in Philadelphia the day my parents arrived in this country.

The Scottish Morrows had for generations been schoolmasters, a closely knit Presbyterian family until dissension over the singing of Watts' hymns brought about an irreparable family disruption, driving my mother and father to America.

In Philadelphia my parents founded a school for young ladies which flourished so long as my mother, who had a good business head, lived. Unable to carry the burden alone, my father sold his school at a high price, no more than a year before the influx of French schoolmasters, who, with their fancy manners, practically drove the more prosaic schools like my father's out of business.

The school sold, my father and I took up lodgings at the Indian King Inn, presumably because my father was a close friend of Benjamin Franklin's and an active member of the Junto. With ample funds on hand my father now devoted his full time to pamphleteering, an effort which brought him academic fame and considerable profit. As for profit—money as such meant nothing to my father, possibly because he never knew what it was like to be without it. I am convinced that it never occurred to him that had he not sold his school when he did, we might well have ended up in the debtors' prison. While he never investigated any of the various investments he made, Midas himself couldn't have done more to improve our financial situation. For example: merely because he had taken a fancy to Stephen Girard, my father invested an unreasonably large sum of money in what at the time was nothing more than that enterprising young man's dream of someday building up a great shipping empire.

My father was constantly dropping and losing things and his study looked as if devastated by a hurricane, but he knew where his papers and notes were amid the debris. He could not drive a nail into a board without smashing his fingers, so he never tried. Since he was the kind who never demanded of others what he couldn't do himself, my training as an artisan was sadly neglected. While it seems impossible, I am prepared to swear that from the day my father and I moved to the Indian King Inn until I married Mary Livingston and had a house of my own, I never once held a tool of any kind in my hands.

The human mind, my father was convinced, was the only important part of a man's body. No stones should be left unturned to improve it. He encouraged me to listen in at the various society meetings held at the inn and took great pride in the fact that I did so with pleasure. Enraged by the inferior manner I was being taught in the school at which I was enrolled, he took it upon himself to educate me. Every morning beginning at six, he tutored me until noon. This was quite a sacrificial undertaking since my father, while stimulated by teaching older students, was driven to distraction trying to cram knowledge into youngsters' heads. It must be remembered, too, that my father was now in his sixties and most anxious to get on with his own writings. Nonetheless our little private school went on and nothing was allowed to hinder its sessions.

If being reared in an inn is unnatural and therefore harmful, I was blissfully unaware of it. My childhood, in my opinion, was most pleasant. I can see now that I did much more reading than most young boys, but

I read what I pleased and never considered it a task. At the usual age
of thirteen I matriculated at the City College of Philadelphia or to give
its proper title: the College, Academy & Charitable School of Philadelphia
in the Province of Pennsylvania, as what is now the University of
Pennsylvania was then called.

Although the War of the Rebellion was in progress when I was graduated,
I took no part in the conflagration. Like my father, I should say I leaned
toward being a Royalist, but was not a very good one. In Philadelphia,
even while General Washington's army wintered at Valley Forge, it was
possible for people, who so desired, to live a life more or less as usual
and that, I should say, is what I desired.

Through my father's and Anthony Benezet's influence I obtained a
teaching position at the William Penn Charter School. Because this is a
Quaker school and most Quakers are against war had nothing to do with
it. We believed the William Penn Charter School was the finest institution
of learning in Philadelphia. I am most proud to have been a member
of Penn Charter's faculty and I must say this: the school's headmaster
never, even by indirection, made an effort to "convince" me, a Presbyterian,
nor did anyone else. I was not required to attend Meetings, although I
frequently did, preferring the simple Quaker services to the long-winded
sermons one became subjected to at Philadelphia's First Presbyterian Church.
Yet, while I listened most attentively at the Meetings and to the sermons
delivered at my own church, I could never become fully convinced there
was a God, although I wished ardently that I did not feel this way.

I was almost twenty-three years old when I was presented to Mary
Livingston, during May, at the season's final Dancing Assembly, or the
"Marriage Mart" as we young men used to call this social event. "Tom,"
John Buchanan, recently married and now turning into something of a
self-appointed marriage broker, said, "I bring you tidings from Mrs. Theopolis
Livingston. She wishes to congratulate you and, it must be presumed, present
you to her daughter."

We both smiled slightly, for this was not the first of such tidings which
John had delivered that evening. Although I was the same person who
had attended previous Dancing Assemblies, times had changed. Suddenly,
in the eyes of mothers with marriageable daughters, I had been promoted
from an ordinary schoolmaster's ranking into one of Philadelphia's most
promising young academic theorists.

This new and exalted position had come about as the result of having
had a widely acclaimed pamphlet published. In it I had charged Thomas
Jefferson's Ordinance of 1784 as being too complicated for prevailing trans-
Allegheny Mountain conditions, a thesis substantiated in 1789 when, as its

final contribution to the nation's welfare, the dying Continental Congress passed new and more enlightened legislation: An Ordinance Creating the Territory Northwest of the River Ohio, frequently referred to as the Great Ordinance of 1789 or simply the Northwest Ordinance.

It was my habit in those days, when aroused, to write out my anger on paper. That is why, during the course of a single evening, I wrote the pamphlet, over five thousand words in length.

Actually years of research went into what erupted out of me within a few hours. Even before entering college I had been fascinated by the Ohio Country. I had read avidly everything in print upon which I could lay my hands. That there was such a dearth of knowledge and specific fact infuriated me. Books written by supposed authorities on Ohio Indians merely called these people depraved savages, then neglected to expound upon these assertions. I am prepared to say that as late as 1790 not a single book was available in Philadelphia which would enlighten a person on this subject and that includes John Filson's work, which sold so many copies not only in America but in France as well.

My pamphlet had nothing to do with Ohio Indians. I am merely saying that I had amassed considerable academic knowledge of the Ohio Country. When I read Jefferson's ordinance, I hit the ceiling!

That my pamphlet was printed was John Buchanan's doing, for he happened to read this particular effort. "Everything you charge is so," John said.

"Of course it is," I said. "You'd think Jefferson was legislating for a town like Philadelphia. That's the trouble with us Easterners, John. When we talk about the Ohio Country, we know better, perhaps, but nonetheless we picture it as being as it is here. Do you, for example, know what the Wilderness Trail is like?"

"The way you pose the question," John said, "I'm sure I don't."

"What's your picture of it?"

"Come to think of it, I really don't know," John said. "I don't think it's Market Street or even the Boston Turnpike, of course."

"Do you think it's travelable?"

"Travelable! Surely it has to be travelable, or it wouldn't be a highway of any sort."

"Most of it's just a blazed trail," I said. "Girdled trees. Not passable for wagons."

"Well, I'll be damned," John said.

"The Ohio Country's nothing but wilderness, John," I said. "Start at Pittsburgh and go all the way down to the Falls of the Ohio where Louisville is. There are a few scattered squatter stations, but not a single *bona fide* settlement in the whole territory."

"Well, I'll be damned," John repeated. "Tom, you should be teaching history, not me. I think your article should be printed. It sounds extremely interesting. I'd say it's quite good."

"A printer has to make money on his pamphlets," I said. "This isn't a popular subject."

"It's a timely one though," John said. "I've been hearing a lot of talk about the Ohio Country lately."

While I was not convinced, John was, so strongly that he took my effort to a printer, who agreed to issue a pamphlet provided he be permitted all profits, should any ensue. To this I readily agreed. Sales eventually went into the thousands, from which I derived not one penny. What happened is that portions of the pamphlet were read in the Continental Congress by antagonists of the Jefferson measure. Angrily the Jeffersonian apologists replied, naming me by name, pointing out that being very young, I was, thus, an immature thinker. As a result of all this, I enjoyed a short reign as a public figure. Invited to read a paper before the Academy of Arts and Sciences, my position as a man of letters became irrevocably established when, at the conclusion of my reading, Benjamin Franklin stood up and voiced his approval.

My first impression of Mother Livingston was that she was one of the kindest and most gracious older women it had been my pleasure to meet. "You are to be congratulated, Mr. Morrow," she said when John Buchanan presented me. "My daughter and Dr. Livingston and I have read your pamphlet with the greatest interest."

I was, of course, presented to Mary. "Mother is telling the truth, Mr. Morrow," Mary said. "I did read your pamphlet, every word of it."

"Now, now, Mary," Mother Livingston chided ever so charmingly, at least so I thought, "you will make Mr. Morrow think that not all the other young ladies present have actually read it."

A striking brunet, Mary was an acknowledged beauty. Fairly tall and slender, she looked simply stunning that night in a pale blue, high-waisted gown which, knowing Mary, I can say, with complete assurance, was in the latest fashion.

Mary and I had an abnormal interest in clothes. In each other's as well as our own. Many a pleasant hour, after we were married, was spent discussing our attire and I might add we both went into our shells when not properly dressed. Mary had a small private income. All of it, we agreed, should go for her clothes. This is the one secret Mary kept from Mother

Livingston and it is a good thing she did for, had Mother Livingston known the truth, she would have died of apoplexy.

With a needle, Mary was simply brilliant. I don't know if it's significant, but if there was a time when Mary and I completely understood each other it was when we discussed clothes. Mary not only altered all of her dresses, but my suits as well. We had implicit confidence in each other's judgments. I remember suggesting that Mary tighten the waistline of a dress. "It will bring out the flow of your hips," I said, "and you do have extremely attractive hips."

I was stating a fact, not making a compliment. Mary studied herself in the mirror. "Yes," she said, pleased as a young girl receiving a doll. "Yes," she said and, before going for her needle and thread, surprised me with a light kiss.

Mary seldom did things like that and I yearned for these slight indications of affection. As an actress Mary would have been a complete failure, for she was self-conscious and always worried about the impression she was making. If, for example, we were at a party she'd be the epitome of charm, but would be utterly exhausted when we arrived home. For her it was work, not pleasure. I should say this attribute had a lot to do with making me think, before our marriage, that Mary was so gay and animated.

Yet when Mary tried on a new dress, all her inhibitions seemed to vanish. While discussing possible improvements, she would pirouette about the room with the natural grace of a gazelle. While altering my jackets, especially the shoulders, she would push me around, tug at this and that and appeared to be an altogether different person. Completely absorbed in the problems at hand there came over her an aura of natural competence, the charm of which she seemed totally unaware.

Although at the Dancing Assembly Mary's card was already filled, Mother Livingston saw to it room was made for me, by the simple expediency of telling others on the list that there had been a mix-up. Mary was an excellent dancer and I knew without being told that she'd been educated in a Frenchman's school because of the studied manner in which she made a point of getting me to talk about myself. The following Sunday I was invited to the Livingstons' for tea and from then on, it seems to me, I spent all my free time with Mary.

I have difficulty recalling any details of our courtship and I wish there were some way for Mary to present her side. There is no doubt I enjoyed being in Mary's company, but that doesn't mean I wanted to make her my wife. Of this much I am certain: I was not mature enough to marry Mary or anyone else. However, since I was not compelled by law or honor bound to go through with the marriage, statements like that haven't much value.

On the day of our wedding John Buchanan, our best man, drove me up Market Street to the First Presbyterian Church. "I've got some whiskey, Tom," John said. "You'd better take a nip. You look white as a ghost."

I don't doubt it. I was wishing that I could sprout wings and fly off to—anywhere. I would have given my soul, assuming I had one, to be going anywhere save where I was. "No, thank you," I said. "I don't need a drink to get married." I did make it to the altar though, calmed down considerably when the final verdict was pronounced, and vowed that I would be a good husband.

I never talked to Mary about any doubts she might have entertained. But, while I do not mean this disparagingly, I am able to say that Mary was in the market for a husband and that on sight, practically, she decided she wanted me. I still have a letter which proves this.

Possibly one year after Mary died Mother Livingston held a tea honoring Mary's aunt, Barbara Coxton of Boston, wife of a well-known surgeon.

Barbara was forty, but I must say I would never have guessed this if Mary hadn't mentioned the fact at our wedding reception and again while we were driving off to Connecticut on our wedding trip. "Did you notice that I never called her 'Aunt' Barbara?" Mary asked.

"No," I said, "I didn't."

"That's because she thinks it makes her seem older. If you call her 'Aunt' Barbara, she won't answer."

"She does have a youthful figure," I said and wondered if now that Mary and I were married I might add: "and also quite a bosom."

"She tints her hair," Mary said. "She's made quite a study of staying young. She naps every afternoon and won't go out into the sun without a bonnet. Did you notice how she smiles?"

"I don't think I noticed anything in particular."

"She smiles like a dead fish so she won't develop wrinkles."

"I thought she was quite pleasant," I said.

"Of course *you* would," Mary said. "You're a younger man."

It wasn't until the tea that I learned what Mary meant by that last statement. By way of making pleasant conversation Mother Livingston began talking about the great pains Mary suffered during the early months of her pregnancy, strongly intimating that it was my fault, so it can be imagined how I felt. I spent that night at the Livingstons'. I was already in bed when Barbara, in her nightgown, tiptoed into my room, bringing with her a bottle of claret and two glasses. "My heart went out to you, Tom," Barbara said. "Mother Livingston is a beast."

"I have become accustomed to her," I said.

"I mustn't stay long, especially like this," Barbara said, indicating her nightgown, "but I did so want to talk to you. You must not grieve too much over Mary. Life is far too short."

"I am not exactly grieving," I said. "At times though I'm sorry that I wasn't what might be called a model husband."

"I'm sure you were a perfectly wonderful husband, Tom," Barbara said. "Will it help if I tell you our dear Mary was incapable of knowing what love is? When I return to Boston I shall mail you a letter which Mary wrote me."

That settled, Barbara, before long, indicated a willingness to demonstrate what true love was like. The following morning she appeared at breakfast with her face bandaged. She had, she said, another one of her miserable toothaches. "I'm so sorry," I said to her. "You horrible man!" she whispered when the opportunity arose. "You weren't shaved! There's no skin left on my chin."

She did, though, send me the letter:

Last week [Mary had written her] I was presented to the man I intend to make my husband. You will see, I am sure, that my choice is an excellent one. He is reasonably handsome, with tar-black curly hair. Slenderly made, he stands over six feet, wears his clothes very well, and would be distinguished looking were it not for a slight tendency toward a scholar's stoop, a minor fault which I'm certain we will be able to correct without too much difficulty.

He has beautifully expressive, artistic hands. His recently published pamphlet, a copy of which I enclose, is ample evidence of the brilliance of his mind. I do wish he would write another pamphlet soon for people, as Mother has pointed out, forget quickly.

Thomas, however, says that at the moment he doesn't know what else to write about. I think he became annoyed when Mother suggested that he compose a reply to his critics, explaining that he need merely re-write the first pamphlet, thus with virtually no effort adding a second publication to his credit list.

He does though have charming manners and he is extremely well-liked by everyone and his father is a very famous man. Yet Thomas makes no effort, none whatsoever, to cultivate the proper people. But Mother says there is no real worry on this account. Although twenty-three, Thomas is very young and unworldly for his age and still overly-idealistic. Given time and proper guidance, Mother is convinced, he possesses all the qualifications necessary to go far . . .

I became engaged to Mary on Christmas Eve, one day following my father's funeral. Over the previous five years my father's health had deteriorated greatly and with it went his good disposition. All through this period we were constantly at odds, a dreadful state of affairs, for we held each other in the greatest esteem and affection.

I realize it is practically impossible to be objective in appraising the worth of one's own father. Yet, without hesitation, I humbly submit that mine contributed greatly to Philadelphia's welfare. I point out that during the five years preceding his death my father did not have a single line printed, nor did he attend any of the various society meetings in which he had been so active. Still, he was not forgotten. I am not now referring to the many illustrious citizens who came to pay their last respects. I refer to what I consider to be his greatest tribute. When the funeral procession left the First Presbyterian Church, the walks along Market Street were lined with Negroes who wept without shame as the coffin passed by.

My father's death left me prostrated with grief and remorse. I do not know what I would have done at this time if it weren't for Mary and Mother Livingston. Mary was constantly at my side; Mother Livingston relieved me of all funeral arrangement duties. "You must help Mary trim our Christmas tree, Thomas," Mother Livingston said when we left the cemetery. "At Christmastime, no one should be alone."

V

When the Christ Church chimes bonged out six times, I stirred drowsily and wiped a strand of red hair from my eyes. Beside me Susan dozed on, her cheek pressed against my neck, her left breast spread out across my chest.

For a moment I gazed at the blissful, angelic expression playing across Susan's face. Although I paid her quite liberally, I did not think of her as a mistress and we'd spent many a pleasant evening without ending up in bed. It was just as well, though, that it was now all over.

I failed in an effort to remove my arm without awakening Susan. "Oh, Tom," she said, "I wish you weren't going away—and for so long."

"We talked about that last night," I said.

"So you remember," Susan said and by that she meant that frequently, after drinking too much, I had no recollection whatsoever of what transpired. There was only this eerie feeling, telling me that I'd made a fool of myself.

"I happen to remember all of what went on last night, Susan, and I meant it when I said I was grateful."

Susan sat up suddenly and threw her arms around my neck. "Once more, Tom," she said. "Just once more."

"No," I said. "Definitely, no."

"Well, give me a big kiss anyway."

"On the forehead only," I said and left the bed. "I'm going to miss the coach."

"It's always late."

"*This* morning, I assure you, it will somehow manage to be on time. That is, if I'm not."

"Tom—"

"Please, Susan, no conversation now. I'm going to shave."

"You ain't got hot water."

"There isn't time to have it sent up."

". . . Tom, are you coming back to Philadelphia?"

"Of course." I was now putting on my breeches. "What a question to ask."

"While I was waiting on the tables last night, I heard Mr. Buchanan say he thought you were tired of being a schoolmaster."

"Well, John's mistaken."

"You're sure?"

"Of course, I'm sure," I said. I turned. Susan was sitting up in bed and looked as if she were about to cry. "Aren't you going to get dressed?" I asked.

"This is the only way you really like me," Susan said.

The coach which I boarded at Second and Market streets, in front of the courthouse, was one of the recently inaugurated Philadelphia-Pittsburgh postal service vehicles, hailed by Benjamin Franklin, Mayor Samuel Powell, and other Philadelphia luminaries as being still another beacon of progress throwing its light across the Alleghenies to our young country's new frontier: the Ohio Country. An hour late, it was filled to capacity, forcing me to ride the driver's seat. By evening we were at Lancaster, the end of the trip for everyone save me, for all the other passengers had come to the city of Amish people to watch the cockfights, illegal in the Commonwealth of Pennsylvania. I spent the night at the Lancaster Inn. Here I learned that

Pennsylvania currency was down and likely to keep on going down all the way to Pittsburgh.

Our Lancaster replacement horses were short-winded and overspent nags, old and weary as Methuselah. A full day passed, afternoon was waning fast, when we reached the last mile post east of Chambersburg. The previous morning was scarcely an hour old before I had realized that our driver, Ambrose Zimmer, was an inquisitive bore. At Lancaster I discovered him to be an out-and-out scoundrel as well. Nonetheless, the day being so divine, I had taken the driver's seat, preferring Zimmer's chatter to being cooped up in the stuffy, flea-infested coach.

We began passing corn fields, neatly painted barns, and many grazing cows. In the distance the Allegheny Mountains loomed up, defiant and formidable. Yet soft now as the Lorelei's song. It was my first view of it and I was drinking in the sight: that breathtakingly beautiful lavender haze which, at the first signs of evening, appears to erupt from the mountains' crests, spills across the horizon like water plunging over steep falls, and eventually comes to rest as a fine mist, tincturing everything below it with its delicate coloration.

"We won't be stopping off at the Chambersburg Inn, Mr. Morrow," Ambrose Zimmer said.

"Is that so?"

"It ain't part of your fare, but if you want you can go to the Chambersburg Inn and take a bath."

Zimmer, who had a snively nose and a snively voice, was a scrawny, little fellow with evasive eyes. In a manner singularly his own, he'd managed to sound both ingratiating and patronizing.

"Thank you for the advice," I said.

Chambersburg, hidden by the folds of a rolling countryside, suddenly came into view. The houses along the Lancaster Highway, mostly constructed of brick, could have been transplanted from residential Philadelphia. The Presbyterian Church, whose white steeple was turning lavender amid the descending haze, was an imposing structure. A stolid, prosperous town, I recalled having read about Chambersburg, inhabited by hard-working, God-fearing people, predominantly Presbyterians.

However the postal coach inn which we approached, off the highway, a half mile from the mall, was a log cabin which had been added to at the rear, cabin by cabin, each one successively smaller. It reminded me of a Chinese festival dragon. "Ain't too clean inside, Mr. Morrow," Zimmer said. "Maybe you'd rather spend the night at the Chambersburg Inn. Won't cost you too much."

"I'll make up my mind later," I said, "but I will go to the Chambersburg

Inn for a bath." I answered offhandedly for my attention was focused upon a young lady leaving the second wagon of a long Conestoga train which had just come to a halt before the postal coach inn. Fairly tall, wearing a dark blue redingote, she walked with becoming dignity. The cords of her bashful bonnet were not drawn. Black-haired, her complexion was extremely fair. She was, I thought, most attractive. So, apparently, did any number of the men sitting on the veranda, for they stopped talking and stared at her.

Zimmer gave his horses the whip and our coach rattled past the inn full speed ahead. "In front of the jail!" Zimmer shouted to people awaiting mail. "In front of the jail!"

"Inside of it! That's where you and your constable friends ought to be," a number of people called back. "Inside of it!"

Halfway to the jail, a stone's throw from the Lancaster Highway and the Chambersburg Inn, Zimmer permitted me to alight. "Thank you most kindly," I said while removing clean linen from my traveling trunk. I spoke coldly and Zimmer knew why.

Although the price of a Philadelphia-Chambersburg letter was less than one shilling, Pennsylvania, payable upon delivery, Zimmer was going to charge whatever he thought the traffic would bear. This, I had learned in Lancaster, was common practice amongst postal service coach drivers, who worked in close collusion with the local constables. If the price demanded was not met, the drivers tore up the letter. Should bodily harm come to a driver, the word was quickly passed along and all mail delivery stopped.

The Chambersburg Inn, constructed of brick with a brown limestone façade, was spacious and respectable. In the foyer I paused momentarily to examine a mural depicting General George Washington crossing the Delaware, the work of a local artist, a pleasing enough endeavor if one weren't too critical. I had, though, some difficulty surmising how my countrymen could have accomplished a surprise since, in the painting, a band of Hessian grenadiers, rifles poised for action, stood awaiting on the opposite bank.

The price of a warm-water bath, soap and towel included, was one shilling which I purposely attempted to pay for with a pound note, Pennsylvania. "I'm sorry, sir," the innkeeper said. "You'll have to pay in coin."

"The situation is that gloomy?"

"Yes, sir," the innkeeper said solemnly. "I have hardly enough money of any kind to make change for my paying guests. In fact money is so scarce that most local trade is being carried on by barter."

Glancing at the inn's currency sheet, I noted that two-pounds-zero-shillings-five-pence Pennsylvania bought only one-pound-twelve-shillings-five-pence Virginia, two pence off the price quoted in Lancaster. "I gather,"

I said, producing a coin, "that with each coach-wheel turn westward, my Pennsylvania will depreciate in value?"

"I'm afraid so, sir. Word coming through from Pittsburgh on Pennsylvania is not good."

"Since I have only Pennsylvania," I said drolly, "it might be good business to return to Philadelphia, buy up Virginia, and start my trip all over again."

"Any number of travelers have done so," the innkeeper said.

In the bathing shed, my mind on depreciating Pennsylvania, I knicked my chin quite deeply while shaving. This added to my annoyance—with my banker, as well as with myself for having listened to him. Before embarking on my trip I had sought out the advice of my banker, a long-time friend of my father's, a man with an enviable reputation in Philadelphia financial circles. "It might be wise," I'd said, "for me to buy up some Virginia."

"In heaven's name, Thomas! How could you possibly arrive at such a conclusion?"

"I've been reading the quotations in the newsprints," I said. "State moneys, I've noticed, seem to have more value the nearer home they are being passed around. Ohio, in many places, borders on Virginia. Since this is so, wouldn't it be prudent to buy up a bit of Virginia here in Philadelphia?"

"That would be most imprudent, Thomas."

"May I inquire *why*, sir?"

"Among other reasons, Thomas, I have just received the latest news from New York Town. The Congress is about to pass a uniform currency act, which means an increase in the value of Pennsylvania because it is the sounder money."

"About to—" I distinctly recalled having said. "It seems to me the Congress is always *about* to pass something."

"Alexander Hamilton is pushing the measure and Alexander always gets what he wants," my banker said. "Even should there be a delay, news travels fast. Word will get around in the west. Virginia will drop accordingly and so will all foreign moneys."

Although I still thought there was a certain merit to my notion, I had to presume that my banker knew more about the financial situation than I. As to his statement concerning news traveling fast in the west—before the day was out, I learned that many, *many* people in Chambersburg did not know yet that General George Washington had in January been inaugurated as President of the United States of America . . .

Now in a penny-pinching mood, I gave up any idea I might have entertained about staying at the Chambersburg Inn. A bath and clean clothes, however, always managed to buck up my spirits. It is quite possible, even probable, that nobody in Philadelphia bathed more frequently than I. As a young lad I had read about the pleasures ancient Greeks derived from daily bathing. While, at first glance, this seemed to be overdoing things, I was nonetheless entranced and it must be remembered that at the Indian King Inn warm water and soap were mine for the asking. Imagining myself a Greek Olympic athlete, I bathed daily for a week and reached the conclusion the Greeks were right. Thereafter, at least every other day I got into a tub, a practice which my father thought bordered on lunacy.

I persisted though and continued the practice during my married life, much to the annoyance of Mary who, every time we discussed household expenses, mentioned the outrageously high price of soap. She was convinced, too, that bathing would cause me to die of pneumonia, so strongly that at Mother Livingston's suggestion she took up the matter with our family doctor, who advised me to forgo this dangerous extravagance at least during the winter months.

Reaching the postal coach inn, I again saw the young lady who'd alighted from the Conestoga train. She was on the veranda, consoling a sobbing gray-haired woman, who sat on a three-legged stool. The lady's eyes, I noted, were hazel, most expressive, and I had erred slightly in thinking her hair was black; it was tinged with auburn, giving it a rich mahogany-red coloration.

Bowing and tipping my Nevernois, in a most gallant manner, I inquired if I might be of assistance. "You can shoot that damned coach driver right through his evil heart," the gray-haired woman cried out and, amid sobs, explained that Zimmer had torn up her letter when she could not meet his price.

"Being a passenger on his coach," I said, smiling my pleasantest for the young lady's benefit, "I have been tempted to do just that on any number of occasions."

"We would appreciate a glass of water," the young lady said. Her voice was well-modulated, her enunciation was excellent. If, however, she was even slightly impressed by my show of gallantry, she gave no indication of it.

"Gladly," I said, hastening to the taproom where the innkeeper, drawing mugs of spruce beer, was in no mood to stop what he was doing. Raising my voice, I demanded a glass of water and finally received service. When I returned to the veranda, the young lady was gone. "I don't know who she was," the gray-haired woman told me while drinking the water in the manner of someone who would have preferred Monongahela rye. "She come through on the train."

The Conestoga train was no longer before the inn. It was, I learned from a lackey, bound for Pittsburgh and had moved to the tethering grounds for the night. Not quite certain what was on my mind, but aware that I was quite taken by the pleasing although impersonal quality of the young lady's voice, I strolled the tethering grounds. I saw the Conestoga train, but not the young lady.

It was dusk and beginning to drizzle when I returned to the inn. On the veranda a lackey was lighting lamps which needed cleaning badly for they contained the bodies of so many singed insects that only dim, yellow rays showed through the dirty glass. The inn looked so dismal that, although the drizzle seemed to be turning into rain, I was tempted to forget that Pennsylvania was depreciating and spend the night at the Chambersburg Inn.

As I stood on the veranda, trying to reach a decision, three young boys and two old men, dirty and clad in bedraggled clothes which defied description, came trudging down the road and halted before the inn. When they did, the lollers on the veranda began whistling "Yankee Doodle Dandy" in a derisive manner. A sturdily built young man, wearing buckskins, strode through the inn's main door. Freshly shaven, queued, and well-powdered, his erect posture and crisp movements made him appear soldier-like despite his attire. When he reached the veranda steps, the whistling stopped. To the five men standing before him: "At ease," he said, an order that had already been carried out. "I'm Lieutenant Ebenezer Denny, General Harmar's aide-de-camp. Which one of you is the corporal?"

No one spoke and nothing happened until one of the older men shoved a barefooted lad forward.

"You're the corporal!" Lieutenant Denny said.

"Yes, sir," the lad muttered. He had an undersized body with a huge cranium and very dull eyes. He was no older, I judged, than fifteen. Had he rolled in mud, he couldn't have been dirtier. I could only guess that the tattered cloth covering the upper part of his torso was once a hunting shirt. His other attire consisted of a breechcloth and ragged flannel leggings.

"I understood there were to be four squads," Lieutenant Denny said.

The corporal shrugged his shoulders and the men sitting on the veranda snickered, but that ceased immediately when Lieutenant Denny turned and glared at them.

"So the rest deserted?" the lieutenant said to the corporal.

"I guess so," the corporal said.

"You guess!" Lieutenant Denny said. "Where in the hell are they? I see they stole all the rifles. Or did you sell yours and buy whiskey? Now don't tell me you weren't issued any, because I know you were."

"I didn't get no rifle," the corporal said. "Over to Carlisle when I joined up they promised me a shootin' iron, but I never got one. If I don't get a rifle, I don't have to stay joined up."

"You're a corporal," Lieutenant Denny said quickly. "You'll get a pistol when you report to Fort Pitt . . . Men, walk down the road to the jail. The sheriff will feed you and put you up for the night. Start walking at dawn. Just follow the Lancaster Highway until you get to Pittsburgh. And don't forget, you're in the United States Army. Signed up and legally sworn in! If you desert, it's treason. They've got your names at the Carlisle Arsenal. They might not catch you for a couple of years, but when they do, you'll be hanged."

Muttering under his breath, Lieutenant Denny went back into the inn.

VI

Historical Background: The Ohio Country was ceded by His Majesty's government to the United States of America, by treaty, following the War of the Rebellion.

Western migration, however, was negligible because of the Indian menace. Constant efforts of the American government to reach an understanding had met with rebuff after rebuff. As I, Thomas A. Morrow, stood on the veranda of the postal coach inn at Chambersburg, there were a few scattered squatter stations, but only two bona fide settlements in the Ohio Country: Marietta and the Miami Purchase.

On January first of the previous year, Brigadier General Josiah Harmar, at Marietta, negotiated the Treaty of Fort Harmar, which in essence said that the Indians now acknowledged the right of the white man to settle north of the Ohio River.

Great rejoicing, all along the Atlantic seaboard, followed the announcing of this treaty. In Philadelphia, for example, there were torchlight parades and the Hibernia Volunteer Fire Company marched down Market Street in full regalia. Our newsprints hailed the event. The Ohio Country, leading statesmen said, was a veritable Garden of Eden where citizens, impoverished by the War of the Rebellion, might start anew on land that was theirs practically for the asking. In New England, so frenzied were migratory plans that newsprint publishers began issuing words of caution, fearing their own areas might become depopulated.

Bit by bit, however, the true facts emerged. Instead of peace, Indian massacres were on the increase. Marietta, the Miami Purchase, and the squatter stations between Pittsburgh and the Falls pleaded for federal military protection. The Treaty of Fort Harmar was worthless. The principal Indian chiefs were not present at the conferences. Those who attended were too drunk to know what the word cession meant. Besides, Ohio Indians, while bound by promises made to other Indians, did not consider those made to white men as binding.

To further complicate the situation British agents, operating at Niagara, egging the Indians against us, could advance a most potent argument. If they were still on soil ceded by His Majesty's government to the white man, why should the Indians vacate lands which had been theirs since time immemorial?

In an effort to safeguard the lives of its Ohio Country citizens and determined to resolve the Indian problem, President George Washington and the Congress appropriated a hundred thousand dollars to finance an expedition, under command of General Harmar. Marching out of Fort Washington, located at Losantiville, it would destroy the Indian villages along the Maumee River and in the Lake Erie region. At this time the entire armed forces of the United States of America numbered only 840 men, including the artillery companies stationed at Springfield and West Point. Thus it would be necessary to recruit six hundred volunteers from Pennsylvania and another six hundred from Virginia . . .

VII

I watched the volunteers until they rounded a bend in the road. "Those fellows we just saw," I inquired of a man sitting on the veranda. "Can they possibly be the usual caliber of recruits coming through?"

"They sure can be, mister," the man replied and the others on the veranda joined in when he laughed. "Matter-of-fact, they're the best batch we've seen in quite a spell. Three came through last week—hunchbacks."

"As I understand it," I went on, "they're only enlisted for three months."

"You understand it, mister."

"Something's wrong," I said. "On July first Harmar's army is supposed to march out of Fort Washington."

"It sure is, mister, and the boys are supposed to be trained at Fort Pitt before they go down the river. Want to make a bet? I say the boys you just saw won't even be in Pittsburgh by July first."

"No, thank you," I said, "but I'll make you that same wager and give you three-to-one odds."

"I won't take it," the man said.

The rain was coming down quite heavily now. Moving into the inn, I made inquiries about sleeping accommodations. As I suspected, only the loft was available. Climbing the ladder, for an inspection before making final arrangements, I stuck my head through the loft hole. The smell of musty hay, which must have lain on the flooring for months, was nauseating. Slit-openings in the wall provided the only ventilation.

There were already two occupants—Lieutenant Ebenezer Denny and a naked young woman who lay on the flooring. The lieutenant, still standing, was removing his buckskins. "I'm delighted to find you available, Madora," I heard him say. "I'll appreciate it greatly if, later, you will let Mrs. Dwyer know that I am here."

Making a discrete and quick departure, I decided to spend the night at the Chambersburg Inn, but again changed my mind when I discovered that it was now pouring rain. Advised that supper would not be ready for at least an hour I wiled away the time on the veranda listening to a committee of Baptists from the backwoods, haggling with a circuit rider, who apparently had just arrived in town.

The circuit rider was a huge man with fiery eyes. He wanted a sound horse for his services. The beast he'd ridden into town, he admitted, was skin and bones but was a willing creature and had possibly a year of light plowing left in him. A sound horse, the circuit rider said, was all he wanted. He was not asking for any share of the collections when the "handle and poke" was passed around, nor would he expect gifts from those for whom he performed special services. In return for the sound horse he was prepared to perform all marriages, christenings, grave blessings, preach a two-hour morning service from the heart, a memorized afternoon service, as well as discuss morals with all those whom accredited officials of the settlement deemed to be sinners.

The parley was still in progress when a lackey blew the dinner horn. The taproom, also the inn's dining room, was empty upon my arrival except for Lieutenant Denny, who sat at a table beside an open hearth in which two pigs on spits were being turned by a lackey. Lonely and anxious to gain firsthand information of the state of General Harmar's army, I considered introducing myself to the lieutenant. However, while I was trying to make up my mind, Ambrose Zimmer, entering the taproom from the veranda door, made for Denny's table and sat down.

Stepping over to the bar, I ordered a glass of claret. "We ain't got nothing but crab apple wine," the barmaid said.

"That is satisfactory," I said.

"It was only made this morning," the barmaid said while filling my glass. "You won't like it."

"You're quite right," I said, after the first sip.

"Want to change to Monongahela rye? I've got some that's eight years old."

"Please."

"That's more like it, ain't it?" the barmaid said after bringing on the whiskey.

Throughout this entire conversational exchange, the barmaid did considerable bending over, showing off tremendous breasts that were sprinkled with beads of perspiration. She was a black-haired, fleshy but still shapely individual, olive-skinned, possibly partly Indian.

"The Monongahela rye is excellent," I said.

"You eating here?"

"Yes."

"It's pork tonight," the barmaid said. "The price is one shilling for dinner, for two shillings I come with the meal. You stay with me till you've had a satisfaction. If you want another, it's half a shilling for each extra time."

"I'll just have the dinner, thank you," I said.

"You want somebody younger?"

"Thank you, no," I said. "I'm afraid I'm too travel-weary this evening."

"It's your pleasure I'm thinking about, mister," the barmaid said. "Do you like your pork well done?"

"Please."

The pork was tasty and tender. For dessert an apple tart, smothered with hot buttered rum sauce, was delicious as any I had ever eaten. Finished with my meal, I ordered brandy and coffee. Filling my clay with exported tobacco, a going-away present from my colleagues at the William Penn Charter School, I moved to the hearth for a straw. Lieutenant Denny, lingering over brandy, still sat at his table and was now alone. "Mr. Thomas A. Morrow of Philadelphia?" Lieutenant Denny said pleasantly.

"You are correct, sir."

"I'm Lieutenant Ebenezer Denny, Mr. Morrow. Coach driver Zimmer told me who you were."

"I had already reached that conclusion, Lieutenant."

"Quite an ass, that fellow Zimmer, isn't he?"

"That is my first impression, sir."

"Will you be so kind as to join me?" Denny said, indicating his brandy glass.

"I'll be delighted. I have already ordered brandy."

"What pleasant-smelling tobacco," the lieutenant said. "I do not recognize the blend."

"It is a Turkish tobacco," I said. "It is rather strong, but smokes smoothly. Would you care to sample it?"

"Thank you, I will do so with relish," Lieutenant Denny said, produced his clay, tamped tobacco into it, stood up, went to the fireplace for a straw, excused himself, left the taproom, and returned shortly with paper, inkwell, and quill. "You are quite right about the tobacco, Mr. Morrow. It is strong, but smokes smoothly." Seating himself, the lieutenant brought out his pen-knife and slit the quill. "Let us get the unpleasant part of the evening over quickly as possible, sir," he said. "Zimmer has formally charged you with being a British spy. Although I have already stated that Zimmer is an ass, I am obliged to take note of the accusation."

"The accusation is utterly ridiculous!"

"I'm inclined to agree, Mr. Morrow. Will you object if I examine your luggage?"

"I will!"

Lieutenant Denny's expression clouded. Subsequently I was to learn he was only twenty-two years old. Thinning hair and the fact that he was General Harmar's aide-de-camp, I suppose, is why I at first presumed him to be somewhat older. He had an honest-looking face, with pleasing but undistinguished features. In due time I would discover that before deciding to become a career soldier, Lieutenant Denny had contemplated being a Congregational minister.

"I wish you would reconsider that statement, Mr. Morrow."

"It's a matter of my rights," I said.

Lieutenant Denny shook his head. "No, it isn't, Mr. Morrow. You've seen the broadsides announcing that British spies are roaming the Lancaster Highway, informing Niagara as to the progress of General Harmar's recruiting?"

"I noticed them."

"Governor St. Clair has declared the Lancaster Highway, from here to Pittsburgh, under martial law."

"St. Clair is governor of the Territory Northwest of the River Ohio, not of the Commonwealth of Pennsylvania," I pointed out. "Has he such authority?"

"I would say that actually he hasn't, Mr. Morrow. But he's done it."

"You may examine my traveling trunk," I said.

"And may I search you?"

"You may."

"Thank you." Lieutenant Denny wrote, permitting me to see, that he had carried out both of these requirements and had found no incriminating evidence.

"I don't understand," I said.

"Zimmer's already gone through your trunk," Denny said. "He showed me your papers."

"What!"

"I reprimanded him for going to such extremes."

"Extremes!" I said. "Martial law or not, he needs a search warrant. I can bring charges against him against such action."

"Yes, before the local magistrate," Lieutenant Denny said and continued writing. "My advice is to forget the matter . . . Have I spelled your name correctly? Will you please sign this document, under the part which says that I did not bully or beat you into agreeing to the accuracy of my statements?"

I could not help smiling. "You did not bully or beat me, Lieutenant," I said as I signed.

Lieutenant Denny smiled ever so slightly then too. "That is that, Mr. Morrow," he said. "You are fortunate I was here. Had Zimmer taken this up before the local militia, the questioning might not have been so—shall we say perfunctory."

"I can appreciate that and I thank you," I said. "May I ask how Zimmer could possibly have reached the conclusion that I might be a British spy?"

"With a five-pound reward in the offing, it pays someone like Zimmer to suspect everyone. The reason he gave me is that no one in his right mind would be going to the Ohio Country these days unless he had to."

"I did want to ask you about the general situation in Ohio," I said.

"It is very bad," the lieutenant said. "The Britishers are fools to keep on sending spies and we are fools for wasting time trying to catch them. That is what is known by everybody, especially the Indians. Our army will not be able to march out on schedule and when it does it will accomplish nothing and probably will be beaten. The Indians will not be subdued until a string of forts is erected from Fort Washington to the Great Lakes. My advice to you, Mr. Morrow, is to return to Philadelphia and go somewhere else on your sabbatical. I can think of no worse place to be than the Miami Purchase. It lies in the direct path of the Miami-Maumee trail to the Indian hunting grounds of northern Kentucky. This is frequently referred to as Slaughterhouse Road."

"Our army will be beaten?"

"Of course. You've seen a sample of our recruits. Our War Department has outdone itself in stupid behavior. The recruits are sworn in at the Carlisle Arsenal, where they are issued equipment. Then they march in squads to Fort Pitt. Is it possible to devise a more ridiculous way to recruit an army? Is it any wonder that we're getting nothing but jail sweepings and drunkards who sell their guns to British agents, who will turn our guns over to the Indians. I am surprised by only one thing. So far our War Department hasn't decided to pay the oafs we're recruiting their three-dollars-a-month in advance. Mr. Morrow, I wish you hadn't mentioned the subject, for it sickens me . . . Do you play chess?"

"A passable game."

"I would enjoy very much an hour of play," Lieutenant Denny said, adding that he could not permit himself more time for he was on his way to Fort Pitt, was leaving at the crack of dawn, and must retire early.

Our match was scarcely begun when my brandy and coffee was served by a tall, buxom, golden-haired, middle-aged woman wearing a striking black brocaded dress adorned with gold-colored roses which fit her Venus de Milo-like figure to perfection. On her a diamond necklace, made up of huge stones, did not seem gauche. Nor did the oversized sapphire on her ring. It occurred to me that I'd noticed this woman in the foyer of the Chambersburg Inn and I'd wondered who she might be. At the time I'd thought she should do something about her perfume, for I could smell it across the length of the foyer. I was still of this opinion.

When upon the lady's arrival Lieutenant Denny stood up, so did I. "Good evening, Mae," the lieutenant said, bowing graciously. "It was most kind of you to come over here. Have you had the pleasure of meeting Mr. Morrow of Philadelphia . . . Mrs. Dwyer, I am honored to present to you Mr. Thomas A. Morrow."

"Morrow . . ." Mae Dwyer said after we'd acknowledged Lieutenant Denny's introduction. "Is it possible you are related to the late Robert A. Morrow, the well-known Philadelphia pamphleteer?"

"He was my father, Mrs. Dwyer."

"I am one of your father's admirers, Mr. Morrow."

"You knew him?"

"Well, no. I did, though, read everything he wrote. Your father impressed me as being an extremely kind man."

"He was, Mrs. Dwyer," I said. "I thank you for speaking so well of him."

Lieutenant Denny said: "General Harmar sends his kindest regards, Mae.

He is most anxious to know if you will be paying him your respects at Fort Washington."

"I doubt it greatly, Ebenezer. I have considered the matter, of course. For the time being, at any rate, it does not seem feasible."

"You have no other choice, I'm compelled to admit," Lieutenant Denny said. "I'm just back from Philadelphia and New York Town. Nothing has changed. We must simply go on with the recruiting as best we can. The General will be greatly disappointed to hear of your decision."

"The General will understand, I trust."

"I'm sure that he will."

Mrs. Dwyer took her leave. While contemplating his next move, Denny said: "You have never, I seem to gather, heard of Mrs. Mae Dwyer?"

"No, I have not," I said.

"Coming from Philadelphia, I am mildly surprised that you shouldn't have."

"Some forty thousand people live in Philadelphia, Lieutenant."

"You are not familiar with the Golden Eagle Inn?"

"I know, of course, that it is on Wharf Street and is a well-known house of ill-repute. It so happens that the course of my life has never taken me there."

"Mrs. Dwyer is its owner. A rather remarkable woman. She owns any number of inns between Philadelphia and Pittsburgh and has just purchased this one. She was born in Holland, of an excellent family, whom she disgraced and was banished to America. Whether she is actually *Mrs.* Dwyer is a moot question. No one has seen or heard of a *Mr.* Dwyer . . . Were you able to follow my conversation with her?"

"Not while it was transpiring," I said. "Now, I am assuming that Mrs. Dwyer had been considering supplying General Harmar's army with women."

"That is correct," Lieutenant Denny said, "and her decision not to should be regarded as still another indication of the deplorable state of our army. I am, however, surprised that being a resident of Philadelphia you are not aware that Mrs. Dwyer performed a similar service for both the British and American military quartered in Philadelphia during the War of the Rebellion. Surely you have heard the ditty being sung everywhere, it seems to me, about: 'Come what may, there is always Mae'?"

"Yes, I've heard that ditty."

"May I inquire what you thought it was all about?"

"If I thought about it at all," I said, "I would imagine I assumed *Mae* was the month of May, the coming of spring, which to poets means winter is over."

"I can see how you could think that, Mr. Morrow," Lieutenant Denny said and made his move.

The young officer played excellent offensive chess, reaching his decisions very quickly. Being a fairly sound defensive player, I managed to hold him off. When the hour was up, the match remained still undetermined.

"Thank you most kindly, Mr. Morrow," Lieutenant Denny said and stood up. "I should say before too long I would have had you."

"I think I'm inclined to agree," I said. "Once or twice I was more fortunate than wise."

"Yes," the lieutenant said, "you were, but you gave a sound performance. I will remember how the board stood. If I'm at Fort Pitt when you arrive, we can finish the match."

"I should enjoy that," I said.

Lieutenant Denny offered me his hand. "It was a pleasure meeting you, Mr. Morrow. Despite my desire to finish this match, I hope you will consider my advice and return to Philadelphia."

"I am at least going to Pittsburgh," I said.

"I have given you excellent advice, Mr. Morrow," Lieutenant Denny said and left.

The rain, I could hear, was coming down harder and there was thunder and lightning. Ordering a cup of coffee, I contemplated Lieutenant Denny's advice. I was going to Losantiville, come what may. That much was that. During the days which followed, I never wavered on this determination. There were times, though, when my common sense fairly shrieked that I was behaving like a fool—and this was one of those times.

Eventually the barmaid asked me if I wanted anything else. "No, thank you," I said.

"I'll close up then," she said.

A bear rug lying before the fireplace looked far more inviting than the ill-smelling loft. "Is it all right if I sleep on the rug?" I asked the barmaid. "It sure is, mister," she said and began extinguishing the lamps.

I slept fitfully. Although I seldom dream, that night I had a wild one. Ambrose Zimmer, laughing and taunting me, was driving off, leaving me stranded in Chambersburg. I mention this merely because it is a fact. I do not place any significance upon it. Yet, the gist of the dream came true. Arising at dawn, I ate an excellent ham and egg breakfast, then moved out to the inn's veranda into a morning that indicated a clear day. Beside the door I saw what looked like my traveling trunk. Examination proved it to be. Ambrose Zimmer, having no new passengers and with no mail to go west, had simply turned around and gone back to Philadelphia. This sort of thing happened all too frequently, I was told. No one had the faintest idea when another postal coach was due or whether, when one did arrive, it would be going to Pittsburgh.

There is no point in elaborating on my anger. Around noon, while I was still telling everyone who would listen how outrageously unjust it all was, a tall, bald-headed man of about sixty, wearing buckskins, came up to me. His name, he said, was Abner Wilson. His twelve-wagon Conestoga train, loaded with flour and beef, was leaving for Fort Pitt in the morning.

"You can ride with me," Abner Wilson said. "Help out and it won't cost you anything. If a postal coach overtakes us, you can board her, but I don't think one will."

"I don't know anything at all about wagons," I said. "Not too much about horses."

"All you need is a little common sense."

"I don't have too much of that either," I said. "May I consider your offer?"

"Sure," Abner Wilson said. "If you decide, yes, be here at five tomorrow morning. Are those the only kind of clothes you have?"

"Yes."

"Buy yourself some buckskins," he said. "Get them at Abraham's General Store." After a moment's hesitation, he added: "Not that I think Abe would cheat you, but you'd better let him know who you're working for."

VIII

Five o'clock the following morning, wearing buckskins treated with bear oil to make them waterproof, I left Chambersburg, riding the van wagon of Abner Wilson's Conestoga train. Though no other means of transportation was available to me, I had, as a precautionary measure, gone to the pastor of the Presbyterian Church for advice. Abner Wilson, I was assured, was trustworthy. A lifelong resident of Chambersburg, he was a pillar of the Presbyterian Church. Twice a widower, he was the father of nineteen children, all girls. His present wife, aged no more than seventeen, was pregnant and Abner hoped ardently that at long last the good Lord would permit him to sire a son.

One day out of Chambersburg torrential rains struck us, muddying the highway and flooding the Juniata, a meandering stream which we had to cross many times, raft-ferrying the wagons on each occasion.

The rains held until we reached Bedford, where the Lancaster Highway divides into the Old Forbes and Glade roads, which unite some twenty-eight miles before Pittsburgh.

We'd taken the Glade Road. Approximately three weeks out of Chambersburg, at a time when, according to my carefully calculated itinerary, I should have been aboard a flatboat no more than a few days above Losantiville, we were thirty miles east of Pittsburgh, rumbling over a fairly level stretch of terrain.

Ahead was a rather steep rise. After that, so Abner Wilson had told me, came a drop, then another rise. About two miles in all. This would bring us to a settlement which Abner referred to as Old Forbes Crossing. As I understand it, had we been traveling the Old Forbes Road, the settlement's name would have been Glade Crossing.

I was still riding the van wagon, which Abner Wilson drove. Here, as had been the case for days, giant trees flanked both sides of the highway. Standing trunk-to-trunk, close enough to form a tolerable stockade, they blotted out a panoramic view of the mountains and a vast expanse of virgin wilderness which by its very nature made an inspiring sight. Ahead the dirt road, hardly a wagon-wide, wove on and on and looked out of place in the deep woods, like an elongated scar of which Mother Nature was ashamed.

It was midafternoon, the dreariest time of day. West of Bedford there'd been no rain and on this humid afternoon a two-inch carpet of dust covered the highway, which the horses were methodically clopping up into my nostrils, like so many explosions from a barker. If there was a comfortable spot on the wagon seat, I had yet to discover it. "It will be a relief to see an inn," I said.

Nodding, Abner pointed to a run of dried bear wallows, axle-deep, potting the road, looking like the craters of miniature volcanoes. Without being told, I jumped from the wagon to guard the wheels. "Bear wallows!" I yelled out and behind me teamsters began emerging from the wagons, like so many jack-in-the-boxes.

Moments later the driver of wagon number six came to the van. "Left rear wheel," he said to Abner.

"How bad?"

"She's ready to cave in. The axle's bent."

"Damn!" Abner said and looked up at the sky, which showed a slight tinge of purple. Jumping to the ground, he piped a halt.

"How long will we be held up?" I asked.

"An hour," Abner said. "Do you mind, Tom? Walk up to the rise and see if there's any sign of Morgan and the packhorses."

"Mr. Morrow won't see any sign of Morgan, Pop," the driver, who was one of Abner's many sons-in-law, said. "That bastard's already at the inn by now, guzzling spruce beer."

"He'd better not be," Abner said grimly.

"You shouldn't have hired him, Pop. You know damned well he's a Harmar deserter and so are his helpers."

"You've been saying that almost daily, William," Abner replied patiently. "I was stuck for a packhorse master and there's nothing we can do about it now."

I'd started off. "Tom," Abner called after me, "when you get to the rise, on your right, there's a lane. It leads to a settlement. Take a look. You can see for yourself what we were talking about this morning."

Welcoming an opportunity to stretch my legs, I moved ahead rapidly. Actually all I knew about packhorse master Jonathan Morgan was that he was a rough-looking fellow with a shaggy brown beard. I'd caught a brief glimpse of him in Chambersburg when he and his five helpers started the twenty-four packhorses on their way, an hour ahead of the wagons.

Abner's own packhorses, in charge of sons-in-law, were already en route to Pittsburgh. An urgent order from Fort Pitt for salt and iron had come through, hence the need to hire horses and a master. Under strict orders never to be more than a rise ahead of the train Morgan, Abner strongly suspected, was racing the packhorses down the long drops, when he couldn't be seen, thus giving him and his men an opportunity to loll and play cards on the far side of the rise.

Reaching my destination, as I had expected, I saw only a steep drop, then a long rise. Since an inn was at the end of this day's trek, I shuddered while thinking of the ordeal Morgan must have put the packhorses through.

The lane Abner had mentioned was the bank of a brook, along which the trees had been girdled. Walking over it, however, was rather pleasant for it was refreshingly cool within the woods and the smell of moss was sweet. The settlement consisted of some two dozen one-room log cabins, circled about a stump-covered clearing, which was crisscrossed with footprints where people had become accustomed to walking. The whole was completely surrounded by a solid wall of trees. Because of this I had come upon the settlement with such sudden abruptness that I was actually startled.

This was what Abner had suggested I take notice of. Like Lieutenant Denny, Abner had urgently advised me to return to Philadelphia. "Tom," he'd said, "you Easterners just don't understand it. Out in the Ohio Country, the Indians have got millions of friends: the trees. The trees hide them when they sneak up on a settlement and they hide them again, after they've struck and are getting away."

Apparently the settlement's menfolks were still at their outlots, planting. Only women and children were present, congregated off the far end of the clearing, near a small stockade where fires were burning beneath four large copper kettles.

Everyone moved about with purposeful efficiency. The young boys were busily engaged feeding the fires and the women were skimming and stirring. Even the small tots had something to do. Under supervision of an elderly lady, who was churning butter, they were engrossed in the project of building houses with corn cobs.

Although I had never before seen soap made by community effort, in fact had never seen it made by anyone, the stench which permeated the entire clearing told me what was taking place. To the rear of the kettles, set on platforms, were a number of barrels in which lye was being made from straw and wood ashes. From behind these came a young boy of about nine, dutifully followed by a fairly young lady. The distance between the two never varied, which struck me as being rather odd, until the pair came closer and I saw the reason why: the young lady had a horse's halter about her neck and the boy was leading her with a rope.

The young lady, barefooted, walked with the caution of someone unaccustomed to being without shoes. She wore a gray linsey-woolsey dress, ill-fitting as a sack. I could not see her face and not much of her hair, for she'd been splattered from head to foot with mud, most of which was now dried.

Despite this masquerade there was a certain litheness of body movement which seemed familiar. "Impossible!" I thought. "This can't be that young lady I saw in Chambersburg." Then the young lady began speaking and I realized it was she.

"My name is Melissa Andrews," she said wearily. "Yesterday my father, Bushrod Andrews of Trenton, was convicted of criminal conniving. He has repaid his theft threefold times and in order to spare him the thirty-nine lashes he legally deserves, I have chosen to publicly announce our shame and degradation in his stead before the Lord and all the God-fearing people of this community."

Finished reciting the words required by law, her drooping shoulders indicating her resignation, Melissa Andrews faced me and it dawned upon me that, in buckskins and with a two-week-old beard, my masquerade was as complete as hers. The boy, a freckled-faced towhead with a compelling grin, said: "You're a stranger, ain't you, mister?"

"Yes," I said, "I am."

The boy's grin broadened and as his countenance took on an expression innocent as a cherub's, my schoolmaster's instincts told me that here stood one of those lovable imps who is capable of disrupting an entire classroom without disturbing the halo constantly hovering above his head. "You know what you're supposed to do to Miss Andrews, don't you?" the boy asked.

"I presume," I said, "that you mean I'm supposed to throw wet mud on Miss Andrews and that the laws of the Commonwealth of Pennsylvania also permit and encourage me to call her any vile name which enters my head?"

"Well, go ahead," the boy said.

"If you have no objections," I said, "I'll forgo the pleasure."

The boy, I could sense, was sizing me up. "Mister," he inquired cagily, "you ain't a great big squealer, are you?"

"Joseph!" Melissa Andrews cried out.

"No, Joseph," I said, "I'm not a squealer. I gather you want to do something."

"All I want—" Joseph said, but before he could continue Melissa Andrews pulled him to her and placed her hand over his mouth.

"Miss Andrews," I said, "rest assured you may trust me not to—squeal." Introducing myself, I quickly told her of our brief meeting in Chambersburg and how I happened to be where I was. Her hand stayed over Joseph's mouth. "I recognize that you should be concerned for Joseph's welfare, Miss Andrews," I added, "and know only too well that the law prescribes ten stripes to children, slaves, or servants who are disobedient. Believe me, I am not trying to trick either of you into further punishment."

"I remember you," she said quietly and removed her hand from Joseph's mouth."

"All I want," Joseph said, "is to get Miss Andrews some water. She ain't had a drink since sunrise."

"It might be safer if I did it," I said. "Where do I get the water and what in?"

"Right behind yonder trees," Joseph said. "That's the dump. You'll find a broken teacup or something." Whispering in my ear, he admonished: "Don't take water from the brook, mister. It gives you the vomits. Find a rotted tree trunk with rain water in it. Plenty are back there."

Moving behind the trees, I smelled lant and realized the dump was also the settlement's latrine, probably its principal one. Locating a cracked cup, I followed Joseph's instructions, returned to the clearing, and cautioned Melissa Andrews to drink with her back to the settlement. "Thank you, Mr. Morrow," she said after gulping down the water.

"May I get you another cup?"

"This is sufficient, thank you."

"I'll refill the cup," I said, "and place it behind the trees."

"Thank you, you are being most thoughtful."

Returning, I said: "I have time. If you're hungry, I can get you a bit of food."

"Thank you, but I shall survive. Fortunately my ordeal ends at sundown."

"May I inquire how it came about?"

Her eyes lighted up and for the first time, despite the mask of mud, her expression showed animation. She seemed faintly amused at the manner in which I had put my question. "That depends upon whose side of the story you wish to hear."

"I should like to hear yours," I said.

"Mine is that—my father was cheated. Yesterday our Conestoga train was passing through. While we halted to rest the horses, a man from this settlement, named Benoni Benjamin, walked up to our wagon, struck up a conversation with my father, and learned that we were going down the Ohio River. Eventually the conversation moved to money and when my father bemoaned the fact that he was carrying Pennsylvania, this Benoni Benjamin said he could arrange an exchange and my father agreed to pay a reasonable commission. I heard every word of the transaction, Mr. Morrow. It was to be an exchange of Pennsylvania for Virginia, but when the time came to consummate the agreement Benoni Benjamin produced no Virginia. Instead, he offered indents."

"Indents!"

"An indent," Melissa Andrews explained, "is the paper money issued by the government after the War of the Rebellion, to pay the soldiers' wages."

"I know what indents are," I said. "I was registering surprise."

"Well, I'd never heard of them before," Melissa Andrews said, "but, of course, my father knew that to him, they were valueless. When he refused to accept such money, Benoni Benjamin insisted that indents are legal tender."

"They are," I said, "but only in payment of debts. Your father wasn't obligated to—"

"Of course he wasn't," Melissa Andrews said, "nonetheless Benoni Benjamin had my father hauled before three local citizens who acted as judges and jury. They decreed that since my father had made a bargain, he was actually in debt and must accept the indents at their face value."

"Preposterous!"

"Not to my father and me," Melissa Andrews said. "My father was accounted guilty. He had to pay threefold and it took all my persuasive powers to convince these rogues that I should be permitted to walk about the settlement with this horse's halter about my neck in the place of my father, who is a sick man."

"You have no redress?"

"Redress!" Melissa Andrews said bitterly. "Yes, we may appeal our case before a circuit judge at Pittsburgh when he arrives within some three months or longer from now. I see clearly now why Benoni Benjamin, while talking to my father, made a point of ascertaining that we were going down the Ohio River. Certainly we can't wait three months for a circuit judge. That made us perfect dupes for him."

"Your Conestoga train has, of course, gone on?"

"Yes."

"How will you and your father get to Pittsburgh?"

"My father is by now at the Old Forbes Crossing Inn awaiting me. We'll hire a chaise and catch up with our train."

"You're here—alone!"

"The experience aggravated my father's illness. I insisted that he go on with the train."

"How do you expect to get to the crossing settlement?"

"I shall walk. It is no more than two miles."

"Alone! After sundown?"

"Joseph's parents have been kind enough to allow me to spend the night with them. I will leave at dawn tomorrow."

"I can't let you do that," I said. "Harmar's recruits—"

The recruits, the few of them coming through, were causing more trouble than enemies. Stopping off at homes, they were demanding food, slaughtering cattle if they didn't get it. They were robbing, plundering, and raping. Because they were needed so desperately, the military was closing its eyes.

"I certainly don't relish the prospect," Melissa Andrews said, "but I don't know of any other way of getting to the crossing."

If I stayed overnight and accompanied her, I would be of no help if we ran into a squad of drunken recruits. While talking we'd been moving slowly in the direction of the lane over which I had just walked. "There is another way, Miss Andrews," I suddenly heard myself saying. "You could ride there on our Conestoga train."

Stopping, Melissa Andrews looked at me as if she hadn't heard me correctly. "You mean—your train will wait until sundown and travel this rough road after dark?"

"No," I said, "come with me right now." I will never know what prompted my proposal. I knew only that, come what may, Melissa Andrews was not going to walk the Glade Road. "My suggestion is quite sound," I continued and built up sustaining arguments as I talked on. "We'll merely walk up the lane. The very simplicity of it will insure success. With no men about, we won't be pursued, even if our departure is noticed, which I doubt. Furthermore, I should say this parading about with a horse's halter around your neck is just so much sauce for the gander anyway. These thieves have your money, which is all they care about. They're wrong and know it. They would be fools, to pursue the matter further."

By the time I was finished talking, I believed implicitly in the feasibility of the plan I was suggesting. The exigencies of the situation had blotted out any thoughts I might have entertained of possible failure. It is quite likely Melissa Andrews was swayed by the conviction in my voice. "But Joseph—" she faltered. "What might they do to him?"

"Nothing!" Joseph blurted out staunchly.

"Oh, my darling Joseph!" Melissa Andrews said. "You don't realize what you're saying."

"I do so!" Joseph said. "My father won't let them lay a whip to me. Miss Andrews, the man's talking sense and a lot of people around here will be tickled pink that you outsmarted those crooks . . . I'll run up the lane ahead of you, to make sure nobody's coming from his outlot."

Without awaiting the words of assent from his elders, Joseph took off.

IX

Goaded into action by what Joseph had done, Melissa Andrews and I started up the lane. Neither of us, surely, could have been thinking too calmly, for we were halfway to the highway before I noticed that Melissa still had on the horse's halter. "Hide it behind the trees," I said and gestured toward the brook. "It might be wise if you washed your face."

"Yes," Melissa muttered and disappeared behind the trees.

She stayed there so long that eventually I called: "Are you all right?"

"I'm trying to get some of the mud off my dress!"

Joseph came running down the lane. "Two men are coming this way," he stage-whispered.

Joseph and I moved behind the trees. As we did, Melissa returned and I bumped into her. Although there were trees galore, Melissa and I, arms wrapped about each other, huddled behind an enormous oak.

Shortly I heard the two men's voices, indistinct at first, then: "There's only one thing to do and that's shoot him."

"I suppose so," the second voice said.

These assertions brought me close to a state of panic, but only momentarily, for the men didn't mean me. They were talking about a tame raccoon belonging to a son of one of the men. "I hate to do it," the first voice went on to say. "He's a cute little rascal and he sure likes frogs. Damned if I ever saw anything like the way he can catch 'em."

"My boy had one too, so I know how you feel," the second voice said, "but I had to get rid of ours because he was forever robbing my hen-roost."

That "crisis" past, we immediately became confronted with another. When the two men were directly opposite us, I felt Melissa tugging at my shirt. Her face, colorless with terror, she indicated with her eyes that I should look downward. When I did I saw a large brown and white snake lying no more than five inches off from my left foot. Silently coiled amongst dried leaves, leering, it was preparing to strike.

Acting with dispatch, I stamped my foot on the snake's head. Some divine power, so I've heard, protects drunkards and ignoramuses. Included amongst the latter, high up on the list, is the name: Thomas A. Morrow of Philadelphia. When the rest of the reptile began squirming amongst the dried leaves, to quiet the noise, I planted my other foot on the rear end. "Get a rock, Joseph," I said when the two men were beyond hearing distance, "and smash its head."

"That's a copperhead, mister," Joseph said, staring with blank amazement at my bare left ankle, plainly visible, for I was wearing pacs, stuffed with leaves to prevent rubbing.

"Copperheads are poisonous!" I said.

"They sure are, mister," Joseph said, "I guess you took this one by surprise." Breaking off a pronged twig, he V-pinioned the snake's head to the ground, picked up the reptile properly by the tail, allowed it to bite itself out of pure spite, then smashed its head against the tree trunk.

Again acting as our van guard, Joseph moved off. This time Melissa and I reached the highway without further incident. Joseph awaited us. "Everything's clear," he said, "but you'd better walk to the train behind cover of the trees."

Taking Joseph in her arms, Melissa kissed him and told him she'd send him a present from Pittsburgh. I shook his hand warmly. Following Joseph's advice, we moved over the highway behind cover of the trees, reaching the train's van wagon just as Abner Wilson came up from the rear.

"See Morgan?" Abner asked and scowled at Melissa.

"No sign of him," I said. Then with so much force that I saw Abner's eyes flick with surprise, I quickly added: "Miss Andrews, may I present Mr. Abner Wilson of Chambersburg, the owner of this train. Abner, Miss Andrews is going to the crossing. I took the liberty of saying she could ride with us."

Abner's glance took in Melissa's attire, which was not completely free of mud. "Didn't I see you in Chambersburg, young lady?"

"It is possible," Melissa said. "Our Conestoga train halted there overnight."

Abner's expression clouded. "Abner," I said, "if you don't want to take Miss Andrews, we'll walk."

"I guess it's all right," Abner said, glowered a bit, then piped the forward.

I gave Melissa my hand as she took to the wagon seat. While riding up the rise, nobody spoke. Melissa, shoulders erect, sat beside me, staring at the road. She appeared to be quite collected and I marveled at her composure. Later she was to tell me that she was frightened to the verge of hysteria and it was my apparent calmness which gave her the strength to control herself.

As a matter of fact, Melissa's diagnosis of my state of mind was as inaccurate as mine was of hers. Any impression of calmness I might have exhibited was, in reality, a form of petrification. I had gone numb. One after another the pitfalls which might have happened passed through my mind. It seemed impossible that I, Thomas A. Morrow of Philadelphia, had actually behaved as I had.

When we reached the top of the rise, Abner studied the drop which, quite steep, was comparatively free of bear wallows. Deciding to make the descent without brakes, he gave his horses the whip and down we rumbled, the other wagons following so closely that if a wheel was lost or a wagon overturned there'd be quite a smash-up.

The momentum of our burst of speed carried us a quarter-way up the rise. While the puffing horses were being rested, Melissa and I moved to the side of the road and sat down, "We haven't fooled Mr. Wilson," Melissa said.

"I'm sure we haven't," I said, "but it's all right or he wouldn't have taken us. He probably knows what the officials of the settlement are like."

"In retrospect," Melissa said and managed a faint suggestion of a smile, "I think we acted rather rashly."

"Yes, we did," I said, "but anything's better than running into a squad of Harmar recruits."

Because the next rise was so abrupt, before piping the forward, Abner ordered everyone but the drivers to walk. To avoid the dust clopped up by the horses, Melissa and I moved to the rear of the van wagon. We'd progressed no more than a few paces before Abner piped an alarm-halt. "He's spotted somebody ahead," I told Melissa. "We'll have to lie under the wagon."

"Officials from the settlement!"

"If they are," I said, "I'm going to lie like a trooper. I have a letter of introduction, signed by the Governor of Pennsylvania. I am going to say that we are engaged to be married and that if any harm or inconvenience comes to you, the governor will hear about it."

Abner's voice rang out loudly. "Hey, you, behind the trees. What do you want?"

By now Melissa and I were beneath the wagon. Crawling to the right front wheel, I could see up the road. Some twenty yards ahead a powerfully built, reddish-bearded man in forest-tattered buckskins had emerged from behind the trees. Waving his coonskin cap over his head, he called back in a deep bass voice: "Hello, strangers."

"Keep your distance," Abner warned.

I whispered to Melissa: "I'm quite sure he's not a settlement official. He's probably a *coureur de bois*."

"A—what?"

"One of those fellows who just roams the woods. Yes, I'm sure of it. I can tell by his hair. It's braided!"

"Braided!"

"If he lets his hair down, it'll reach almost to his hips. Abner was telling me about these fellows only this morning. When they trade with Indians, they let their hair down—to impress them."

The red-bearded man called out: "Everything's all right, strangers. No cause for alarm. You're looking at a friend. My name's Phineas Ford."

"If you're coming up here," Abner replied, "put down your rifle."

"Not me, my friend," Phineas Ford said. "Where I go, so does this rifle. Tell you what I'll do though. I'll sling her over my shoulder and if I so much as touch her with my hand, you can shoot me dead."

"Where are you headed?"

"The crossing."

"What do you want?"

"I'm figuring maybe you'll give me a drink."

"Sure," Abner said. "Sling your rifle and come on up."

Phineas Ford moved forward with long, jaunty strides. Standing well over six feet, even in pacs, the man's shoulders were enormous. He was, I judged, about thirty-five. Arriving at the van wagon, he grinned roguishly and clicked pearly white teeth whose incisors looked like hounds' fangs.

There was an arresting bestial appearance about Phineas Ford's teeth, of which their owner seemed proudly cognizant. With exaggerated movements, using his forefingers and thumbs, Phineas Ford took hold of his rifle by the end of the stock and the tip of the barrel and presented it to Abner.

"A nice gun," Abner remarked and returned the weapon.

Indeed that rifle was. It was a Jacob Feree, clean as a whistle. Fancy carving on its stock indicated that at one time it had belonged to an Indian.

"Finest rifle ever made," Phineas Ford said, clicking his teeth. "Show me half an Indian's head at two-hundred-fifty yards and I'll kill him deader than a nigger in a woodpile."

"I'll believe that when I see it," Abner said good-naturedly.

"Want to wager," Phineas Ford said, also good-naturedly. "Any time, any place, no matter what the wind or snow or rain I'll wager whatever you want and I can cover. One shot only."

"Damned if I don't believe you could at that," Abner said, piped the all clear, and Melissa and I crawled from under the wagon. "I'm sure Phineas Ford isn't from the settlement," I whispered to Melissa, "but you'd better stay out of sight."

Apparently Abner had handed down the whiskey jug, for I heard him say: "Help yourself."

"You won't find me bashful," Phineas Ford replied.

Moving to the rear right wheel, I could see Phineas Ford. He had our whiskey jug to his lips and held it there so long I became convinced his ultimate objective was to gulp down all the contents. The reason he finally stopped drinking, so far as I could tell, was because he was out of breath. "Mighty fine Monongahela rye," he said, smacked his lips, clicked his teeth, and punched himself hard enough in the stomach to knock the wind out of an ordinary man.

"Take your fill," Abner said.

"Had enough," Phineas Ford replied. "I'm much obliged."

As was customary an exchange of news followed. "Are you a Harmar recruit?" Abner asked.

"Hell, no," Phineas Ford said. "I'm supposed to scout for the General, if he ever gets his damned army. I'm due in Cincinnati right now, but with the recruiting so far behind schedule—what's the hurry."

"Cincinnati?" Abner asked. "Where in the hell's that?"

"You don't know about Cincinnati?"

"Never heard of it."

"It's a new settlement. Harmar's going to march his army out of there."

"You don't say!" Abner said. "The word around here is that Harmar and the federals left Marietta for Losantiville."

"They did," Phineas Ford said, "but Losantiville's gone. Wiped right off the map."

"Good, holy God!" Abner said and I heard Melissa, who stood beside me, gasp.

"Yes, sir," Phineas Ford drawled, "nothing's left of Losantiville. She's wiped clean off the map."

Because Phineas Ford had turned, I couldn't see his face. There was, though, something about his manner of speaking. Abner caught it too. "You bastard," Abner said, "you're baiting me, aren't you?"

"Now would I do a thing like that?"

"You're damned right you would," Abner said. "Now quit stringing it out. I admit you hooked me neat. How?"

Bowing with the flourish of a scientist making the announcement of an important discovery to a group of learned colleagues, Phineas Ford said proudly: "All done fair and square, my friend. Didn't even stretch the truth. General St. Clair, or I guess he likes to be called Governor St. Clair these days, came down the river a while back. He figured Losantiville was too hard a word to say, so he changed the settlement's name to Cincinnati."

"Well, I'll be damned!" Abner exclaimed and chuckled. "You sure pulled that one off smooth as silk, Phineas. I freely admit you had me hooked. You could have walked off with me none the wiser."

"I wouldn't have done that to a dog," Phineas said.

"When did you last go through—Cincinnati?"

"Six weeks back."

"Harmar and the federals *are* there?"

"They're there," Phineas said, "but there's a lot of sickness and desertion."

"How's Fort Washington coming along?"

"Most of it's up and it's being built fine. Major Doughty's doing the building."

"The volunteers from Virginia? Any coming through?"

"Just as slow as the boys from Pennsylvania."

"Nobody could be that slow!"

"The hell they can't! It's crazy. The army Harmar's getting couldn't fight its way out of a rotten barn. And don't think the Indians don't know it."

"Crazy is right," Abner muttered. "Want to ride with us to the crossing?"

"Hell, no," Phineas Ford said. "I can foot it through the woods faster than you buggers can roll."

X

While walking up the rise, Melissa and I constantly looked back to see if settlement officials were in pursuit. The density of the surrounding woods, so we reasoned, made the highway the only means of travel. Thus, so long as no one overtook us, we felt reasonably safe. If Bushrod Andrews were well enough to travel, we decided, a chaise should be hired. Departure from the crossing settlement should be made quickly as possible.

Although our conversation concerned itself principally with our predicament, I did learn a smattering of the Andrews' plans. Bushrod Andrews was a land operator and a general investor. Just outside of Pittsburgh he planned looking over a glass manufacturing plant which had failed. He bought up establishments in run-down conditions, Melissa explained in a manner which indicated that she was not too familiar with Bushrod Andrews' business dealings, then put them on their feet and sold them at a profit. The Pittsburgh matter resolved, they would go to the Miami Purchase for a short stay, while Bushrod Andrews bought up lots, to be held as an investment. Thereafter they'd be going to New Orleans where, so far as Melissa knew, they expected to be residing for an indefinite period.

Dusk was fast approaching when we reached the outskirts of the crossing settlement. Suddenly that depressing solid wall of trees vanished and song birds, shunners of the deep forest, began chirping melodiously.

Now the highway took us through well-tended apple tree orchards, in resplendent full-bloom, the blossoms filling the air with their sweet aroma. The Allegheny haze was in complete descent. It had tinted the apple blossoms into a rich blood-violet. Its delicate coloration had wiped away all signs of weariness and worry from Melissa's face, softening her features, and rendering her beautiful. The distinctive hue was everywhere. I could see it on my own hands. Even the dust under my feet had absorbed a tinge of lavender and no longer looked so deadly drab.

While the setting of our entrance to the crossing settlement might be accounted regal, arrival was proletarian. Dreary-looking, the settlement was comprised of some three dozen log cabins, a blacksmith's shop, a general

store, and an inn. The inn, like the postal coach inn at Chambersburg, was
a log cabin with additions. Here, however, the cabins had been added side-
by-side and were all approximately of the same size.

Being a junction settlement, an air of bustle prevailed. The general store
was crowded and possibly a dozen horses were tied up in front of it. Men
occupied all the stools on the inn's veranda and at the near end I saw Phineas
Ford rolling dice with a group of local militiamen, at least that is what
I presumed them to be for they wore regulation blue Pennsylvania uniforms
with white linings, faced with red buttons. Seeing our train Phineas Ford
called out: "Hello, friends!" and went on with his play.

"I'll have to go with the train to the tethering grounds, Miss Andrews,"
I said. "Go straight to the inn. Make arrangements for hiring a chaise. I'll
get there quickly as possible, to give whatever help I can."

"Yes . . ." Melissa said and left.

When we reached the tethering grounds, Jonathan Morgan and his helpers were unloading the twenty-four packhorses. "Those conniving bastards!"
Abner muttered.

Reeking of spruce beer, Morgan told Abner he'd just arrived. Nobody
in his right mind would have believed him. Obviously Morgan had raced
his charges into the settlement, gone straight to the inn, and was just now
getting around to hurriedly brushing the sweat from the packhorses' flanks.
The foamy heaps, looking like dirty soap suds, hadn't lain on the ground
long enough to even begin settling.

Sharp words ensued between Abner and Morgan and when Abner's son-
in-law projected himself into the argument I thought physical encounter
was inevitable. Abner, however, managed to restrain William. "Everybody
help unload the packhorses!" Abner called out, an order which brought about
considerable grumbling from the wagoneers, who feel such tasks are beneath them.

What a heartless fellow that Jonathan Morgan was! Who knew how long
the poor beasts had stood by with some two hundred pounds of salt and
iron, plus sundry household belongings weighing on their backs? These hired
packhorses did not have conventional saddles. Flat boards, with sheeps' pads
under them, provided the only protection against saddle burns. Over and
over again Abner had admonished Morgan to regularly inspect his charges.
What I saw was gruesome. All the horses' backs had been rubbed raw
and the open wounds were black with hovering flies.

The horses unloaded and the saddle burns greased down, we all made for
the inn which, from the outside, was ugly looking as a monster. Inside, its
builders had managed to carry on with this general motif. Uneven puncheon
floors wobbled with each step I took. The furniture was, for the most part,

rudely constructed. One reached the sleeping loft by climbing up ladders made of boards nailed to the wall.

Yet, there was a certain utility in the manner of erection. Each cabin, enterable from an aisle or from the veranda, served a particular purpose. The one we'd gone into, located at the west end, was a dining room reserved for wagoneers and packhorsemen. Then came the kitchen and taproom. Next: cabins reserved for higher class guests, Negroes, and town gatherings. The final one was the settlement's school and also its church, when a circuit rider passed through.

I located Melissa in a cabin room reserved for higher class guests. She sat at a table with a middle-aged man, whose face was pitted with the pox. He wore city clothes. Staring glassy-eyed at a bottle of Monongahela rye, which was knocked over, he was muttering something to Melissa. Lunging forward suddenly, his chin cracked so hard onto the table that the impact knocked off his wig, exposing a bald crown deeply marked with flea bites.

Sighing visibly, Melissa placed the wig back on the man's head and made an effort to get him to his feet. At this moment, she saw me. "May I help?" I asked.

"Please," Melissa said, her cheeks turning crimson with embarrassment. "As you can see he—my father is not well."

While in a sense this was the fact, it is possible to be more specific. Bushrod Andrews was drunker than a lord. "You're too tired to drive a chaise, Miss Andrews," I said. "I'd better do it."

Melissa shook her head.

"It'll be all right," I assured her. "Your train can't be too far ahead. I won't mind waiting until Abner Wilson catches up with me."

Melissa shook her head again, wearily. "It will soon be too dark," she said. "The highway is too bumpy. The inn will not let us hire a chaise until tomorrow morning."

The color was beginning to drain from Melissa's cheeks. They were turning a ghastly white and her eyes were becoming glassy. "You'd better lie down," I said.

"I'm all right," Melissa said and pointed to Bushrod Andrews. "There are no sleeping quarters other than the loft."

Glancing doubtfully at the boards nailed to the wall, I placed my hands under Bushrod Andrews' armpits. The man gave me no cooperation at all. He was dead weight and it occurred to me that we couldn't get him to the loft without the aid of a pulley.

"I don't see how we'll be able to manage it," I said.

"I don't either," Melissa said.

A simpering, freckled-faced, buxom barmaid, carrying a tray of empty flip glasses, passed through the aisle. "Take him down to the last cabin and let him lay on the floor," she suggested. "If he pukes, though, you'll have to clean up the mess. I ain't got time to go there tonight and there's an early Mass tomorrow morning."

Following the barmaid's suggestion, I took Bushrod Andrews under the armpits and dragged him down the aisle. En route, he did not utter a sound. A wooden statue of the Virgin Mary, rudely carved from a tree trunk, stood in the last cabin. A bear rug lay before it. When I deposited Bushrod Andrews on this rug, he lay there inert as a half-filled sack of flour. Had he not been breathing, I would have thought surely he was dead.

Melissa sank to the floor, buried her head in her hands and began sobbing. For some moments I stood there, feeling utterly helpless. At length I had sense enough to realize that this poor girl must be utterly famished. "I'll be right back with food," I said, but I doubt if Melissa heard me.

I moved to the dining room, via the veranda. Apparently a dice game had just concluded. The militiamen, glowering dourly, were taking their leave. Phineas Ford, a smug expression playing across his rugged face, sat on the steps, passing the time cleaning his fingernails: first with the nail of his right forefinger, then with the left. "Hello, stranger," Phineas Ford greeted and clicked his teeth. "You look in a big hurry."

"I am," I said and went into the taproom where the simpering barmaid was now placing cups of pepper pot soup onto her tray. "Thank you," I said and took two cups off her tray. "Well, if you ain't—" the barmaid said, but I was gone before she could finish her sentence.

As Melissa drank the first cup of soup the color came back into her cheeks and it was almost possible to see her strength returning. "This is so good," she said.

"I'd try to drink this other cup more slowly," I suggested.

"Yes," she said.

"Meanwhile, what else may I get you?"

"Nothing, thank you, this is thick soup. A meal in itself." While sipping that second cup, Melissa, from time to time, looked up at me. There was infinite tenderness in her eyes. It was not merely an expression of gratitude some instinct told me and, to my great surprise, I felt a shock of sheer elation surge through me, pronounced as if it were caused by that new invention of Benjamin Franklin's, called electricity.

"I don't cry often, Mr. Morrow," Melissa said. "I do not believe in it."

"I believe in it," I said. "Unfortunately, I have never been able to. My deepest feelings seem to stay inside of me."

"You've never cried? Even when you were a little boy?"

"I don't remember crying, even as a little boy," I said. "I used to read a great deal about the ancient Greeks. The Spartans especially. Spartan boys were taught it was effeminate to cry. I modeled myself after them, although today I'm more the Athenian than the Spartan."

"I hated the Spartans when I was little," Melissa said, "because they took their sick babies into the mountains and let them die . . . I'm getting dreadfully sleepy, Mr. Morrow. May I rest my head against your shoulder?"

"Of course, but possibly I should leave?"

"No, please, stay a little while," Melissa said. "Tell me about when you were a little boy. You read a great deal, didn't you?" (How could she possibly have known that!) "If I close my eyes, it won't mean I'm asleep." She laughed softly. It was a melodious, happy laugh. "I used to say that to my mother, Mr. Morrow, when she was reading me to sleep."

This time, though, Melissa was mistaken about not being asleep because her eyes were closed. The moment her head touched my shoulder, she was dead to this world.

Easing Melissa gently onto the bear skin, I climbed to the loft, located a dirty blanket and covered her with it. There were no windows in this room, merely slits in the wall. Light rays of a veranda lamp, coming through one of these slits, lit up Melissa's face as she slept ever so peacefully. Curled up, her knees almost touching her chin, she looked more the little girl than a grown woman. For quite some time I stood by, simply looking at Melissa, wondering if I were falling in love with her.

Taking my leave, I moved over the aisle. Laughter and shouts from the dining room indicated that the wagoneers were already in their cups and over the din I could hear Phineas Ford's voice, the loudest and most commanding of all.

Reaching the dining room, I saw what I expected to. Three wagoneers already lay on the floor, dead drunk. The others were shouting and carrying on the way drunken wagoneers all over the country do when they stop off at an inn. Phineas Ford had the buxom barmaid raised over his head and was spinning her around. Simpering and giggling, the barmaid was pretending she enjoyed being shaken up. Seeing me, Phineas put the barmaid down. "Drink up, Mr. Philadelphia!" he said and slapped me so lustily across the back that I was moved three steps forward.

These three steps brought me to a table and I sat down. Filling a large pewter mug with Monongahela rye, Phineas shoved it toward me. "Drink up, Mr. Philadelphia," he repeated and I did.

I was still thinking about Melissa. While falling in love at first sight is, in my opinion, something of a mirage, it cannot be denied that mirages do appear to be real. I *was* falling in love, I strongly suspected, and in a way I had never felt about any woman. It was a frightening prospect to be contemplating. There were so many other things I wished to do. I did not want to fall in love with anyone.

"You deaf, Mr. Philadelphia?" Phineas asked me.

"No," I said, "I'm not."

"You must be," Phineas said, giving me what he considered to be a playful nudge. I thought of it as a hard body blow to the ribs. "I've been shouting my head off at you."

"I'm sorry," I said, "I was thinking about something. What is it you wished to know?"

"Damned if I can remember now!" Phineas said.

The arrival of the barmaid with my dinner put an end to this snatch of brilliant conversation. "Miss me, honey?" Phineas said to the barmaid.

"I sure did, you great big brown bear," she replied with professional impishness.

The barmaid's statement pleased Phineas. "G-r-r-r!" he said and clicked his teeth. "That's me, honey. A great big brown bear!" Phineas' hand went to the back of his head and his great shock of red hair fell down well past the top of his shoulders. Pulling the barmaid to him, Phineas flipped his hair from his back to over the top of his head. Phineas' hair was long and thick enough to cover his own face and the barmaid's head. Under this hood, it must be presumed that Phineas was kissing the barmaid. His hands roamed over various strategic parts of the barmaid's body. It was quite an exhibition to be staging in public and at the time I thought Phineas must be very drunk.

The barmaid had brought me a piece of pork, carved from the inner depths of the pig, so raw that I could not eat it. Eventually Abner Wilson came to my table, to collect a shilling-six. Meals at inns were not included in the wagoneers' wages, nor in my arrangement with Abner. The shilling was the price of the meal, the sixpence went to local constables, stationed outside the door, under orders to stop anyone attempting to inflict himself on the local citizenry.

Abner's face was aglow and he looked twenty years younger. Although Abner had imbibed freely here at the inn and was constantly nipping a whiskey jug while we traveled, he never became drunk. He was the steadying influence on such evenings, the arbiter of fights, the man who remembered exactly how much furniture was broken, so the innkeeper couldn't overcharge us.

"What a man!" Abner said and pointed beyond my table where Phineas Ford now had the barmaid. Phineas' hands were under the barmaid's dress. He seemed unconcerned that he was surrounded by a circle of wagoneers who were watching him.

The lustful expressions on the onlookers' faces made their states of mind apparent. "I don't know why Phineas doesn't take her to the loft," I said.

"Don't worry, they'll get there," Abner said drolly. "Right now he needs pasture room. It's still the mating season." Tapping his bald head, he added somewhat ruefully: "Hair like Phineas Ford's drives women crazy. They can't keep their hands off it."

What I saw seemed to verify Abner's observation. Shrieking with delight, the barmaid was tugging at Phineas' hair and rubbing it against her breasts. While she would, of course, expect to be reimbursed for her performance, her heart and soul *did* appear to be in her work.

A wagoneer staggered up to Phineas and mumbled something which was unintelligible. "Get your trotters moving, friend," Phineas growled.

"I sure hope Sam does," Abner said, mainly to himself.

Sam, however, made a lunge for the barmaid.

"Now watch what happens to Sam," Abner said, shaking his head dolefully.

Phineas' right leg lashed out. Its movement was basically angular, as if Phineas' limb members were joined by strings, like those of a huge toy. So perfect was Phineas' one-legged balance, he did not have to remove his hands from beneath the barmaid's dress. A man needed big feet to achieve such balance and Phineas had them.

"I figured Phineas was a good leg man," Abner remarked.

Phineas' foot had caught Sam flush in the face, knocking him halfway across the room. "Real neat," Abner went on to say. "Even on the lookout, I couldn't tell which leg it was going to be."

"Sam's getting up," I said.

"If he goes back again he'll really get the hell knocked out of him," Abner said. "The jackass *is* going back . . . Tom, get over there and try to stop Sam."

The reason Abner had delegated the task to me was because his presence was needed elsewhere. Three nearby wagoneers, bemoaning the fact the barmaid was the only member of the opposite sex available, had decided to go into town and seek out a female goat.

I experienced no difficulties with Sam. "Phineas Ford," he shouted at me upon my arrival, "I'm callin' you a God damned stinkin' leg man. You ain't fit to spit down a rat hole." Sam's fist missed its target, my face, by a good foot-and-a-half and his around-the-barn swing threw him off balance. Reeling about, seeking his adversary, he bumped into other wagoneers, who took him into tow.

Abner, on the other hand, was having his troubles convincing the three

wagoneers that local farmers frowned upon behavior such as they were contemplating. "You damned fools!" Abner was saying. "Do you want to get
yourselves shot?"

"What the hell, Abner!" the wagoneers' spokesman protested. "You heard
what Phineas Ford said. Nobody's even allowed second dips. He figures to
ram it into that damned barmaid all night."

"Phineas paid her everything he won in the dice game," Abner said. "Can
you come close to matching that?"

"Phineas horned in! That stinkin' leg man don't belong to the train."

"I wouldn't bet on him just being a good leg man," Abner said. "I know
how you feel, boys, but you've got to figure this was just one of those
nights when the cards didn't fall right."

"To hell with Phineas Ford!" the wagoneer said and called his two com-
panions into consultation.

"I'm warning you, boys!" Abner said sharply. "Don't go after Phineas
Ford!"

"To hell with Phineas Ford!" the trio shouted, practically in unison, and
sprinted for the door. With a loud thud, they went sprawling on the veranda.
Aware, of course, that constables were stationed outside, the wagoneers hadn't
realized a rope was stretched across the doorway.

"Well, that shoots their night of fun," Abner said, a trifle sadly. He was referring to the penalty for trying to leave the dining room: offenders,
tied up, gagged if necessary, spent the night stretched out on the veranda.

Actually, except for the presence of Phineas Ford and the relatively minor
commotions he'd aroused, the evening was progressing in what might be
called the accepted manner. As time marched on there were the usual
number of arguments and fights. Abner, however, was able to break up
most of the latter before they got out of hand.

At previous inn stop-offs, I had imbibed sparingly and acted as Abner's
aide-de-camp. On this occasion, though, I wasn't of much use to Abner for,
in almost no time, I became quite drunk. While I might say the reason
I reached this stage so quickly is because I had had no solid food since
noon, the real reason is that I drank a great deal of Monongahela rye in a
very short span of time.

Phineas had left with the barmaid, then come back to join in the
festivities, then returned to the barmaid, then come back again. "Ain't you
finished yet, Phineas?" I recall someone asking him. "Hell, no!" Phineas
replied. "I'm good till early morning."

At the moment I was simply roaming about, discussing this and that with
anyone willing to listen to the words of wisdom which I felt were making

a contribution to convivial conversation. Since nobody paid attention, it made no difference what I said.

Phineas had sat down at one of the tables. More profit, I overheard Phineas telling a wagoneer, could be gained taking pigs rather than flour down the Ohio River. This matter of moving goods down the Ohio River for profit intrigued me. Moreover, I fancied myself as having a certain knowledge of the subject. Only that morning Abner, who had a bid in to supply Harmar's army with packhorses and flour, had spent possibly twenty minutes telling me something of the trials and dangers of river transportation.

Flour, Phineas was saying, admittedly could be bought, if available, in Pittsburgh for four dollars a barrel and sold for eight in Marietta, as much as ten at the Miami Purchase. The army, however, had first purchasing rights and made payment in government promissory notes, which had to be discounted greatly, for it took forever to collect upon them. On the other hand, young pigs, and they were plentiful, could be bought in Pittsburgh for fifty cents each. "At the Miami Purchase," Phineas said, "hogs bring twenty-five shillings a hundred."

"That's interesting," I said.

"You're damned right it is," Phineas said without looking up. "What's more, young pigs turn into little hogs while going down the river. You got to figure on being held up one, two, maybe three or four times. While you're waiting around, the pigs are growing. Sure, you're losing time, but not money."

"You have a rather brilliant idea there, Phineas," I said. "Unhappily, it is currently impractical."

Phineas turned. "Well, now, Mr. Philadelphia," he said, good-naturedly, but in the manner of a St. Bernard noticing a poodle, "who in the hell asked you?"

"Nobody," I said. "Out of pure generosity of my soul, I am offering you this free advice."

"Have a drink," Phineas said, "but stick your free advice up your ass."

"I'll have the drink," I said and sat down beside Phineas, "but I can't stick free advice where you suggested—it's too intangible a commodity."

"Are you daffy?"

"Please—no begging the question."

"What the hell are you talking about?"

"I'm very serious, Phineas," I said. "With the Indians acting up the way they are, the army's warning all downriver riders to travel only while there is no moon."

"Don't you think I know that!"

"Hear me out, Phineas. Abner just told me this morning. You probably haven't heard it. The army's just forbidden any craft to leave Pittsburgh with animals having tongues aboard."

"Animals . . . with tongues!" Phineas sputtered.

"I know that sounds a little silly," I said, "but that's the army's way of saying it. Even pet dogs have to be left behind. Pigs would squeal, Phineas. Indians would hear this squealing, no matter how black the night."

"Well, I'll be damned!" Phineas drawled. "What about one jackass, Mr. Philadelphia? Would the army let *him* go down the river?"

"One jackass?" I said. "He'd bray, wouldn't he?"

"How should I know, Mr. Philadelphia? You're the jackass I'm talking about."

"I beg your pardon!"

"Have another drink, Mr. Philadelphia, and don't get sore," Phineas said. "But you're arguing like a jackass. You're talking about *one* flatboat going down the river. I'm talking about a flotilla with an army escort."

The debate lost, I had no recourse but to laugh at my own stupidity. "You're all right, Mr. Philadelphia," Phineas said. "Have another drink." In its own peculiar way I should say this was the beginning of my friendship with Phineas Ford and within a few minutes I managed to get in a lick of a sort on my own. Phineas and I began talking about Ohio Indians. The Indian language, Phineas contended, was much more practical than English because it was simpler.

"The Indians are smarter than white men," Phineas said, "because of the way they talk. Take when an Indian's fishing with a rod, he's got one word for that. If he's fishing with a net, he's got another word for that. Or let's say he's spearing a fish. He's got—"

"I understand the point you're making," I said. "But it's only practical because Indians don't live in the complicated world we white people do."

"Well, I'll be damned!" Phineas said. "I never gave that a thought. Mr. Philadelphia, you're pretty smart at that."

Coming back to the dining room for his third recess period, Phineas looked somewhat peaked. His pride was hurt though when someone said: "What's the matter, Phineas? Is the tree's sap startin' to run slow?"

"Can't a man even take a minute to catch his breath?" Phineas said, climbed up on the table and began singing Ohio River songs.

Phineas' voice had a booming quality, if not a particularly good tone, and soon everyone, including myself, joined in. This was the first time I had heard an Ohio River song. Most river songs are nothing but chanteys; they teem, though, with the primitive wildness of the region. One especially, which goes:

"Some row up,
Some row down,
All the way—
To Shawneetown,
Pull Away—*PULL AWAY!*"

It does not call for much imagination to guess at the number of variations a group of drunken wagoneers are able to devise when they come to the "Pull Away—*PULL AWAY!*" part. The words of that chantey, I admit, do not make too much sense, especially when you bear in mind that flatboats are never rowed and don't go upstream, but I submit that if you have any love of the river, instinctive or from actual experience, you need only to be slightly drunk and you are right there—pulling away.

I was far more than slightly drunk. Climbing onto the table, I took my place beside Phineas and joined him in leading the song. "God damn, Mr. Philadelphia!" Phineas said. "You've got a good voice. Have another drink."

Somebody—it could well have been me—made the suggestion that a group of us sit on the floor, the thought being that we should climb aboard an imaginary boat and "pull away" like so many slaves on an Egyptian galley. The suggestion struck the popular fancy. Tables were knocked over to give us rowing space. I should say all wagoneers still physically able to row became members of the crew. Phineas took his place at the bow. "Pull Away—" he sang out. *"PULL AWAY!"*

XI

To get the Conestoga train under way in the morning, Abner Wilson followed the procedure of an army breaking camp. It was, thus, the beating of reveille by the train's drummer that awakened me.

I lay on a dew-damp bearskin beneath the van wagon. There was nothing unusual about this for, because of fleas, no one slept in the wagons. While I knew where I was, I could not recall anything evenly remotely connected with my arrival. It was necessary, I realized, to get up. However, the desire to continue sleeping was overwhelming and I succumbed to it.

Eventually reawakening, I still lay on the bearskin. Opening my eyes I saw a vast expanse of cloudless sky. "Good morning, Mr. Philadelphia," I heard Phineas Ford say.

Startled, I sat up. "You sure timed things smart, Tom," Phineas said good-naturedly, and pointed to Abner's twenty-four packhorses, standing docilely some fifteen yards off, lined up, tied tail-on-tail, and ready to move. "I just loaded the last one."

I looked toward the tethering grounds. "Where's the train?"

"Gone maybe three hours ago."

"I overslept!"

"Like a log," Phineas said, handing me a cup of coffee and a platter of fried ham and grits.

"Thank you," I said. "How did I get here?"

Phineas indicated the bearskin. "Abner and I carried you."

I looked, inquiringly, at Phineas. "While you were sleeping it off," Phineas explained, "there was a big fight. Abner caught Morgan stealing salt and kicked him and his boys off the train. You and I are taking the packhorses to Fort Pitt."

"Phineas!" I said. "Abner must have lost his mind. I'm no packhorseman."

"Hell," Phineas said, "anybody can be a packhorseman."

This was not the moment to discuss my qualifications. As a result of eating, my head was beginning to clear. Actually, all in all, I felt quite well. The previous evening's events began flashing through my mind. Recollection stopped abruptly with me sitting on the dining-room floor and starting to pull away.

"When do you plan on leaving?" I asked.

"Right now," Phineas said.

"No," I said. "I have to go to the inn first. I'll be back in less than ten minutes."

Moving at a fast trot, I made for the inn. Only the barmaid, going through the motions of sweeping up, was on the veranda. She looked at me through bleary eyes, of which the left one was so dark it could well have been hit with a fist. "Well, if it ain't you," she said.

"The two people you saw me helping last night?" I said. "The middle-aged man and—"

"They're gone," the barmaid said. "Left two hours ago."

"Thank you," I said.

"You must have missed the train," the barmaid said.

"Yes, I did," I said. "Did the young lady leave a message?"

"No message. You ain't one of Morgan's helpers, are you?"

"No, I'm not."

"Then you must be goin' to help Phineas Ford with the packhorses?"

"As a matter of fact, I am."

"I'd be ever so much obliged, mister," the barmaid said, "if you'll tell Phineas Ford I hope he rots in hell."

"I would imagine Mr. Ford would prefer such a message as coming directly from you."

"I already gave him that message," the barmaid said. "I'd like for him to hear it again."

Phineas, when I returned, was tying two bulging gunnysacks on the last packhorse's back. "Just follow behind this last horse, Tom," Phineas said. "And *watch* those two sacks! They're filled with gold."

"Gold!" I said.

"Same as," Phineas said and clicked his teeth. "Those sacks are crammed full of young beavers. They're going down to Cincinnati with me."

"*Furs* to Cincinnati?" I said. "Isn't that like taking coals to Newcastle?"

"What the hell are you talking about?"

"I thought the Ohio Country abounded with furs."

"Young beavers aren't like regular furs," Phineas said. "Nothing sells like young beavers from Pittsburgh to the Falls, all the way to Cairo for that matter. A young beaver's harder than hell to trap, Tom! Rich ladies in New Orleans will pay out their eyeteeth for them. Could be, after I'm through scouting for Harmar, I'll go all the way to New Orleans with them myself."

"How'd you get them?"

"From a trapper friend of mine who's too old to travel. That's why I was stopping off at the crossing."

We started off, taking to a packhorse trail which ran through deep woods. A shortcut, Phineas told me, this route would save us a half day.

My assignment was simply to walk behind the last packhorse. During the earlier stages of the day's trek, I gave considerable thought to Melissa Andrews. The danger of falling in love with her, I admitted freely, was real. It might be circumvented though, I reasoned, by studiously avoiding her while we were both in Pittsburgh. I should say that before I became physically weary from walking and stopped thinking about anything, I had more or less decided to follow such a course of action.

We experienced no difficulties while trudging along, saw no one. By sundown we'd covered fifteen miles and could have made possibly another mile, had not Phineas decided to stop where there were what he called "unloading" trees, but never "loading" trees. They were large trees sawed

off to the proper height, enabling packhorsemen to slide their charges'
loads onto and off the stumps.

Our unloading chores completed, Phineas and I ate, then stretched out
on the ground, using the sacks of young beaver furs as pillows.

"Tired?" Phineas asked me.

"I hope so," I said.

"What the hell are you talking about!"

"If I'm not tired," I said, "it means my legs are paralyzed."

"God damn, Tom!" Phineas said. "You sure do say funny things."

"Aren't you tired?" I asked him.

"I guess so," Phineas said. "Hell, I never think about it. Have a drink?"

"No, thank you," I said. "I had enough last night."

"That God-damned barmaid," Phineas said after taking a healthy swig.
"I sure could use her right now."

Nothing would be gained, I felt, by mentioning my conversation with
the barmaid.

"That lousy little bitch," Phineas said. "I really gave her a smack in
the eye."

"You hit—a woman!"

"Sure," Phineas said. "Why not?"

"I'm not certain I can answer that," I said.

"She said she was fed up with the crossing and wanted me to take
her down the river with me."

"Because of that—you hit her?"

"No, no," Phineas said. "I hit her because she wanted to be paid before
we did anything."

"Isn't that the usual way?"

"Not with me it isn't," Phineas said. "I lay, then pay. I give them what
I figure they're worth when we're finished. They've got nothing to worry
about because if they give me a good show, I pay them aplenty . . ."
His voice trailed off. "But I did pay her in advance. And I'm not complaining. Where do you think we did it?"

"In the loft?"

"No," Phineas said. "In a shed back of the kitchen."

"On the floor!"

"Yes and no," Phineas said. "Damned if she didn't show me a new
place to do it! We pulled up a couple of puncheons and laid a deerskin on
the ground. It was damned near soft as doing it in a bed, a hell of a
lot better than doing it in a tree."

"I'm afraid I don't understand," I said.

"That's the last place I had it," Phineas said, "in a tree. I was over to

Lancaster and run into this Amish girl at a fair. She wanted to get laid, but the only place we could go was up a tree."

"You lay on a branch!"

"For Christ's sake, no," Phineas said. "Standing up. On two branches that stuck out."

I said nothing. Phineas took another swig of whiskey and began reminiscing. "You know, Tom, of all the times I've laid women on a hard floor, it never entered my mind to pick up the puncheons. A simple thing like that and I didn't have the brains to see it."

"Well," I said, "you're still young. There's plenty of time to put your new discovery to use."

"Not so damned young any more, Tom," Phineas said. "I'm forty-six."

"Forty-six!" I said.

"You didn't think it?" Phineas said and looked at me hopefully.

"I thought you were no more than thirty-five."

"I look younger because I lived with Indians," Phineas said. "They got me when I was fifteen. I was still living with my family near Fort Pitt. That was thirty-odd years ago and it was still called Fort Duquesne. 'Phineas,' my pop said to me one morning, 'Mathilda's strayed again. Go fetch her back.'"

I asked Phineas who Mathilda was.

"Mathilda was our cow," Phineas said. "I got my brother, Potter, and we headed into the woods, breaking bush branches so we'd be sure to find our way back. Well, pretty soon we heard Mathilda's bell and it was ringing regular . . . You know what that means, don't you?"

"No," I admitted, "I don't."

"If a cow's bell is just ringing every now and then," Phineas explained, "it means she's feeding; if it's ringing more or less steady, it means she's walking. Well, from the ring we could tell that Mathilda was walking pretty fast, but Potter and me didn't give it a thought. We busted into a run and before we knew it, we caught up with Mathilda all right, but she was in the company of a half-dozen Delawares who'd taken her bell off and tricked us."

"Good Lord!" I exclaimed.

"The good Lord didn't have anything to do with it that morning," Phineas said, "it was the Devil himself who was in charge. Now my brother Potter—he never did have a sense of caution. Right off the reel when he saw those Delawares, he busted into a run. He made for the trees, but was going so fast he didn't watch his footing. Blow me down if he didn't step into a swamp and sink up to his chin. The Indians never did find him.

"But as for me," Phineas said, emitting a deep sigh, "I used caution, so I was taken. Of course, my luck was worse than Potter's. He was standing where he had a chance. I was right under a Delaware's tomahawk and if I'd have tried for a get-away, he could have brained me.

"The Indians took me to a village on the Maumee. They were all right to me while we were on the move, but every village we passed through they made me run the gauntlet. I sure got beat up aplenty, but I can see now that they were testing me to see how strong I was.

"Finally we came to the main village where all the chiefs were. I ran the gauntlet and all the squaws were on hand to take a swat at me too. After I was out of it a renegade by the name of Jack Johnson came up to me. Jack was the skinniest fellow I ever saw in my life. He looked like his skin was glued on his bones. He had a wolf's head on his own head and the rest of the skin, tail and all, was dangling down his back. Of course, he could talk English. He told me that if I could jump over a road-wagon the Indians stole from some Britishers, things might not go so bad for me.

"He led the way over to the wagon. The covers were stretched up and I'd say the wagon and bows were eight feet off the ground. Don't ask me how I did it, but I jumped over it with something to spare and all the squaws who were watching stopped looking solemn and cheered like they were crazy.

"Right after that I saw about a dozen chiefs sit down in a circle and begin passing around a war club. I don't mind admitting that I started to sweat. If just one of those varmints decided to rap the ground with the club it meant that I was going to get it good—maybe be burned at the stake if they couldn't trade me, which wasn't so easy then as it is now. But the club was passed all the way around and the chiefs got up and went away.

"Jack Johnson came over to me again after a bit and said I was supposed to sleep in a lodge that night. It suited me all right, but about ten o'clock I got the surprise of my life. An Indian girl came into the lodge and lay down beside me. Her name was Ayomah and it's a funny thing— excited as I was when I was running the gauntlet, I'd noticed Ayomah because she was pretty as the sunset. And it was some hard lick she'd given me—right between the shoulder blades.

"I couldn't speak a word of Indian and as I say I was only fifteen— so I don't have to tell you that having a woman Indian lie down beside me had given me quite a start.

"Ayomah was twenty. She'd been married before but her husband was killed over in the Wabash country hunting bison. She ran her fingers through my hair and when I shied away she started to laugh. Honest, Tom, when Ayomah laughed it was like someone singing, she was always that happy.

"She put her arms around me and pulled my head against her soft breasts. She sang a while and started whispering something into my ear. I didn't know what she was talking about then, but I do now. She was giving me an Indian greeting.

" 'The birds sing more sweetly, my brother,' she was saying, 'now that you are here. The squirrels chatter a welcome from the treetops. And our own hearts are glad to see you at our council fire, and hear your message. Speak and we will listen.'

"Now I call that real pretty, Tom! I'm telling you, when Indians like you they can be awfully nice. Ayomah was gentle as a shivering doe and she showed me what to do. She stayed with me until the crack of dawn, part of the time singing me songs.

"The next morning she put a stone in a young hickory tree, to let a handle grow around it. I knew she was making a tomahawk, but I didn't suspect why. It was going to be for our first son and every day she'd walk over to that hickory tree and watch how it was growing.

"I guess it was about noon when Jack Johnson came to me again. He was friendly this time and told me he was captured near Carlisle when he was six and while he could have been traded plenty of times he always said *no* because the Indians were fine people, much better than us whites.

"He was being nice, but I could see that he was worried too. He was worried because he thought the world of Ayomah, the same as did everyone else in the village. She wasn't a chief's daughter and didn't hold any rank, it was just because she was so pretty and nice to everyone.

"I know now why Jack Johnson looked worried and I also know what he was thinking. He was thinking that the Indians hadn't got me soon enough. If Indians get a white boy when he's young enough they'll have him for life, but I was fifteen and no matter what came about I wasn't likely to forget my color.

"Over by the river drums started to beat and the Indians started to yell and carry on. Jack Johnson led me toward the noise and the whole village was there, all dressed up and painted. Everybody was dancing and singing and cutting up as Jack Johnson took me over to the chief.

"The chief dipped his fingers in ashes so he could get a better hold and started to pull out my hair, one strand at a time, until it was all gone except for a lock across the crown. Then the chief made a sign and Ayomah came over, all dressed up in white buckskins and looking happy as a lark. She tied up what was left of my hair with a bead string and silver brooches. I wasn't wearing anything but loincloth; she gave a signal to the medicine men and they came over and painted my face and body.

"When that was over with, Ayomah took me by the hand and led me to the river. I jumped in and that meant my white blood was washed away. After that we went to the council house in the village where the chief gave me a new ruffled shirt and fancy leggings and a pair of moccasins that Ayomah had embroidered with porcupine quills. They painted my face again and tied red feathers to my scalp lock. They gave me a pipe and tobacco pouch, had me sit on a bearskin, and then the chief spoke to me and Jack Johnson told me he was saying that I was adopted into the tribe.

"That same night Ayomah and I were married . . .

"Well, I don't know—" Phineas continued, "it took me a while to learn how lucky I was, but I know now I could never give a real tinker's damn about any other woman but Ayomah. Tom, you'd have loved her too. She was the sweetest thing that ever lived. Remember me telling you about the tomahawk she made? Well, it takes about three years for one to grow right. By the time it was ready to be cut we had Sooke and Lahcopis and the handle was hardly cut off before Waconsta was born. Then we had a girl, Methoataska, and after that another boy, Puckishenoah.

"I loved them all, Tom, but my favorite was Sooke. Honest, Tom, there wasn't a cuter little devil in the whole world. Always cutting up and raising hell and when I'd catch him at something he'd grin at me and I couldn't get mad no matter what he'd done. Ayomah used to say I was spoiling him, but she couldn't get mad at him either.

"Sooke was just turned seven when we lost him. The little rascal climbed into a hollow tree to get some bear cubs and while he was there the she bear came back. Sooke fought her back like a man, cut her to ribbons, but the bear was getting in her licks too and our Sooke died.

"I often wonder if I'd left if Sooke had lived on. That's a hard one to answer. I don't really know how it all came about. Sometimes at night when I'm all alone I try to piece it all out, but I can't ever get it to make sense. It just seems that bit by bit I got fed up with being an Indian. It came to a head one winter night when some British traders got drunk, raped two squaws, and the Indians killed them for it.

"Now don't get me wrong, I was glad to see those damned Britishers killed. I even helped to cut them to bits and throw what was left of them to the dogs. But that night we had a feast and ate the dogs that had eaten the British traders. I put the food into my mouth, but I couldn't swallow, and I spit it out. Ayomah saw what I'd done and for weeks afterward she didn't smile, she'd just look at me like she was about to cry and all the while she broke her neck trying to be nice . . . Well, there isn't any more to tell you, Tom. We all went sled riding one afternoon. I kissed Ayomah and our children, got on the sled, rode down the hill, and never came back."

XII

The following morning I awakened to find Phineas, chin sunk to his chest, staring morosely into the fire. He'd filled a cup of coffee, but it stood on the ground beside him, untouched. "Phineas," I asked, "has something gone wrong?"

Without replying, Phineas arose, moved to the van packhorse. "Damn!" he said and punched the horse between the eyes with such force I thought surely he'd fracture the animal's skull. "Damn!" he said and struck the animal again. "Phineas!" I cried out and grabbed his arm. "Have you lost your mind?"

"He's not sore," Phineas muttered and gave the horse an affectionate slap on the flank. "Horses understand, Tom. They know when it's not *them* you're sore at."

"What in the world's the matter with you?"

Phineas sat down beside the fire and stared blankly into space. "I'm worried sick, Tom," he said eventually. "About my brother, Potter. I think he must be dying."

Although it would have been difficult to picture a more grief-stricken man than Phineas Ford at this moment, it was equally difficult to understand how—here, on the packhorse trail—he could have reached the conclusion that his brother was dying.

"Dying!" I said.

Making a futile gesture with his hands, Phineas said: "While you were sleeping, a mail carrier rode by."

"He brought you a letter?"

"I think so."

"You *think* so!"

"I guess I'm sure of it," Phineas said miserably.

To say the least, all this was rather confusing. "May I read the letter?" I asked.

"You can't," Phineas astounded me by replying, "because the carrier's still got it."

Phineas stood up and began pacing to and fro about the fire. He was so distraught that it was some time before I was able to piece together a logical sequence of events from what appeared to be a chaotic conversation.

"My brother Potter lives in Chambersburg now," Phineas explained. "I just paid him my first visit in six years and found him sick unto death with the malaria. Damn it, Tom! I wanted to stay with him. But how could I? I'm supposed to scout for Harmar. The God-damned army never'll be ready. But I have to report in."

While I now understood the nature of Phineas' predicament, there appeared to be a great many gaps in his story. "The letter?" I said. "I'm unable to comprehend what happened to it."

Phineas sighed deeply. "You know what those mail carriers are like? They're God-damned robbers."

"Yes," I said, "I know that."

"Well," Phineas continued listlessly, "Potter's wife and I agreed that if Potter took a turn for the worse she'd write me at Fort Pitt. I've been stopping all the carriers I saw coming over the highway and I'm sure the one that passed by this morning was carrying a letter from Potter's wife."

"Phineas," I said, "I still don't understand you. Why wouldn't you *know* whether or not the mail carrier had a letter from your brother's wife?"

"Because I can't read," Phineas said, "and neither could the mail carrier."

"Then why do you believe there was a letter for you?"

"Potter's wife and me did what a lot of people do," Phineas said and explained that since the mail carriers charged such exorbitant prices, it was common practice for people to address their letters with telltale marks on the envelope. A certain mark might mean that the letter contained only the news that everything was well at home and need not necessarily be purchased. Another kind of mark, however, would mean that the letter contained important information and must be bought no matter what the cost.

"And that's the reason I'm sure of it," Phineas said grimly. "I pretended I knew how to read and had the mail carrier show me all his letters. I saw one with two dots in the left-hand corner. That was our signal. One dot meant Potter was better, two dots meant he was worse, three dots meant he was dead . . ."

"You saw the two dots!" I said. "And you *didn't* buy the letter?"

Through pursed lips Phineas said: "I'm ashamed to admit this, Tom, but I'm traveling sort of light. I used up every penny I owned buying up those young beavers. What I won at dice, I handed over to that damned barmaid."

"Oh, Phineas!" I exclaimed. "Why in the world didn't you ask me for the price of the letter?"

"In a way I wish I had now," Phineas said ruefully. "I even thought about it. But you're carrying Pennsylvania and if the carrier found that out—he'd have bled you white. I guess I was also figuring that we'd be at Fort Pitt tomorrow and I could pick up the letter there, maybe get permission to go back to Potter." He looked at me appealingly. "God damn it, Tom! To tell you the God's truth—I was afraid to find out what was in that letter."

I poured Phineas' coffee, which had cooled, back into the pot. Walking over to our supplies, I got flour, jerked venison, and bear oil. Mixing the flour, I shaped dough on a peeled twig and made stick bread. I fried the jerk. All the while Phineas stared at me, as if he were in some kind of a trance.

"Phineas," I said, "you'd better eat something."

"I guess so . . ."

We loaded and tied up the horses. "Giddap!" Phineas shouted. Before the horses had taken five steps, Phineas called out: "Whoa!" When I came forward, he said hoarsely: "Tom, I can't do it. Potter's all I've got left in the world. I've got to go back to him."

"Yes, I think you should," I said. "At Fort Pitt, if the army won't lend you a horse, I'll give you the money to hire one."

Phineas shook his head. "I won't be given a leave of absence. Ebenezer's a bastard when it comes to regulations."

"Ebenezer?" I said. "Do you mean Lieutenant Denny?"

"That's right. It just struck me, Tom. Ebenezer'll be the ranking officer at the fort. No federals are there, only militia. I know Ebenezer's still there because he's supposed to wait until two companies of recruits are ready to move out. Two companies! Hell, there aren't two squads ready to move out."

"Under those circumstances," I said, "Lieutenant Denny will recognize there's no real hurry and will give you a leave."

"Like hell he will," Phineas said. "I'm supposed to be at Fort Washington right now. Harmar wants me to take north into the woods to see what I can find out. Ebenezer knows that and will give me holy hell for being late as it is . . . Good-bye, Tom."

"Wait a minute, Phineas!" I said and it seemed impossible that I had heard him correctly. "Do I understand you properly? Are you planning upon leaving right now?"

"Sure."

"Phineas, that's desertion!"

"I know it."

"The packhorses?"

"You can take them through, Tom."

"Phineas," I said and began to tremble. "I never so much as touched a packhorse before the day before yesterday. I haven't the faintest idea how to get those horses to Pittsburgh."

"You won't have to take them to Pittsburgh," Phineas said. "The trail crosses the highway about twelve miles from here. There's a station there. Put up the horses with the blacksmith and wait for Abner's train."

"Phineas!"

"There's nothing to it, Mr. Philadelphia," Phineas said and gave me a gentle nudge in the ribs. "Horses have tongues, but it won't make any difference if they neigh on the packhorse trail. Just let them walk. They'll take care of themselves."

Phineas offered me his hand, started off, then turned. "Those young beavers, Tom," he said. "They're yours now."

I had forgotten about the beavers. Actually I was too dazed to be thinking clearly about anything. "I'll give you what you paid for them," I said.

"No, Tom," Phineas said, "they're yours."

"You're penniless," I said.

"Hell, Tom, I've been broke so many times I'm used to it."

"How much did you pay for the beaver?" I asked.

"Forget it."

"How much did you pay for the beaver?" I asked again, firmly.

"Thirty-five pounds Pennsylvania," Phineas conceded reluctantly. "It was a real bargain. They'll bring fifty pounds in Pittsburgh without a hassle."

I reached into my money belt and brought out thirty-five pounds. "I'll mail you half of any profit I make," I said. "I'll send the money to you at the Chambersburg postal coach inn."

Tears welled up in Phineas' eyes as I pressed the money into his hands. "Good luck to you, Phineas," I said.

"I sure appreciate this, Mr. Philadelphia," Phineas said. "I don't figure it can mean too much to a gentleman like you, but—you've just made yourself a friend for life."

Phineas disappeared behind the trees and it became necessary for me to take some positive form of action. "Giddy-up!" I said and slapped the lead horse smartly across the hind, for I recalled that Phineas always did this when he got the horses under way.

The animals, to my great relief, began plodding ahead. "Just let them walk," Phineas had advised and this, come to think of it, succinctly states my plan of procedure.

While en route, I did not worry about what to do if my charges became panicked by a wild beast—for it did not occur to me that such a contingency might well have arisen at any moment. My sole concern was to keep the horses moving. Phineas, after a rest period, frequently had to push, beat and yell at the horses in order to get them going again. Doubting my abilities in this field of endeavor, I did away with all rest periods.

This was a hot, sticky day. In due time the horses began glancing at me appealingly. By late afternoon the hurt look in their patient eyes had torn my heart to shreds. Since the poor creatures, innocent victims of my incompetent management, had neither rest nor drink, it was only proper that I should not take sustenance either. "My unfortunate friends," I said out loud, more than once, "I can assure you that you cannot possibly be more hungry and thirsty and weary of all this than I."

Shortly before dusk, the twenty-four packhorses and I turned a sharp bend in the trail. We were now back on the Lancaster Highway. Ahead, I saw a blacksmith shop, a general store, and three log cabins. After ascertaining that Abner Wilson's train had not yet arrived, I acquainted the blacksmith with how I happened to be where I was. "You brought those horses all the way through without a stop!" the blacksmith exclaimed, and he was amazed not only because I had done it without helpers, but also because most of the route was up steep rises.

"It sometimes helps to be a neophyte," I said and made for the general store, where I was served an excellent roast beef dinner.

XIII

Following a sound night's sleep in the loft of the blacksmith's stable, I awakened at dawn completely refreshed. This was a beautiful day. The dew had freshened the violets and red and white trillium which abounded in the surrounding woods. As I walked about after breakfast for want of something better to do, the air was permeated with the fragrance of these pleasant-smelling flowers. Until the sun arose, the aroma was so pronounced the station settlement seemed to be enveloped by a sweet-smelling fog.

During this stroll, I must confess to being quite pleased with myself. Since all things are relative, I was able to convince myself that persuading twenty-four packhorses to walk twelve miles constituted something of an accomplishment. While it is difficult to understand the mental processes involved, it now no longer seemed outlandish to presume I might be able to move goods down the Ohio River for the purpose of turning over a profit. As a matter of fact, I became fascinated by the notion. The opportunities seemed endless. In Pittsburgh I fully expected to pursue the matter further.

At noon, while eating lunch in the general store, I overheard someone say that a Conestoga train was halted about a mile east, the reason being that this day was Sunday. Melissa Andrews' train, I told myself, would surely be farther along than this and dismissed the possibility from my mind. However, shortly the speaker remarked that the train had been where it was since before Friday noon, the reason for this earlier halt being that the wife of the train association's president was giving birth to twins.

After shaving with the blacksmith's razor and tidying myself well as I could, I walked two rises west. Abner Wilson's train was not in sight. Turning about, I walked east.

Although still of the firm opinion that prudent behavior dictated keeping distance between Melissa and me, I could feel myself becoming unduly excited when I noted the halted train was of some forty wagons, approximately the length of the one Melissa was riding. Off the final wagon a white-haired woman had a deer's stomach, filled with clabbered milk, tied to the branch of a tree. Beating the deer's stomach with a stick, she was making butter. "Are a Mr. Bushrod Andrews and his daughter, Miss Melissa Andrews, members of this train?" I inquired of this woman.

"That they are, my good man," the woman said, "and Melissa's all right, bless her sweet soul. Nary a bone of the dear girl's body was broke."

"I beg your pardon?" I said.

"Ain't you heard!" the woman said. "Melissa, the dear child, almost blowed herself to bits this morning while we were at the services. Such an explosion—"

"Where is Melissa?" I asked.

"At wagon number two. And a sheer miracle, 'twas God Himself—"

"Thank you," I said and rushed off.

Melissa, a patchwork quilt thrown across her legs, sat half-dozing on a bearskin placed on the sunny side of wagon number two. Although a trifle pale, she appeared to be intact and, in my opinion, looked rather lovely.

Melissa's expression brightened up beautifully at the sight of me. "Tom!" she exclaimed and despite my concern I noted with pleasure that, for the first time, she had called me by first name. "I was told you almost blew yourself to bits," I said. "Are you all right?"

"Quite," Melissa said, "except for an extremely sore right shoulder. I have been ordered to sit here quietly and to rest. While I see no real need for this, I confess to finding it rather pleasant."

"What in the world happened?"

"A comedy of one error, in which I played the principal role," is what Melissa called it. That morning the more religious members of the train had considered it an act of God that a circuit rider happened by. Bored by long-winded sermons, Melissa was delighted to be delegated the task of looking out for the young children. There were nine babies in cribs, plus a dozen very lively youngsters, none older than four, but all possessing sturdy legs capable of allowing them to roam about. Included was a small pig, a pet belonging to one of the children.

"The pig was in a make-shift pen," Melissa said, explaining that it was hoped some of the youngsters, interested in watching the pig, might remain stationary for a short time. "While I was changing a baby's diaper," Melissa went on to say, "one of the older children began tugging at my dress. 'Miss Andrews,' she said, 'look what's crossing the road.' I thought she meant a turtle or something like that. 'It's a great big brown bear,' the child said and when I looked it *was!*"

"Good heavens!" I said.

"I'm told the bear was after the pig," Melissa said, "but the pig's pen stood in the midst of the cribs and I was certain he had one of the babies in mind." She pointed to her father's rifle, lying on the wagon driver's seat. It was, I could see, a Kentucky rifle, or a "Kaintuck" as so many people in the West called this firearm.

"I had never shot a rifle," Melissa said. "The children had begun to scream and this may have confused the bear. At any rate, he stopped and looked at us. I had seen my father and wagoneers fire their rifles and I went and got my father's. Having heard our men talking about 'two fingers' of powder, I poured two fingers full, drove home the ball, and waited for the bear to come forward." Looking at me, she smiled slightly.

"Yes?" I said.

"When he came forward," Melissa said, "I pressed the trigger. The rest of my story is pure hearsay. My body, so I am told, was discovered on the far side of the highway. Upon regaining consciousness, I lay on this bearskin. Very little of my caller, I have been assured, is left."

"That much backfire!" I said. "It seems incredible."

Melissa held out her right hand with the fore- and middle-finger pressed together and extended horizontally. "This is two fingers of powder, is it not?" she inquired.

"Yes," I said, "it is. Two inches of powder is about right. Even a bit more shouldn't make too much difference."

Raising her left hand, Melissa held up both her forefingers, perpendicularly, one atop of the other. "This would also be two fingers of powder, would it not?"

"You didn't!" I said. "You didn't pour that much powder?"

"Yes," Melissa said, "I did, with a bit extra for good measure."

With that much powder she could well have blasted her way through a stockade's gate. "I'm surprised you aren't already in Pittsburgh," I said.

"I was not going that way," Melissa said. "I was hurled in the direction of the Allegheny River. Yonder trees arrested my progress."

I sat down beside Melissa and we began talking about our mutual experiences. While I do not remember much of the actual conversation, I do remember how much I enjoyed it and that, while it progressed, I found Melissa to be more and more charming. It may also be said that now all thoughts I might have entertained concerning the prudence of keeping distance between us, vanished.

Eventually, although I would have preferred staying on longer, my sense of propriety asserted itself and told me it was time to leave. "May I look forward to seeing you in Pittsburgh?" I requested.

Seemingly in doubt, Melissa hesitated and before she could reply, from behind the wagon, I heard someone cough in the provocative manner of a person wishing to make his presence known. "My father," Melissa said and I stood up.

Almost immediately Mr. Andrews, whom I strongly suspected of eavesdropping, came around the front of the wagon. His strides were not those of a sober man. When he came close to me, I could smell whiskey on his breath.

This was my first unimpeded view of Mr. Andrews. He wore knee breeches with silver buckles, silver shoe buckles, three high collars to his coat, a queue, and a voluminous neckcloth. While he was shorter, slighter of stature, and more dumpy than I had realized, the man's legs were thin as stilts. One of those people who don't appear to have hips, Mr. Andrews' legs went straight into his body, like a stork's. His pinched, pointy, solemn face with a rather large nose and not much of a chin gave added credence to the analogy.

"Father," Melissa said apprehensively, "this is Tom—Mr. Thomas A. Morrow of Philadelphia."

Mr. Andrews regarded me with a withering dignity which made him seem taller and me feel uncomfortable. "I had presumed as much," he said. "Mr. Morrow, my daughter has already fully informed me of the service you rendered us. Since what you did turned out well, I add my thanks to hers." Bringing out first his spectacles, which he placed on the far end of his nose, then his timepiece: "I noted when you arrived, Mr. Morrow. You have been here almost two hours. You will understand, I am sure, that I must ask you to leave very shortly. My daughter is far more shaken up then she realizes. She was not injured, the good Lord be praised, but it is imperative that she have quiet and rest."

"I fully understand, sir," I said.

"I was certain you would, Mr. Morrow," Mr. Andrews said, and turning about-face with the precision of a well-drilled soldier, he moved to the rear of the wagon.

I confess to being somewhat taken aback. "I had no idea we'd talked so long," I said to Melissa.

"Nor had I," she said.

Melissa's eyes were trained on her father and I could see that her lips were quivering ever so slightly. "I am hoping, ever so much," I said, "that I may plan upon seeing you in Pittsburgh."

"Our train is not going to stop at Pittsburgh," Melissa said. "We are going beyond, to the Little Beaver River Station or possibly to Steubenville. Better facilities for downriver travel, as I understand it, are available at these places."

"I imagine I could manage to be at either of the two settlements," I said.

"If so, I shall be most pleased to see you," Melissa said.

Upon taking my leave, Mr. Andrews was not to be seen in the vicinity of wagon number two. He did, however, call out to me when I passed wagon number six. "I would appreciate it, Mr. Morrow," he said, "if you will await me at the rear of the train."

The meeting took place on the side of the highway, out of Melissa's sight. "I am going to assume that you are a gentleman, Mr. Morrow," Mr. Andrews said.

"Thank you, sir," I said, "I do make the effort."

"As one gentleman addressing another," Mr. Andrews said, "I am requesting that you do not see my daughter again." Before I could reply: "You deserve an explanation, sir. My daughter is betrothed to a young, healthy, well-educated man of excellent family, residing in New Orleans. Since I have not long to live, a fact unbeknownst to my daughter, I am most anxious that nothing shall come in the way of the consummation of this marriage. I believe you are capable of understanding my feelings?"

"I should say, yes, I am, sir," I said.

"Thank you, sir," Mr. Andrews said, and once more making a quick and precise about-face, walked away.

XIV

It was midmorning of the following day before Abner Wilson's Conestoga train arrived at the station settlement. During this interim, jolted by Mr. Andrews' dictum, I had thought of virtually nothing else. So varied were my initial thoughts that there is no use attempting to evaluate them. However, of this much I was certain: I was going to see Melissa at least once more. While in the course of our get-togethers nothing of a definite nature had transpired which actually indicated either of us was even considering the possibility of falling in love, there had been innumerable innuendoes passed out, by both parties, which to me did not seem to come under the general heading of mere flirtatious banter. If this were wishful thinking on my part—so be it! I must find out from Melissa's own lips that she was in love and wished to marry this young, healthy, well-educated man from New Orleans.

After stating in strong language his disapproval of what Phineas Ford had done, Abner Wilson, like the blacksmith, expressed his amazement that I had managed to bring through the twenty-four packhorses on my own. While inspecting the animals and making arrangements to get them to Pittsburgh, Abner noted the two gunnysacks, now my private property. "What have you got in those?" he asked me.

"The equivalent of gold," I said.

"That lousy bastard!" Abner exclaimed almost immediately after I began relating my transaction with Phineas Ford.

Pulling out a pelt, Abner threw it onto the ground and spit on it. "Tom," he told me, "Phineas Ford suckered you slicker than a wet perch. That's a muskrat with the tail cut off."

Muskrats, even with the tails appended, Abner informed me, were next to worthless.

Except to be infuriated, there was nothing I could do. In due time the train began rolling, with me again a passenger aboard the van wagon. Approximately three hours later, still riding across high country, we passed a steep bluff. A formidable stream flowed below us. "The Ohio?" I said to Abner.

"Hell, no," Abner said, "that's the Allegheny."

Shortly we rounded a bend and now I saw the Ohio River for the first time. Although three miles off, I could see how avariciously she gobbled up the waters of the Monongahela and Allegheny rivers and surged out from the Point at Pittsburgh, a splendid "liquid highway to the west," moving through an endless wilderness of tree-covered hills—on and on, right into the far-off horizon.

On this day she was the exact color of unsweetened chocolate, running considerable driftwood, shimmering like a canopy of glistening spangles under the bright afternoon sun. Not a watercraft of any kind was on her.

"A beautiful bitch, isn't she?" Abner said.

"Yes, she is," I said and at the time I did not realize Abner meant his statement to be taken literally.

Pittsburgh was down there too, an irregular, rudely constructed settlement whose some two hundred houses, built mostly of logs, were clustered about Fort Pitt like so many baby chicks hovering beneath the protecting wings of a mother hen. Yet such was the sheer, wild magnificence of the Ohio River, I was scarcely aware that the settlement of Pittsburgh existed.

Within an hour we were at Pittsburgh's outskirts. Our reception committee was two dozen or so dogs, mostly hounds, left behind by people who'd gone down the river. Thinking we were their masters, at last returning for them, the forsaken animals yelped and leaped at our wagons.

With the dogs yapping at our wheels, we rolled over a corduroy road toward Fort Pitt. Although the fort stood out huge and imposing, as we moved along its high walls of reinforced logs and massive gates at the sally ports, I noticed that much of the timber needed to be replaced, for it was rotting.

Outside the main gate a large broadside, crudely illustrated but sparing none of the gory details, announced a hundred-fifty dollars reward for an Indian scalp with both ears appended. Another forbade the shooting of firearms within the settlement limits except as a warning of Indian attack. Still another, written in English, told Indians to stay out of Pittsburgh.

A half-asleep militiaman sentry, sitting on a powder keg, condescended to inform Abner that Lieutenant Ebenezer Denny was at headquarters.

On the parade two squads of Harmar recruits, old men and young boys, dressed in various garbs and carrying boards for rifles, trudged up and down, presumably drilling. Before the barracks a dozen other recruits, also sorry-looking chaps, lolled about. It is possible they were policing up. The blacksmith shop was cold. As we passed the latrine, the smell of lant ate into my nostrils.

"A sickening sight, isn't it?" Abner said.

"Yes, it is," I said. Yet you needed only to glance about to understand that Fort Pitt, built upon the burned-out ruins of Fort Duquesne, possessed the wherewithal to have been the citadel which held out and won for us the western phase of the War of the Rebellion. Some two dozen nine-pounder cannons on her Allegheny-Monongahela sides rendered her impregnable against attack from the Ohio. Rows of six-pounders protected her rear. Her rifle platforms were sturdy, her sentry towers high. She was well-contained with barracks and stables and storage houses. Her three ammunition dumps could hold enough powder and shot and cannon balls to see her through a whole year of siege.

Abner halted the van wagon before headquarters, signaling the rest of the train to move on to the stables. "I shouldn't be here too long, Tom," Abner said. "I want to see Ebenezer about that contract."

Actually Abner did not want the contract to supply Harmar's army with packhorses and flour. Anxious to return to Chambersburg in order to be on hand when his wife presented him with what he was certain would be his first son, Abner's bid was so outrageously high that "even the army," to quote Abner, would be compelled to say no.

"The way things go," I said, "you'll be sure to get it."

"If I do," Abner said, "God help the nation's tax rate."

Abner must have been in headquarters at least an hour. "Did you get the contract?" I asked when he returned.

"I'm the only bidder so far."

"Then you've got it?"

"Maybe not," Abner said. "Ebenezer knows what I did. He's going to send out another call for bids . . . Tom, step into headquarters. Ebenezer wants to talk to you."

The time had come to bid Abner good-bye. He and the wagoneers were going to spend the night at Houlens, a settlement directly across the Monongahela River from Pittsburgh. In no mood for another night of revelry, I planned upon staying at the Pittsburgh Inn. At dawn the train would be returning to Chambersburg.

"I probably won't see you before you start for home," I said and left the wagon.

"No," Abner said, "I guess not." He extended his hand. "You're a jackass to be going to Cincinnati, Tom, but good luck anyway. Oh, by the way! I asked Ebenezer about that damned name. Phineas Ford wasn't lying. St. Clair did make the change. People kicked so much though that St. Clair let it out that Losantiville was too hard to say. The real reason for the change is that St. Clair is a member of the Order of Cincinnatus. The settlement's name honors the society."

While Abner spoke it struck me Melissa had mentioned that, when you thought about it, Cincinnati was no easier to pronounce than Losantiville. This is how it had been with me all day. A casual word from Abner while en route, something I saw along the highway. In one way or another I was being constantly reminded of what Melissa had said or there seemed to be things she might be interested in hearing about.

"Perhaps I'll be seeing you in—Cincinnati," I said.

"If you do, I'm a bigger jackass than you," Abner said and got into the wagon.

"Abner," I called out as he started off, "I hope it's a boy."

"He sure better be," Abner called back.

Headquarters, a bare room with puncheon floor, was furnished with a hutch table, a number of three-legged stools, and two large wooden cabinets. Lieutenant Denny, seated behind the table which was cluttered with papers of all sorts, stood up upon my arrival. Powdered, immaculately attired, he looked quite the young dandy in his white double-breasted vest, white pantaloons, and highly polished half-boots.

Greeting me with crisp, military warmness, Lieutenant Denny motioned that I be seated. "Ridiculous! An utter waste of my valuable time, Mr. Morrow," he said, indicating the pile of material on the table. "Yet my immediate attention is required. Will you be so kind as to not mind waiting a few minutes?" Dipping his quill into an inkwell: "Damn!" he exclaimed and told me that because there was no ink at Fort Pitt, he was compelled to use gunpowder mixed with water. His signature, he felt, would not remain on the foolscap very long.

Working rapidly, impatiently, Lieutenant Denny's face frequently showed his displeasure with what he read. Eventually finished, he stuffed a batch of papers into a large leather portfolio and had them taken away by his orderly. "They'll go to Carlisle," he said, emitting a deep sigh, "where they'll be placed somewhere where nobody can find them . . . Abner tells me you are still determined upon going to Cincinnati."

"Yes," I said, "I am."

"May I repeat my suggestion made in Chambersburg, Mr. Morrow. I strongly urge you to reconsider."

"Thank you, but I am going anyway."

"I'm wondering how you plan getting down the river?"

"By flatboat, of course! Abner told me that, with the Indians acting up, I might have to wait a while before a flotilla is assembled."

"You will have to wait two weeks at least," Lieutenant Denny said, "probably longer."

This, of course, was most unpleasant news.

"I understand," the lieutenant said, "that you were fleeced by Phineas Ford?"

"I most certainly was," I said. "Among other things, Phineas Ford told me he was a Harmar scout. May I inquire if in this instance he happened to be telling the truth?"

"He was and, unhappily, General Harmar is in most dire need of his services."

"Then he *will* be in Cincinnati?"

"Yes, he will be."

"Thank you," I said.

Permitting himself a slight smile, Lieutenant Denny said: "Am I correct in presuming that in Cincinnati you expect to take up the matter with Phineas Ford?"

"You are," I said. "In one way or another, I intend to get back my thirty-five pounds."

Lieutenant Denny clapped his hands. Almost immediately his orderly appeared in the doorway. "Herman," he said, "I want a squad of militiamen. At once! They will report to me at the Allegheny River gate."

Lieutenant Denny stood up and when he did, so did I. "If you will come with me, Mr. Morrow," he said, "we shall see what we can do about your general situation."

With no more knowledge than this at my disposal, I accompanied Lieutenant Denny across the parade. At the Allegheny River gate we were met by a squad of puffing, buckskin-clad, armed militiamen whom I'd seen coming up on the double. Moving possibly a half mile up the Allegheny River the six of us arrived at a row of at least three dozen flatboats, lodged on the river's rather steep embankment, a good six feet above the water's edge.

Pittsburghers, I learned before the day was over, built their flatboats here and awaited a rise of the river to launch them.

Dried mud was visible on the flatboats' sides, which indicated they'd been built prior to a rise of the river. As if waiting for the Indian menace to subside so they could become useful, the flatboats simply stood there, forlorn-looking as the empty chicken coops one sees when passing an abandoned poultry farm.

Although burning with curiosity about what Lieutenant Denny intended to do, it was impossible not to experience a certain feeling of apprehension upon what was my first face-to-face encounter with an Ohio River flatboat. It must be borne in mind that fifteen years would pass before barges and keels and the so-called "floating-farmhouse" flatboats became a common sight. The craft I saw, equipped with bow and stern oars, were built of oak, of varying sizes, ranging from forty to ninety feet in length and from twelve to twenty feet in width. I did not get the impression that their construction was sturdy. My immediate thought—and I recall this vividly—was that I was contemplating going almost five hundred miles down the Ohio River aboard what could have well been a large crate, sawed away so as to leave a small and low cabin at the bow with a two-foot fence around the open part.

While telling myself that surely such means of water transportation would not fall apart before floating to Cincinnati (or why else would people build them!) we reached the final flatboat. "Please, stay out of sight, Mr. Morrow," Lieutenant Denny said. "Do not be surprised at anything which happens, for I know what I am doing."

As the lieutenant and the squad of militiamen went ahead, I moved to the final flatboat's stern, taking a position where I could see without being seen. Phineas Ford, stripped to the waist, was digging under the flatboat's bow, wielding his shovel with the feverish haste of someone who deems it prudent to get out of town in a hurry. Two logs, already beneath the flatboat's bow, made it abundantly clear that Phineas planned to launch this particular craft on rollers.

"Good afternoon, Phineas," Lieutenant Denny said.

"Hello, Ebenezer," Phineas said over his shoulder and went on with his digging.

"Since you are already a month late in honoring General Harmar with your presence," Lieutenant Denny said, "I am somewhat surprised that you aren't awaiting a rise of the river before taking your leave."

"If I'm going," Phineas grumbled, "I might as well get started."

Moving toward the river, the militiamen took up a position behind Phineas. With Lieutenant Denny at the flatboat's stern, Phineas was completely hemmed in. "A commendable thought, Phineas," Lieutenant Denny said. "However, I bring you unhappy news. You're under arrest."

"Under arrest! Ebenezer, what in the hell are you talking about?"

"I've got a warrant here," Lieutenant Denny said, and held up a piece of paper, folded thrice, which *did* look like an official document. "A Mr.

Thomas A. Morrow of Philadelphia has accused you of fleecing him. Apparently your oft-repeated young beaver skin bamboozle has backfired, Phineas. I must take you to the local magistrate, who will send you to Bedford for trial before the circuit judge."

"Circuit judge in Bedford!" Phineas said and slammed his shovel onto the ground. "Ebenezer, are you crazy! I'm a member of the United States Army. Sworn in right and proper. I'm under orders to report to Fort Washington."

"This is a civil action, Phineas. It supersedes the military."

Phineas moved up to Lieutenant Denny. Lowering his voice, in order that the militiamen could not hear: "Now look here, Ebenezer. The General needs me bad. He's down to nothing when it comes to scouts and you know it."

"Only too well," the lieutenant said. "Phineas, I've warned you over and over again about bamboozling gullible travelers."

"Never mind the sermon," Phineas growled. "You're the big cheese at the fort. You can get me out of this if you want." His face lighted up. "Say you just missed me! Tell your flunkies to help me get this God-damned boat in the water and I'll be gone before anybody knows the difference."

"Impossible," Lieutenant Denny said. "I did explain to Mr. Morrow how much General Harmar needs your services and have asked him to drop his charges. He is rightly incensed, so I don't know what his final decision will be. However, no power under the sun can keep you from being taken to jail right now . . . I take it, you have bills of sale for this flatboat and cargo?"

"Certainly I've got them!"

"Where are they?"

"In the flatboat."

"Get them."

While Phineas carried out this instruction, Lieutenant Denny moved over to me. "Everything seems to be going well, Mr. Morrow," he said. "Stay out of sight. Meet me at headquarters."

At least an hour must have passed before Lieutenant Denny joined me at headquarters. While I waited the lieutenant's orderly, Herman, inquired if I desired whiskey. "No, thank you," I said. "Is a map of the general vicinity available?"

"No, sir," Herman said.

"Are you familiar with the area?"

"Yes, sir."

"I have been told the Little Beaver River Station is about twenty miles from here."

"Yes, sir, by road," Herman said. "Forty miles by the river."

"The river's bends are that abrupt?"

"Yes, sir."

"Steubenville? Is it thirty miles off, by road?"

"Yes, sir. Seventy miles by water."

"Can you recommend a reliable hostler? I expect to ride to one of the settlements, possibly to both."

Herman shook his head in the negative. A tall, gaunt man with an Adam's apple large enough to be a hen's egg, he never smiled. One of the saddest-looking individuals I have ever seen, Herman spoke in a low monotone, dreary enough in sound to make announcement of the coming of the Messiah seem to be bad news. What he told me meant it would take considerable doing on my part if I expected to see Melissa before arriving in Cincinnati:

Local hostlers, Herman informed me, would not rent horses to people riding west, unless accompanied by military escort. I could expect none for three weeks, since the monthly supply train had gone out only a week before.

Reaching the settlements by water, Herman added, was an unlikely hope. Rivermen were not going downstream these days. Only army flotillas were leaving Fort Pitt. Bound for Fort Washington in Cincinnati, they did not put to at the settlements or even at Marietta, for fear of desertions.

"Mail?" I asked.

It only went off, Herman said, with the supply trains.

However, this particular predicament was soon quickly resolved. Returning to headquarters Lieutenant Denny handed me what upon examination proved to be bills of sale for Phineas Ford's flatboat and cargo, notarized and properly signed over to me.

Lieutenant Denny had gone to his table for a whiskey bottle. His face, I noticed, was quite flushed and his hair no longer looked neatly brushed and combed. Perspiration circles, under the armpits, showed on his shirt. Taking a stout swig, he handed me the bottle, which I declined. "In today's army," Denny said and took a second drink, "an officer must be a man of many parts."

"So I am beginning to gather," I said.

"Phineas Ford and I have discussed things at length," the lieutenant said. "In return for not having to go to jail, Phineas is more than pleased to pilot you to Cincinnati on your flatboat." Adding that there was no better riverman on the Ohio than Phineas Ford and that my flatboat's cargo would more than double in value at Cincinnati, showing me a handsome profit: "I therefore suggest, Mr. Morrow," Lieutenant Denny said, "that you consider what I have done as being the solution to your present problem."

My reply, in the affirmative, was made immediately. The young officer seemed quite pleased and thought, so I gathered, that he had managed things rather neatly—the army would not lose a valuable scout and a robbed civilian had been placated. I did not feel it necessary to tell Lieutenant Denny that the all-compelling reason for my ready reply was that as master of my own flatboat I could order my pilot to put to at the Little Beaver River Station and if need be, Steubenville.

XV

Lieutenant Denny would not hear of me staying at the Pittsburgh Inn. I must have dinner with him, he insisted, and be a guest of the United States Army for so long as I tarried in Pittsburgh. Providing me with an orderly, to be at my disposal around the clock, he had my traveling trunk, still on Abner Wilson's train, taken to a room in the officers' quarters. There was nothing unusual about this, he assured me. More than ample sleeping room, he remarked drolly, was presently available at Fort Pitt. The United States Army, he said, was only too glad to give what aid and comfort it could to "better class" citizens going to the Ohio Country.

Within the hour, shaved, bathed, and wearing a suit for the first time in a month, I dined with Lieutenant Denny in a small room within the headquarters building. This room had paneled walls and a carpeted hardwood floor. It was luxuriously fitted out with Chippendale furniture, China plates, silverware, and linens—all borrowed from the official residence, presently closed up.

Lieutenant Denny, upon my arrival, sat at the table, sipping wine while reading a Bible. "I read a chapter daily," he told me, "for I find it soothes my nerves."

At the moment, he went on to say, his nerves were badly in need of being soothed. While he was settling the Phineas Ford matter a barge had put to with a hundred barrels of flour. Or rather paste! Delivery was late because for two solid weeks the barge and flour had rested sunken on the bottom of the Monongahela River. "And where do you think the accompanying shipment of cannon powder is?" Lieutenant Denny asked and answered his own question. "Still at the bottom of the Monongahela! The haphazard way things are done here, Mr. Morrow! It is almost as bad as at Fort Washington, but there it is not our fault. On my own time I am preparing a critical report, accompanied with recommendations, which I will send directly to Mr. Washington, not as President, but as Commander-in-Chief of the United States Army."

Lieutenant Denny calmed down when Herman brought in our dinner, and turned out to be quite a gourmet. The entrée, served on a tremendous silver platter, was a baked catfish that must have weighed at least fifty pounds and was a good eight inches between the eyes. Tender, it was delicious and did not taste of mud as did catfish caught back home in the Schuylkill River. There were baked potatoes, wild asparagus, an excellent dandelion salad with radishes, and a raisin pie for dessert. It was a superb meal except for a murderous wine which puckered my lips with the first sip.

The wine, Lieutenant Denny told me, was made from winter grapes, so-called because they were too sour to eat until sweetened by a number of frosts. "It is quite palatable," he said, "once you become accustomed to it."

Apparently Lieutenant Denny had become so, for he drank eight or nine glasses during the course of the meal. Half-tipsy, he monopolized the conversation, yet I found him interesting and rather engaging.

Born in Boston, he'd almost followed in his father's footsteps and become a Congregational minister. "There is," he said, "a striking similarity between the work of ministers and dedicated army officers, for we are both attempting to rid the world of those who do not see the light."

As we'd seated ourselves Lieutenant Denny mentioned that it was an unwritten rule, amongst career officers at least, never to mention "shop" while dining. Adhering scrupulously to this practice, our talk moved from one subject to another.

The lieutenant, I learned, was a lover of the theater. He had seen Royall Tyler's The Contrast performed with applause at the John Street Theater in New York. (While this play was forbidden in Philadelphia, during January Susan and I had listened to Mr. Wignell's reading of it at the City Tavern.) Mr. Wignell, Lieutenant Denny felt, was a most accomplished comedian and character actor, there being no better proof needed than that Mr. Dunlap, obviously jealous of Mr. Wignell's popularity and The Contrast's success, had stooped to issuing disparaging remarks about both. In this I agreed and, listening further, I was surprised to discover that Lieutenant Denny's knowledge of the theater went considerably beyond merely liking or disliking this or that performance.

We also discussed Henry Fielding's *Rape Upon Rape,* currently riding a rebirth in the popular fancy since it was being published in parts in Eastern seaboard newsprints as a means of increasing circulation. Here Lieutenant Denny made a most interesting aside observation. "This business of stopping the story in the middle of a sentence!" he fumed. "I know it's because that's when the column is filled, but I find this ever so exasperating. It would seem to me, if the printers had any brains, they'd close at a high point in the tale. Wouldn't that make the reader more eager to find what is to follow?"

The feasibility of this suggestion *did* impress me and I recall that I planned writing Benjamin Franklin's son about it, although I never got around to doing it. "Yes, it would," I said, "and I predict that one of these days an enterprising printer will hit upon your suggestion."

"And I will receive nothing," the lieutenant said, laughing, "for having thought of it first."

We discussed Dante, Shakespeare, Thomas Paine, Adam Smith, the young Corsican, Napoleon. There was no doubt that the young officer was well read. Yet somehow I was gathering the impression that he wished to impress me with the range of his knowledge.

Mrs. Mae Dwyer entered our conversation, too. When Herman brought in the pie, Lieutenant Denny raised the upper crust with his fork and poured wine onto the raisins. "It is surprisingly good this way, Mr. Morrow," he said. "If you are wondering why I have not suggested completing our unfinished chess match, it is because at nine o'clock I am expecting a visitor—Mrs. Mae Dwyer."

"Mrs. Dwyer—she is in Pittsburgh!"

"In all her finery, Mr. Morrow."

"Does this mean Mrs. Dwyer has reconsidered and is going to provide General Harmar's army with women?"

"Now, now, Mr. Morrow," Lieutenant Denny chided playfully. "It was agreed we would not discuss anything even remotely connected with shop. But heavens, no! The situation has become worse, not better. It merely means Mae has acquired an inn here. She is bringing me one of her young ladies. You may have one too, if you so desire."

"Thank you, no," I said. "For me this has been a long and rather trying day. I am looking forward to sleeping in a real bed—alone."

"You may be missing what could well be an interesting and novel experience, Mr. Morrow," Lieutenant Denny said. "Have you ever gone to bed with a quadroon?"

"No," I said, "I have not."

"Neither have I," he said, "but Mae is supplying one for me this evening. In her typically enterprising fashion, Mae has brought in a dozen quadroons, at least their skins are light enough, so it makes no real difference if actually they are most probably mulattoes. They are real beauties, Mae says, imported from Jamaica at a ridiculously low figure and their white blood, in most cases, is French. Mae will observe how they are received here in Pittsburgh, before deciding whether or not to move them East. Should her thought catch the popular fancy, her sizable fortune will be increased commensurably, I should say, wouldn't you?"

"Yes," I said, "it would certainly seem so."

At five minutes of eight, explaining that between eight and nine he always worked on his critical report, Lieutenant Denny begged to be excused. "Possibly," he said, "while we are both in Cincinnati, you will be willing to read what I have written and offer constructive criticism as to its presentation."

"I will be most happy to be helpful in any way that I can," I said.

"I will appreciate that greatly," the lieutenant said, giving me his hand. "Tomorrow, I shall be arising at dawn." This apparently reminded him of the miserable state of General Harmar's army, for he suddenly became what I had at first thought constituted the all of him: an intense, young army officer. "I am going up the Monongahela River," he told me, "and will find out what is what about that sunken powder. The recruiting! Our supplies! Indescribably disgraceful, Mr. Morrow, and there's a lot of overcharging that I've unearthed besides. Speaking for General Harmar, you may be assured Carlisle will hear a word or two from me."

The room assigned me had a comfortable bed, a pleasant change, yet sleep did not come to me readily. The abandoned dogs of Pittsburgh began howling and were answered by those of Houlens. While in Pittsburgh, I discovered, one must learn to accustom himself to this disturbance, for it was a regular nightly occurrence.

In the light of what happened elsewhere that night it seems almost sacrilegious that I should even mention such a minor inconvenience. At the very time I was attempting to get to sleep, a mile beyond Pittsburgh's limits, Indians struck. They burned down two cabins and killed seven people. A young mother and her infant son, who'd hidden in their potato hole, were the only survivors. At noon this woman, carrying her baby, came running into Fort Pitt, hysterical to a point of shock. She eventually managed to tell that nothing was left of her cabin except the frame of the door. Through it, stuck on a pole, she saw her husband's scalped, decapitated head, his mouth stuffed with soil and his eyelids cut off.

The frequency of such tragedies had turned Pittsburgh into a settlement of extreme unrest. Outlying factories were abandoned. Farmers could not get on with their spring planting. Most of them had come within the settlement limits to live with friends or in lean-tos set up along the banks of the Monongahela. This, of course, meant trading was at a standstill. Money had all but disappeared. No CREDIT signs were on all shop and tippling house doors, many of which were closed. Yet none of the displaced men could be induced to sign up for General Harmar's army.

Finally getting to sleep, I did not awaken until midmorning and even then did not arise immediately, for it was a most luxurious feeling to be again lying in a bed. Hearing a knock on my door, I said, "Come in," and presumed the orderly assigned me was wondering when I planned having breakfast.

My caller was Phineas Ford. "For Christ's sake, Tom," he said, "are you still asleep?"

"Good morning, Phineas," I said.

"Now look here, Tom," Phineas said. "I hope you're not sore?"

"Of course not," I said. "I'm filled with rapture at the sight of you. What could possibly be more pleasing than a surprise visit from someone who only recently has cheated me out of thirty-five pounds?"

"Tom," Phineas said, "I was never going to cheat you. I gave you my hand, didn't I?"

"I vaguely remember such a gesture—an indication, was it not, of lifelong friendship?"

"I just *had* to have the money, Tom," Phineas said. "Hell, when you got to Cincinnati I figured on paying you back, double. Ask anybody along the river. When I give a man my hand, I'm his friend. I don't cheat him."

Despite the dictates of common sense, I found myself believing him.

"Tom, I was dead broke," Phineas pleaded. "What the hell else could I do?"

"You might have stated the case," I said. "As a matter of fact, had you offered to pilot me down the river, I would in all probability have been only too glad to say yes. The idea of taking a cargo to Cincinnati and turning over a profit appeals to me. We could have reached some kind of an arrangement, I'm sure."

"Now how in the hell was I supposed to know that!" Phineas said.

The expression of amazement on Phineas' face was genuine. I was convinced of that. How, I wondered, was it possible to cope with a mind like his?

"I have just finished making a plausible suggestion," I said.

"I wish now I had spoken up," Phineas said, shaking his head ruefully. "Damn it, Tom, I almost did. When you said you'd send me my share of the profits I came close, awfully close."

"But you didn't."

"No," Phineas said, "I didn't. But that's water over the dam by now! The big reason I came here this morning is because I can't figure out what Ebenezer Denny's got up his sleeve. He's a slick one, Tom. All he thinks about is being a general before he's thirty. I know why he was glad enough to get a chance to flog me, but it doesn't come to me yet why he's so damned anxious to get *you* down the river."

"He flogged you!"

"Sure," Phineas said and lifted up his shirt. His back, covered with newly formed scabs, was black as if coated with tar.

"Good Lord!" I said.

"Fifty lashes," Phineas said. "Ebenezer gave me twenty himself, trying to get me to whine. It's hard to say if he was worn out or got his satisfaction."

"Phineas!" I said. "What are you saying about Lieutenant Denny?"

"He's one of them, Tom," Phineas said. "Maybe not all the time, but ask any whore in Pittsburgh and she'll tell you she's scared to death when she pays him a call. Mostly he's satisfied to act regular, but plenty of times he beats the hell out of them."

"Phineas," I said, "I had no idea you'd be flogged."

"Hell, Tom, I know that. Don't look so worried! I've got the whole story about what Ebenezer pulled. Those twenty stripes didn't bother me too much. The militiaman who took over the strap was a friend of mine. He threw the leather around me and I hardly felt the rest."

"When we get to Cincinnati," I said, "Lieutenant Denny is certainly going to hear it from me about that flogging."

"Forget it. I'll take care of the lieutenant good and proper in Cincinnati," Phineas said. "But figure out what he's got up his sleeve. Damn it, Tom, he's got to have something up there or he'd tell you you're a jackass to be going down the river."

"He did tell me that," I said, "any number of times."

"He did! Well, then he figures you were going down anyway, no matter what he said. He's like that, Tom. Religious."

"What's religion got to do with it?" I asked.

"A lot. He knows damned well he ought to make you go back home. Now he can say to himself that he did try."

"He has no authority to *make* me go back to Philadelphia," I said.

"But he could pull strings!" Phineas said. "He could God-damned well see to it the only way you'd get to Cincinnati, is to walk. Instead, he's helping you out. Tom, I'm telling you. Watch that man, he's half crazy. He prayed before he flogged me. For *my* soul! Ask the whores! He prays for theirs before he beats them up."

Eventually we began talking about taking our leave from Pittsburgh. "Just what are our traveling plans?" I asked.

"There aren't any," Phineas said. "We wait for the rain. When the river rises, we go."

"Now—about the cargo . . ."

"Don't worry your head, Tom," Phineas said. "I'll do all the loading."

"That's not what I'm talking about," I said. "I don't want to be a Shylock."

"What's that?"

"Shylock was a blood sucker," I said. "What I mean is that I have no desire to be one. As I understand it, I now own the flatboat and cargo?"

"That's right."

"This is fair," I said, "since both were bought with my money."

"That's right too," Phineas said.

"The cargo—it's to be flour and whiskey, isn't it?"

"Unless I can think of something else."

"Whatever the cargo," I said, "when we get to Cincinnati, we'll discuss sharing the profits. But it must be clearly understood—first of all I'm to get back my thirty-five pounds, Pennsylvania."

"I wish you'd make that thirty-six pounds, Tom," Phineas said.

"Thirty-six pounds! Why?"

"Because I'm dead broke," Phineas said. Grinning and clicking his teeth: "You want me to have a chance to look over the town, don't you?"

I gave him the pound.

"Tom," Phineas said, "this pound will bring you better than two in Cincinnati."

"Is that so? How?"

"I'm letting you sell the flatboat when we're through with it."

"I thought the flatboat was already mine," I said.

"It is," Phineas said, "but the oarsman's always allowed to sell it for planks. All the boatowners do that, Tom, but since you loaned me this pound, I'm going to let you pick up that profit."

A flatboat, Phineas told me, cost a dollar a linear foot in Pittsburgh.

Ours was a sixty-footer. At Cincinnati, the planks could be sold for at least fifteen dollars, come what may. They'd bring considerably more, Phineas said, if there was still no sawmill in the settlement, which would most likely be the case.

XVI

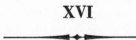

Two days of waiting for rain was enough for me. Seeking out Phineas at the tippling house where, without benefit of clergy, his pound note Pennsylvania permitted him to live the life of Nebuchadnezzar: "Tomorrow," I said firmly, "we'll launch the flatboat on rollers."

"Whatever you say, Tom," Phineas replied readily enough, which was somewhat surprising, for I had anticipated considerable protest.

Two hours later the skies darkened and the rain came. Phineas, I learned, could sense the imminence of rain by the stiffness in his left shoulder blade which had been dislocated during a tavern brawl. And I never found him to be wrong!

We got a torrential downpour, accompanied by thunder and lightning so violent that Fort Pitt seemed to be under attack. It lasted three days, ending close to evening. At this time Phineas came to my quarters for my traveling trunk, saying he'd put it aboard now and would float our flatboat to the Point, thus saving an hour's traveling time. He handed me an army promissory note for two-and-a-half shillings, endorsed by a local farmer. Being a carrier's fee, he said, this rightly belonged to me.

"Is somebody going with us?" I asked.

"Two cows," Phineas said.

I knew of course that it was safe enough to travel during daytime to the Little Beaver River Station, which we should reach before evening. While Phineas actually would deliver the cows to someone at the station, their real purpose was to make Indians, watching from the hills, think we were local farmers. Since he was personally known to many Indians, Phineas said, he'd add to the deception by shaving off his beard.

Shortly after dawn of the following morning, wearing new buckskins bought in Pittsburgh for fifty cents, half the Chambersburg price, I sloshed across Fort Pitt's muddy parade. Outside the main gate, I paused and looked ahead in amazement. The Ohio River, a bloody-brown under the rising sun, had doubled in width. Along her shores, trees cropped up unnaturally out of the water. The river, I should say, had risen to within five feet of the fort's main gate. She'd crept up high into Pittsburgh.

Our flatboat, the cows aboard, was moored well out in a cove. Be it a ship of the sea or a sixty-foot flatboat, rudely constructed of green oak planks, there always seems to be an aura of excitement when someone leaves land and takes to the water. At least two dozen people had congregated to see us off. Emerging from the group, Phineas motioned to a two-seated birch-bark canoe tied up beside a small plank-pier in the cove. "Let's get started, Tom," he said.

So help me, had I not recognized the voice, it might have taken me a while to guess the speaker's identity. To hide his great shock of hair, Phineas had on an oversized Mennonite hat. He wore homespuns, a blue shirt, and gray trousers. Not only had he shaved, but also, by means of rabbit fur, he'd given himself a Mennonite beard.

As was customary in Pittsburgh, when Phineas and I got into the canoe, the people ashore began singing:

> "The river is up, the channel is deep,
> The winds blow high and strong,
> The flash of the oars, the stroke we keep,
> As we row the old boat along,
> DOWN THE O-Hi-O!"

Although usually irked by good-byes which smack of the ceremonial or the sentimental, in this case I was quite touched. The singers weren't compelled to be here, they didn't know me from Adam, yet they knew what a trip down the Ohio River was like and were wishing Phineas and me well.

Taking the bow position in the canoe, I picked up the paddle. Phineas, shoving us off, hopped onto the aft seat so expertly that the craft didn't so much as quiver. I put my paddle into the water and began—to paddle. A squad of husky men, pushing with full might, couldn't have capsized us more neatly or quickly. Into the water Phineas and I plunged. "For Christ's sake, Tom," I heard Phineas calling out as I struck out for shore. "You don't have to swim, it's not two feet deep here." Within moments I discovered this on my own, for with my arms and legs still in locomotion, my torso was on the muddy river bottom.

"Haven't you ever been in a canoe before?" Phineas asked me.

"No," I said, "I haven't."

"If you paddle too hard on the same side I do," Phineas said, while righting the canoe, "we'll tip."

"I can see how that would be so," I said.

Once aboard the flatboat, Phineas took over the bow oar. No complications ensued when he entrusted me with the task of untying the mooring rope, off our stern. Slowly Phineas circled us into midstream. The planks of our flatboat were fastened with wooden pegs, not a hundred iron nails went into her entire construction. When the current gripped us she creaked and groaned so loudly that it seemed most unlikely that she'd remain intact. The cows, already set into a dither by the movement of the craft, became quite upset by the noise and made it evident that they would have preferred being on dry land. They had no recourse, though, but to moo, for they were tightly wedged in the aisle between flour and whiskey barrels piled up on the afterdeck.

The creaking and groaning stopped once we were attuned to the current and now we glided along smoothly. We carried some fifty tons. Such a load, Phineas had told me, drew two-and-a-half feet. This is correct, but where I was, sitting on a whiskey keg beside the flatboat's stern oar, I thought surely Phineas must be in error. By merely bending over slightly, I could cup up river water in my hand. Our deck wasn't two inches above the waterline.

Fort Pitt and the settlement disappeared from sight as we rounded the first of the Ohio's many bends. This one was so abrupt that it was almost possible to believe that we had come about and were floating back to Pittsburgh. Now there was nothing to see but river, sky, endless forest.

Although Phineas had called for me to come forward, I had stayed where I was. The vast expanse of virgin wilderness surrounding us! We seemed to be floating off into nowhere. I needed to be alone for a while.

When Phineas called to me the second time, climbing over the barrels, I moved forward. Phineas sat on the leeward rail, with his knee crooked over the oar. A happy, contented expression played across his clean-shaven face. Shaved, Phineas actually came close to looking distinguished. He had good features, a strong chin, broad brow and until he clicked his teeth or began talking the inherent intelligence of the man showed all over his countenance. Whether he would be happier or better off is something else again, yet one couldn't help wondering what he might have been like, reared in another environment. What pleasure he derived, simply by being on the water! He, the boat, and the current seemed to have become combined in a silent, self-contained partnership.

"Take a drink, Tom," Phineas said, pointing to five whiskey jugs lined along the starboard rail.

"It makes me sleepy in the daytime," I said.

"Well, get out of your wet underwear then," Phineas said, "If they're not dry, you'll get the damps tonight when it's foggy."

The advice was good and I followed it, placing my buckskins and underwear on the top of the cabin. "You ought to get the habit, Tom," Phineas said. "A little nip now and then through the day. It fortifies you at night."

"I'll wait and see what happens on that score," I said. "How fast are we moving?"

"Four miles. Maybe a little more."

"Is that good time?"

"Good time!" Phineas said and clicked his teeth. "If I got down on my knees and prayed to God, I couldn't ask for better."

It appeared to me, though, that we were scarcely moving. When I looked straight down at the muddy water, we seemed to be standing still. However, every now and then on the hillsides there were great patches of color made by masses of blue larkspur, purple phlox, and yellow celandine poppies. These would suddenly loom into my direct line of vision, then I had to turn my head to see them, then they were gone.

We rounded bend after bend, so abrupt that by merely riding the current, our course took us alternately closer to the Ohio and Virginia shores. Shortly before dusk: "One more bend," Phineas announced, "and we'll be at Little Beaver."

"Excuse me," I said and went to the cabin, to shave and comb my hair.

I had not mentioned to Phineas that I hoped to see Melissa Andrews at the Little Beaver River Station, thus he was somewhat surprised by what I had done. "You planning on visiting in Little Beaver?" he asked.

"Yes."

"A lady?"

"Yes."

"The one you were with at the crossing, I'll wager," Phineas said and clicked his teeth.

"As a matter of fact, yes, it is she," I said, "but her train may have gone to Steubenville." I spoke with such resolution that Phineas realized I was in no mood to hear snide remarks, no matter how jocular or harmless their intent.

"I doubt if she'll be at Little Beaver, Tom," Phineas said. "The road to Steubenville's better and at Fort Steuben there'd be more of a chance to hook onto a flotilla."

Phineas' appraisal was correct. Melissa was not at the Little Beaver River Station.

We, of course, tarried at the station until darkness set in. Approximately at nine o'clock we took our departure, riding into a night so tar black that I could scarcely see my own hands. Being of no use to Phineas, I lay down on a bearskin placed in the aisle between the afterdeck barrels.

I slept soundly until awakened by a pair of annoyed goatsuckers, flying almost directly above me. My hair, my face, and the bearskin wrapped around me were soaking wet and sticky. We seemed to be circling. Arising, I walked forward. Fog had made the whole flatboat wet as if it had been sloshed by a heavy rain. Phineas, pressing on the bow oar, was guiding us shoreward in a series of sweeping arcs.

Although it was not quite so dark and I could see my way about, the fog was so thick that I could not tell how close it was to morning. "What time is it?" I asked Phineas.

"Daylight'll break in maybe a half hour."

We rode through an unusually heavy fog puff. Phineas become enveloped by it and I could not see any part of him, then none of myself. When we pulled through, fog still lingered in Phineas' hair, making it appear as if smoldering.

"Aren't you tired?" I asked Phineas.

"I'm maybe a little ass-weary," he said.

We continued to circle. Although I could not yet see them, on the bank sycamores and cottonwoods grew to the water's edge. Our starboard gunnel bumped against one of these trees. Phineas lashed the bow oar and started for the stern. "Tom," he advised, "you'd better lie down, so you won't get scratched by branches."

I could hear Phineas tugging as the flatboat zigzagged slowly ahead. Branches swept across the deck and a number of hummingbirds buzzed about me. The aroma of honeysuckle was strong. Gnats and other insects quickly discovered my presence and began descending upon me in droves. The fog, trapped in the boscage, was thick as glue.

The flatboat stopped. Phineas came forward, yawned, and said: "I'm going to sleep a while."

"I'm wide awake," I told him.

"It's all right if you want to go ashore," Phineas said, "but don't roam too far." He added sharply: "And *don't* show yourself on the riverbank."

Wrapping himself in a bearskin, Phineas went to sleep immediately. Gnats, swarming all over his face, did not disturb his blissful repose. That he was able to get to sleep at all was a feat in itself. The insects were so numerous, I was removing them from my nostrils and spitting them out of my mouth.

Pouring a small swig of whiskey, I drank it slowly. With the breaking of dawn, the thickets became loud with the drone of cicadas. Although completely hidden from river view, we were possibly a hundred feet from the riverbank itself, which rose abruptly. We were moored in what looked like a swamp. The roots of the trees beside our flatboat were exposed and their trunks were covered with dried mud. The mud went up a good forty feet, twice as high as the riverbank. At first striking me as being somewhat of an oddity, it suddenly dawned upon me that this was an indication of how high the Ohio River was capable of rising when she flooded.

In due time, I became restless. A sycamore stood close enough to the flatboat to touch. Stepping onto the gunnel, I climbed this tree. Below me I saw an Ohio River steaming under the morning sun. The fog was lifting, but here and there clumps were still stuck on the water. They rode downstream like so many miniature, dirty-looking icebergs.

The current told me we were tied up on the Virginia side. On the Ohio shore a herd of at least two dozen buffaloes frolicked about in the shallow water, the dames having great fun ducking their young offspring. I, however, having gleaned my knowledge from Eastern seaboard newsprints, labored under the impression I was watching wild cows. "These wild cows," I had read in the Boston *Gazette*, "are larger than oxen, have short black horns, with a large beard under their chins. Their heads are so full of hair that it falls over their eyes and gives them a frightful look."

Elsewhere, no matter where I looked, I saw only: sky, trees, and the Ohio River.

BOOK TWO

---·◆·---

DOWN THE O-HI-O!

I

Phineas, who required little sleep, awakened shortly after midmorning. He came ashore, carrying his rifle and a whiskey jug. Glancing about he noted the wherewithal for breakfast, which I'd already taken from the flatboat. "Haven't you eaten yet?" he asked.

"I was afraid to make a fire," I said.

Nodding, to indicate his approval that I possessed this much common sense, Phineas showed me how to build a smokeless fire. Digging a hole some six inches deep, he filled it with a soft lining of white oak bark. The pit he covered with earth, leaving holes at each end to provide a draft. When he applied his flint, there was fire but no smoke and the bark burned even when covered with ashes. Such a fire, Phineas mentioned, was also useful in the woods during the winter. By sleeping atop it, you could keep from freezing.

Instead of the jerk I'd brought out, we had fried crawfish, big as Boston lobsters, which Phineas caught by probing under rocks along the riverbank. Fried in bear oil, they were most tasty. Breakfast concluded, Phineas scooped up the ashes from the fire and dumped them into a pail of river water, to settle the mud. For a fleeting moment, I confess, I thought he planned to drink this, at least to provide us with clean washing water. I was, however, mistaken. He poured the water into the whiskey keg from which he'd filled our five jugs.

From now on there was nothing to do but await the coming of darkness. Phineas wiled away the time taking nips of whiskey. Every hour or so, he'd climb up the riverbank to look about. For me, the wait was maddening.

In desperation I finally went to my traveling trunk for the only reading material at my disposal, the texts I'd need to teach school in Cincinnati: Dillworth's *Speller*, the *Columbian Orator*, Pike's *Arithmetic*, Murray's *Reader & Grammar*, the *American Preceptor*. Already quite familiar with these works, nothing therein provided me with stimulating reading.

Since the crawfish were so filling, we did not eat lunch. Announcement by Phineas that it was time to prepare supper, meaning also that at last I had something to do, came as a great relief.

Phineas went to the flatboat for a spear, a fishline of twisted fiber, a bone hook, a cork, and a cleverly carved stone sinker. Keeping the spear, he handed me the fishing gear. "Try to catch a perch if you can, Tom," Phineas said and told me a cove was only a short ways downstream.

Lifting rocks along the riverbank, in short order we had a dozen squirming night crawlers, my bait. As I moved off toward the cove, Phineas walked in the opposite direction. The cove was a fisherman's paradise. Within a few minutes, I hooked and landed a twenty-five-pound perch. Unable to resist, I threw in again to see what else I could do. A pike this time, then a sturgeon. Another perch, three catfish, and a quillback. I lost a muskellunge, a tremendous fish that looked big as a hound as it leaped out of the water. All this in less than an hour.

I'd immediately thrown back all my catches except the first perch. Returning, I held up my fish, proudly. The expression on Phineas' face indicated amazement that it had taken me so long. A spirited account of my other catches left him unimpressed. "You can throw away the perch," he said and indicated the going fire, from within which I got a whiff of roasting meat.

"What is it?" I asked.

"Young beaver tails," Phineas said, his broad smile making me think a touch of the whimsical lurked in the man's soul after all. The smile, however, merely meant that he was pleased to be serving a real delicacy. The secret of making young beaver tails a dish fit for a king, Phineas explained, lay in the way Indians did it. You roasted the tails first. *Then* you fried them in bear oil.

We took off into another tar black night. Although I had no idea of the time, it was an hour before daybreak when Phineas awakened me. "You'd better come forward, Tom," he said and hurried back to the bow oar.

The moment I stood up, I saw it. To our starboard, downstream, how far off, I could not tell, but it was a great distance away: a blotch of scarlet. Bright, in the darkness, as an Alpenglow.

I moved to the bow oar. "Steubenville's out there, Tom," Phineas said.

"An attack!"

"No," Phineas said. "You'd see more red than that. Indians sneaked up on an outlying cabin."

"The people in the settlement?"

"They're all right," Phineas said. "Indians aren't going for forts these days. This was a hunting party, feeling frisky. They were drunk or they wouldn't have come that close to the stockade. They sure did come close though, it's a wonder they didn't run into a patrol."

Phineas spoke with the assurance of someone already fully apprised of the facts.

"I'll be honest with you, Tom," Phineas said, "it figures the Indians hit and took off fast. There's an outside chance, though, that they're still hanging around. It's just plain common sense that we put to in Virginia and forget Steubenville."

I shook my head in the negative.

"Tom, I've got to follow the river. I can't hit Steubenville on the nose and wouldn't want to anyway because we'd be spotted surer than hell. We're off Virginia now. I can't say for sure where we'd land in Ohio. It'd be a couple of miles above or below Steubenville. There'll be a walk through deep woods."

"Phineas," I said, "we're going to Steubenville. From then on I won't open my mouth until we get to Cincinnati—you'll give all the orders."

"Are you that daffy about the girl!"

"I'm not certain," I said. "It's quite possible that I am."

Our putting-to on the Ohio shore was a re-enactment of the previous night's arrival on the Virginia side. There was just as much fog, just as many insects, we again had fried crawfish for breakfast.

We were surrounded by dense forest. Steubenville, Phineas said, should be about a mile-and-a-half below us. It had already been established that Phineas would accompany me to the settlement. I had protested. "As you said," I'd told Phineas, "the highway runs parallel to the river. All I have to do is walk straight up the bank and I'll reach it."

"Through these woods! Tom, you'd end up back at Little Beaver."

"You need sleep."

"I'll grab some right now." My impatience amused Phineas. "Dawn's a hell of a time to *start* courting."

This gave me ample time not only to shave, but also to bathe in a cove. At midmorning we were on our way, moving through woods so dense that the rays of the sun, forcing their way through the boughs, were broken up and seemed to be coming from under the ground rather than from above. The broken-up light, coupled with the solemn deep forest silence, made it seem as if I were in the cloister of a great cathedral. Phineas had not overstated the situation. Every other step I took was around a tree, knocking asunder my sense of direction. Without Phineas along it is possible I might have eventually arrived at the Little Beaver River Station, but almost certainly not at the Steubenville highway.

Reaching the thoroughfare, we were still in the deep woods. We turned in the downstream direction, which was to our left. Phineas laughed when I asked how he could be certain this was the proper way. In what other direction, he wanted to know, could Steubenville be? The highway ended at Steubenville. After Steubenville there was nothing but trees, all the way to Marietta.

A half mile later, we met four militiamen. All was now clear, we were told. There were no casualties and Phineas' pronouncement, made on the flatboat, proved to be correct. Out of sheer malice, the Indians had thrown a lighted torch onto the cabin's roof, then taken off. The cabin wasn't a quarter-of-a-mile from the stockade. How the Indians had slipped past the patrol, which the militiamen insisted hadn't been sleeping on the job, remained a mystery. The settlement's council members were quite incensed about this and a general meeting was scheduled for that evening. The militiamen spoke bitterly and talked of taking reprisals against Indians held captive at the fort.

Upon reaching Steubenville's outskirts Dame Fortune, or whoever decides such things, treated me most benevolently. Coming over the highway, carrying a fishing rod, I saw a young lady wearing a blue gingham dress. It was Melissa. Recognizing me she stopped in her tracks, staring in frozen amazement. I, if Phineas may be believed, began trembling like a "faun doused with a bucket of ice water." Then Melissa and I started talking at once, expressing our surprise and pleasure upon seeing each other. Amid this hodgepodge of words, Phineas managed to say he'd meet me at the tippling house. Grinning and clicking his teeth, to show his approval of Melissa, he added while exiting, that it was all right with him if we forgot he was alive until darkness set in.

Until he clicked his teeth, Melissa had not realized that my beardless companion was Phineas Ford and I explained the circumstances which had brought us together. Motioning to a lane, which led to a river cove, Melissa suggested that we talk there, while she fished. The moment we were behind the trees, I took Melissa into my arms and kissed her. Melissa, I should say, was surprised as I by my impulsive behavior, but her response was most warm, once she realized what was happening. This pleased me greatly. "Melissa," I said, "I am in love with you." While I hadn't counted upon making such an assertion in Steubenville, I meant it, and I was glad to have the matter brought out into the open.

Melissa said it was more than possible that she was in love with me too and we kissed each other again. "I have been thinking of you constantly," I said and Melissa said that quite a bit of her thinking had been centering around me also.

That was that, wonderfully so. Moving to the cove, we sat in a secluded spot and spent considerable time marveling about how it had all come about. In an effort to be sensible, we did take note of the fact that we had seen each other only on three occasions, four if we counted our brief meeting in Chambersburg. We must take time, we both agreed, to become better acquainted before considering so important a step as marriage. "We will be able to see each other in Cincinnati," I said. "In due time I can propose marriage there and you can say yes. I am not required to stay in the settlement. We could leave immediately after being married, if you desired."

I am aware this was the brash statement of a young man very much in love, yet it did form the basis of our decision. Sometimes I have wondered what such an arrangement might be called. Betrothal by amortization? But that is unimportant, for Melissa and I knew what was meant. We were certain our love was real and that the passage of time would merely prove it all the more.

Melissa knew what her father had said to me. As might be expected, we talked about the young man from New Orleans. "He is, of course, alive," Melissa said. "Other than that, I know nothing of him except what my father has told me. Naturally, I *was* somewhat curious."

"Were you planning upon marrying him?"

"If I loved him, yes," Melissa said. "I am almost twenty-three years old. The thought of someday becoming married *has* upon occasion crossed my mind." Placing her hand ever so gently upon mine: "However, I must confess, my darling, since our meeting in that awful settlement, I haven't known anyone else was alive but you."

The young man from New Orleans thus disposed of, we began trying to pinpoint the exact moment we'd fallen in love. Laughing, saying it was asking the impossible, we nonetheless pursued the subject. "I suppose," Melissa said, "it was when—the gentle way you put that blanket around me at the crossing inn."

"You were sound asleep!"

"I couldn't have been," Melissa said, "because I remember the all of it."

"I fell in love with you, I can now see," I said, "in Chambersburg. At first sight."

"Tom!" Melissa said and she looked so beautiful as her expressive face lighted up with pleasure. "When you talk like that, I'm compelled to doubt your sanity."

"There was this feeling of being helpful to you," I said. "Of *wanting* to be. And not failing! May I tell you something that sounds silly? That glass of water you asked for. I *had* to have it immediately. The innkeeper was drawing mugs of spruce beer. Paying customers were waiting. Yet, I raised my voice, demanded and got that glass of water, not for the gray-haired woman, but for you."

"That doesn't sound silly, Tom," Melissa said softly.

"I can see it in other ways too," I said. "In the wildest fancies of my imagination I can't conceive of doing what I did to get us out of that settlement—except for you."

I don't know why I am rambling on like this. Lovers, the world over, talk in this manner. And I am glad that they do. Most of what else Melissa and I said in Steubenville has faded away with the passage of time, but the spirit of it remains with me, very much alive, and it is precious.

"If you fell in love with me at the crossing settlement," I *do* remember saying, in playful rebuke, "I must say that such emotions were well kept in abeyance."

"And so were yours, my darling."

"That is not quite so," I said. "In Chambersburg I bowed my head off and put on my best Sunday manners trying to make a good impression, but you didn't even notice."

"I am not blind, my darling. I noticed."

"I will have you know," I said, "after you took flight, I walked the tethering grounds, looking for you."

"I saw you," Melissa said, "from behind the flaps of our wagon."

"You did!"

"You looked so disappointed, my darling. So honestly disappointed."

"In heaven's name," I said, "why in the world didn't you drop a bucket out of the wagon, or fall out yourself—anything, so I could have come to your assistance and then asked you to have dinner?"

Melissa's head was resting in my lap as I put this question. Now she sat up. My arm was still about her and I could feel her whole body becoming tired. "My father, Tom," Melissa said. "He lay in the wagon. He needed me."

We had already spoken of Bushrod Andrews in a cursory manner and

Melissa had told me how enraged he'd become when she'd defied him and said that she would and wanted to see me again. It was the first time in her life, she said, that she'd come out in direct opposition to one of her father's demands.

"I think I should speak to your father," I said. "Right now."

"He is in the woods. All men have been asked to go there—on patrol . . . Tom," Melissa said, "about my father—"

Bushrod Andrews, Melissa told me, had only begun drinking heavily during the past four years, following the death of her mother. At first Melissa had thought the drinking was the result of sorrow, now though she was beginning to suspect that financial worries had become a contributing factor. "He will not tell me anything," Melissa said sadly. "He keeps on insisting that I must not bother my head with such matters. Yet every now and then he says something that makes me wonder. Tom, do you know anything about the Holland Company of Amsterdam?"

"There was a great deal written about the company in the newsprints about a year ago," I said. "It's an investment house with many interests such as shipping and trading in general."

"A legitimate house?"

"Oh, yes, but they made a frightful error. As you know, no doubt, all sorts of outlandish statements are being made about the possibilities in the Ohio Country. One was that in Ohio there was an abundance of maple trees from whose branches sugar could be scraped off with a shovel. The directors of the Holland Company purchased 132,000 acres, right here in the vicinity of Steubenville. They sent over a sugar refiner to make plans for starting a factory which would undersell sugar made from cane. Initially the printers of our newsprints lauded the foresight of the Holland Company and many Americans bought the company's stock. Of course, when the refiner arrived and investigated—the bubble burst."

"Tom, only yesterday my father became—he drank too much. Getting an axe, he went into the woods and began chopping down maple trees." Melissa looked at me beseechingly. "That would indicate, wouldn't it, that he invested too deeply in this Holland Company?"

"Yes, my dear," I said, "I should say it would."

We managed to erase Bushrod Andrews temporarily from our thoughts. The rest of this day was simply glorious. We strolled about the settlement, which was only Fort Steuben and some log cabins, but with Melissa along it became a quaint and most interesting place. At the tethering grounds we found the women of Melissa's train agog with excitement over good news. Word had been received that arrangements for assembling a flotilla had been completed. Departure shouldn't be more than a week or so off.

Melissa and I did not make an effort to avoid Bushrod Andrews and if he returned, I was going to speak up. However, we did feel that it might be better, on the whole, if Melissa broached the subject, approaching it by degrees and at the best time.

When at supper time it became apparent that the men were staying over for the general meeting, Melissa and I sought out Phineas and the three of us had dinner at the inn. To show his approval of our happiness, Phineas did something most thoughtful. He announced that he would attend the general meeting, talk with members of the patrol, and arrange things so he and I could ride back with them over the Steubenville highway. This meant Melissa and I had an extra two hours of being together.

II

It was close to midnight when Phineas and I took to the river. I sat with Phineas at the bow oar, being far too exhilarated to think about sleep. Actually, I told myself, it was better to stay awake at night, for by sleeping during the day there wouldn't be so many long, dreary hours of sitting on the riverbank with nothing to do.

While not grieving, Phineas was in a somber mood and had I been thinking about anything else but Melissa, while riding back from Steubenville, I might have wondered why the patrol members appeared to be rather subdued too.

"Talk about your Indians!" Phineas eventually said with a surprising display of vehemence. "White men are just as big jackasses."

A number of Steubenville citizens, he told me, drunk, and demanding reprisals, had brought Indians from the jail and flogged them. "When that didn't satisfy them," Phineas went on to say, "they held a chase-the-doe."

A chase-the-doe, previous conversations with Phineas had taught me, was a man's game presumably so-called because someone in the Ohio Country had at one time fancied a naked squaw, running through the woods, resembled a fleeing doe.

Simple enough, the rules of the game could be easily understood. To play you needed only naked Indian women and clothed white men. Since there was almost always more men than squaws, a barrel of whiskey was rolled out. The female participants were allowed only enough "fire water" to make them feel, as Phineas described it, "frisky." The males all drank equal amounts, in large quantities, under careful supervision, in order that there would be no cheating. This latter proviso made it a contest as well as a game. The males, best able to stave off drunken stupor, had earned the right to be on the steadiest feet when word was given for the "does" to run into the woods, to be chased after.

Phineas, who was very much against the molesting of Indian women by white men, said quite bitterly: "Some drunken jackass really got it." The man, Phineas went on to say, had been clawed to death by a puma. Precise details were still lacking when Phineas left. What had most likely happened, Phineas told me, was that the man, hearing a noise in a tree, had assumed a "doe" had taken refuge there. In quest of his game, the man had climbed up the tree.

III

With no rain, the current fell off, and the moon became unfavorable. Although Marietta was only slightly over a hundred miles below Steubenville, it took us better than six completely uneventful nights to reach this settlement.

We planned putting to at Williamstown, a squatter settlement directly across the river from Marietta. Here Phineas expected to pay his respects to a young lady whose charms, described in the fullest detail, became the principal topic of his conversation during the two nights prior to our arrival.

On that sixth night we were close enough to Marietta to be safe while riding into the dawn. With the rising of the sun, as the wind broke up the fog, I saw jagged tree-covered hills, a rugged but mellowed countryside whose general topography reminded me of the Catskills.

"Damn!" Phineas muttered, leaned over the gunnel and doused his head into the river.

"Why did you do that?" I asked.

"I've got one hell of a toothache." His mother, Phineas had suddenly recalled, always told him to stick his head in a bucket of water when he had a toothache or the hiccups.

Taking a healthy swig of whiskey which, apparently, did not bring relief, Phineas said, "It started three days ago. Now it feels like somebody's smacking me in the mouth with a mallet."

I went into the cabin, for my traveling trunk, to get cloves. The traveling trunk was wedged between two crates, so heavy it took all my strength to move them. "What's in those two crates," I asked when I returned, "iron?"

"Yes," Phineas said.

"I didn't know we were carrying iron," I said.

"Well, we are," Phineas grumbled. "What'd you get for my toothache?"

"Cloves," I said. "Chew them."

"It still hurts just as much," Phineas said after two clamps of his teeth.

"Keep on chewing," I said. "You mustn't expect immediate results."

We were approaching Kerr's Island, which Phineas called "The Long Finger." This strip of narrow land, a mile-and-a-half long, ran down the middle of the river. The island's lower end was just off Marietta and Williamstown.

After gazing mournfully in the direction of Williamstown, Phineas rode us on the Ohio side of the island. "These damned cloves!" he said. "They aren't any good. I'm going to the fort. I figure Jeremiah'll still be there."

"Who," I asked, "is Jeremiah?"

"The army surgeon," Phineas told me and went on to say that Dr. Jeremiah Allison, the sole surgeon attending General Harmar's some four hundred federals, had been left behind to cure those too sick to go on down to Cincinnati.

Phineas' thought caused me to shudder. As was well known, army surgeons didn't even pretend to know more than how to bandage and amputate. "I'd give that some consideration, Phineas," I said. "Reputable doctors admit they don't know much about teeth. The best thing to do, they say, is stand the pain long as you can and hope it'll go away. I'm almost certain this Dr. Allison won't be able to help you. He'll probably want to yank out the tooth and you can't even be sure he'll get the right one the first time."

Phineas shook his head doggedly. "If anybody can stop the pain, it's Jeremiah Allison. Jeremiah's smart as they make them. He comes from Scotland."

"What's coming from Scotland got to do with it?" I asked.

"They've got a fine doctors' school over there," Phineas said. "In Edinburgh."

"Are you saying this Dr. Allison was educated at the Medical College of the University of Edinburgh?"

"That's the place," Phineas said.

"Why is he an army surgeon?"

"He got into some kind of a row with the doctors over there. I never did know what they were fighting about, but Jeremiah came to America, Boston, and got mixed up in another doctors' row. So he ended up in the army. Everybody swears by him. Harmar lets him do what he pleases and no officer's allowed to pull rank on him. Jeremiah's even got his own orderly."

Fort Harmar loomed into view. Well-situated, she stood in a commanding position atop a high bluff which rose like a pinnacle on the lower bank of the Muskingum River.

Marietta's Campus Martius and the Ohio Company buildings, located on flatter terrain quite a way up the upper bank of the Muskingum, were hidden by trees. From the flatboat all I could see of the first *bona fide* settlement in the Territory Northwest of the River Ohio was a picket fence, built at the public landing. And, of course, the settlement's landmark: her gigantic sycamore, acknowledged to be the biggest tree east of the Mississippi.

A dozen or more flatboats and as many canoes and rowboats were tied up at the public landing. Early in the morning as it was, people were already moving about. By calling out to them, we learned that Dr. Allison was still here. And that we were just in time. An army flotilla had been sighted four bends upstream. Dr. Allison and the twenty-two federals he'd restored to health would be boarding her.

Riding across the mouth of the Muskingum, we put to below Fort Harmar. "I think I hear-ed someone say the doctor went over to Marietta last night on an ailing call," a fisherman told Phineas. "I ain't seen him come back yet."

The fisherman could not guarantee the accuracy of his information. "Wouldn't administering to civilians be against Army Regulations?" I said as Phineas and I discussed what to do.

"Sure," Phineas said, "but Harmar's got sense enough to know that's a jackass rule. Besides, Jeremiah'd do what he pleased anyway . . . Tom, I'm going to the fort. You wait here. If Jeremiah comes by, tell him to come to the fort, fast as his legs will carry him."

Phineas was scarcely out of sight when I saw three men get into a canoe on the Marietta side of the Muskingum. "Nope," the fisherman told me, "them wouldn't be the doctor."

Paddling only a short way into the stream, the men threw over a rope and grappling iron. "Them's lookin' for him who drowned last night," the fisherman informed me.

The deceased, the fisherman went on to say, was a Dutchman from Connecticut. Before allowing search to begin, the man's widow had insisted upon wrapping a loaf of bread in the last shirt her husband had worn and setting it afloat, on the theory that the parcel would sink when it floated over the lost man's body. "Crazy, ain't it?" the fisherman said.

The parcel, the fisherman added, was already sunk. It had, though, by that time worked itself free from the line to which it was attached. This, the wife was convinced, meant it was God's will that her husband's body should not be recovered. "Them's his sons," the fisherman explained. "Them thinks they'll find him anyway. Them won't though because him's already in the Ohio River by now, afloatin' downstream."

Shortly before midmorning, the fisherman said, "That would be him," and pointed to a buckskin-clad man getting into a rowboat on the Marietta side of the Muskingum. In this case "him" meant Dr. Jeremiah Allison.

"So Phineas Ford has a toothache," Dr. Allison said after I had introduced myself and explained the situation. His slight smile an indication that he knew how proud Phineas was of his teeth, he added: "You were right in giving him the cloves, Mr. Morrow. Had we any cloves here, I would have done the same thing."

Dr. Allison spoke softly. His enunciation was superb. Phineas had mentioned Dr. Allison's age: seventy-two. He did not look it. Slenderly made, in fact quite thin, six feet tall, his movements were agile, almost youthful. His nose was prominently large. Actually Dr. Allison had a homely face, but such was its kindly expression that he didn't seem to be a homely looking man.

While climbing the bluff, I asked Dr. Allison about the state of affairs at Marietta. "Direful," Dr. Allison said and told me Wyandots had struck Williamstown two nights before, which was alarming news for the Wyandots were the most ferocious of all the Ohio Country tribes. "They struck boldly, burned four cabins, and killed twelve people." The Wyandots, Dr. Allison added, had behaved in a most beastly manner, even for them. A witness, presumed to be dead after having had a spear driven through his chest, had survived. Women were scalped while still alive. While still alive their ears were cut off, also their noses until they dangled down over their mouths. A man's head had been chopped off. The Indians had kicked and tossed it about in the manner of a favorite game of theirs, played by men and women, called football. An Indian had grabbed an infant, not a year old, by the ankles, swung him over his head and dashed the child's brains out against a cabin wall. The Wyandots were not drunk, the witness insisted. This was not an orgy, it was studied behavior calculated to terrorize.

"Apparently the Wyandots were of sufficient strength," Dr. Allison went on to say, "to show no fear of counterattack by the Williamstown Rangers, in fact seemed anxious to engage them. It's almost certain they're raiders, not a hunting party seeking diversion."

Were the citizens becoming discouraged, I asked Dr. Allison. One might surmise they were not, he said, for that evening a protest meeting was being held at Campus Martius, demanding that the directors of the Ohio Company stop following the New England plan of settlement, which means lots can only be bought in the vicinity of the center of population.

However, Dr. Allison told me, the Williamstown massacre had a most unfortunate aftermath. Following the raids, Williamstown Rangers had chanced upon two wounded Indians. One had hurled himself into the Ohio River, preferring death by drowning to capture. The other, whose leg was broken, feigned death and fatally stabbed a Ranger before being shot down. Infuriated, the Rangers had scalped this Indian, skinned him and tanned his hide. It had been proposed that the hide should be auctioned off to be used for bullet-pouches, the proceeds to be contributed to Williamstown's church fund.

"The proposal has split Williamstown into two opposing camps, creating much ill-will," Dr. Allison said. "The schism goes far deeper than the proposal itself. Involved now is the torturing of Indian captives and whether or not white men shall repay Indian atrocities in kind."

In the course of the conversation I mentioned something about myself and it turned out that Dr. Allison, an avid reader, was a great admirer of my father's writings. "I was quite interested in your father's remarks on Dr. Benjamin Rush's pronouncement that Negroes' color and the shapes of their noses are caused by a wholesale affliction of leprosy," Dr. Allison remarked.

The article of which he spoke had caused quite a stir. Since Negroes' color was actually the result of disease, Dr. Rush had contended, a remedy must be found. This would destroy a most potent argument against slavery. It would clearly demonstrate that the claims of superiority of whites over blacks were founded on "ignorance and inhumanity."

A slight twinkle showed in Dr. Allison's gray eyes. "May I inquire if you are familiar with Dr. Rush's reactions to your father's article?"

"You refer, I take it," I said, "to my father's statement that whether or not Dr. Rush was right about the leprosy theory, his general thesis and belief that Negroes are our equals was lofty and sound and should be applauded?"

"I do," Dr. Allison said.

"My father's statement," I said, "was not meant to be derogatory. It was merely made in passing."

"That is the way it impressed me," Dr. Allison said.

"To my father's great surprise," I said, "Dr. Rush was infuriated. He

behaved as if it were a cardinal sin for anyone to intimate it was even remotely possible that his medical conclusions might be subject to doubt. He
refused, after the publication of my father's article, to speak to either of us.
One afternoon my father and I approached Dr. Rush on Market Street.
The moment Dr. Rush saw us, he turned about abruptly and walked hastily
to the other side of the street."

"How very interesting," Dr. Allison said.

Square in design, with sturdy blockhouses at the angles, Fort Harmar
was a formidable and well-constructed fortification. That, though, is all she
was. General Harmar had taken her heavy guns with him to Fort Washington.
By the next day, she would have no professional soldiers.

The height of the grass on her parade made it evident drilling had been
kept to a minimum. Phineas, having seen us enter through the main gate,
came ajog from the northwest blockhouse and was awaiting us at Dr.
Allison's quarters. "Am I glad to see you, Jeremiah!" Phineas said. "I've got
one hell of a toothache."

"So Mr. Morrow has already informed me," Dr. Allison said.

"Well, for Christ's sake, Jeremiah, do something!"

"What, Phineas? Mr. Morrow tells me you've already been chewing cloves."

"Those things! You mean to say you can't figure out something else?"

"No, Phineas, I can't."

"Well, damn it, you can at least look at the tooth, can't you?"

"Yes, I can do that."

Going to his knees, Phineas opened his mouth.

"There's a rather large rotted portion extending between both your front
upper teeth," Dr. Allison said.

"Rotten!"

"Quite."

Standing up, Phineas put his hand to his mouth. An expression of utter
disbelief clouded his face, as if it were impossible for anything to happen
to his pearly, white teeth, of which he was so peacockishly proud. "What's
going to happen to them?" he muttered.

"The rotting will undoubtedly spread, Phineas," Dr. Allison said. "Before
too long, I can almost assure you, somebody will have to yank the teeth."

"You're not yanking out my teeth, Jeremiah!"

"Certainly not here, Phineas," Dr. Allison said, "even if you wanted me
to. I have only a pair of pliers. Were I to use them, the chances are excellent that I would fracture your jaw. The army flotilla is expected at about
three o'clock. I suggest you join it. Daytime travel will get you to Cincinnati
quicker. If the pain isn't gone by then, we can reconsider yanking the
teeth."

"I'm not hooking up with any army flotilla," Phineas grumbled, "and nobody's going to yank out any of my teeth."

"That is that then, Phineas."

Phineas' voice came out in a hoarse whisper. "Does this mean they'll turn black on me?"

"Beyond a doubt."

"If I did let you yank them out," Phineas said warily, "what about the holes?"

"You could put in a cow's tooth or a sheep's, if you were able to find the right size. They'd be loose though and since only one side is enamel, they'd corrode quickly. Ivory could be carved to the proper size, but an ivory tooth would be loose too."

"God damn it!" Phineas said and began pacing up and down, like an enraged animal in a cage. "Can't you do something?"

"I could fill the teeth."

Phineas came to Dr. Allison with a bounding leap. "Why in the hell didn't you say so?"

"It means burning off the rotted portions."

"Do it," Phineas said.

"The pain will be excruciating."

"Do it."

"The teeth, of course, have to be filled. Tinfoil doesn't stay put very long in any kind of a filling. In your case, it wouldn't hold at all. I'd have to use melted lead. Gold, if you had some, would be much better."

Reaching into his money pouch, Phineas produced a Spanish Joe that had been cut down to about half-dollar size. "Is this enough gold?"

"Yes, it's more than enough."

"Start and get it over with," Phineas said.

Dr. Allison shook his head. "We'll have to wait until you're at Fort Washington. The army flotilla, as I have just stated, is due to pass here around three o'clock. She's carrying recruits and won't stop. I'll have to row out to board her."

"Three o'clock!" Phineas said. "It's only noon. How in the hell long does it take to fill a couple of teeth?"

"Ten or twelve minutes, I should say, but you must be dead drunk."

"The hell I do," Phineas said. "I can stand pain and you know it."

"I can't have you jerking your head, Phineas," Dr. Allison said, "and, believe me, you would. You would have to be drunk, dead drunk, or I wouldn't even attempt to begin."

"Three o'clock . . ." Phineas said. "Could you do it on the flatboat?"

"Yes."

"I'll go down right now and start getting drunk," Phineas said. "You come down with your baggage at half-past two. I'll be dead drunk by then."

Dr. Allison regarded him doubtfully. "Dead drunk, Phineas, and I mean precisely that."

"Dead drunk," Phineas said. "If I'm not and the flotilla shows up, you board her. No hard feelings on either side. Deal?"

"Deal," Dr. Allison said, after looking at his timepiece.

"Anything else I'm supposed to do?" Phineas asked.

"Have the gold melted and a hot fire going."

"Maybe we ought to do it at two o'clock to be sure?"

"Phineas," Dr. Allison said patiently, "I have a number of other things to do. Also I was up all night with a patient. I'm somewhat tired and would like a bit of rest."

"Sorry, Jeremiah," Phineas said quickly. "I'll be damned! For some reason I never figured you ever got tired."

"You may take my word for it," Dr. Allison said, "that I do."

I must say that Phineas made a valiant effort to carry out Dr. Allison's instructions. The moment we arrived at our flatboat, he began drinking whiskey. How much, exactly, I do not know. He emptied one full gallon jug and was well into a second one before he collapsed. Unhappily, he was not dead drunk. In a stupor, he muttered incoherently and fought off my efforts to induce him to drink more whiskey.

There was no change in Phineas' general condition as half-past two o'clock approached. By now, for news has a way of traveling fast, a dozen or so citizens of Marietta, the majority of whom being women, were on hand to offer their services and to watch. The rest of the settlement's hundred residents were at the public landing, to cheer the army flotilla. On the bank, across the river, Williamstown's citizens were watching and waiting too. All militiamen and Rangers were armed, under orders to shoot on sight any Harmar recruits attempting to desert by swimming ashore.

Almost simultaneously with the arrival of Dr. Allison and the twenty-two federals, the shouts, "Flotilla around the bend!" started at the public landing, were relayed on, and came to me in waves, like so many echoes.

This meant the flotilla would pass at approximately the expected three o'clock. It was now a few minutes after half-past two o'clock. Dr. Allison needed a quarter of an hour, at the least, to row out and be in position to effect a boarding.

After examining the fire, which the fisherman had made for us in a large iron kettle, Dr. Allison boarded our flatboat. A glance told him, Phineas was not dead drunk. "That's better than I expected," he said tersely. Feeling Phineas' pulse: "The man's strong as a horse."

Federals carried Phineas ashore. Laying him out on his back, his limbs stretched out, the federals tied Phineas' wrists and ankles to stakes.

"When we're finished," Dr. Allison told me, "cover him with bearskins." Giving me a package containing hartshorn and feathers, he said, "Try to bring him to by burning these and waving them under his nostrils." He handed me two bottles. "I have no idea if Phineas will be feverish or have chills. He may have neither. In any case, keep him well covered. If he has fever, give him no cooling drinks. Do give him this calomel in generous quantities regardless of the ill effects upon his gums and teeth. If he has the chills, give him liberal doses of these bitters."

Dr. Allison and I went ashore. Federals sat on Phineas' arms and legs and held his head. Others kept sponges between his fingers and toes. Mercifully, I did not have to watch. I sat on Phineas' stomach, with my back to his head. Dr. Allison sat on Phineas' chest. "Can you hear me, Phineas?" Dr. Allison called out and I heard Phineas' incoherent mutterings. Dr. Allison asked for his mallet, I heard a thud of leather against skull, and could feel Phineas' body go limp. A red hot brass wire was passed to Dr. Allison. Phineas' whole body quivered, as if struck by lightning. Then it took the strength of the combined manpower of us all to hold that powerful, contorting body still.

But at last it was over and when it was Phineas lapsed into a deep sleep. Returning him to the flatboat, we wrapped him in bearskins. There was scarcely time to thank Dr. Allison and bid him safe journey, for the army flotilla was already in sight.

"Drunken broadbrim!" the roar, starting at the public landing, reached me as Dr. Allison and the federals were getting into their rowboats.

"Drunken broadbrim," I learned later, referred to brevet Brigadier General Josiah Harmar, blamed by the citizens of Marietta and Williamstown for the moving of the federal troops to Fort Washington. The General, I would be told, was a "drunken Quaker," incompetent, suffering from the gout, and generally more interested in returning to private life than carrying out his present assignment. General Harmar's real interests, it was being said, lay in horticulture and the collecting of Indian relics. Pursuing the latter, the General had unearthed a number of burial grounds which had infuriated the Indians. In the case of the other, a so-called "Harmar Peach," now growing along the banks of Muskingum, was cited as indication that the General's thoughts were not solely concerned with military matters.

"Drunken broadbrim!" I have never heard a cry quite like it. Anger mixed with frustration. Somehow the citizens of Marietta and Williamstown had reached the conclusion that the arrival of the flotilla meant the coming, at long last, of General Harmar's army. They saw fourteen flatboats, loaded with provender, but carrying only thirty-nine Harmar recruits.

IV

Carrying out Dr. Allison's instructions, I attempted to rally Phineas with the hartshorn and burned feathers. It was almost midnight before he opened his eyes. "Hello, Mr. Philadelphia," he said, grinned boyishly, and made an effort to click his teeth. Moving his hand to his mouth, he appeared to be satisfied with what he felt and dropped off into a peaceful sleep.

Phineas, so far as I could tell, had neither fever nor chills. His recovery, I should say, followed the pattern of normal drunken men. It was accomplished by degrees, accompanied by the passage of time.

We left Marietta on the third night. Although fully recovered, Phineas considered himself in dire straits. He had completely lost his taste for Monongahela rye. The mere smell of it nauseated him. "If I can't 'fortify' myself," he grumbled, "I'll come down with the damps or the ague for sure." The enforced abstinence tended to make him irritable.

The three hundred miles between Marietta and Cincinnati constituted the extremely dangerous phase of our trip. From now on Phineas, rather than riding the crest of the current, frequently hugged the Virginia shore. A precautionary measure, he told me, for Indian hunting parties customarily returned to the Ohio side after the day's hunt, camping on the riverbank.

Also, deeming it unsafe that I should be left alone at any time, Phineas insisted I accompany him as he surveyed the areas where we put to. We began seeing the ashes of Indians' recently made campfires and the entrails of animals they had killed.

Traveling in this prudent but slower manner, it took us nine nights to reach the mouth of the Kanawha River, some seventy miles below Marietta. Under these circumstances it seemed to me that Melissa's flotilla, strong enough to travel by day, should be catching up with us. Any number of times, while ashore during the day, I climbed trees and looked up the river.

There was only the familiar sight: trees, sky, river, and an occasional osprey. Phineas kept telling me not to worry, for flotillas never got off as soon as was expected. This was probably what had happened, I tried to assure myself, yet I couldn't still a growing sense of uneasiness.

A single cabin, serving as a trading post for a salt factory located about fifty miles inland, stood at the mouth of the Kanawha. The factory's representative's name was Caleb Carter. Now friendly with the Indians, Phineas told me, Caleb Carter had survived after being scalped. Dissatisfied with the looks of his pate, painted black, Caleb Carter had come through a second raid unscathed because he'd purchased a wig. An Indian had grabbed what he thought was Caleb Carter's hair. When the wig came off, the Indian ran away in a state of complete confusion.

"I'm going to see Caleb," Phineas said. "Tom, you stay on the boat. I don't think Caleb'll come back with me, but if he does, lie down in the cabin and pretend you're sick with the ague. Don't talk to him."

"May I inquire why?"

"Sure," Phineas said. "Caleb plays on both sides of the fence. If he hears the way you talk, he'll know damned well you're not a riverman like I'm going to tell him you are. Let Caleb get the notion I'm running a gentleman down the river, he'll figure you're taking news to the General and he'll tip off the Indians for sure."

"If he's that sort," I said, "how can you believe anything he says?"

"I'll have to figure," Phineas said. "Caleb'll be lying through his teeth to me and I'll be lying through mine to him. Some of the time, both of us'll be telling the truth. It's up to each to figure out when."

Upon taking his leave, Phineas lifted onto his shoulders one of the whiskey kegs which was half-filled with water. "Caleb," he explained, "will probably expect a little something in the way of thanks for telling me he won't let the Indians know that we're passing through."

Within the hour Phineas returned, looking extremely concerned. "Caleb says the woods are full of Illinois," he said.

"An intertribal war?"

"Caleb says, no," Phineas said and told me the Illinois were here by invitation. "What Caleb says makes sense," he added. "If ever there was a time when the Indians wouldn't be fighting among themselves, it's now."

"I'm not sure I understand you, Phineas," I said. "The presence of the Illinois by invitation would have to mean, wouldn't it, the Indians are on the warpath?"

"That's what it ought to mean," Phineas said, "but it can't. The Indians know they can't take Fort Washington, even with their Illinois cousins helping out. Harmar's army hasn't marched out, so they can't be waiting for him. Besides, the Indian planting season isn't over yet. They'd be taking care of that before calling in the Illinois."

"What was Caleb Carter's explanation for the presence of the Illinois?"

"He says he can't figure it out either."

"Do you believe him?"

"I guess I do. I'm the first white man he's seen in a month. The Indians know what Caleb's like. They'd only tell him what they'd want him to know."

"Then General Harmar's army must have marched out?"

"With four hundred federals! Tom, do you think the General'd be that crazy?"

"I know the Pennsylvania recruits haven't come through," I said. "Maybe those from Virginia did?"

Phineas shook his head, picked up a whiskey keg, and took a healthy swig. This was his first drink of Monongahela rye since Marietta! "Those buggers are signing up slower than the Pennsylvanians," he said and took a second swig. "They haven't showed up at Fort Washington yet, but let's say they did. What would they use for guns and supplies? Nothing's come through yet from Carlisle."

"The presence of the Illinois has to mean something," I said.

"It sure does," Phineas said, "but damned if I can figure out what."

During the next three days Phineas spent practically all his waking hours attempting to figure out what was what, but was unable to arrive at a passable conclusion. However, again drinking Monongahela rye in the manner to which he was accustomed, he was no longer irritable.

After putting to on the third morning after leaving the Kanawha River, while scouting through extremely dense woods, we reached what I thought was a dried-up pond. An acre at least in size, its cracked surface was baked hard as a tile floor. "Stay away from that," Phineas warned sharply. "It's a live mudhole."

When Phineas tossed out a rock, it broke through the dried mud and sank with the finality of something dropped into a vacuum. He raised one of the mud pieces with a branch. Underneath was a greenish slime, over whose surface myriads of tiny insects, confused by the sunlight, skittered about, looking like a whirlpool. "Those little bastards," Phineas said, "can bite the holy hell out of you."

"How deep is it?" I asked.

"Damned if I know." Spotting a six-foot sapling, Phineas threw it, spear-like, into the mudhole. Down it went, as if meeting with no resistance, until no more than two inches showed. "God only knows how deep she'd be in the middle," Phineas stated.

Circling the mudhole, we were again in the semidarkness of the deep woods. Suddenly Phineas stopped and froze, alert though as a pointer flushing a quail. Halting me by raising his hand: "Tom," he whispered, "stand beside yonder tree." Slinging his rifle, Phineas moved forward a few steps and waited. Eventually a buckskin clad, stoop-shouldered, incredibly old-looking Indian of short stature emerged from behind the trees.

In his left hand the Indian carried a musket, a Brown Bess, I would guess, quite battered, in keeping with red men's haphazard manner of caring for firearms. In his right hand, which he raised in greeting, the Indian held a large skinned and gutted opossum. Showing off the animal proudly, he grinned broadly and began talking rapidly in a shrill voice. His teeth, I could see, were black stumps.

Neither Phineas nor the Indian had exhibited visible surprise over having met. Although I could not understand what was being said, the tenor of the rather extended conversation which took place seemed to be entirely amicable. The conversation concluded, the Indian moved on his way, we on ours. Once out of sight behind the trees, Phineas stopped, listened, then said: "Tom, what in the hell do you think that old bugger told me?"

I, of course, hadn't the faintest idea.

"He said Harmar marched out of Fort Washington and the Indians are all set to beat the hell out of him."

"Do you believe him?"

"Yes, God damn it," Phineas said, "I do."

The Indian's name, Phineas told me, was Mesass. "A chattering magpie, if ever I heard one, Tom." Over eight hundred moons old, senile and rheumatic, Mesass had only recently been told he must soon join the council of ancient men, which meant no more hunting and fishing. "Indians hate that, Tom. Even the worst of them are proud." Most of Mesass' talk, Phineas said, had centered upon the opossum. "That was some big possum, Tom! Must have weighed over seven pounds." Mesass, Phineas went on to say, planned showing the opossum to the young bucks and challenging them to say when they'd brought back one as big. With this in his favor, Mesass fully expected to win a reversal of the tribal judgment that he must sit on the council of ancient men.

"It was the way the old bugger talked, Tom," Phineas said. "Nobody could be that cagey a liar. But I say it again—Harmar's not crazy. He wouldn't have marched out."

"Old men's minds wander," I suggested. "Maybe Mesass was just wishing the Indians were on the warpath."

Phineas shook his head. "If that were so, I'd have caught on to it."

Moving to a nearby, fairly slender trunked sycamore, Phineas removed his pacs, shinnied up the tree trunk, and was soon lost among the branches. When, a good half hour later, he came down, he said soberly: "Mesass didn't sample our whiskey."

"He was on our boat!"

"Of course! He was checking up on some of the things I told him."

"What has not sampling our whiskey got to do with it?"

"He's a Shawnee, Tom. A Shawnee on the warpath won't drink whiskey."

"Mesass might have strongly suspected or even known you were watching him?"

"No," Phineas said. "It's part of the Shawnee religion not to drink whiskey while on the warpath. When it comes to fighting, Indians are the trickiest rats alive. But when it comes to their religion—you can count on it, they never monkey around."

"Is it possible," I said, "that Mesass just didn't feel like taking a drink?"

"Monongahela rye!" Phineas said and smiled slightly. "Not that old bugger."

Although Phineas was answering my questions his thoughts, it was plain to see, were miles off. "What difference will it make," I asked, "if the Indians are on the warpath or not? Under either circumstances Mesass will tell his fellow tribesmen we're here, won't he?"

"Sure he will," Phineas said somewhat impatiently, "but I told him we were traders, working out of Niagara, running rifles to the Look-Out. If the Indians are on the warpath, they'll let us go through. If they're not, they'll be over here after us."

"Rifles to the Look-Out!"

"Don't worry about that part of it," Phineas said.

"But, Phineas!" I said. "Mesass was on our flatboat. He'll have verified your story."

"Tom, I told you not to worry about that part! He'll think those two crates of iron are filled with rifles."

"Good Lord!" I said.

"Harmar can't be marching out," Phineas muttered, more to himself than to me. "The old bugger has to be lying through his teeth . . . Tom, wait here. I'll be right back."

Within about an hour Phineas returned and told me we might as well go back to our flatboat. Phineas, I could tell, was not in a talkative mood. When we reached the mudhole, I discovered why. Not too far from where Phineas had hurled in the sapling I saw a freshly opened area in the sun-baked surface, big enough to have been made by the body of a short-statured man.

V

The Scioto River enters the Ohio ninety miles below the Kanawha. It is a clear and beautiful stream which creeps lazily along its pebbled bottom through the extremely fertile Scioto Valley.

The Indian Look-Out is a cave located halfway up the wooded bluff above the lower bank of the Scioto River, from which Indians pounce upon flatboats coming down the Ohio. Since it was completely hidden from view, Phineas had told me, most white men, including General Josiah Harmar and Governor Arthur St. Clair, were still unaware of the Look-Out's existence. When I'd asked Phineas why he didn't inform the General, he'd shrugged his shoulders. "If Josiah asks me, I'll tell him," he'd said. "If he doesn't ask, I'll keep my mouth shut."

Shortly after midnight, one uneventful week after our experience at the mudhole, we put to on the Virginia side, a quarter-of-a-mile above the Scioto's mouth. I was sleeping at the time. With the coming of the false dawn Phineas, returning from the riverbank, awakened me. "Tom," he said and pointed toward where he had just been, "if you want to see something, take a look."

When I did, across the river, rising up from the Ohio hills, I saw Indian smoke signals. Forty, at least. Thin as pencils, they rose high into the sky, stopped abruptly, then rose again. This was a cloudless morning. The sky could have been a huge slate upon which giants were drawing lines, erasing them, then drawing others. The signals streaked all of the visible Ohio sky, those in the distance being mere slivers that faded away into the horizon.

Phineas had gone ashore. Preparing breakfast when I reached him, he was humming while so doing: "Some row up, some row down, all the way to Shawneetown."

You could always know Phineas' mood by the way he hummed. His rendition of the popular river chantey made it sound like a funeral dirge. "What," I asked, "do the smoke signals mean?"

"Biggest powwow I ever saw," Phineas said. "Damned if I know what it means. Mesass could have been telling us the truth, but I still say the General wouldn't have been fool enough to march out."

"All those Indians!" I said. "They'll be coming over here to hunt, won't they?"

"In droves," Phineas said.

"We have no chance," I said. "We're good as captured?"

"If Mesass was lying," Phineas said, "I'd say we're all right."

"What do you mean?"

In the guise of representatives of British agents at Niagara, Phineas informed me, we were going to the Look-Out. "On that we've got no choice, Tom. They'll find us here for sure." We were going to trade off two crates of rifles, Phineas told me. If the Indians were not on the warpath, we would be honored as traders and allowed to go on our way. If on the warpath, coming under the general classification of white men, we'd be taken captive.

"To trade rifles!" I said. Then it dawned upon me. "Iron! Those two crates of iron? They *are* filled with rifles? Those are rifles bought from Harmar recruits, aren't they? You planned trading them off all along?"

Phineas admitted all this was so. "Treason, hell!" Phineas said. "It's how we'll maybe get past the Look-Out. And don't go preaching a sermon on me, Tom, you ought to be damned glad we've got those rifles. They'll save our necks at any rate. Even if the Indians are on the warpath, they'll be grateful and take us to Niagara to be traded. Maybe I can even talk them into letting us pass through."

I haven't the faintest recollection of discussing treason with Phineas, or preaching a sermon. Surely I must have been relieved to learn we probably wouldn't be tortured and killed, but I do not recall experiencing such an emotion. "Phineas," I said, "if we're taken captive, Melissa won't know where I am. And she can't be too far behind us! With all those Indians about, no matter how strong her flotilla—it will be attacked."

What I had said was so. Phineas made no effort to deny it.

VI

I had climbed a tree, seen no signs of Melissa's flotilla. Yet when we were on our way, I kept peering upstream, as if expecting its arrival at any moment.

To impress the Indians, Phineas had let down his hair. "Tom," he'd said, "don't let on to the Indians that you're scared."

Phineas, I must say, was following his own advice. Exuding confidence, he stood proud and erect at our bow, while guiding us with the oar between his knees. With a fairly smart breeze sweeping his reddish-brown mane majestically across his broad shoulders, he looked impressive as a heroically proportioned statue.

Circling us twice, Phineas caught the current expertly and headed us for the lower bank of the Scioto's mouth. While not so rugged as those about Marietta, the hills here were as forest-covered. I could see nothing that indicated the existence of the Indian Look-Out, although Phineas had pointed out where it was. With the rising sun driving away the fog, the conglomeration of insect noises mingling with the buzz of hummingbirds, everything seemed to be so serene and peaceful.

There was no indication that our approach had even been noted until we were close enough to the mouth of the Scioto to be able to see her clear water being absorbed by the muddy Ohio. Then they came out from under the boscage on the riverbank: three birchbark canoes, each carrying eight, solemn-faced, armed Indians, stripped to the waist, wearing only buckskin trousers.

Heading out to quarter-stream, the canoes separated and converged upon us in such a manner as to be able to rake us from three sides. Raising his right hand, Phineas shouted out in the Indian language. An Indian, presumably a chief, stood up, a small man, sunken chested, with fiery buckeye-brown eyes. After uttering a few crisp words, he sat down again. Phineas continued to talk.

When we'd pushed through the boscage and bumped against the shore, the chief boarded our flatboat. Launching into a lengthy tirade, he spoke in a high-pitched voice, oozing with hatred. "Harmar," I was certain I heard him say any number of times, also "Oh, ho, ho, ho!" which is the Indian equivalent of our "Amen." Constantly, as he spoke, the chief, with angry gestures, pointed downstream.

While the chief was having his say, Phineas sat on our starboard gunnel, smiling, nodding his head frequently as if in hearty approval, looking complacent as a Buddha. Eventually the chief concluded his statement, sat down, arose immediately, raised his right hand, and left our flatboat.

"We're all right, Tom," Phineas said when the chief and his fellow tribesmen were beyond hearing distance. "Mesass wasn't lying. Harmar *did* march out but, like I said, he had too much sense to make it an expedition. There were so many scalpings and raids, Harmar had to do something to ease people's minds. The Indians know all about that and are laughing their heads off over it. Harmar marched around the woods for ten days, didn't see a single Indian and got back to Fort Washington yesterday."

"Yesterday!" I said. "If we'd gotten here a day sooner than we did—"

"We'd be on our way to Niagara by now," Phineas said. "That chief's a stubborn old bugger. I couldn't have talked him into anything."

"Melissa's flotilla!" I said. "We've got to warn it somehow."

"There's nothing we can do," Phineas said. "Tom, I know what you've been thinking about all day. I couldn't be too nosy with the chief, or he'd got suspicious. I did find out, though, that the Indians want to get on with their planting. They'll be pulling out fast as they can. If the flotilla doesn't show up in the next day or so, I'd say it'll be too strong to be attacked."

I stood up and started for a nearby tree. "Where in the hell are you going?" Phineas growled.

"I want to see if the flotilla's in sight."

"No climbing of trees here!" Phineas said. "Tom, you'd just as good as be telling the Indians that you're on the look-out for somebody."

Shortly the Indians returned, bringing payment for the rifles: three packages of beaver skins, the size of cotton bales.

They were worth a small fortune!

A beaver skin brought twenty shillings, even in Cincinnati, where there was no real demand for them. In New Orleans, you could virtually name your own price.

Phineas had handed over thirty-six Kentucky rifles, in good condition. For each firearm, sixty inches in length, he had received the prevailing price: a pile of dressed beaver skins, stacked up to the height of the rifle.

Thus, at the Cincinnati price, the Indians were paying twelve hundred shillings for a rifle a Pennsylvania gunsmith could make in a week with about fifty shillings worth of material. Phineas, I would learn, had so far paid nothing for the rifles. Having merely given a man in Pittsburgh his hand to seal the bargain, he'd promised him a fair return when the beaver skins were finally disposed of. The Pittsburgh man had paid Harmar recruits, on the average, two quarts of Monongahela rye per rifle. The cost of a barrel of Monongahela rye in Pittsburgh: ninety-six shillings, the equivalent, at Pittsburgh's rate of exchange, of sixteen American dollars.

The formalities of the trade completed, the beaver skins stowed in our cabin, Phineas lay down on a bearskin and went to sleep. Ordinarily a quiet sleeper, he tossed and turned. "Mesass!" I heard him murmur any number of times.

Conscience-stricken over having killed Mesass needlessly, Phineas lost interest in food, but not in Monongahela rye. He was in a brooding, masochistic mood when, that night, we took our leave. At the moment the Ohio woods were full of Indians, called by the smoke signals to the Look-Out rendezvous. Being below the Scioto and without the two crates of rifles as substantiating evidence, it was no longer possible to say, if captured, that we were traders working out of Niagara. Nonetheless, overcome by retribution, Phineas now chose to guide our flatboat in the devil-may-care manner of someone determined to let the Indians know we were about. Riding the crest of the current, frequently flapping the bow oar noisily, never taking to the Virginia side, he floated us hour after hour beside the Ohio shore.

Another reason we shouldn't have been so close to the Ohio shore is because here the river was full of what we called "planters" although dictionaries say they are "sawyers"—trees which have fallen into the water and become stuck on the bottom, with their branches projecting through the surface. Around late midmorning we hit a "planter" and, in veering off, Phineas rammed us into a mudbar.

"It's nothing, Tom," Phineas said. "We'll be free inside of ten minutes."

Armed with shovels, Phineas and I climbed overboard and began digging. Phineas' prediction was correct. Within ten minutes our flatboat began swaying. "Board her, Tom," Phineas said, "and handle the bow oar. Just keep her steady. The current'll do the rest."

After digging a bit more, Phineas pushed. The flatboat swung around from the stern, gathering momentum with an alarming rate of speed. Not daring to yell out his warning, Phineas had to run through shin-deep water from the flatboat's stern to her bow. "For God's sake, Tom!" he stage-whispered. "Push on that damned oar."

Actually I *was* pushing with all my might, however the flatboat continued to swing around. Mush! Her entire leeward side became firmly lodged in the mud. Making a quick appraisal: "Tom," Phineas said, "we've got to lighten cargo."

My first task was to put barrels on the gunnel, for Phineas to take off and stack up. "For Christ's sakes, Tom," Phineas said, keeping his voice muffled. "Are you taking a snooze?"

It was, of course, dark and foggy. "I'm trying to locate the whiskey barrels first," I said, "to go on the bottom, so the flour won't get wet."

"To hell with where to put the flour!" Phineas said. We were going to have to remove our entire cargo, he told me, also mentioning that if the task weren't completed before daybreak, we would become a pair of sitting ducks.

Working with the fervor of two men having no desire to become a pair of sitting ducks, we cleared the deck of barrels. Then, when we'd pushed the flatboat free, we put them all back aboard again. Losing no time getting over to the Virginia shore, we put to a quarter-of-an-hour before daybreak.

After this experience Phineas again became a cautious flatboat pilot. However, his remorse over killing Mesass continued to prey upon his mind, making him most despondent. "I couldn't have done anything else, Tom, could I?" he kept asking me and went on what was the equivalent of a Monongahela rye regimen of nourishment.

While perfectly willing to gain relief by confessing his woes to me, Phineas would not listen when I wished to give expression of my concern over the safety of Melissa's flotilla. "There's nothing we can do about that, Tom," he'd tell me. "What good will it do to worry about it?" Then he'd begin talking about Mesass.

This brought about a strained relationship between us, on my part at least. Phineas, I am convinced, was too absorbed with his own thinking and drinking, to be aware of my state of mind.

VII

One week after leaving the Look-Out, I was awakened from a sound sleep by what sounded like incessant shrieks. Assuming an attack by Indians, I rolled from my bearskin to the protection of the leeward gunnel. We were riding through the dawn, I now realized, and knew we should be close to Limestone, a squatter settlement sixty-two miles above Cincinnati.

The shrieks which had aroused me were being made by a flock of chattering parakeets that had descended upon our flatboat, covering the deck with their rich purple and golden plumage. Just what had prompted the birds' visit is hard to say, for there was nothing to eat on the deck. But there they were, unperturbed by my proximity, hobbling about, pecking at the air, and leaving their calling cards.

"Why in the world would they light on a flatboat?" I asked Phineas when the birds had flown away.

"Damned if I know," Phineas said rather irritably. "They do it all the time around here, but nowhere else I ever heard of. Maybe somebody on a flatboat gave them some grain one day and they still remember."

Here, on both sides of the river, you could see what geologists call the Great Cincinnati Peneplain and come from all over the world to see it.

Sliced by many valleys, the tops of the hills run flat as a table. The once jagged crests, we are now being told, were crunched off and smoothed down by a series of prehistoric glaciers which altered the original course of the Ohio River.

"How far to Limestone?" I asked.

"She's just around the bend."

Phineas' eyes looked so glassy that I became alarmed. His face was quite flushed. When I placed my hand on his forehead, he brushed it off. "You've got a bit of fever," I said.

The way to cure an illness, Phineas staunchly believed, was not to admit you are sick. "It can't be fever," he grumbled and took a swig of whiskey. "I feel fine."

We approached Limestone, which has since been rechristened Maysville, Kentucky, on a wide sweep. From the river all you could see of the squatter settlement was her stockade and a well-banked public building. Behind the trees were possibly some fifty cabins and over six hundred acres of cleared land. When we'd put to and tied up, Phineas sat down beside the bow oar and stared vacantly into space. "Aren't you even going to have a cup of coffee?" I asked.

"Sure," Phineas muttered, stood up, and came ashore on extremely wobbly legs.

Only the previous night I had learned that Phineas had two friends living at the inland settlement of Washington, one masculine, one feminine. With the masculine friend Phineas planned making arrangements to store the beaver skins, to be retrieved after the Harmar campaign was concluded.

The less said about the rights and wrongs of that beaver skin transaction, the better. After considerable coaxing on my part, Phineas ate a mite of breakfast. "Phineas," I said, "whether you'll admit it or not, you do have a fever. You're simply not well enough to rent a horse and ride to Washington. You should lie down and wait until tomorrow at least."

"And lose a whole day!" Phineas said. "This is the slowest trip I ever made down the Ohio in my whole life. Christ, as it is, I'll never hear the end of it from the boys at the fort."

"Blame it on me," I said. "You can say that it was I who was sick."

"Sure," Phineas said. "You were sick, so I let you lie in the woods instead of running you down the river to where we could get some medicine. Tom, that excuse is older than the hills."

"If you insist upon going to Washington," I said, "I certainly should go with you."

"Are you crazy! And leave the flatboat alone? By the time we'd be back, the buggers around here'd have her plucked clean."

Phineas left on a hired horse. While never permitting our flatboat to be out of sight I had, at the public landing, the opportunity to speak to a number of Limestone's inhabitants. Since the passing by of the army flotilla I had seen at Marietta, I was told, Phineas and I were the only "outsiders" who'd come through from upstream.

One of my conversants was the captain of the Limestone Rangers, a red-faced Irishman, most solicitous and well-meaning by nature. "I wouldn't worry too much if I were you, mister," he said, "if a flotilla big as the one your friend's riding on was attacked, the chances are good we'd have gotten wind of it in one way or another."

By this he meant that usually, but not always, Indians, after an attack, sent a flatboat with a crew of dead people, scalped and mutilated, floating down the river for the purpose of discouraging settlers from writing to relatives back East, suggesting that they come to the Ohio Country. "Such a flatboat," I said. "Wouldn't it bump against the shore and ground itself?"

"Yes, but the current would work her out into the mainstream again. When'd you leave the Scioto?"

"A week ago."

"You put to at night?"

"Yes."

"Well, she'd be going day and night. I'd almost swear she'd be here by now."

"Almost!"

"I hate to say this, mister, but you'd have to figure if she wasn't too far from here, our hunters might have spotted her. They'd burn her and give everybody a proper burial. We wouldn't know about it until the hunters came back."

"When will they come back?"

"Can't say. They only went out a couple of days ago."

What worried me even more than what might be implied from the information received was that Phineas, most surely knowing all this too, had seen fit not to alarm me by mentioning it. There was no opportunity to go into the matter further when, at dusk, Phineas returned. So weak that he almost fell off his horse, Phineas looked positively ghastly. His face had turned as yellow as a dandelion and the vacant, glassy look of his eyes told me his fever was worse.

The trip, to add to Phineas' woes, had been fruitless. His feminine friend had moved off, to who knows where. The masculine friend now resided at the squatter settlement of Bracken, some eighteen miles below Limestone. "It's an easy run to Bracken," Phineas said. "Let me sleep till eleven o'clock."

Shortly before eleven o'clock, Phineas began moaning loudly. Although his forehead was hot as a burning coal, he began insulting me when I tried to apply a wet rag. Jumping up, calling out to Mesass for forgiveness, he threatened to leap overboard and drown himself. Reaching the conclusion that he actually planned upon carrying out his threat, I went to the cabin for a hammer, about whose head I wrapped a rag. By clonking Phineas on the back of his head, I managed to get him to sleep.

The night was so pitch dark that I couldn't have found my way to the settlement to seek help, even if I had known where to go. And there was no one to ask. While Limestone had a company of Rangers of whom its citizens were justly proud, the members were not paid. They did not patrol at night, which at first glance may seem odd to someone unacquainted with the unorthodox manner in which Ohio Country Rangers frequently performed their duties.

At dawn, with Phineas no better, I found a settler who told me to go to a Mrs. Andreson, the settlement's midwife, for help. "The hell you say!" Mrs. Andreson said when I explained my presence. "Phineas Ford sick! Let him alone. He'll be all right."

"I think you should see him, Mrs. Andreson," I said.

Mrs. Andreson was an Amazonian-statured, big-boned woman who, apparently, did not believe in combing her hair. Our conversation took place in front of her trading post, a hewed-out fallen sycamore tree big enough in circumference for six horses to have ridden into abreast. Mrs. Andreson, I would learn, had done all the chopping-out herself and, claiming original occupancy, was challenging the settlement's governing body's right to make her move in order that a street could be laid across the area upon which the sycamore had fallen.

Shrugging her shoulders, Mrs. Andreson pointed to a notice stating that she charged from a shilling to two shillings a visit, according to the patient's ability to pay, plus a shilling per mile for travel. Mrs. Andreson, I could not help noting, had kept abreast of the times. Her fees were on a par with those of accredited Philadelphia doctors.

"Do you wish to be paid now?" I asked.

"I would be very much obliged," Mrs. Andreson said, and her eyes opened rather widely when I handed over actual money. Reaching behind her counter, she brought out a cloth satchel. "Medicine'll come extra," she added.

"I understand," I said.

When we reached the flatboat, Phineas, moaning in a manner which was terrifying, was calling out to Mesass. When I explained what this

meant to Mrs. Andreson, she said, "Phineas needs a faith healer. I ain't one
and we ain't got one here."

"I do think he's also sick," I said.

"He sure is," Mrs. Andreson said. "He's got jaundice and cholera for certain, diarrhea and dysentery, too, I would strongly suspect. It don't come to
me though why he should be delirious."

"What can you do for him?"

"That's hard to say," Mrs. Andreson said and began rummaging in her
satchel. "He's got a lot wrong with him. I'd say his delirium was the
worst, wouldn't you?"

"I would imagine so," I said.

"Well, give him some of this," Mrs. Andreson said, handing me a small
bottle. "This here's a special delirium healer. It's going to have to run you
three shillings, you get one back if you return the bottle."

The special delirum healer, I would discover, was made up of a mixture of
powder of jalap, rosin of jalap, vitriolated tartar, mercurious dulcis, amber
powder, oil of cloves, powdered crabs' eyes, and conserve of rosemary
flowers.

"And here," Mrs. Andreson said, giving me a bottle containing a mixture
concocted mainly from puccoon root, "that's for his jaundice."

For Phineas' diarrhea and dysentery, Mrs. Andreson gave me a bottle
containing a mixture of rhubarb and geranium roots. Her remedy for the
cholera was the conventional one, a mixture of calomel and opium. "And
lay a wet towel on Phineas' belly to cool him off," Mrs. Andreson instructed
me. "Too bad folks don't get cholera in the winter when there's ice, but I
never yet seen anybody get it except in the summer. Chilling the belly, to
my way of thinking, does more good than the medicine."

The price of the medicine, Mrs. Andreson said, would be eight shillings.
"If Phineas don't get better," she added, "there ain't nothing nobody can do,
so don't pay no heed when folks start coming around and telling you about
some fancy, pet cure."

"How big a dose," I asked, "shall I administer?"

"You got a ladle?"

"Yes."

"Fill her about half full."

"In all cases?"

"Certainly!"

"How often should I administer the doses?"

"Whenever you think he needs one."

"At first—am I to give him all these medicines at once?"

My barrage of stupid questions was beginning to irk Mrs. Andreson.

"Why not?" she said. "He's got everything they're supposed to cure, ain't he?"

"I was thinking," I said, "that all this, administered at one time, might upset Phineas' stomach?"

Mrs. Andreson's brow puckered. "Damn if you mightn't be right at that," she said. "Give him the delirium healer first. Wait a while, then feed him the others."

Phineas' delirium lasted three days. The week which followed this phase of his recovery was, for me, a most trying one. Phineas was not a model patient. Convincing him to take the various remedies prescribed by Mrs. Andreson became a major undertaking. He couldn't possibly have what Mrs. Andreson said, Phineas insisted. He knew what ailed him. He had a touch of the damps and the ague. It had come about, precisely as he had predicted in Marietta, as a direct aftermath of not being able to fortify himself.

I took up Phineas' self-diagnosis with Mrs. Andreson. "If he thinks that, it means he's getting better," she said and handed me a quart bottle. "Give him as much of this as he wants."

This latest remedy was Mrs. Andreson's private brand of bitters. Conventional bitters, considered a cure for almost everything in the Ohio Country, are a combination of whiskey and tansy. Mrs. Andreson had substituted a local weed for the tansy, which made the concoction taste far more bitter.

"Bitters!" Phineas said triumphantly. "That's what I should have had all along."

Is it possible the whiskey in the bitters stimulated Phineas' appetite? At any rate, after having within half a day consumed the entire bottle of bitters, Phineas announced that he was ravenously hungry. Thereafter, following two days of gluttonous eating, Phineas was again hale and hearty.

VIII

During the ten days of our enforced stay at Limestone, I watched constantly for the arrival of Melissa's flotilla. It did not come and the Limestone hunters did not return. When Phineas was well enough to discuss the situation, he told me that long ago he had learned so many causes for delay could come about during a trip down the river that it was a mistake to imagine the worst. He could offer me no more comfort than that. By the night of our departure from Limestone a certain spurious heartiness had crept into Phineas' manner of speaking which was frightening.

IX

After a leisurely run, it was well after dawn when we approached the squatter settlement of Bracken, presently called Augusta, Kentucky. We were now only forty-four miles above Cincinnati.

While from the river, Bracken looked scarcely different from Limestone, her cabins and inlots were more isolated. Any number of her outlots were located deep in the woods.

Bracken, we discovered, was agog with excitement. During the night Indians had struck an outlying cabin, killing a mother, father, and three small children. Flushed with their success, the Indians had been unable to resist the temptation to set the cabin on fire. Roosters, seeing the flames and thinking it was dawn, had started crowing. This had warned the inhabitants, an alarm was sounded and everyone else had reached the stockade safely.

Only a short while before our arrival the marauders, some twenty Mingos and their renegade, had come up to the stockade. At Limestone, the renegade shouted out that white men had cheated the Indians in a horse trade. For this he demanded repayment. He also protested the practice of whipping Indian children captives as a disciplinary measure. This was humiliating, he contended. Indian children should be punished by ducking their heads in a bucket of water.

The citizenry of Bracken was quite proud of the way the captain of its Rangers had handled the situation. There were no Indian child captives at Bracken, he'd said, and the settlement's inhabitants could not be blamed for injustices perpetrated by others. After throwing out a British army officer's uniform as a gesture of good will, he'd held up an American coat of arms. While the branches meant peace, he'd stated most firmly that the eagle also had claws which could scratch. And they would, he'd warned, unless the Indians agreed to leave.

The Indians had left.

When Phineas heard that the renegade was a tall, white-haired man, who could roar like a bull: "That's Crazy Izzy," he said.

Crazy Izzy, Phineas told me, was a former Catholic priest who had gone berserk brooding over the injustice of the white man stealing the red man's lands. "Crazy Izzy's tricky as they come," Phineas said. "Showing up with Mingos . . . He's tied up with the Wyandots, one of their big men at that. The old boy's up to something, that's for sure. Tom, we'll have to hang over here a day at least. Crazy Izzy knows me." Making a sweeping gesture which took in all the surrounding hills: "We've got to figure he'll be up there somewhere's, watching this place."

Phineas knew Crazy Izzy from back in the days when he was still living with his family outside of Pittsburgh. "I guess he was a pretty good priest," Phineas went on to say, "but he couldn't keep his hands off the girls, so finally he got chased out of town. By now I'd been with the Delawares for maybe a year. Damned if one day Father Donovan didn't show up at our village. He wasn't called Crazy Izzy then, of course. He said he wanted to hook up with our tribe.

"When he saw me, he figured his goose was cooked because I knew all about him. He's a slick talker though, Tom. He told me he was all through playing around, so I said I'd keep my mouth shut.

"Two days later I caught him fondling a squaw, one of the chief's daughters at that! Christ, he pulls something like that with Delawares. Delawares believe in marriage and really get sore if somebody plays around with their women, Indians as well as whites. 'Father Donovan,' I said, 'you'd better get your trotters moving from here fast or you'll end up burned at the stake.' I guess he was already turning crazy. He told me he felt so sorry for the Indians because they were losing all their lands, he couldn't help himself. Whenever he got around a squaw, he wanted to be nice to her. He wasn't so crazy though not to have sense enough to leave the next day."

"You'd think he'd be most grateful to you," I said.

"You would," Phineas said, "because what I really did was save his skin, but it didn't work out that way. He hates me worse than poison."

Phineas accounted Crazy Izzy to be a most astute adversary. To give him the impression we'd be here some time to trade, Phineas auctioned off ten barrels of flour for salt at a rate which would have made the flour worth ten dollars a barrel, almost two-and-a-half times more than we had paid in Pittsburgh.

He made a great show of transporting the beaver skins to his friend's cabin. Crazy Izzy, knowing what was being done, would have no trouble surmising how the beaver skins had been obtained. This, Phineas hoped, would add to the general impression that he was not connected with General Harmar's army.

To abet his general strategy of subterfuge Phineas, the following morning, hired a horse and rode into the woods. "I'm not going anywhere in particular, Tom," he told me, "I just want Crazy Izzy to think I'm heading inland to do some trading." He'd return after dark, he said, and that we'd be leaving that night.

Phineas was scarcely on his way when I heard the shout: "Flotilla around the bend!"

This has to be Melissa's, I thought.

However, only four flatboats rounded the bend. Surely Melissa's flotilla would be stronger that this! Then it occurred to me that the flotilla might have been attacked and this was all that was left. As the boats neared the public landing those aboard waved to those ashore. There were as many women as men riders, that much I could see although the distance made individual identification impossible and many of the women wore sun-bonnets. When the boats began sweeping toward shore, the sunbonnets still hid most of the women's faces. Aware that Melissa would have no idea I was at Bracken, I climbed atop our cabin and began waving my arms. A number of men waved back. There was, though, no indication that Melissa was aboard.

For quite a while after the boats put to, some two hundred yards off, I stayed where I was. Something told me this was part of Melissa's flotilla. This feeling was so strong, I became actually afraid to go and find out what had happened to the rest of the boats.

Eventually I did. Off the first flatboat, a white-haired woman was prodding a fire beneath a large iron kettle. After regarding each other in the dubious manner of people who are certain they have met before, but cannot recall where, the white-haired woman exclaimed, "Say! Damned if you ain't Tom, the young man Melissa's so daffy over."

The woman's name was Mrs. O'Toole. The moment she spoke, I realized it was she who had directed me to the Andrews wagon, on the day Melissa overloaded her father's rifle.

Before I could say anything Mrs. O'Toole told me, "Melissa's still sleeping." When I started for the flatboat, she grabbed me by the arm. "You can look at her, but don't wake her up," she ordered in an authoritative voice which, despite my excitement, commanded obedience.

Melissa, lying on the deck under a bearskin, was sleeping soundly. She looked peaceful as a cherub. "See them rosy cheeks," Mrs. O'Toole said.

"Ain't she a pretty little chicken? And she's just as sweet. All the fever's gone. She ought to be close to all right again, when she wakes up."

"Fever!"

"She had the cholera. Everybody had it one time or another. Except me." Mrs. O'Toole extended a wrinkled, bony hand. "See them little bones. I'm made like a sparrow. Weigh next to nothing. Don't eat hardly, so I never get sick. I'll live to be a hundred. But who wants to? Because what good are you? My mister's dead twenty-two years come this July. I'm from Bedford. Never set foot out of the place before. My boys all moved away, so did my girls. I had nine altogether. Don't even know how many grandchildren, though there's aplenty. None of them write me, but I suppose if I passed away they'd some of them come to my funeral. I got a little money saved up. So I figured, what the hell! I'll go and see what Ohio's like." Cackling slightly: "From what I've seen so far, it ain't nothing but a lot of trees."

"How long has Melissa been ill?" I asked.

"Ten days, maybe eleven. She's strong, so don't worry about it. You planning on marrying her?"

"Yes," I said, "I am."

"You'd better," Mrs. O'Toole said, "because if you don't I'll be damned if I won't pick up a rifle and shoot you right through the heart."

"If the Indians will only assume your point of view, Mrs. O'Toole," I said, "my chances of living a long, but not necessarily a useful life, will be greatly enhanced."

"You think I'm a-joshing, don't you?" Mrs. O'Toole said.

"Until now I did, yes," I said.

"You're damned right I'd shoot you," Mrs. O'Toole said. "Melissa's stubborn as a mule when it comes to taking on a husband. She's got her heart set on you. If you threw her over it'd be years before she'd have sense enough to know there's always another bird in the bush. By then she'd be too old. And with next to no money left and nobody left to—good God! You wouldn't know it. Melissa's father is dead."

"Dead!"

"It happened the night you left Steubenville. A puma clawed him to death. Awful thing to happen just when the dear girl had found happiness."

"I'd heard about the tragedy," I said. "The last thing I suspected was that—"

"Then you know what people figure Mr. Andrews was trying to do when he was killed?"

"Yes, I suppose I do."

"Melissa doesn't believe it was that way."

"She was told—everything?"

"Not at first. That is, what folks say really must have happened. But you know how people talk, so Melissa soon got wind of it. She doesn't think it happened that way at all. Did you know about how Mr. Andrews lost most of his money, buying up a tract of maple trees?"

"I knew he was probably having financial difficulties."

"You know how he'd get drunk and start chopping down maple trees?"

"Yes, Melissa told me about that."

"Well, he was drunker than a lord that night and it was below a maple tree that they found Mr. Andrews' clawed-up body. Melissa's sure he was off on one of his maple tree chopping sprees. With him being drunk as he was, it wouldn't make any difference whether he had an ax with him or not."

"Melissa could very well be right," I said.

"Well, he's dead and to me it makes no difference how he died," Mrs. O'Toole said. "But I'm here to tell you Melissa's got spunk. There she was. All alone. Everybody started telling her to go back and live with her aunt in Trenton. A minister even came down from Little Beaver to try to convince her. She was taking too big a chance, everybody was saying, because all she had was your word and you could just have been playing with her affections.

"Melissa didn't budge an inch though, Mr. Morrow. She was real polite when people talked to her, thanked them for thinking about her well-being, but it was damned clear from the very first that she was going after you, even if she had to swim to Cincinnati.

"Well, the flotilla finally started off, twenty-seven boats strong. Melissa and I had took to each other from the first, but by now I loved her like she was my own flesh and blood. When we got to the Muskingum River we heard all about a big massacre over to Williamstown and word from Pittsburgh had it Harmar's army still hadn't come through. Everybody but us four boats got scared and bought up lots at Marietta. To tell you the truth, I was so fed up with the Ohio Country that I was ready to go home myself, but I couldn't leave Melissa alone, could I? Mr. Morrow! If you ever tell that to Melissa, I'll skin you alive."

"I promise you, Mrs. O'Toole," I said, "that will be one of the few secrets that will be kept from my wife."

"At least so long as I'm alive," Mrs. O'Toole said. "Look! I think Melissa's starting to wake up. Yes! See? She blew that strand of hair out of her eyes. She always does that. Now she'll stretch and yawn for quite a spell. She's a slow waker, Mr. Morrow. You'd think the dear girl was drugged."

There was no doubt of it. Melissa *was* a "slow waker." Mrs. O'Toole and I watched and waited with the loving concern of young parents looking at a newly born baby lying in a crib. "Ain't that beautiful hair she's got?" Mrs. O'Toole whispered. "See that touch of red? She combs it a hundred strokes every morning. I did it for her while she was ailing and it pleased her so much! If she gets sick again, Mr. Morrow, you do it for her. Wouldn't take long and maybe you'd be surprised how happy it'll make you too. My mister never did anything like that for me, but of course I never did anything like that for him. We kept everything inside us. Funny about some people. They want to do something nice, but until they get old as me they're afraid to . . .

"She's almost awake now, Mr. Morrow. Go back of that barrel and keep out of sight! I've got to find out if she's well enough to stand excitement. If she ain't, you can't talk to her till later. You heard me, didn't you?"

"Yes, Mrs. O'Toole," I said, "I did."

Mrs. O'Toole laid her rough, working-woman's hand on mine. I could feel its soft tenderness through the calluses. "Cholera makes a person weak, Mr. Morrow," she said gently, "even when they think they're better. I want Melissa to eat her breakfast."

Melissa awakened by degrees. Her eyes still closed, she nodded when Mrs. O'Toole told her to go into the cabin to freshen up. "I'll fix you some breakfast, dearie," Mrs. O'Toole said.

"I can do it, Mrs. O'Toole," Melissa protested sleepily. "If you keep on waiting on me, *you'll* be sick next. I feel quite strong this morning. What time is it? Did I oversleep again? We should—"

"Now, now, dearie," Mrs. O'Toole said, pushed Melissa into the cabin, and went ashore to the fire.

Melissa had slept in a blue dress. When she came out of the cabin, she had on a dark red one. Calico. It was a store-bought dress, but I could see where it had been taken in here and there. The net result was that it fit Melissa's trim figure extremely well and I have always felt that a plain calico dress, if not too plain, has a subtle softness about it which many dresses of more expensive materials lack.

Melissa, now wide awake, looked ever so fresh and wholesome. She began combing her hair, which hung down well beyond her shoulders. "Seven, eight, nine . . ." the movement of her lips told me she was counting.

Although I recognized the wisdom of Mrs. O'Toole's order and had fully expected to carry it out, I simply could not wait longer. I stepped forward. "Madam," I said, "I understand you have been ill. Possibly it might be better if I took over the hair brush."

Melissa's lips moved, but no words came out. Then we were in each other's arms. In no time Mrs. O'Toole came aboard. Her frail body showing amazing strength, she wedged herself between us, the way I sometimes had to do when a recess-period fight occurred in the play area of the William Penn Charter School.

"You see!" Mrs. O'Toole fumed. "I knew this would happen. Hugging and kissing, the way you're going at it, tires a person out. I ain't sure Melissa's strong enough for it yet."

"Oh, but I am, Mrs. O'Toole," Melissa said. "I am!"

The sheer happiness that exuded from Melissa's whole being would have melted a heart of stone and, of course, Mrs. O'Toole's was fashioned of pure gold. "Well, maybe it's all for the best," she said grudgingly. "But mind you, Melissa dearie, I want you to eat your breakfast, every last speck of it. And I'll be back in one hour, to find out if you've got fever."

X

After standing by until Melissa had eaten her breakfast, Mrs. O'Toole took her leave. Moving to the side of the flatboat which gave us a view of the river, Melissa and I sat down with our backs against the cabin wall. Thanks to Mrs. O'Toole, we enjoyed complete privacy. "No," we could hear Mrs. O'Toole saying from time to time on the shore, "no, you can't go on the boat now. Miss Andrews is entertaining her gentleman friend." When Mrs. O'Toole spoke, people paid heed.

There was, of course, a great deal for Melissa and me to talk about. Of Bushrod Andrews' death, I shall only say that I was quite proud of Melissa's reaction to it. I do not say she was as yet completely recovered from her shock. However, she had managed great strides in putting everything into its proper place.

Not too long after sitting down, I suggested that it might be advisable for us to be married in Cincinnati, if not on the day of our arrival at the settlement, certainly on the next. This startled Melissa somewhat, for it had been agreed in Steubenville that, while neither of us entertained doubts of being in love, we would wait a bit, since we wished to think of ourselves as being prudent people.

Melissa did mention what had been said in Steubenville and we talked some time on the wisdom of holding to our original thought. This conversation was getting us nowhere. "Have you any doubts?" I eventually asked Melissa.

"None," she said.

"Good," I said. "Let us, then, stop beating around the bush. Melissa, I love you beyond all power of description. I will hold sacred the love which you now have for me and will fight the rest of my life to be worthy of it. Melissa Williamson Andrews of Trenton, will you marry Thomas Andrew Morrow of Philadelphia? In Cincinnati? Tomorrow, if possible, certainly no later than the day thereafter?"

"Yes, my darling," Melissa said. "Yes, yes, yes! And I pledge you my undying love, for so long as I shall live."

That settled I became engulfed in a crescendo of happiness and it is reasonable to suppose that Melissa was experiencing a similar gamut of emotions. Immediately after Melissa's reply, we embraced. Then we spent considerable time talking about how much we loved each other, in a general way. After a while the subject of where we would live came up.

"Temporary quarters will be available for us at Fort Washington," I said. "With Harmar's army in the state it is, I'm certain that Phineas Ford will have enough free time to run us to Louisville. From there a flotilla will take us to Cairo. At Cairo we can board a Mississippi River schooner. These are excellent craft, I'm told, with good quarters. Once in New Orleans, we can take as long as we wish getting back to Philadelphia. My sabbatical runs until March first."

"Do you plan upon leaving Cincinnati quickly as possible?" Melissa asked.

"Yes."

"May I inquire why?"

"Why?" Melissa had suddenly become quite serious. The manner in which she posed her question gave me something of a start. "Certainly you have no desire to remain in a place like Cincinnati a minute longer than is necessary?"

"You have never asked me for a direct answer to that question, my darling," Melissa said gently.

"That's so," I said. "I haven't."

"You might, then, do so now."

"Of course," I said. "Melissa, do you want to stay a while in Cincinnati?"

"Yes," Melissa said. "I think we should. And for the greater length of your sabbatical, at least."

"At least?"

"At least," Melissa said quietly.

"I am not certain I understand you," I said.

"I am convinced that you do not want to leave the Ohio Country," Melissa said. "I am almost convinced that you no longer wish to be a schoolmaster."

How very true it all actually was!

"Please go on," I said.

"There is nothing more to say, my darling. You love the Ohio Country and what it is like. You prefer it to Philadelphia."

"That is so . . ." I said. "Yet until this moment I haven't dared admit it, even to myself."

"And now you have. Isn't it, actually, simple as that?"

"I am having difficulty believing I am in fact awake," I said. "You are saying that on what may well be merely a whim on my part—you are willing to endure the privations of living in Cincinnati?"

"I will have you know," Melissa said, "that I hadn't thought of my life with you as 'enduring' anything. And I shall be greatly obliged if you will tell me you will not be 'enduring' anything with me."

"Melissa," I said, "this is a most serious decision."

"I am well aware of that, my darling. I have been thinking about it, almost daily, since I last saw you."

"Harmar's army—" I said. "We, people with our experience, have no conception—Phineas and others who know have been continually telling me this—what it will be like."

"I am sure that is so," Melissa said. "My many advisers have gone into it all with me too."

"Well, I also believe in making my own decisions," I said. "I can't, though, stop thinking you're doing this because of me. You are right about me loving the Ohio Country. You are right, too, in being almost convinced that I no longer desire to be a schoolmaster. Yet I do not think of remaining in the profession as condemning myself to a life of quiet desperation. I swear to you, I could be happy in Philadelphia, with you."

"And I swear to you," Melissa said, "that I can be happy with you in Cincinnati, if that is where you decide you wish to remain."

"Melissa," I said, "if we decide to stay in Cincinnati, I would never want to leave, the Ohio Country at least. On the rack, I couldn't explain how I know this. It's probably what you said, I love the Ohio Country. It is probably as simple as that."

"Then we have reached a decision?"

"Only if you are able to tell me there is within you, too, such a feeling."

"I am able to," Melissa said.

About this time Mrs. O'Toole returned to say the first hour was up. A glance at Melissa was all she needed. Her withered cheeks aglow, she exclaimed, "It's all settled! You're getting married, ain't you?"

"Tomorrow, Mrs. O'Toole," Melissa said. "Tomorrow! Or on the next day at the very latest."

After embracing Melissa, Mrs. O'Toole felt her forehead and looked at her tongue. "No fever, but your tongue's a mite coated," she pronounced. "Melissa'll have to lie down a while this afternoon." Then she said: "You be a kind husband to her, Mr. Morrow." Then she began talking to Melissa about what they'd wear at the wedding.

This wonderful day simply rolled on. By noon Melissa was forced to admit that she was becoming somewhat weary. "Drink this broth, dearie," Mrs. O'Toole told her. "I can't keep the men off the boat all afternoon. Go and sleep on Mr. Morrow's boat. You and him can have supper together." She chuckled. "That way neither of you won't die from not seeing each other."

"Why couldn't Melissa ride to Cincinnati with Phineas and me?" I suggested. "You'd come along too, of course."

"You crazy!" Mrs. O'Toole snorted and her reasoning was irrefutable, "you two'd be talking the whole night through and I'd be sending a walking cadaver to her own wedding . . . And you stay off the flatboat while Melissa's sleeping, Mr. Morrow. If she sort of wakes up and spies you, she'll never get back to sleep again. Mind you, Melissa's a bright girl, quick as a whip too, but she's got no sense when it comes to taking care of herself. Mr. Morrow, after tomorrow, you'll be the boss. If she starts wearing herself out, you put your foot down."

Well before dusk Melissa was up and about again, doing this and that, and not obeying when Mrs. O'Toole kept telling her to conserve her strength. Mrs. O'Toole had told a young boy from the flotilla, whose name was Enoch Kitchel, to go into the woods and shoot something. "Fish, fish, fish!" Mrs. O'Toole grumbled. "That's all we've been eating. All them tasty birds in the trees and we didn't dare shoot them."

Enoch brought back a turkey and two geese. Although this was June, the turkey was so plump that the fall from its roost in a tree had broken its skin. Proudly Enoch announced that he'd brought down the two geese with a single ball. The flock had flown so low, he said, that he'd been able to see the shining gray of the birds' breast feathers.

Mrs. O'Toole and Melissa examined the three birds with the perceptive care of housewives making a purchase in a poultry market. Their final decision was to take one of the geese.

The fog set in earlier than usual that evening. Wind-blown, it hit us in chilly dank puffs. "Get my shawl, dearie," Mrs. O'Toole said to Melissa, "and you'd better put on the blue dress and the quilted petticoats."

"I had that in mind, precisely," Melissa said gayly.

While Melissa was in the cabin changing her clothes, Mrs. O'Toole said, "Wait'll you see them petticoats, Mr. Morrow. I mean how they fit! Gorgeous. Simply gorgeous! My own great-grandmother made them in Ireland. Handed down from daughter to daughter. But nobody wore them more than once or twice. So they're like new. Me! I never even got into them once because my mister and me didn't have no wedding. I was saving them for my oldest granddaughter. Now don't tell that to Melissa or I'll skin you alive! I had a hard enough time making her take them as it was. What the dickens, I figured. Beautiful petticoats like those! It's a crime to just go on saving and saving them."

The petticoats were superb. When Melissa came out of the cabin and pirouetted gracefully, they swished loud as a gust of wind. The blue woolen dress was actually quite plain, but the petticoats made noticeable Melissa's slender waist and accentuated the soft contours of her hips. In its own quiet way the dress did a great deal for Melissa and she knew it. She was so pleased when I told her how well she looked.

We ate on the riverbank. The goose, roasted, was excellent. I had bought a bottle of the only kind of wine purchasable in Bracken: blackberry. Wrong, of course, for fowl, it would have also been wrong for anything else. While expert distillers of Monongahela rye and better-than-average brewers of beer, citizens of the Ohio Country were atrocious winemakers. We circumvented the wine's sickening-sweet, dried-fruit taste by not drinking more than a sip as a toast, after which I tossed the bottle into the river.

There is nothing more to say of the dinner other than that it was a most pleasant occasion. Despite insistence to the contrary, Melissa showed signs of fatigue as we washed and dried the dishes. By now darkness was setting in fast and people were moving about, getting the flotilla ready to move off.

"Melissa," I said, "as an indication that I possess at least a modicum of common sense, I am going to say: 'good night.' Lie down, won't you, darling, and get a good night's sleep. I'm rather looking forward to seeing you tomorrow."

"Yes, my darling," she said. "Tomorrow and tomorrow and tomorrow."

XI

Phineas returned from the woods shortly after I reached our flatboat. He was in high spirits. "Damned if I didn't run into somebody I knew," he said and clicked his teeth.

"I have a bit of news for you," I said and told Phineas that Melissa and I were being married the next day in Cincinnati.

"Well, I'll be!" Phineas said and shook my hand warmly. "She's a fine girl, Tom. I liked her the minute I laid eyes on her. She'll make you a fine wife."

"I just hope I can make her a fine husband," I said. "You'll be my witness at the wedding, won't you?"

"I sure will," Phineas said. "Now let's go and get the beavers."

"The beavers?" I said. "Why?"

"I'll run you and Melissa and the beavers to Cairo. Hell, I can be back in plenty of time to scout for the General! You sell the beavers in New Orleans and send me one of those papers you told me about." By this Phineas meant a letter of credit, such as I had, issued by the Bank of North America. "You keep whatever you figure is your fair share of the deal."

"That's awfully kind of you, Phineas," I said, "and I know that all along I've been worrying about the difficulties of getting to Cairo, but the situation has changed. Instead of wanting to get out of Cincinnati quickly as possible, Melissa and I have decided to stay on there for quite some time."

"Well, I'll be damned," Phineas said.

When we shoved off, I lay down, thinking it might be wise to get in a good night's sleep. I was, however, far too excited and restless. Shortly I was at the bow, with Phineas.

This foggy night was unseasonably chilly and I kept thinking it was fortunate Melissa was wearing the woolen dress with the quilted petticoats. Around midnight Phineas and I were talking about where Melissa and I would live.

"You'll be all settled, snug as a bug in a rug, by the day after tomorrow," Phineas said.

It was customary in Cincinnati, Phineas explained, for local citizens to clear an inlot and raise a cabin for newcomers. Work started at dawn. By late afternoon, the task was completed. "Nothing for you to worry about, Tom," Phineas said. "All you have to do is bring a keg of whiskey. Hell, we'll give them a whole barrel."

Although touched by this expression of welcome, I was not quite certain how I felt about it. At night, Phineas had told me, Indians regularly walked the girdled lanes which in Cincinnati were called streets. The inlots on which cabins stood were isolated oases in a desert of gigantic trees. While, in most cases probably no more than half-a-mile apart, amid all those trees distance meant nothing.

"How do the Indians get through the army patrols?" I was recalling having asked Phineas.

"They just do," he said. "One night I ran into a Miami not a hundred feet from Fort Washington's main gate."

"What happened?"

"Nothing. We just said 'hello' and kept on going."

Because of the proximity of the fort, Phineas had said, there had so far been no scalpings or cabin burnings in Cincinnati, but such incidents had occurred in the Miami Purchase's other two settlements, Columbia and Northbend. "With the way Indian minds seem to work," I distinctly recalled having observed, "there's no way of knowing when they'll suddenly decide to cut loose."

"That's why you keep the doors bolted at night and the chimneys plugged up in the summertime," Phineas had said.

While I was thinking about all this, Phineas touched my arm. "I hear something off our stern," he said.

Although I listened with all my capabilities, I could not make out what Phineas was talking about. It was not that Phineas' hearing was actually more acute than mine. He could, though, differentiate and evaluate the various noises of the night.

"Hear it?" Phineas asked me.

"I didn't hear anything out of the ordinary."

"It was a couple of oar flaps, I'm pretty sure. Didn't sound light enough to be a paddle."

"It might well be the four flatboats of Melissa's flotilla catching up with us," I suggested.

"*Four* boats!"

I explained how this had come about.

"My holy God," Phineas said more to himself than to me. "Tom, I figured with forty wagons there'd be twenty-five boats at least." He spoke pathetically: "Why in the hell didn't you tell me? Four boats! No cover-up. They just start out. Didn't anybody tell them about Crazy Izzy? Tom, if Crazy Izzy hits them, they don't stand a chance."

The bend of the river was such that the current was moving us toward the Ohio shore. Phineas pushed the oar, easing us toward Virginia. "About a mile ahead," Phineas said, "you damn near bump into the Ohio shore before the current moves you over. That's where Crazy Izzy and his boys will be waiting."

I experienced a moment of panic when all sense of reason left me. "Listen to where Melissa's flotilla is, Phineas," I said. "I'll swim and warn them."

"Bucking the current in this black night! Don't be foolish, Tom." Phineas spoke softly. "They're a mile back and you wouldn't know where in the hell you were going."

Phineas' patient manner of speaking restored me to my senses. "Twenty Mingos," I said. "There are at least eight men on each of the flotilla's boats. Armed. Couldn't they, with our help, fight them off?"

"Twenty Mingos? Sure, Tom, we could fight them off. But I told you Crazy Izzy's tied up with the Wyandots and that he's tricky. You've got to figure Crazy Izzy and his Wyandots ran into the Mingos. Crazy Izzy showed up with the Mingos to make it look like it was a hunting party. God knows how many of his own bastards he's got with him waiting in the Ohio woods."

As we moved toward the Virginia shore, I went to our stern and peered into the blackness, hoping to see signs of Melissa's flotilla. I saw only utter blackness between mountains of heavy fog. I could hear nothing. "Melissa," I began saying to myself, over and over again.

I returned to the bow, well aware that if I kept on repeating Melissa's name, I would soon be calling it out loud. I was becoming panicky again. The worst part was that while I recognized the state I was in, I had no desire to control it. "Phineas," I said, "you're not God almighty. You could be wrong. Crazy Izzy and his boys may have pulled out."

"Sure, Tom," Phineas said. "Sure, I could be wrong."

We bumped against the Virginia shore and tied up. "All we can do," Phineas said, "is wait and see if anything happens."

I started for the stern. It was useless, utterly foolhardy, I knew very well, to jump overboard and swim to Melissa, but that is what apparently I had in mind. Certainly Phineas was convinced that was my intention. "You'd better stay here with me, Tom," he said.

Phineas had stood up and shifted the position of his feet. Another step from me and I knew one of his legs would lash out and knock me flat. Fear of this is not what stopped me. Rather it was Phineas' general demeanor, his forbearance and kindly understanding that calmed me down. "I'm all right, Phineas," I said. "Thank you. I may have come awfully close to completely losing my head, but I'm all right now."

Phineas nodded and sat down.

"What are we going to do?" I asked. My whole manner had changed. I had become deadly calm.

"If we're sure it's just twenty Mingos, we'll help."

"What would our chances be?"

"We could beat the hell out of them. We'd ride right through them. Their only chance would be getting us ashore and making a land fight of it."

"And if it's Crazy Izzy and Wyandots?"

"Then it'll be a question of how long the flotilla can fight them off, Tom. All we can do is get to Columbia fast as we can and call for help."

Columbia, the upstream settlement of the Miami Purchase, was six miles closer to us than Cincinnati. At best, Phineas told me, it would be dawn before we could get to Columbia.

"The chance of getting help back here in time," I said, "would be practically a forlorn one?"

"Yes," Phineas said, "it would."

We waited. The fog was thickening, but the wind, blowing downstream, carried considerable spank. As I peered toward the Ohio shore, I could see great masses of gray dim the blackness of the night, then float on.

"In this fog," I said hopefully, "they might be able to slip through."

"Maybe," Phineas said. He'd sat down and was drinking whiskey. Apparently he felt nothing could be gained by looking toward the Ohio shore.

"If it's Crazy Izzy and the Wyandots," I asked, "will they have canoes in the river, waiting?"

"I doubt it," Phineas said. "They'd lose a canoe crew for sure that way. One thing about Crazy Izzy. He loves to go back to his village and say he did it without hardly losing a man."

"Then how can he tell when the flotilla passes by? Especially if it swings wide of the bend. Surely the flotilla's oarsmen have been told about the bend?"

"Maybe they have and maybe they haven't. Doesn't make too much difference, Tom. The Indians know when the flotilla left. Their scouts will be following her down the river. They'll lose her when she swings over to Virginia, but they'll pick her up again when she's riding nearer Ohio. If I could hear something, what the hell do you think the Indians can hear? And you've got to figure on the last night's run oarsmen think they're home and get careless. Tom, it's not like them spotting us. They *know* when the God-damned flotilla left."

From the Ohio shore a frantic voice pierced the blackness of the night. "Save me! I'm a Harmar federal. Come ashore." The voice rang out again and again: "Save me. In God's name, come to my assistance!"

When the voice finally became silent: "Well, they at least didn't bite on that bait," Phineas said.

"Was that Crazy Izzy trying to lure them ashore?"

"No, it was probably the Mingos' renegade. Crazy Izzy can yell twice that loud."

"Phineas? This attempt to lure the flotilla ashore? Could it mean only Mingos are about? You did say, didn't you, they'd have to make a land fight of it?"

"I guess it could mean that, Tom," Phineas said, but his voice carried no conviction whatsoever.

Suddenly a series of tremendous bonfires blazed, lighting up the Ohio shore. A dozen or more shrieking Indians began running up and down before the flames, exposing themselves to perfect pot shots.

Although you could see the Ohio shore plain as day, midriver remained black as the depths of a deep abyss. You could see nothing out there.

"Jesus!" Phineas muttered. "Crazy Izzy lost them. He's had to figure they're just about due. Look!"

The Indians had stopped running. Standing still, they were beating their chests with their fists and taunting those presumed to be riding through the blackness to fire at them.

A loud voice boomed out. "That's Crazy Izzy," Phineas said. The voice seemed to be coming from above. No doubt he had climbed a tree. "White men! Sinners!" The tremendous carry of the man's voice made it clearly audible over the din. His enunciation was simply superb. Each word came out with crystal clarity. "Robbers of land! Here stand your enemies. Shoot them down. They are nothing but miserable animals. No better than skunks and snakes. Kill them. Your consciences may remain clean, so said the Lord. Their blood will not be on your hands."

"I'll be God damned," Phineas said tensely. "Crazy Izzy got fouled up some place. He doesn't know where they are and he's guessing like holy hell."

I peered into the midstream's blackness. "Can you see any signs of the flotilla?"

"Hell, no," Phineas said, a trace of triumph in his voice, "and if it's there, those bastards can't see it either."

"Then the flotilla may be able to slip through?"

"Tom, it just might at that unless some jackass gets rifle crazy and takes a pot shot."

The shot came within minutes. "That God-damned fool!" Phineas muttered. "They're good as dead now."

The shot had gone wild. No Indian was hit. "You're sure it came from the flatboat?" I said. "I didn't see a flash."

"Of course you didn't!" Phineas said. "The jackass put a blanket around his rifle. The Indians can smell the powder. It's the smell that'll tell them exactly where the flotilla is."

Even as Phineas spoke, shrieking Indians began pouring out of the woods. A good hundred, at least. Probably more. They got into canoes. You could see them paddle out, then disappear in the darkness.

Jumping overboard, Phineas and I began pushing and bushwhacking our flatboat to a more favorable position to catch the current. The firing had begun. Such was the fury of the volleys that the flashes of the discharges blended and flared up like the aftermaths of so many violent explosions.

We caught the current. I had been pushing so furiously, all my strength was spent. Phineas had to pull me over the gunnel. I lay on the deck, gasping for breath.

The noise of the volleys was deafening. Pulling myself up, I looked back. The flashes of the discharges provided enough visibility to enable me to see that the flotilla had no chance. Woefully outmanned, completely surrounded, she was being raked unmercifully from all sides.

We rounded a bend and became enveloped by blackness. I could still hear the volleys. They became dimmer and dimmer, then faded off completely.

Our flatboat scarcely seemed to be moving, but I knew it made no difference how fast or slow we went. When the flatboat quivered a bit, I knew that Phineas had left the bow oar. "You all right, Tom?" he stage-whispered from the top of the cabin.

"Yes," I said, "I am."

"There was nothing we could have done," Phineas said.

"I know it," I said.

I lay on the deck, almost beneath the lashed stern oar. All sense of feeling seemed to have drained out of me. It was as if, although conscious, I was in a state of coma. The sky was brimful of stars. When I was eight or nine I first read of the ancient pagan belief that the stars are brave warriors, marching off on parade to the glory of Valhalla. Pagan or no, I still think this is a beautiful thought. Surely it must have been caused by the movement of our flatboat. Yet I swear it was so. The stars were no longer stationary. They were pressing ahead, in a direction away from me, like a horde of people, marching and marching, on and on, into eternity.

The false dawn streaked the skies, then daylight broke on a river steaming with mist. We reached the mouth of the Little Miami River. Here, hidden by trees, is where the settlement of Columbia was located. Phineas shot his rifle. On the Ohio shore a deer leaped gracefully from the water's edge and disappeared in the woods. A covey of passenger pigeons, populous enough to cast a great shadow, flew over our flatboat, so low I was able to note the pink of the birds' breasts. When they were gone on osprey sailed majestically overhead, surveying us haughtily. I saw it all, yet I didn't see it.

A single man appeared on the riverbank. Phineas yelled out what had happened and said we were going on down to Fort Washington. I had sat up. "Phineas," I said, "aren't we going to put to? I want to go up with them."

"They'll go up on horse, Tom," Phineas said. "Through thick woods. You're not a good enough rider. You'd only slow them up."

"How do we know they'll go?"

"If they've got the horses, they'll go." Phineas pointed to the Ohio shore. Flags were being waved from the lookouts in the treetops.

"What does that mean?" I asked.

"They're sending news to the fort."

"Does that mean nobody's going up from Columbia?"

"Tom, how would I be able to know? It could mean that. It could mean Columbia's asking for protection from the fort while her Rangers are away."

"But somebody *will* go?"

"Yes, Tom, that much you can be sure of."

We floated six more miles. Aport, I saw the Licking River, entering the Ohio. To starboard, nothing but dense forest. Then we passed Eastern Row, Cincinnati's only street which was not a girdled lane. Now I caught a glimpse of a Fort Washington blockhouse.

To put to Phineas made a complete circle. Like Rome, Cincinnati is surrounded by seven hills. So flat did the prehistoric glaciers grind down the hills' crests that, as we revolved, I could see all of the Great Cincinnati Peneplain without moving my eyes.

We entered the brackish water of Yeatman's Cove. Nobody, civilian or soldier, was present as we put to. The riverbank was a solid forest of willows, cottonwoods, and sycamores with green parasite mistletoe growing from their smooth white barks. Sunlight, having difficulty penetrating the trees' foliage, cast weird shadows. It was as if dusk had suddenly descended upon us.

While Phineas tied us up, I stayed seated, staring at the floating debris, my attention focused on a drowned opossum. Phineas brought me a whiskey jug, said nothing, but regarded me with a concern he was unable to disguise. "There's no need to look at me that way, Phineas," I said. "I'm not on the verge of panic."

"Your face is all screwed up, Tom. You look tighter than a drum."

"That may well be," I said. "I assure you, I have never felt saner in my whole life. There are a number of questions I wish to ask you and I expect honest and straightforward answers. There is no hope, is there, that Melissa may be alive?"

"No, Tom, there isn't."

"You have told me a Wyandot will die rather than surrender? Also, that he does not take captives? He kills on the spot?"

"That's so."

"You told me, too, that it is a favorite trick of Wyandots to offer safety to those who will surrender peacefully?"

"Yes, that's one of their tricks."

"Then, in violation of their promise, they torture their captives to death and leave them hanging by their feet from trees?"

"Yes."

"Phineas, at this very moment Melissa may be hanging by her feet from a tree."

"No, Tom! You mustn't think things like that."

"But I am."

"It was a river fight, Tom. Believe me, the Wyandots would board the boats, scalp, and throw the bodies into the river. It's part of their religion. They'd have lost some braves, that's for sure. Those braves are floating down the river without a proper burial. If the Indians send a lot of white people floating after them their god, Moneto, will see them and it'll be the same as a proper burial."

"Even so, a flatboat might have surrendered peacefully?"

"Nobody'd be that crazy, Tom!"

"Somebody was crazy enough to put a blanket around his rifle and fire," I said. "Somebody might have been crazy enough to surrender peacefully."

"I'll grant that, Tom, but the Wyandots would have killed them the minute they took over the boat."

"But the Wyandots might have run the boat ashore, to make the other boats think their promise would be kept."

"Wyandots' minds don't work that way, Tom."

"It might have happened as I said."

"Not one chance in a million, Tom. Believe me, not one chance in a million."

"Phineas, I won't take that one chance. I want you to go with me to the scene of the action, in order that we may be certain."

"Oh, God, Tom! You won't find anything. It had to happen like I told you."

"It didn't happen exactly the way you said it would, when we got to the Indian Look-Out," I reminded him.

Phineas sighed deeply. "If I'm wrong this time, Tom, you wouldn't want to see her. You'd want to remember her the way she was. Tom, leave it all to the Rangers. If they find her, they'll bury her."

"In a ditch with everybody else!" I said. "You once told me this was the only practical thing to do. I will not take a chance that Melissa is lying in a ditch."

"You mean, if she's buried—you want to dig her up?"

"I do," I said, "and bring her to Cincinnati for burial." Going into the cabin, I came out carrying our two spades. "Melissa's not going to lie in a ditch overnight, Phineas," I said. "I'm leaving now. If you don't come with me, I'll go it alone."

"I'll come with you," Phineas said quickly.

The riverbank rose in three terrace-like steps. Traversing these we were on Water Street, a girdled lane, running parallel to the river, not wide enough for Phineas and me to walk side by side. Eventually we reached Eastern Row. Fort Washington, covering some fifteen acres, stood beyond Cincinnati's only *bona fide* street. "We'll save a lot of time," Phineas said just a trifle too cagily, "if we walk through the fort instead of around."

"No, no, Phineas," I said. "I know what you're up to. When we get into the fort you'll take me to Dr. Allison. He'll think I'm overcome by grief. I'll be forced to take a sedative."

Phineas grounded his spade and shifted his feet. "You're worse off than you think, Tom," he said. "It wouldn't hurt to talk to Jeremiah, just for a couple of minutes."

I grounded my spade too. My mind was behaving with animal clarity. I knew how much I needed that spade, but if need be I was prepared to dig up Melissa with my hands. Phineas' legs must not be allowed to lash out and knock me down. He must not get me into the fort. "Look!" I cried. "Phineas, somebody's in back of you." Then I bolted.

I should have had more sense. At a time I was just about learning to read and write, that trick was old saw to Phineas. His feet caught me just above the kidneys, knocking me flat. A sharp blown to the nape of my neck rendered me unconscious.

XII

When I returned to a world in which I could think with reasonable clarity, I knew only that I lay in bed. About me everything was jet black except for a slight red glow, possibly four or five feet off. "Are you awake, Tom?" a well-modulated voice inquired, which I recognized as Dr. Allison's.

"Yes. Where am I?" Dr. Allison lit a candle. I was in a small room, I could now see, and the red glow came from smoldering ashes in the fireplace. "I thought I heard drums," I said.

"You did," Dr. Allison said. "The beating of taps. You're in an officer's quarters."

I began remembering and sat up. "Dr. Allison—"

"The patrol has returned, Tom," Dr. Allison said. "There is no indication whatsoever that anyone was taken captive." The search, he went on to say, had been most thorough. The woods were scoured. The patrol had gone far and wide enough to locate where the Indians had buried their canoes. These had been destroyed.

"Dr. Allison, is there any possible chance that Melissa may be alive?"

"From what Phineas tells me and my own judgment confirms, there is not, Tom." Moving to the fireplace, Dr. Allison ladled out a cup of soup. "Drink this," he said. It was turkey soup. I was, I realized, ravenously hungry.

Dr. Allison asked me how I felt. "Rather drowsy," I said.

"I'm going to give you another sedative," Dr. Allison said.

The forgetfulness of sleep was most welcome. Although I heard the beating of reveille, it was the banging of hammers and men's voices that, shortly thereafter, fully awakened me. My traveling trunk (Phineas had brought it) was at the foot of my bed.

Arising, I stepped onto solid flooring. Officers' quarters at Fort Washington were quite adequate. My room, I should judge, was nine by twelve feet. Besides a comfortable bed, there was a washbasin, a spacious closet, two chairs, and a well-made black walnut highboy. Since there wasn't a single window pane in all of Cincinnati, in the whole Miami Purchase as a matter of fact, here the usual wrapping paper, greased with bear oil, had been substituted.

Although mirrors were most scarce, one happened to be at my disposal.

While drying my face after shaving, someone knocked on the door. "Come in," I said.

My visitor was a ruddy-faced, eager-looking blue-and-white uniformed chap in his early twenties, wearing a shiny brass helmet decorated with white horse feathers. "I am Ensign Asa Hartshorn, sir," he said amicably enough, but with the official bearing of a young officer. "Mr. Morrow, General Harmar sends you his greetings and offers you his deepest sympathy. May I add mine, sir, and that of the entire staff's."

In due time I would learn that Asa Hartshorn had recently been named Captain of the Horse, an appointment of which he was most proud. No matter where or how hot the day, you never saw Asa without his shiny brass helmet. "Thank you, sir," I said.

"The General will consider it an honor, Mr. Morrow," Asa said, "if, at your convenience, you will be so kind as to call upon him."

"I shall be pleased to, sir," I said. "Will you be kind enough to convey my appreciation to the General?"

Almost immediately after Asa left, Phineas put in his appearance. "You all right, Tom?" he inquired.

"Yes," I said, "I'm sorry I caused you and Dr. Allison so much trouble."

"There's some more news," Phineas said gravely.

The Indians, Phineas told me, had sent one of the flotilla's flatboats down the river, with a dead crew aboard. "No, Tom!" Phineas said quickly. "Melissa wasn't one of them. There were only two dead people on her."

Although federals had already burned the flatboat in order that the sight would not prompt more people to leave Cincinnati, the settlement's some hundred citizens, as well as everybody else on the whole Miami Purchase, quickly learned the details. So shot up was the flatboat's outer structure that a man could not have laid the palm of his hand thereon without touching a bullet hole.

The flatboat's captain, scalped, his face black from powder except for white rings about his eyes, was tied to the lashed bow oar. The man's mouth had been stuffed with flour, turned to paste; his eyelids were cut off. A "tiny little old lady," is what people called the other crew member, who was Mrs. O'Toole. Mrs. O'Toole had been standing erect beside the stern oar, impaled to a flour barrel by arrows. Also mutilated, a shot had damaged her hip so badly that only skin held on her right leg. Another ball had caught her flush in the mouth. Her chin was gone.

"A boy came through it alive," Phineas said. "When the shooting started, he was hit in the shoulder. The captain told him to hide in the cabin and the Indians missed him. He saw most of what happened. His name's Enoch Kitchel and he says he knows you."

"Yes, I know Enoch," I said.

"Jeremiah's got him over at his quarters. You can talk to him if you want."

"I would like to," I said.

We left my quarters, located along the eastern wall, and moved across Fort Washington's spacious parade. While I doubt if I could have described what I saw at this moment, Fort Washington could accommodate fifteen hundred soldiers, with officers' quarters. Built of hewn timber her design, like Fort Harmar's, was a perfect square. Two-story blockhouses stood at her four angles, with projecting upper stories, so constructed as to command completely, by direct and raking fire of cannon and musketry, each of the four walls of the fortification. Acknowledged to be the most solid and substantial wooden fortress beyond the Alleghenies, she was now just completed. The hammering, which I could still hear, came from behind the north wall. Here a triangular-shaped palisade, extending from the northeast to the northwest side of the fort, was being built with a small blockhouse at the triangle's apex. Shops would be constructed in this area for the accommodation of the artificers.

Except for a large, fully stacked bookcase, Dr. Allison's quarters were furnished exactly like mine. Enoch Kitchel, his shoulder bandaged, was drinking a glass of milk. He was about ten, a bright lad. "Good morning, Mr. Morrow," Enoch said.

"Good morning, Enoch," I said.

"Zeepers!" Enoch said. "When I brought you the turkey and those two geese in Bracken, we sure didn't think all this would happen, did we, Mr. Morrow?"

"No, Enoch," I said, "we certainly didn't."

"I can't believe my mom and pop are really dead," Enoch said. "I keep thinking I'm dreaming."

"I imagine we all feel that way, Enoch."

"But we're not," Enoch said.

"No, we're not dreaming, Enoch," I said, "and we might as well stop wishing we were."

"You and Miss Andrews were going to get married, weren't you?"

"Yes, we were."

"Zeepers, but she was a nice lady, Mr. Morrow, and real pretty too. Everybody liked her."

Dr. Allison spoke up: "Enoch, tell Mr. Morrow what you saw. Then I'll give you some more medicine and Phineas will take you to the hospital. You can lie down on one of the cots that officers in the army use."

"The jackass who fired the shot that gave us away wasn't from our boat, Mr. Morrow!" Enoch said. "We were the first one. The shot didn't come from the second boat either."

"That part isn't too important, Enoch," Dr. Allison said gently.

"We could see them get into their canoes and start paddling out," Enoch said, "then we lost them in the darkness. For the longest time you couldn't see anything or hear anything. Captain Walters told everybody to take shooting positions and wait. I wanted to load for my pop, but he wouldn't let me. When the shooting started, from the flashes we could see canoes all around us. I was hit in the shoulder right away. It didn't hurt hardly at all and Captain Walters had told us not to talk, so I didn't say anything.

"I was standing right next to Miss Andrews, Mr. Morrow. She was loading for Mrs. O'Toole.

"Miss Andrews told me to go into the cabin, but I didn't until Captain Walters ordered me to. I could see most everything that was going on though.

"The Indians were shooting like mad and we were shooting right back. It sounded like firecrackers going off all over. So far, though, I was the only one on our boat who'd been hit.

"Our second boat came abreast of us and an Indian canoe was caught right between us. We were all so close we could have shook hands. I mean we could have shook hands with the Indians and so could the men on our number two boat. We killed all eight Indians in the canoe. Our bullets tore up the canoe like it was made of paper! A couple of wounded Indians tried to swim for it, but we got them too.

"The Indians had a renegade with them, but he'd stayed ashore. It sounded like he was yelling out from a treetop. He sure had some loud voice. You could hear him plain as anything. He said that if we'd give up, nothing would happen to us except that we'd be taken prisoners and traded off. Captain Walters said the renegade was a liar and not to believe him, but the men on our number two boat did.

"The Indians boarded her and right away shot all the men and scalped them. Soon as they did, they stretched out the scalps on hoops. Didn't hardly take them a second to do that, Mr. Morrow! It was like a butcher in his shop, cutting up meat and and wrapping it up. Behind me I could see our number three boat was on fire. People were jumping off, but they were getting shot just as fast as they showed themselves over the gunnel.

"When somebody'd fall into the river, the Indians would fish him out, scalp him, then throw him back in again.

"After the men on our number two boat were scalped, the Indians lined up the women along the gunnel and shot at us from behind them. 'Kill us! Kill us!' the women yelled out, then they started singing *Faith of Our Fathers.*

"'Shoot!' Captain Walters ordered, but the men firing from that side of our boat wouldn't. Then Mrs. O'Toole, who was firing from the other side, stood up, and came over. 'You damned fools!' she yelled out. 'Do as your captain says.' Captain Walters yelled for Mrs. O'Toole to get behind the gunnel, but it was like she didn't hear. She raised her rifle and started to fire. At that very second an Indian ball smacked her rifle and took away the lock. 'Melissa, dearie,' Mrs. O'Toole said to Miss Andrews, 'hand me another rifle. No, never mind, I can get one more shot out of this one.'

"Then cool as a cucumber Mrs. O'Toole picked up a brand of fire from the kettle we were using for a caboose, lit the pan, and got off her shot.

"Suddenly Mrs. O'Toole went down on one knee. I think she was shot in the leg.

"After that our men started firing too and right away the singing got quieter and quieter. Pretty soon I could only hear Mrs. Oberman's voice. I knew that because Mrs. Oberman used to lead the singing at our Sunday services. She got hit just as she was starting singing the hymn over again. 'Faith of our fathers,' she sang, 'holy faith.' Then she stopped. Then she started again. 'We will be true to Thee—' she sang, but that's as far as she got.

"Captain Walters went down and my pop took over the command. Pop got hit in the chest and I could see the blood spurting out like somebody was under him with a pump. Mom was holding him and crying. Then she slumped over on top of Pop. I guess Mom was hit in the back of the head, because I saw her hand go to her neck.

"By now most of the men were dead or lying wounded on the deck. The Indians began boarding and I went to the far end of the cabin and hid behind trunks. I could hear though. The Indians were shrieking and our women were crying and begging to be shot before they were scalped. But from the way it sounded to me, the Indians were scalping them alive, then tossing them into the river.

"I stayed where I was. An Indian looked in the cabin, but didn't see me. Then it was quiet and I kept wondering who was keeping us going.

"When morning broke, I looked out. Flour barrels hid Mrs. O'Toole. I didn't know she was on the boat. Nobody was on the deck, but it sure was covered with a lot of dried blood. I figured an Indian must be at the bow, taking us downstream to somewhere and from the way we were bobbing about I thought to myself he sure couldn't handle a boat smooth as Captain Walters.

"The thing to do, I figured, was let myself overboard, swim to the Ohio side, and walk down to Columbia. I looked over the side of the cabin, to see what my chances were, and there was Captain Walters, leaning over the bow oar. I could see how red his head was, but the way the Indians had him trussed up, I first thought he was still alive and guiding the boat."

XIII

In spite of what Enoch had related, I could not stop hoping that by some miracle Melissa might be alive. When the boy and Phineas left for the hospital, I said: "Enoch didn't actually see Melissa killed."

"Tom," Dr. Allison said, "you must not cling to such a hope."

"Yes," I said, "I know that."

"You must be hungry," Dr. Allison said.

I said that I was, extremely so. Calling his orderly, Dr. Allison instructed him to bring me breakfast and told me that I must not think it an oversight because there would be no bread. The fort's last shipment of flour, he explained, had arrived sour. Dr. Allison then mentioned that Phineas had informed him that I had planned upon staying at Cincinnati for quite some time.

"I still plan upon staying here," I said, "for quite some time."

"What do you intend to do?" Dr. Allison asked me.

"Teach, I suppose," I said. "Although I have all but forgotten it, that is the reason I came here in the first place, one reason at any rate."

"Cincinnati already has a school and a schoolmaster," Dr. Allison said.

This surprised me. A contributing factor in my decision to come to the Ohio Country was a speech delivered at Carpenter's Hall in Philadelphia by General Arthur St. Clair. At this time the Continental Congress, of which the General was president, was considering passage of the Northwest Ordinance. The need for schoolmasters beyond the Alleghenies was most acute, General St. Clair had said, and I had been quite stirred as he told of the services members of my profession might render. Before leaving Philadelphia I had written to the General, who was now Governor of the

Territory Northwest of the River Ohio. In a warm reply he had expressed his personal thanks, stating that mine was the only such letter he had received.

"May I suggest going to Losantiville," General St. Clair had written me. "This settlement is peopled predominantly by former inhabitants of that portion of Virginia which they generally refer to as Kentucky. They are tradesmen, almost entirely. My observation of them leads me to conclude that they have not concerned themselves greatly with acquiring even the rudiments of a formal education."

"I labored under the impression," I said to Dr. Allison, "that Phineas had described for me every square foot of Cincinnati. He didn't mention a school. In fact, he said there wouldn't be enough pupils to conduct one."

"The school is now one week old," Dr. Allison told me. It was held outdoors, weather permitting. When it rained the five pupils moved into a Conestoga wagon which had floated down the river. "John Riley, recently an itinerant welldigger by trade," Dr. Allison went on to say, "is the schoolmaster. Riley, I understand, formerly taught in Lexington and is most pleased to return to his chosen profession. A loud school is presently being conducted, but I have heard books have been ordered."

"I have a number of texts," I said. "Mr. Riley is most welcome to them."

"They will be greatly appreciated, Tom."

I said nothing.

"What do you plan to do?" Dr. Allison asked me.

Actually I hadn't the faintest idea and, at the moment, I didn't even wish to think about it. "Look about a bit, I suppose," I said. "It strikes me it's not unlikely that's what Riley was doing when he gave up teaching for welldigging. Possibly after a while I'll be most pleased to return to my profession."

"With nothing to do," Dr. Allison said, "Cincinnati can be a very dreary place."

"With plenty to do," I said, "I found Philadelphia to be a very dreary place."

"I think it most advisable, if you decide to stay on here," Dr. Allison said, "that you find something to do."

"Something to do?" I said. "Isn't it a fact that you're always doing something, even if it is merely riding to hell in a chaise-and-two?"

"Yes," Dr. Allison said, "but one should be at least my age before adopting such a philosophy. Would you object to working for General Harmar?"

"Join the army!" I said, aghast.

"Not exactly," Dr. Allison said, smiling slightly at my reaction. "A dearth of people exists here who are able to write legible English, in fact write at all. The General's need for a scribe is seriously acute. To have available your abilities in this field, I should say would be looked upon as being a manna in the wilderness. You have no idea how greatly the efficiency of the General's offices would be enhanced."

While Dr. Allison spoke with quiet humor, I gathered he was not over-stating the situation. "The General's scribe would not be in the army?" I said.

"I should say the General is not in a position to bargain," Dr. Allison said. "If it should be your wish to be designated on the rolls as a civilian scribe, only temporarily employed with no tenure set, I am certain such an arrangement could be arrived at."

"I confess the thought does have a certain appeal," I said. "At the moment I am overcome with surprise."

"Weigh over the matter," Dr. Allison said. "I would certainly suggest that it might be well worth your time to discuss it with the General."

"The General has already asked me to pay my respects," I said.

"On that occasion," Dr. Allison said, "the General would be embarrassed if the matter were brought up. He comes from Philadelphia, Tom, is a gentleman, and was acquainted with your father. His earlier request, as you will discover on your own, was an expression of good will. Under no circumstances does he ever, with anyone, use such requests as pretexts to further his needs or as a means of presuming upon friendship."

"To whom," I asked, "would I go to arrange an appointment with the General?"

"If you wish, I will arrange it."

"I would appreciate that."

About this time Dr. Allison's orderly brought me four fried eggs, a thick slice of ham, and a pot of delicious smelling coffee. Rising: "Albert," Dr. Allison said, "will you be so kind as to bring up my horse?"

Excusing himself, Dr. Allison walked across the parade to headquarters. When he returned his horse was awaiting him and I had finished break-fast. "The General will be most pleased to see you at four o'clock this afternoon," Dr. Allison told me.

"Thank you," I said.

"If you feel the need for a sedative tonight," Dr. Allison said, "go to the hospital and get one."

"Thank you," I said again.

Before mounting his horse and leaving, Dr. Allison told me he was going to Columbia and might be gone for as long as two days. An epidemic of ague had broken out there. "It comes from the clearing of land," Dr. Allison said. "All kinds of bugs. Apparently they're harmless enough in the deep woods. The sun, however, stirs them up and they spread their ague-breeding miasmas."

Dr. Allison rode out through the rear gate. When Albert returned to clear away the breakfast dishes he told me that Phineas had gone into the "woods," meaning the settlement of Cincinnati, to visit his friends Kitty and Emil Kummerschmitt. Coming out of Dr. Allison's quarters, Albert also was carrying a medical book. Albert was about sixteen, a gangling youth with big ears, but extremely alert blue eyes. "If you need that sedative tonight, Mr. Morrow," he said, "I'll get it for you."

Albert was making it most apparent that I should notice he had the medical book. "Are you studying to be a doctor?" I asked.

"Yes, sir," he said eagerly. "Dr. Allison's my preceptor."

"Well, good luck in your chosen profession, Albert," I said. "You've got a fine preceptor."

"I sure have," Albert said. "He doesn't teach me like most doctors do. I'm not allowed to read anything in this book until I've seen it happen first. Then I read about it. Then Dr. Allison and I talk about it. A lot of things in this book aren't exactly right, Mr. Morrow."

"No," I said, "I suppose they aren't."

"Take the ague," Albert said. "While we were waiting for you to come out of sedation, Dr. Allison and I were talking about that. This book says there's one way to cure ague. We've got another that tells still another way. Neither say you can get it from bugs."

I was thinking that Dr. Allison was an extremely busy man. "When are your instruction periods held?" I asked.

"Whenever Dr. Allison has a spare minute. It's mostly early in the morning."

"Doesn't the man ever sleep?"

"Not like most people," Albert said. "He says he knows his body. He keeps going until he's tired, then he naps a while. He eats that way too, just when he's hungry."

While waiting for my four o'clock appointment with General Harmar, I wiled away the time strolling about the fort, not thinking much about anything, gaining a certain amount of comfort from merely walking. Becoming General Harmar's scribe did appeal to me and I recognized the wisdom of Dr. Allison's advice that I must find something to do. Yet, without Melissa, nothing seemed worth the effort.

Fort Washington was not an active place, for everything had been done which could be, and there was nothing more to do but await the arrival of the volunteers, who at the moment were not yet assembled at Fort

Pitt or the various recruiting places in Virginia. By now General Harmar's federals who'd planned upon deserting, had. Those remaining were competent and loyal, resigned though to the knowledge that until a string of forts was built between here and the Indian villages along the Maumee River, the enemy could not be beaten.

I sensed though, during cursory chats with various soldiers, not only an intense loyalty to General Harmar, but what amounted to actual affection. This came as something of a surprise, for I had unconsciously jumped to conclusions after hearing the general talk in Marietta.

I could sense, too, that an excellent discipline of an informal nature prevailed at Fort Washington. The enlisted men, although attired in various state uniforms and carrying inferior arms, were all well-groomed and comported themselves with soldierly dispatch. The gunsmith's shop, whose molds were idle for lack of lead, was spick and span. There was pleasantry when patrols relieved each other, but no signs of indolence. The latrines could not have been kept cleaner. Their walls were whitewashed and no obscene writings appeared thereon.

Around three o'clock, while moving along the wall walk, I saw a tall, thin man in buckskins leave headquarters and prepare to mount a horse. Immediately he was surrounded by a group of officers, who shook his hand and bade him farewell. "That's Lieutenant Harrison," the sentinel on duty said and told me that Lieutenant Harrison was being transferred East, upon orders from New York Town, much to General Harmar's regret.

Later I would learn that Lieutenant Harrison had been in command of the stockade at Northbend, the Miami Purchase's downstream settlement. He had fallen in love with Polly Symmes, Judge John Cleves Symmes' favorite daughter, and the two wished to become married. Opposing the match on the ground that Lieutenant Harrison was lackadaisical and would get nowhere, Judge Symmes had used his influence as a former member of the Continental Congress and recently appointed judge of the Territory Northwest of the River Ohio, to bring about the transfer. The lieutenant's full name was William Henry Harrison.

At exactly four o'clock I presented myself at headquarters, where I was greeted by Ensign Cornelius Sedam, an artillerist, who, in the absence of Lieutenant Denny, was General Harmar's aide-de-camp. "Go right in, Mr. Morrow," Cornelius said. "The General is expecting you."

The headquarters' walls were lined with piled-up stacks of earthenware, shrunken human heads, and a variety of Indian weapons, clothes, and relics. This was a large room with four black walnut desks and possibly a dozen or more chairs. At the time I was not aware this was actually a staff meeting place and that the General's private papers and confidential files were in an adjoining room.

General Harmar sat at the central desk, a broad-shouldered, well-featured man in his late forties. He was smoking a clay, turned coal black, which gurgled with each puff. That the clay should stink to high heaven, was not surprising. During my morning stroll I had learned that with no tobacco available in Cincinnati, men and women were fueling their clays with dried willow bark.

"You will please excuse me for not rising, Mr. Morrow," General Harmar said most pleasantly and motioned for me to be seated at one of the desks. "Yesterday, while investigating a leak in the roof of the enlisted men's quarters, I slid off and sprained both my ankles. I must not put weight on them for at least a week, Jeremiah has decreed. It is most annoying."

"I would suppose so, sir," I said.

"I am aware," General Harmar said, "that this is not a happy time for you, Mr. Morrow. Yet I haven't the faintest idea what to say to you, except that you have my deepest sympathy."

"Thank you, sir."

Having never met a general before, I hadn't quite known how I should behave and confess to having experienced an original feeling of awe. Already, however, General Harmar had put me at complete and natural ease. This man, I was fast concluding, was one of those rare individuals who can command and hold his co-workers' respect simply by being himself.

"At another time," General Harmar said, "I should very much enjoy hearing the latest news of Philadelphia. As I understand it, this is to be an official rather than a social call?"

"Yes, sir."

"Jeremiah has explained the situation?"

"Yes, sir," I said. "If you feel I can be of help, I shall be honored to be permitted to do what I can."

"That is splendid, simply splendid!" General Harmar said. "You have no idea how pleasing I find your reply, Mr. Morrow. I am assuming that you do not wish to be commissioned an officer?"

"I should prefer not to be, sir."

"I will set you down on the rolls as a civilian adviser to the General, with the assimilated rank of lieutenant. This permits you to leave us when you choose. Do you object to wearing an army uniform?"

"Why, no, sir."

"I would prefer that you did, Mr. Morrow. Not at the moment necessarily, but when the volunteers begin arriving. Your pay will be that of an army lieutenant, twenty-one dollars a month." Smiling slightly, he added: "Payable in army script."

"That is more than satisfactory, sir," I said.

"The script is acceptable for the purchase of lots here," General Harmar said. "That is what most of us are doing with it. Should you desire to use yours that way, speak to Ensign Sedam. Cornelius understands the lot situation better than the rest of us and will be able to explain what to you and me on the surveyor's plat looks like a form of hieroglyphics."

"Thank you, sir," I said. "I had intended to consider the purchasing of a few lots."

"When will you be prepared to begin the task of working with us?"

"Immediately, sir," I said. "Soon as you wish."

"Tomorrow morning then," General Harmar said. "However, I would appreciate it if you will compose one letter this afternoon, to Dr. Wistar."

I looked up.

"You are acquainted with Dr. Wistar?" General Harmar inquired.

"The curator of Philadelphia's Museum of Natural History? Yes, sir, I am acquainted with Dr. Wistar. That is, we know each other to speak to."

"Please inform Dr. Wistar that the shipment of his Indian pots must be on one of the flatboats bringing in the Pennsylvania volunteers, for no other craft is available. Therefore, he must not expect his relics for quite some time."

I looked up again.

"Apparently, Mr. Morrow," General Harmar said, "in Marietta you were told that rather than carrying out my duties as general of this army, I employed my energies digging up Indian burial mounds?"

"Yes, sir, I heard that being said."

"The mere sight of the things drives me to distraction, Mr. Morrow," General Harmar said. "I do it on orders from New York Town. In your letter please state firmly but with tact that, as I have previously pointed out, we are giving the Indians a legitimate cause for grievance by this action, worthy as on the face of it it may appear to be."

At this moment I heard a commotion outside headquarters. Phineas Ford's voice. Ensign Sedam's, telling Phineas that General Harmar was busily engaged.

Phineas burst into headquarters. "Phineas—" General Harmar began.

"I'm sorry, Josiah, but this is important." Phineas turned to me. "Tom, they've found Melissa!"

I jumped up, thinking that Phineas meant Melissa's body had been discovered floating down the river. "She's alive, Tom!" Phineas said. "She's

at Columbia, delirious, calling for you. Jeremiah says it's important that
you get there right away."

"In heaven's name, Phineas!" General Harmar said. "Get Mr. Morrow
a horse."

"He can't, he's not a good enough rider to go through the woods,
Josiah."

"Then get somebody he can ride with."

"I've already got Asa Hartshorn waiting outside," Phineas said and grabbed
me by the arm, for when the two men finished talking, I continued to
stand still as if in a trance.

Of the six mile ride through deep woods to Columbia, I remember only
hanging onto Asa Hartshorn's waistline and tree branches and the horse
feathers of Asa's brass helmet brushing my face. Melissa was in a one-room
log cabin, lying on a bed which was a deerskin tied to the corners of
the room and supported by saplings. Melissa's face was very scratched and
she appeared to be in a coma.

"Just tell her you're here, Tom," Dr. Allison said. "Then you must
leave."

Melissa recognized my voice and threw her arms around me. "Mrs.
O'Toole," she said. "When the Indians boarded, we were all going to kill
ourselves. 'Not you, dearie,' Mrs. O'Toole said. 'Swim to him, dearie,
you can make it.' I told Mrs. O'Toole I couldn't swim. 'The quilted
petticoats, dearie,' Mrs. O'Toole said. 'They'll keep you afloat.' Then she
pushed me overboard."

How long Melissa had floated, she had no idea. In due time the current
had bumped her ashore. Following the river, she'd run through the woods.
Reaching Columbia, she'd fought those who wished to help her. "I must
get to Cincinnati," she'd said.

BOOK THREE

EXPEDITION

I

Melissa had contracted pneumonia. On a stretcher made of deerskins tied to poles, Phineas and I carried her to Fort Washington, lodging her in the quarters vacated by Lieutenant Harrison. Feverish, frequently delirious, she seldom recognized me. She would recover, Dr. Allison assured me.

Although my confidence in Dr. Allison was boundless, it was impossible not to worry. It is most fortunate that I was General Harmar's scribe, for while my duties were far from exacting, they at least gave me something to do.

The only tedious part of my work was preparation of the army payroll. For the four hundred enlisted men as well as for the officers, it was necessary to write out individual notes of credit, to which I signed General Harmar's name. If done a bit each day, the task would be simple enough. However, at the moment, the payroll was two months in arrears and had been kept in such haphazard a manner that most of the list had to be decoded.

A further complication was added because any number of the soldiers had gone to Israel Ludlow, the town surveyor, to purchase lots, pledging money due them. From Mr. Ludlow I received a list of the soldiers with lot stoppages against their pay. Individual credit slips then had to be made out to Mr. Ludlow, as treasurer of the proprietors of the Miami Purchase. It was necessary to do it thus in order that land payments still due the United States Congress could be met.

On the second morning after bringing Melissa to Fort Washington, while I was laboring over the payroll, Ensign Cornelius Sedam brought in a mail pouch from Fort Knox, which was located at Louisville. "The General's in headquarters," I said, indicating the adjoining room.

"Now that you are his scribe," Cornelius said pleasantly, "this sort of thing becomes your task."

"Shall I take it in now, or wait?" I asked. "At the moment the General's talking with Major Doughty. Dr. Allison's in there too, binding the General's ankles."

"I'd ask him if he wants it now," Cornelius suggested. "John Doughty's here!"

"The major arrived about an hour ago."

"Any news from Fort Pitt?"

"If you mean have any Pennsylvania volunteers arrived there yet, the answer is no," I said.

"That bit of news, since I drew September fifteenth, will cost me exactly three dollars," Cornelius said. He was referring to an officers' pool, on when the army would actually march out.

I knocked on the headquarters' door. "What is it, Tom?" General Harmar called out.

"A mail pouch from Fort Knox, sir," I said.

"Bring it in, please."

Headquarters reeked with the smell of burning dried willow bark, for the General and Major Doughty were smoking clays. In his midforties, Major Doughty was a rugged-looking, stockily built man, an artillerist and engineer, the designer of both Fort Harmar and Fort Washington. It was not only my opinion, but also that of everyone else at Fort Washington: Major John Doughty was a brilliant soldier.

"Open it up, please," General Harmar said. "What's in there?"

"There's a letter from President Washington," I said.

"Read it, please."

The letter stated that General Harmar's request for the means to build a string of forts from Fort Washington to the Maumee River had been denied. The reason given was that such an action would make the British uneasy.

"What else, Tom?"

"A letter from Secretary of War Henry Knox."

This letter, dated three weeks prior to the President's, was also a denial of General Harmar's request for the means to erect a string of forts.

"Well, there you have it, gentlemen," General Harmar said.

"Are you surprised, Josiah?" Major Doughty inquired mildly.

"No, I suppose not," General Harmar said. "But I can't understand it,

John. The President fought the Indians. Knox was certainly a reasonably competent general during the War of the Rebellion. Yet—"

"You've got to protect yourself, Josiah," Major Doughty said with considerable unction and Dr. Allison nodded in agreement. "When this thing's finally over with, there'll be Court of Inquiry. That's certain as the sun will rise tomorrow."

General Harmar nodded wearily. "Tom," he said, "when you have time, please go through the files. Gather up every communication I've written and those which Major Doughty has written, stressing the need for a string of forts."

"Yes, sir," I said.

"And while you're at it, Tom, you'd better begin gathering all other relevant material. Think of yourself as an attorney, preparing my defense."

"Yes, sir."

"What else?"

"A letter from Major Hamtranck, sir," I said and handed the letter to General Harmar. "This one is marked personal."

Major Hamtranck was in command at post Vincennes. As a divergency force he and three-hundred-and-thirty men were supposed to march into the Indiana and Illinois Country to keep the tribes of those areas occupied while the Harmar Expedition was under way. Under strict orders from New York Town, Major Hamtranck had marched out as per the original schedule, despite the fact that General Harmar's army was not yet assembled.

General Harmar read the letter rapidly. Smiling sadly: "The major has a rather wry sense of humor," he said. "He begs to inform me that my earlier suggestion of not marching out has in effect been carried out. He left post Vincennes, with one day's provisions, all that was available. Hunting was bad. The men refused to go on and are back at the post."

I told the General that all other communications were either bills for the quartermaster or enlisted men's mail and hurriedly left headquarters, for there was a letter addressed to me, the handwriting looking like that of a young child's.

The letter was from Susan. She missed me "something terrible," Susan said, "because with you, Mr. Morrow, I never had it so good." She had left the Indian King Inn, Susan went on to say. If I wished to see her again upon my return to Philadelphia, I should seek her out at the Golden Eagle Inn where she was now working as a hostess, employed by a Mrs. Mae Dwyer. There was some talk among Mae's girls that they might be coming to Cincinnati to entertain the army. If so, Susan said, she would come too. She concluded her letter with: *"Love and x-x-x-x's."*

II

The following day, around midmorning, Phineas Ford came into head-quarters. "Josiah wants to see me, Tom," he said. "How's Melissa?"

"This hot, humid weather is certainly hard on her," I said. "Her breathing's awfully labored, but Dr. Allison insists he's satisfied with her general condition."

"If Jeremiah's satisfied, you don't have to worry," Phineas said. "I was talking to him yesterday. He was telling me he wished he had a woman nurse to bathe Melissa. Bathing her every day! Tom, I don't think it's right that Albert should do it."

While it was merely a sponge bath, I confess to having been entertaining a few qualms over a sixteen-year-old boy bathing Melissa. "Well, we can't get a woman nurse," I said. "Somebody has to do it."

"I'm getting you a woman nurse from the woods," Phineas said.

"You are!" I said. "I asked Dr. Allison if a woman willing to nurse Melissa might not be found in Cincinnati. He told me that because of the usual antagonism between towns people and the army, no self-respecting woman would come into the fort."

"Well, Kitty Kummerschmitt is self-respecting," Phineas said. "She and Emil are married right and proper. Kitty's expecting in late September. Nobody can blame that on the army."

"Kitty Kummerschmitt . . ." I said. "I have a quartermaster's invoice saying a Kitty Kummerschmitt just sold a flatboat load of flour to the army at the rate of twenty-five dollars a barrel."

"That's Kitty," Phineas said. "The flour's yours."

"Mine!"

"You're in the army, Tom," Phineas said, lowering his voice. "You're not allowed to sell the army anything. When you pay off Kitty, she'll sign the script over to you. Don't worry about that part, Kitty and Emil are my best friends."

"I'm talking about twenty-five dollars a barrel!" I said. "That's highway robbery."

"Damned if it isn't," Phineas said and clicked his teeth. "I hear, too, that salt's running low in town. We'll hold onto yours for a while. We can store it in Emil's loft. Emil'll know the best time to sell."

"Twenty-five dollars for a barrel of flour!" I said.

"What the hell's the matter with you, Tom? Don't tell me you're sore because I made you a nice profit. What did you want me to do? Barter it off by the pound and fill up the flatboat with junk? I figured you could hold onto the script until it could be turned into real money. If you don't want to, a bank at Cairo will take the script at a twenty percent discount. That's still twenty dollars a barrel."

"I'm not complaining, Phineas," I said, "believe me, I'm not."

"Well, what the hell's eating you then?"

"Nothing," I said. "I'm in a philosophical mood, that's all. It's dawning upon me that while I can forgive myself for gouging the government, I don't think it's right that anybody else should."

"Are you daffy?"

"Probably. I just can't help thinking that eventually the United States government is going to have to pay out twenty-five dollars for barrels of flour worth no more than ten. Has it ever occurred to you what will happen to the government's financial structure if this sort of thing goes on all over? And it *is* going on all over."

"What the hell have we got a President for?" Phineas said. "That's his worry."

When I ushered Phineas into headquarters, General Harmar was studying a map. Earlier in the morning, the General and Major Doughty had been drawing up a route of march. "Thank you for stopping by, Phineas," General Harmar said and pointed to a place on the map. "This stream? Do you recognize it?"

"Sure," Phineas said. "It runs into the Maumee."

"Into the Maumee!" General Harmar said. "It's on this side of the water shed."

"The map's wrong," Phineas said.

"Well, where should it be?"

"Up about there," Phineas said.

"That would put it in Lake Erie!"

"You need a bigger piece of paper," Phineas said, "or you ought to make everything else smaller."

General Harmar frowned deeply. The map had been drawn by United States Geographer, Thomas Hutchins. While it is possible to imagine that upon due reflection the General would recognize that Mr. Hutchins had his troubles too, it was also possible to imagine this was not the General's present reaction. "Has the stream a name?" the General inquired.

"I never heard if she has."

"How deep is she?"

"Four, maybe six feet right now. There's been a lot of rain. You figuring on running supplies over water when you can, Josiah?"

"Yes."

"I wouldn't count on it if you don't march out before the middle of September at the latest."

"The streams will be dry?"

"I'd say so, Josiah."

"With all the rain we've been having lately?"

"Once they start drying up, the water goes out fast."

"I have a report on those streams from Ebenezer Denny," General Harmar said. "Ebenezer consulted with Tom Hutchins at Fort Pitt. There's supposed to be plenty of water."

Phineas shrugged his shoulders. "By the way, Josiah, did you know Hutchins was dead?"

"No! When did it happen?"

"He died at Fort Pitt, the day before Tom and I left. He'd been sick for quite a spell."

"I'm sorry to hear that," General Harmar said. "Is—was he wrong in giving Ebenezer that information?"

"I hate to speak bad of the dead, Josiah, but I've got to say he was."

"Thank you, Phineas," General Harmar said. "Tom, I'd appreciate it if you'll send for John Doughty."

"Yes, sir," I said.

Taking leave of headquarters, I immediately sent one of the General's waiters after Major Doughty. "This Kitty Kummerschmitt," I said to Phineas. "If she's going to have a baby in September, will she be well enough to take care of Melissa?"

"Why not?" Phineas said. "Kitty's strong as a horse. Right now she's clearing maybe half again more land than Emil."

"What will Emil have to say about her leaving home?"

"That's part of it," Phineas said. "Emil and I are going into the woods tomorrow. We want to look over a piece of property. We'll be gone maybe ten days. Emil wouldn't want Kitty living in the cabin all alone."

"A piece of property?" I said. "I'd more or less assumed you meant Emil was also one of the General's scouts."

"Emil a scout!" Phineas said and laughed. "He doesn't know any more about the woods than you do, Tom. Emil's my partner."

"Partner in what?"

"Trade," Phineas said.

"Trading in what?"

"We don't care," Phineas said, "so long as we can turn over a profit."

"Is it all right, at a time like this, for you and Emil to—simply take off for ten days on a private venture?"

"Why not?" Phineas said. "Josiah knows I'm going. I'm on my own until the volunteers get here."

My face, I'm certain, indicated that I was somewhat surprised. "Why should I go scouting now?" Phineas wanted to know. "I can tell you from here what's happening. Little Turtle's boys are around, watching. When the volunteers start coming through they'll tell Little Turtle what's what. Little Turtle'll figure out how far he'll let them come into the woods before he hits them. You think the General's too easygoing, don't you?"

"Not exactly," I said. "I do admit though I didn't expect to see an army managed the way the General's doing it."

"It's the only way, Tom," Phineas said. "Look around. Isn't everything spick and span? Isn't everybody drilling? Aren't patrols out?"

"I should say so."

"What else do you want the General to do?"

"I don't know," I said.

"If the General played it any other way," Phineas said, "he wouldn't have an army left. There's hardly an enlisted man here whose time hasn't run out. They can all go home tomorrow if they want. Why are they staying on? I'll tell you why. Because the General asked them to. It's hard to believe, but that's all that's holding the army together. When the boys talked about going home, Harmar said his enlistment period was over too. He wanted to go home as much as they did, he said, but he figured he was stuck with a job and had to see it through. 'If I don't have you boys here to help out when the volunteers come through,' he said, 'I'll be in one hell of a mess.' Hardly a man walked out on him, Tom."

"I got the impression," I said, "that the General isn't playing any sort of a game. He's simply behaving, well—naturally."

"You hit the nail smack on the head, Tom! He knows who he's dealing with. The enlisted men are professionals. They know when they're being treated like gentlemen and appreciate it. The jackass volunteers won't know that, so the General'll have to clamp down on them. And he'll have every enlisted man helping him out. You just watch. The General'll get twice as much out of those volunteers as somebody like St. Clair could."

"St. Clair . . ." I said. "I've gathered from bits of conversation passed about headquarters, that General St. Clair, or rather Governor St. Clair, doesn't exactly approve of General Harmar?"

"If you ask me," Phineas said, "St. Clair's jealous because the General can get discipline without acting like he's God o'Mighty. You should of seen the way St. Clair went over the fort, trying to find something wrong, but he couldn't and in the end he had to compliment General Harmar.

"Now get me straight, Tom," Phineas went on to say. "I'm not like some around here who hold that St. Clair doesn't know anything about soldiering and showed he was a coward for giving up Fort Ticonderoga without putting up a fight. I've talked over Ticonderoga with John Doughty and John says St. Clair did right up there. Tom, pay heed to anything John Doughty says! He's a smart man and one hell of a good soldier. But I *am* saying that St. Clair doesn't know how to use his brains."

Phineas pointed to the sentry on duty at the southeast blockhouse. "See that young boy up there? That's Abel Cobbleman. Abel and six other fellows came to the fort from the Falls and said they wanted to join the army. That was when St. Clair was here. St. Clair told them if they wanted to join they'd have to cut their hair and wear queue ties. Abel and his friends told St. Clair to go to hell and didn't join up."

"Abel has a queue tie now," I said.

"Sure, he has," Phineas said. "After St. Clair left, the General told Abel and his friends they could join up and if they didn't want to, they didn't have to wear queue ties. Inside of a week, they wanted to be like all the rest of the soldiers.

"And take the way St. Clair treated me," Phineas said. "There was this young soldier. Johnny Mathews. Only thirteen years old. Johnny was running a fever. Jeremiah said he ought to be put to bed, but St. Clair said Johnny was faking and ordered him to go out on a three-day patrol.

"Johnny got lost in the woods and the patrol came back without him. General Harmar asked me if I could find Johnny. I said I'd give it a try, but it figured that Johnny'd gone woods crazy, so it wouldn't be easy."

"What exactly," I asked, "is meant by being woods crazy?"

"Some people lost in the woods just go plain batty, Tom," Phineas said. "And get tricky as an animal. Even Jeremiah can't explain what goes on in their heads. Maybe they do sort of turn into animals, Jeremiah says. Anyway, they run away and hide from anybody who's trying to find them.

"It took me a week to catch up with Johnny. He'd roamed to the other side of the water shed! Fast on his feet, that little bugger. I knew where he was, but I couldn't catch him till he started circling. I waited and let him bump into me. I had to knock him out and bring him back on my shoulders. After I turned him over to Jeremiah, I stepped into headquarters to let Josiah know I was back. St. Clair was there and, of course, I was all messed up from going through the woods. 'Mr. Ford,' St. Clair said, 'you will remove that lice from your hair and tidy up before presenting yourself to a general of the United States Army.'"

Phineas grinned broadly. "But three days later I got back at him. He needed a scout bad and there wasn't anybody but me. 'Sure, Governor,' I said, 'I'll go, but since you're paying a dollar a day to rent packhorses, I figure I'm worth three.'"

"Three dollars a day!" I said. "That's more than St. Clair was making!"

"That's why I named the figure," Phineas said. "And you should have seen St. Clair's face. It turned so red I thought that big wig of his was going to explode right off the top of his head.

"When St. Clair left," Phineas said, "the General asked me if I wouldn't go into the woods. 'Sure, Josiah,' I said, and didn't charge him a penny."

III

It was agreed that Phineas and I would go for Kitty Kummerschmitt at the conclusion of my day's work. "I'll be staying over with Emil," Phineas said. "You can bring Kitty back to the fort."

At the moment I was still wearing buckskins. Sometime during the afternoon Quartermaster Markheim came into headquarters. "Stand up, Tom," he said. "I want to size you up."

"Why?" I asked, as I stood up.

"The General's orders, I'm bringing you a lieutenant's uniform."

"Have you any idea what it's all about?"

"Not the foggiest," Quartermaster Markheim said.

Quartermaster Markheim left and almost immediately thereafter one of the General's waiters took a freshly pressed dress coat, adorned with two gold epaulets showing a gold star and white feather, into the principal office. Coming out emptyhanded, the waiter was gone only a few moments before he returned, this time bringing the General's dress wig.

Shortly Quartermaster Markheim was back, with a complete lieutenant's attire, including a long horseman's sword, steel mounted. "Everything'll fit, Tom," Quartermaster Markheim said, "but while I'm here, you'd better try it on to make sure."

It was a light dragoon's uniform, the whole blue, faced with white, white buttons and linings. Apparently the former owner of the uniform had served four years in the army, for a service stripe of white tape was on the left sleeve, a few inches from the shoulder. "It fits perfectly," I said.

"Danned if you don't look like a real soldier now, Tom," Quartermaster Markheim said.

"Am I supposed to wear the sword all the time?"

"Damned if I know," the quartermaster said. "According to regulations, you're supposed to wear it whenever you're on duty."

Leaving this matter pending, Quartermaster Markheim took his leave. I must confess the uniform seemed to add an aura of the military to my whole feeling of comportment and I realized I was making an effort to improve my posture. The desire to see how I looked was overcompelling and I succumbed to it. There being no mirror where I was, I walked over to my own quarters. While en route a corporal, changing the guard, saluted. Turning to see who was in back of me, I realized the corporal was saluting me. I did have the presence of mind to return the greeting.

Although unable to see the all of me in my mirror, I could see my upper portions. There is no doubt of it, epaulets do help a man's shoulders! Now, being only a few paces from where Melissa was, I moved to her quarters, most anxious to get her reaction to me in uniform. She was, however, sleeping soundly at the moment.

Returning to my desk, I went back to work. Not quite certain what I should do about the sword, I kept it on. Possibly a quarter of an hour before the day's work would be concluded, the General called for me.

"Good afternoon, Lieutenant," the General said pleasantly.

"Good afternoon, sir," I said.

The General's dress coat hung on the wall. His wig stood on a nearby table. "Take a seat, Tom," the General said. "I'd appreciate it if you'll wear the uniform tomorrow. We'll be entertaining a distinguished visitor. Lieutenant Colonel Commandant Robert Trotter."

I had not seen Trotter's name on any of our lists.

"Please make a point of rising and saluting when Colonel Trotter puts in his appearance tomorrow, Tom," the General said. "From what I gather Trotter may well be heading the Virginia volunteers, whom he prefers to call 'his Kentuckians.' I've only met Trotter once. On that occasion he was kind enough to tell me how I should run my army."

The General added somberly: "We may have our troubles with Trotter, Tom. Colonel Hardin's the one who ought to lead the Virginia volunteers, but I gather Trotter's arranged things, or is trying to arrange things, so the volunteers will elect their officers. In that case—well, Trotter's by far the better politician."

"Does this mean the Virginia volunteers are at last assembling?" I asked.

"Only in so far as they are beginning to talk a great deal about doing so," the General said. "Trotter's object in visiting me is to get my endorsement to the election plan of procedure. He can't have it, of course, but the man must be placated. He carries considerable weight in Louisville and I have it on the best authority that if he doesn't get some kind of command, we'll only get about half the expected Virginia volunteers. That the man's a sublime egotist, I'm quite certain. As to how he's actually to be dealt with, I don't yet know. The meeting tomorrow will be quite important. The Hardin-Trotter rivalry is extremely acute. At this moment it looks as if, at best, we'll end up wih a divided command."

I was experiencing considerable difficulty in manipulating my sword. While seating myself, I'd forgotten I had it on and it had clanked against the floor. Now, arising, to take my leave, it got between my legs.

"You'll get used to it in time, Tom," the General said, smiling slightly. "Am I correct in assuming that you don't know how to salute with a sword?"

"Yes, sir," I said, "you are."

"Excuse me for not standing up," the General said, gesturing toward his ankles. "It is actually quite simple, once you get the hang of it. Suppose you try it now? Bring your sword up in front of your face . . . Keep the blade straight up . . . Knuckles of the right hand a bit more to the left. That's better . . . Now lower the blade flat-side upper-most. Good. Extend your arm to form a straight line. No. Higher. At an angle of about forty-five degrees . . . Now bring your sword up in front of your face . . . Good . . . Now return it to your side and that is all there is to it."

"I think I should write down those instructions and practice a bit, sir," I said.

"Yes, it might be wise to do so," the General agreed.

At the conclusion of my day's work, Phineas awaited me outside of head-quarters. "Well, I'll be damned!" Phineas exclaimed. "Tom, so help me, I didn't know you at first in that uniform."

"Do I look like a soldier?"

"Damned if you don't at that!"

"I'm going to take my sword to my quarters," I said. "Then I'll have a quick look at Melissa."

"I was just talking to Jeremiah about her, Tom. He says she had a good afternoon."

I got this impression too. Melissa was still sleeping. Quite peacefully. Her breathing no longer appeared to be labored and the feverish look had left her cheeks. When I touched her forehead, it seemed to me that her temperature must surely be at least close to normal.

Leaving the fort, Phineas and I crossed Eastern Row to a girdled lane called Hill Street. Soon we were flanked by a cluster of buckeyes, still in partial bloom, the fetid odor of the blossoms permeating the entire walk. On the trunks of these trees, I could see ax scars. Because their wood is so soft, Phineas informed me, buckeyes are not killed by ordinary girdling.

Then we came to a run of dead girdled black walnuts whose trunks, one tree after another, measured twenty or more feet in girth. While the trees were dead, wild grapevines, festooning themselves from the branches, made it seem, at times, as if we were walking through a covered bridge.

"You'll like Emil and Kitty Kummerschmitt," Phineas said. "Emil was born in Germany. Used to be with a traveling circus. A juggler. A damned good one too. Wait'll you see how he can keep four balls going at once. Blindfolded! But Emil's like me. He likes trading. Doesn't really care what. Just so there's a chance to turn over a profit. One day in a German newsprint Emil saw a drawing of a possum, carrying a baby in its pouch. The newsprint told all about what a great country America is and how plentiful possums were. But the drawing was all wrong. The possum was too big. Do you know what I mean?"

"I think so," I said, "you mean the drawing was out of perspective?"

"Yes, that's what Emil said it was. What's that you called it again?"

"Out of perspective."

"Out of perspective . . . Out of perspective," Phineas said. "I want to remember that. Emil thought possums were the size of kangaroos. He figured he'd come over to America, catch himself a couple of dozen possums, and make a fortune showing them off all over Europe. Of course, that was one of Emil's dumb ideas, but he gets plenty of smart ones too."

Since Emil didn't have the passage money, Phineas explained, he had joined up with the Hessians, deserted the day they landed in America, headed west, and ended up in Pittsburgh which is where Phineas had met him.

"Could Emil speak English?" I asked.

"Good as you can, Tom," Phineas said. "Emil's bright as they come. He can read and write fine. The circus played a couple of years in London. That's where Emil learned our talk.

"It's funny how things go," Phineas went on to say. "I'd run into a streak of bad luck and landed in Pittsburgh with hardly a penny to my name. There was this cockfight. 'What the hell,' I said to myself, 'I might as well be all busted.' So I bet against a heavy favorite and damned if I didn't win, almost a pound. 'This is my lucky day,' I said, went to the inn and threw dice. Inside an hour I had ten pounds. 'That's enough,' I told myself and for once I had sense enough to quit while I was ahead.

"By now I was feeling top of the morning. I walked down the street and ran into this young girl who had Pennsylvania Dutch country written all over her rosy cheeks. She was Kitty, Emil's bride, but I didn't know it at the time, nor that a couple of months before Kitty had run away from her father's farm to marry Emil.

"Kitty gave me the eye, but I could tell she was plenty nervous and I was pretty sure she hadn't been out peddling very long. She had on a nice clean dress and talked real lady-like. Being flush, I figured I'd do it up right and rented us a room at the Pittsburgh Inn.

"Once we got inside, Kitty wouldn't take off her clothes. When I asked what the hell was the matter, she busted out crying and said she couldn't go through with it because of Emil. Emil, Kitty said, was lying sick in a lean-to along the Allegheny. They were dead broke, she said, and had to have money for medicine.

"'Sister,' I said, 'I pay what you're worth, so don't try buttering me up. You're lying through your teeth. Anybody who's sick can go to the fort and get medicine free.'

"When Kitty heard that, she really bolted for the door, but I slapped her down on the bed. She came back at me strong and put up about the best scrap I ever saw, that is for a woman. But what the hell chance did she have?

"I slapped her back onto the bed, so hard the wind was knocked out of her.

"I was turning sucker, I was pretty sure, but somehow I believed she was on the level and I did admire her spunk. 'Sister,' I said, 'I'll make a deal with you. Take me up the Allegheny. If you've really got a sick husband, I'll buy you some food and get him medicine. If not, you come back here and that damned dress comes off and stays off for a week.' Kitty agreed and I'll never forget how grateful she looked at me. 'You are a very kind man, Mr. Ford,' she said.

"On the way up the Allegheny Kitty told me Emil'd been working two solid weeks, eighteen hours a day, at a sawmill and then wasn't paid. That I figured was the truth, because from the way Kitty told it, the sawmill was Sam Abramson's and I knew Sam liked to hire passers-through. Just before the job was finished, Sam'd go off on a long purchasing trip. Before he was back, a couple of his workers couldn't wait around and were down the river. That way Sam figured he could cut down his overhead by five percent.

"Kitty was telling the truth about Emil all right. Emil was lying in a lean-to, moaning so loud I thought Kitty'd be a widow for sure before the night was over. Emil had the ague and I guess the jaundice too, for he was yellow as stale butter. I kept my end of the bargain, Emil got well, and after Emil got over being sore at Kitty for trying to save his life, we all became friends.

"Emil couldn't get it out of his head that if you got in on the ground floor in the Ohio Country, you had to make money. To tell you the truth, Tom, I think so too. Even with things looking black as they are right now. It's like Emil says. All you have to do is keep your eyes open.

"Emil sure can do that. You watch, Tom, he'll get you a top price for your salt. He's the one who put it into my head how to sell your flour to the army. Anyway, in Pittsburgh we didn't have enough money to buy a flatboat. Emil raised some by penning letters for people who couldn't write. I ran into a couple of suckers who fell for the young beaver skin bamboozle and when Sam Abramson finally got back, we collected Emil's pay. By then we had enough to buy three young pigs and a broken down flatboat that'd just barely made it down the Monongahela with a load of flour."

"Three pigs!" I said. "What about the Army Regulation against taking animals with tongues down the river?"

"It wasn't issued yet," Phineas said, "but even so only a fool would take squealing pigs down the river unless he was smart like us. I told you Kitty'd been raised on a farm. She told us all we had to do to shut up a little pig was to scratch his belly and it'd go right to sleep. Each of us had his pig to watch out for and we didn't have any trouble. But that flatboat! We barely made it to Cincinnati before she fell apart.

"Those were the first pigs ever to be in Cincinnati, Tom. Emil auctioned them off and that's how he got the money to buy up his lots. St. Clair was in Cincinnati when we got there. Tom, did you know St. Clair is as bald as a bat is blind? He's ashamed about it and doesn't want anybody to know. When he comes through again, watch the sneaky way he lifts his wig to cool off his head. Always pushes it up from the back and pretends he's got the itch. Everybody knows what he's doing though and it's a big laugh all over the fort.

"On the day before St. Clair left, he called out the army and gave them a talk on how to be good soldiers. It was hotter than hell that day and right in the middle of his talk, St. Clair pushed up his wig. Everybody started snickering and a couple of the younger fellows busted out laughing.

"St. Clair never did find out really what was what, but he was madder than a wet hen with pepper up her ass. The next day he was stopping off at Northbend, to say good-bye to Judge Symmes before going on down to the Falls. Instead of getting on his boat, he went by horse far as Northbend and made three squads of the laughers march with him, armed, equipped and accoutred. It's sixteen miles to Northbend, Tom. And it was another boiling hot day. St. Clair wouldn't let those boys have water until they were damned near to Northbend. Then he let them take a drink from a stream that flows out of a cave. The stream's got bitter-tasting water that gives a person the runs real bad. The boys didn't know what they were drinking and really lapped it up. When St. Clair got them to Northbend, he made them stand at attention for the two hours he was saying good-bye to Judge Symmes. Of course, they all pooped their pants.

"Afterward everybody was talking about what a big louse St. Clair was. Everybody but Emil! And it shows you how his mind works, Tom. Quick as a whip Emil saw that if he and I bottled up the water from that stream, gave it a fancy name and sold it in New Orleans, we'd make a fortune. That's the reason I was East when I met you, Tom. I was raising the money to get us into business.

"What," Phineas asked me, "do you think of the idea?"

"I really don't know," I said, "but if the water actually does what you say it does, I have to admit your plan would seem to have possibilities."

"It sure does the trick all right," Phineas said. "I know because I tried the water out on myself. So did Emil and Kitty. It works on women as well as men. There's only one catch. The God-damned stream isn't in Northbend and it isn't in Cincinnati. There's no way to get title to the land around it."

"What will you do?"

"Emil says the only thing we can do is build a cabin and maybe a stockade there. We'll start a little station and put in to buy the land. You don't need any money to do that. With squatter's rights, we ought to have first choice.

"God damn it," Phineas went on to say, "whenever a man tries to make an honest living there always seems to be something that stands in his way. But we'll get that title mess cleaned up in one way or another. Selling the water would just be the start, Tom. We can sell Indian medicines too. That was my idea! I know all about them. The water first, then the Indian cures. Tom, the water's free and the Indian medicine costs next to nothing. Emil says we'll charge a dollar a bottle for the water. Will you tell me where you can latch onto a better deal than that?"

IV

While Phineas talked, we passed any number of upriver girdled lanes, but saw no cabins. A number of inlots with cabins thereon, Phineas told me, were behind the trees.

Approaching what was called Filson Street, I saw what at first glance appeared to be a miniature stockade. It was in fact a kennel in which two brown bears were lodged. So fat they couldn't move, the animals simply lay where they were, in a state of complete inertia, looking like huge mounds of fur-covered flesh. One of the bears was smugly permitting ants to crawl over its paw and when the paw was covered with the insects, it licked them off. The other bear was making a whining sound, as if in great misery.

"Another one of Emil's dumb ideas," Phineas said and told me Emil had allowed the bears to gorge themselves on mast. When Emil dissected their alimentary canals, he expected to get at least double the usual gallon or two of oil. The bear steaks ought to be more tender, Emil also figured.

"What's the one whining about?" I inquired.

"July's the mating season," Phineas said. "He's so fat he can't get up and hop the she-bear. Emil'll slaughter him next month."

"Why not now," I asked, "and put the poor fellow out of his misery?"

"He-bear meat's not good eating during the mating season," Phineas informed me. "It's tough and tastes strong."

Moving off Hill Street we walked a quarter-of-a-mile through deep woods to the Kummerschmitt half-acre inlot. We approached the one-room log cabin from the rear. At first glance something seemed out of the ordinary, then I noticed why. "There's no chimney!" I said.

"Emil won't have one on purpose," Phineas told me. "That's his way of saying that we'll be in New Orleans before the cold weather sets in."

"Suppose he wants to sell the cabin?"

"Emil figures that's not important. The big thing is—get to New Orleans and start selling the water. It's just the way Emil's mind works, Tom. He doesn't want to even think that something might hold us up. If we have to stay here this winter, he still won't have a chimney. He'll raise the floor."

"Raise the floor!"

Not having a chimney, Phineas explained, was to Emil Kummerschmitt a symbol of straight direction toward a given goal. It, like the goal itself, must remain inviolate, a constant reminder that attainment of the goal was merely being temporarily postponed. When the cold weather came, the cabin floor would be raised. Stones would be placed thereunder. These, heated, would warm the cabin. Should the cabin become too hot, it could be cooled by sloshing water over the floor.

When we arrived at the cabin's front side Emil Kummerschmitt, wearing buckskins, sat on a split log beside the door, hollowing a bowl out of dogwood with a barlow knife. Arising as we put in our appearance, Emil brought his heels together and greeted us with a formal half-bow. His age, Phineas had mentioned, was thirty-nine. His slender, muscular body looked much younger. The extremely serious expression on his face made him appear to be, possibly, ten years older. He was an average-sized fellow, unmistakably a Teuton, blue-eyed, fair-complexioned, with wavy blond hair that was almost golden.

"Emil," Phineas said, "this is Tom."

"I am honored to meet you, Mr. Morrow," Emil said without the slightest trace of a German accent. "Kitty is somewhat ill-disposed and is resting. She assures me, however, she will be well by tomorrow. We will bring her to the fort, the first thing in the morning."

"You have no idea how much Melissa and I appreciate what Mrs. Kummerschmitt is willing to do," I said.

"Kitty will be delighted and is looking forward to it, Mr. Morrow," Emil said. "It will be good for her to be in the company of a woman."

The customary jug of Monongahela rye stood beside the door. Phineas handed it to me. I took a swig, so did Phineas, but Emil Kummerschmitt merely placed the jug to his lips, as a gesture of hospitality. He was a teetotaler, I learned subsequently. He did not smoke and until he came to Cincinnati, where there were no cows except at the fort, his diet consisted mainly of vegetables and cheese. The man's favorite meal was mashed turnips, a piece of rye bread, and a glass of milk. He could eat this combination three times daily, day after day, with complete enjoyment.

Sitting on the log bench, we engaged in general pleasantries. The complete absence of cows in Cincinnati entered the conversation. "That is another reason I am pleased that Kitty will be at the fort," Emil said. "In her present condition, she should have milk."

"I don't need the army's milk!" Kitty Kummerschmitt called from within the cabin. She had a soft, pleasant voice. The Pennsylvania Dutch accent was, however, quite noticeable.

"You must learn not to be so independent, my dear," Emil said.

"The army could sell us a cow," Kitty said.

"That is impossible," Emil said. "Please ask Phineas if I am not correct?"

"Can't be done, Kitty," Phineas said after Kitty had put the question. "For one thing there aren't enough cows without playing favorites. For another, stick a cow out here and the Indians would grab it for sure. As I told you yesterday, you should have gone to Jeremiah Allison. I know he's a man, but you wouldn't have to tell him in so many words you were expecting. He'd know it and he'd see to it that you'd get some milk."

"And why couldn't Emil tell him?"

"He could," Phineas said patiently, "but it wouldn't do any good because too many men are pulling that one. All Jeremiah'd have to do is see you. You wouldn't have to say anything."

"Well," Emil said, "Dr. Allison will see her tomorrow and the matter of her getting milk will be settled."

When this conversation began, thinking I was being privy to a family squabble, I had been somewhat embarrassed. By now, though, I realized that Kitty and Emil and Phineas were simply holding a general discussion of a situation.

"I don't understand it," Emil said in that serious manner of his. "American women. They stay secluded while awaiting to give birth. One would think it should be presumed that American husbands and wives go to bed merely to sleep."

I was prepared to smile at this statement, but did not, for it was apparent Emil did not think he was being droll.

"It has nothing to do with being ashamed," Kitty said, "at least that is not what we think where I lived. It has to do with how horrible we women look."

"I don't understand that either," Emil said. "A woman, happy to have a child, looks beautiful. At times there is a certain sublime facial expression which—"

"And at times," Kitty said, "there is an expression which would frighten a band of wild Indians."

"I hadn't thought of that," Emil said and now, while it was impossible not to think he was being droll, the grave expression on his face gave no indication of it. "Possibly Phineas should suggest to General Harmar that he use pregnant women as a vanguard when he attacks the Indians."

"Emil, you promised not to use that word!"

"I only promised that I would *try* not to use it," Emil said. "This is the first time it has slipped out in over a week. Will you please admit that, on the whole, I have been doing very well?"

"Yes, you have, my dear," Kitty admitted and it struck me that throughout the entire conversation, neither Kitty nor Emil had raised their voices.

The conversation shifted back to generalities. Eventually I said that I ought to be getting back to the fort. "Good afternoon, Mrs. Kummerschmitt," I called into the cabin. "And thank you again, ever so much."

"I'll be pleased to come, Mr. Morrow," Kitty replied.

There was a great deal of warmth in Emil Kummerschmitt's hand shake and there was a certain brightening of his eyes as he bid me good-day, but the solemn expression did not leave his face. Phineas said: "I'd better walk you through the woods to Hill Street."

"Yes," I said, "I think you'd better."

When we were in the woods, Phineas said, "Emil's worried about Kitty."

"This, of course, is their first child?"

"Sure."

"Well, it's natural for a prospective first father to worry, isn't it?"

"It's not that way," Phineas said. "Emil's got no faith in Mrs. Robinson and can't stand her besides."

"Who is Mrs. Robinson?"

"The only midwife in town," Phineas said. "To tell you the truth, I don't like her very much either. Damned, but she's got dirty hands. And the way she's always picking her nose, makes me sick at my stomach."

"I gathered," I said, "that Mrs. Kummerschmitt is very much against men doctors for the delivery of babies."

"Kitty thinks that would be sinful. She says she'd rather die than have any man except Emil see her naked."

"Is this Mrs. Robinson experienced?"

"Christ, yes," Phineas said. "I know her from Louisville. She must be sixty years old. I'll bet she's delivered a couple of hundred babies. But she's one of those loud-mouthed jackasses who knows everything. When Emil tries to ask her a sensible question, she just laughs and tells him she was delivering babies before he was born. Emil's sure hoping that while Kitty's at the fort, she'll get to know Jeremiah and change her mind."

"Some women feel awfully strong on that subject," I said.

"Maybe Melissa can talk to Kitty," Phineas said. "Women listen to women better than they do to men."

"To be quite frank," I said, "I don't know Melissa's feelings on the subject."

"Well, there's still some time," Phineas said. "Emil's doing a lot of figuring. Maybe he can think up something that'll change Kitty's mind."

When we reached Hill Street, in order that I'd be certain to go the right way, Phineas pointed out the proper direction of Fort Washington. "We'll bring Kitty to the fort first thing in the morning," he said.

V

There was considerable redbud amid the trees flanking Hill Street and I recalled, while en route to the Kummerschmitt cabin, that I'd caught sight of a magnolia tree whose pink and purple blossoms were simply beautiful. I was on the lookout for this tree as I walked back toward the fort, thinking that a bouquet would brighten Melissa's quarters.

When I reached the intersection of Cider Street, four men stepped from behind the trees, hemming me in. They wore buckskins and such was my surprise that, at first glance, I didn't realize they were Indians.

Moving with quiet efficiency, one Indian went to his all-fours behind me. Another shoved me over this Indian and, jumping atop me, wrapped a rag around my mouth. Jerking me to my feet, two Indians grabbed me by the wrists and ran me over Hill Street.

We ran, in my opinion, quite rapidly. Not at what to me would be a racing pace, perhaps, but almost that fast. In a short time, gagged as I was, breathing became most difficult. I thought surely I was going to faint and my legs began wobbling. I must keep them going, I realized, for if I fell or tripped one of my captors, I was familiar enough with Indian behavior to know that my life was as good as over. Eventually, catching my second breath, my legs began moving mechanically.

Circling Fort Washington, we took to the riverbank, moved upstream toward Columbia, at length coming to a halt beside a corn field. Released by the Indians, I dropped to the ground, quite exhausted. I had lost both my half-boots. Nothing was left of the bottoms of my stockings. My feet were bleeding and punctured with thorns.

The Indians did not lie down. Standing about me, they inhaled and exhaled deeply. I did not see so much as a single bead of perspiration on any of their faces. They were little men, sunken chested, almost emaciated-looking. But they were sinewy and tough.

Scowling at me fiercely, an Indian waved his arm in an angry gesture toward the corn field. I was now certain that I was going to be killed and propped up in the corn field as a human scarecrow.

Citizens of the Miami Purchase called this corn field the "Indian Cemetery." Seven acres, it had been planted originally by the Indians. In their usual haphazard manner of farming, they'd given it no attention, being content to harvest eighty bushels an acre, despite the ravages of squirrels and crows. When Ben Stites and the founders of Columbia had arrived, the field was discovered and the corn was appropriated. Calling it a manna in the wilderness, Ben Stites and his fellow citizens had gone to their knees and thanked God. As an indication that they did not share this point of view, the Indians at regular intervals killed somebody and stuck him in the field as a scarecrow.

Shortly a tall, extremely thin, withered-faced, fiery-eyed white man emerged from the corn field. His hair, snow white, hung over his shoulders, long as Phineas Ford's. He wore magnificent albino deerskins. Nodding his approval to the Indians, he beckoned one to remove the rag around my mouth. After doing so, the Indian stood beside me, a raised tomahawk in his hand. "It would be folly to shout out, Lieutenant," the renegade said and I recognized the deep, sonorous voice as being that of Crazy Izzy's. "Do you understand that?"

"Yes," I said, "I do."

"Lieutenant," Crazy Izzy said, "we know that Colonel Trotter is on his way to Fort Washington. Believe me, it will behoove you to speak freely and with complete honesty. I wish to know the purpose of Colonel Trotter's visit."

"I do not know the purpose of his visit."

"That is difficult to believe, Lieutenant."

"It is nonetheless, the fact. While I wear a lieutenant's uniform and hold the rank, I am not actually a military man. By profession I am a schoolmaster. I am temporarily employed as General Harmar's scribe."

"It would seem to me that the General's scribe would know what is going on?"

"I have held my position for only a few days and, in any case, am not privy to the General's plans. As for Colonel Trotter, I did hear it said that he was expected. I know nothing more than this."

Crazy Izzy regarded me shrewdly. "Your name, then, is John Riley?"

"I am Thomas A. Morrow of Philadelphia," I said. "I arrived in Cincinnati only a few days ago, unaware that the settlement already had a schoolmaster."

Crazy Izzy turned, spoke in a whisper to the Indians, then gave his attention to me. "You say you arrived in Cincinnati only a few days ago? You came from the East?"

"Yes."

"By what means did you arrive in Cincinnati?"

"By flatboat."

"That statement interests me, Lieutenant. Who was the captain of your flotilla?"

I was able to diagnose the manner in which Crazy Izzy's question was progressing. "There was no flotilla," I said. "It was a single flatboat."

"You piloted her yourself?"

There was no point in lying, I told myself. The Indians knew everything which was taking place in Cincinnati. I must mention Phineas Ford's name and hope that Crazy Izzy's antagonism toward Phineas would not produce an unfavorable reaction. "No, I did not pilot the flatboat. I was a passenger. A man named Phineas Ford was at the oar."

"I'm afraid I believe what you have told me, Mr. Morrow," Crazy Izzy said and shook his head sadly.

Suddenly the Indians began chattering excitedly and pointed toward the river. Midstream I saw a flurry of splashing water. What I saw next made me think I was losing my mind. The head of an osprey emerged from the water. It sank, re-emerged, sank . . . By now I realized the bird had underestimated the size of its prey and sunk its talons into a fish that was big enough to drag it under.

Chattering vivaciously, laughing, and making derisive gyrations for my benefit, the Indians noted what was taking place with the eagerness of young boys. The bird's head emerged again. A terrific struggle was ensuing. The Indians became grimly silent as they looked on. Somehow the osprey managed to free its talons. After two efforts, it got up into the air, flew a wobbly course toward shore, dropped to the ground, completely exhausted.

The Indians stood still as statues as they watched. "Brace yourself, Mr. Morrow," Crazy Izzy said. "You must expect to be beaten up unmercifully."

"May I ask why?"

"My friends were telling you that your army is like the osprey. It is sinking its claws into a fish too big to subdue. Should the bird recover and manage to fly away, their fury will be vented out on you."

"The bird will surely recover!"

"I should say so, Mr. Morrow."

I have no idea from whence my inspiration came. "Tell an Indian to kill the osprey," I said. "It will show that, no matter what, the red man will prevail in the end."

Crazy Izzy nodded gravely. "An excellent and timely suggestion, Mr. Morrow." Stepping over to the Indians, he spoke a few words. Immediately an

Indian went to the osprey, grabbed the bird by the talons, beat its head against a fallen log, then decapitated it with his tomahawk and threw the battered remains, except for the bird's head, into the river. The head, its mouth stuffed with soil, he stuck on a sapling, which he planted in the ground beside me.

"Your adroit thinking, Mr. Morrow," Crazy Izzy said, "has saved you from being beaten."

"I thank you for helping me."

"Unhappily your situation remains most precarious, Mr. Morrow." Crazy Izzy pointed to the corn field. "When I tell my friends you are useless to us and they must catch me another officer, they will want to kill you."

"But apparently you do not wish that to happen to me," I said. "Do you, Father Donovan?"

"No," Crazy Izzy said, "I do not."

I will never know what prompted me to call him Father Donovan. The name simply left my lips. When I'd mentioned Phineas Ford's name, Crazy Izzy had given no outward indication that he was acquainted with the person of whom I spoke. Now there was no outward indication that Crazy Izzy had ever heard of Father Donovan.

Turning abruptly, Crazy Izzy disappeared behind the corn stalks. "Merciful God," I heard him cry out, "give me Your divine guidance." In essence, he then stated that he did not wish to see a schoolmaster killed for the salvation of the world lay in the hands of Catholic priests first, then schoolmasters.

Returning, Crazy Izzy's eyes glowed like burning coals. After making a lengthy statement to the Indians, he spoke to me. "I have told my friends it is advisable that you should be questioned further by their chiefs. They are taking you to one of their villages. What will happen to you there, since we will soon be at war, I do not know. I have done the best I could for you."

"Thank you, Father."

"*Pax vobiscum*, Mr. Morrow," Crazy Izzy said and made a sign of the cross.

After saying a few more words to the Indians, Crazy Izzy disappeared into the corn field. Almost immediately thereafter two Indians tied buffalo thongs about my wrists. Grabbing these, they pulled me forward. Moving through the corn field, we took to the woods, heading north.

VI

We ran at a rapid pace until darkness set in. Deep as the woods were, we seemed to be following some kind of a path, which eventually I realized was a buffalo trace.

When we finally halted, my face was bloody from being whipped by branches, my uniform was badly torn, my stockings were gone entirely, my feet were lacerated and full of thorns.

None of us ate that night. Driving four saplings into the ground, the Indians tied my ankles and wrists to them with buffalo thongs, so tightly that I could not sleep. By dawn, when we were again on our way, my ankles and wrists had turned black as tar.

There was still no food for any of us. We were walking now, in single file, two Indians ahead of me, two behind. Whenever it was possible, we waded streams. Circling frequently, we walked on fallen logs, crawled out to the extremity of branches and let ourselves to the ground, the last Indian expertly covering our tracks with a sapling.

I was being watched most carefully, I was aware, to make certain I would do nothing which would permit possible pursuers to pick up our trail.

When I dropped from a branch to the ground, the pain in my feet became unendurable. In desperation, throwing myself to the ground, I pointed to my feet, then to the Indians', as an indication that while they had on pacs, my feet were bare. Following an exchange of glances amongst themselves, an Indian, nodding gravely, ripped off half my shirt. After removing the larger thorns, he bound up my feet. "Thank you," I said. For a brief moment I thought the Indian was going to raise his right hand to acknowledge what he surely must have guessed I was saying. If, however, I was correct in thinking the impulse was there, the Indian resisted giving it expression.

We pressed on. The woods were too deep to be able to see the sun. At what may have been close to noon, I noticed a quickening of the Indians' steps, a certain aura of excitement about their general demeanor. We came to a fallen log. Eagerly two Indians began digging a claylike soil from each of the log's extremities. The other two started a fire.

The diggers brought out earthen pots, gourds. Food! There was jerk, flour for stick bread, and dried flower petals, mostly those of roses it seemed to me, for tea. An Indian handed me a sapling, indicating that I should make my own stick bread. There was ample jerk for all of us. We gorged ourselves.

That night I was tied against a tree in a resting position, permitting me to sleep. At dawn we were again on the move, walking until darkness set in. On this day, there was food. Logs, such as I described, were in abundance.

Late afternoon, two days later, we reached a supply camp, ingeniously hidden behind gigantic beeches. Here rifles were stored in trees. Taking one, an Indian moved into the woods. Shortly he was back, with a cock turkey, which was roasted and we all shared.

Meanwhile, after bringing down rifles and stacking them, the Indians had brewed a concoction of some sort in a large copper kettle. I recognized wild cherries, red oak, and dewberry bark as each was tossed into the kettle. What else went in, was unfamiliar to me.

Once the concoction came to a boil, an Indian skimmed off a mixture of twigs and a ghastly looking reddish scum. Sipping the remainder, the Indian nodded his approval, with me being included in the nod.

When the concoction cooled, we all sampled it. It was bitter, but potent stuff. After two swigs, I could feel myself becoming heady. That is all I drank. Imbibing freely, the Indians were soon laughing and making jokes among themselves. They did not tie me up. However, amid all their fervency, it was noticeable that one Indian was always beside the stacked rifles.

There were two stacks, each with four rifles. They stood side-by-side.

That night I was tied in a comfortable sitting position to a tree, with the Indians sleeping encircled about me. During the day I had taken off the bandages from my feet and removed as many thorns as I could. While being tied up for the night, the Indian who had bandaged my feet while we were en route, brought me two bowls containing the concoction we had been drinking. Shaking my head, but making it evident I appreciated the gesture, I indicated that I did not wish to drink. Shaking *his* head, the Indian placed the bowls on the ground and indicated that I should sleep with my feet soaked in the concoction. In the morning, most of the swelling of my feet was gone.

After breakfast, I spent the morning with my feet in the bowls. I was not tied up. The Indians wiled away the time drinking the concoction and playing cards. The cards were laid on the ground, face upward, enabling me to see. Yet, try as I did, I could not fathom how tricks were being taken. Time after time the loser was determined by what, to me, appeared to be sequences similar to those which had previously produced winners. The penalty for the loser was that all the others pinched his nose and made wry faces at him. If the loser laughed at these antics, his nose was pinched again.

At noon the Indians gorged themselves on cock turkey and corn bread, baked on a hot shovel. Then they lay on the ground beside their rifles, half-dozing. Thereafter they went back to their card playing. They enjoyed this game immensely, playing it hour after hour, laughing uproariously when their antics compelled a loser to break out in laughter.

The next day was a replica of the preceding one. It was after lunch, during the Indians' siesta, that I noticed that their stacked rifles were charged but not primed. "In another day," I heard myself saying in silence, "my feet will be practically healed." I began toying with the notion that it was not preposterous to think about making my escape. A possible plan began evolving in my mind. With the Indians, half-dozing and full-bellied, I could outrun them. I could make for the stacked rifles, grab one, knock the others down, club the nearest Indian over the head. By the time the surprised Indians were up and had primed their rifles, I could be behind the shelter of the trees.

Fantastic as my thought seemed, I continued to consider it. We were, I estimated, some sixty, no more than seventy miles north of Columbia. That we were not beyond the water shed, I was certain, for all streams we'd passed had flowed toward the Ohio. While I had sense enough to know I was incapable of finding my way through sixty miles of woods to Columbia, this would not be necessary. The Little Miami River, to our east, couldn't be more than a mile or two away. Phineas Ford had told me that moss grew only on the northwest sides of pines. By this means I could find the Little Miami and follow her course to Columbia.

I told myself that I was daydreaming. Yet I could see no flaws in the plan. Suppose it took me a week, even ten days to reach Columbia? A man could survive that long without food. There would be plenty of water. And there would be plenty of wild berries. It was not beyond the realm of reason to presume I'd come across an Indian food log.

It could be done, I kept hearing myself saying. In my mind I spent the afternoon rehearsing the proposed role, counting the number of steps required to get to the trees, weighing this against that. I slept very little that night. Part of the time was spent telling myself I was out of my mind to even consider attempting to escape. During the greater part, however, I was admonishing myself that if the attempt were made, it must be on the next day. While I had no idea why we were tarrying at the supply camp, it had to be presumed that most assuredly we were waiting for somebody who would soon be coming along.

The following morning, I was still attempting to reach a decision. My feet were bare. The Indian who had shown me kindness had indicated that I should allow the sun to play on my bare feet. If I bound them up now, I wondered, would it arouse the Indians' suspicions? I decided that it would.

I ate a hearty breakfast, only a bite of lunch, and pretended to drink the concoction. It seemed to me on this morning the Indians drank more of the concoction than usual. At noon they'd again gorged themselves on turkey and corn bread and lay down beside their stacked rifles. The Indian who had been kind to me was closest to the rifles. It was he whom I would have to club over the head.

Was it indecision or compassion? I do not know. I did not make a move while my benefactor lay where he was. He had been drinking more than the others and seemed to be sound asleep. He rolled over against one of his fellows. This Indian made a remark indicating his annoyance and moved over, making him the man nearest the rifles.

Is it possible that something like this motivated my decision? Sauntering to the rifles, I grabbed one and rapped it against the second stack. Clubbing the Indian at my feet over the head, I made for the trees. In my careful calculations, I had overlooked an important factor. I had not taken into account that the red-hot shovel upon which the corn bread was baked lay in my direct line of path. I stepped on it heavily with my bare left foot. A sliver of pain raced up my limb, bringing me to a momentary halt. Recovering, I ran for the trees, approaching their shelter amid a volley of shots. A ball missed my scalp by inches, lodged in a tree. Another pinked my left arm. Still another found my left shoulder and came out of the top. A third struck my queue tie, the shock stunning me momentarily. Thinking I was mortally wounded, I kept driving my legs, wondering why I did not fall dead.

I ran like someone demented, not thinking about direction, not thinking about anything except that I must keep trees between me and the shots. The pain of my burned foot began asserting itself. With each step I took, my left leg raked my entire body.

The pain became so intense that my every step, I thought, must surely be my last. Behind me, I heard no shouts or shots. Surely, I was being followed! I continued to push ahead, still giving no thought to direction. As the darkness of twilight began casting its weird shadows about the forest, I suddenly collapsed, my limbs trembling violently.

With a cloth from my tattered trousers I bound my burned foot. A desire to fall into deep slumber was all but overwhelming. With the greatest effort, raising myself on my rifle, I gained my feet and trudged on. At dusk I reached a large, swamplike pond which barred my path. Now I knew why the Indians weren't at my heels. They had spread out. I was hemmed in. It was only a matter of time before they would have me.

Determined to drown myself if discovered, I placed my rifle in a tree, then entered the pond, swimming to its center where there were many lily pads and dead trees, their roots exposed. Placing lily pads on my head and in my collar, my body submerged, except for my head, I held myself against a tree root.

Eventually I heard an Indian shout out. Apparently, he'd discovered where I had entered the pond. Soon I heard the voices of other Indians, coming from various areas about the pond. Shortly their voices told me they had assembled and were holding a discussion of some sort. Then I heard nothing.

I was listening so intently that I didn't see a water moccasin until it was no more than six inches from my nose. It had simply stopped and was looking at me. After a moment or so, it turned around and swam away. This snake must have been at least four feet long. As it slithered off, its wriggling rear end slapped against my forehead.

I could hear nothing indicating that the Indians were still present. As time passed I dared hope that they had reached the conclusion that, being a white man, I had taken the coward's way out and drowned myself. It was more likely, however, to assume that they were behind the trees, waiting. Not only in the vicinity of where I had entered the pond, but at other places from which I might emerge, if I were still alive.

Darkness came and frogs began croaking and leaping about around me. Long before mosquitoes had discovered my presence. They feasted on my scabbed face. If I submerged my head, they could survive under water longer than I.

That night it rained rather hard, giving me relief from the mosquitoes. I considered leaving the pond under cover of darkness, but discarded this thought, "figuring," as Phineas Ford would have put it, that this was precisely what the Indians would be on the lookout for.

The rain stopped around the false dawn and the mosquitoes came back. At the real dawn a large three-pronged buck emerged from the woods, erected his stately head as he sniffed the air and looked about cautiously. Wading into the pond, he drank his fill. Bounding off gracefully, he moved to the far end of the pond and stood by while a herd of deer drank.

Now reasonably certain the Indians were gone, I swam for the shore. My left leg had gone numb. Reaching the bank, I saw that my left foot was swollen to half the size of a water bucket. In blank amazement, I stared at my foot, wondering why it did not hurt. While going to the tree for my rifle, I stepped on a sharp stone. Such was the sliver of pain that ripped up my leg, I had to throw myself to the ground. Hobbling to the tree,

I recovered my rifle. With its flint, I pricked my swollen foot. From my trousers, I made bindings for both my feet.

While my burned foot was painful, I could walk on it. My pinked arm appeared to be healing itself. Except for a slight but steady ache, my shoulder wound was not unduly painful. I bound up this wound, using twigs for splints and white oak leaves for dressing. At the moment I was too excited to think that I had had no sleep and was hungry. Surely I must have known that my ordeal was far from over. Yet, it actually seemed to me as if it were.

Nearby I saw a run of pines. Directing myself by the moss growing on the northwest side of the trunks of these trees, I moved eastward. The Little Miami River, I felt confident, could not be more than five miles away no matter how far off I had wandered.

By noon I thought surely I must soon be arriving at the Little Miami. When darkness came and I had seen not so much as a stream, I became somewhat worried but not actually alarmed. Even if I had not been able to walk in a due-east route, I assured myself, surely I had to be going in an easterly direction. The river meandered. No doubt, I told myself, I was moving toward one of the river's wide bends which swung away from me.

Throughout the day I had eaten dried wild raspberries and gooseberries. Sometime during the afternoon, I had become extremely hungry. Now, however, I seemingly had no desire to eat. I did, though, for I was in the midst of a wild raspberry patch whose fruit was lusciously ripe.

With a small log for a pillow, I slept well that night. At the false dawn I was again on my way. As the hours went by with nothing but trees around me, it became necessary to wonder if possibly I was making an error of some sort. My answer came with the approach of dusk. I was back at the swamplike pond from which I had started.

Determined not to permit myself to become panicky, I sat down, made an effort to discover what I had done incorrectly. I could think of nothing other than that in stepping around the trees, my direction was thrown asunder.

I was certain Phineas had told me that moss grew on the northwest sides of pines. He had mentioned this while we were in the woods, en route to Steubenville. In my mind I could hear Phineas saying northwest and could see him waving his arm downstream.

I can't be wrong about this, I told myself.

I slept fitfully that night, for my wounded shoulder had begun to ache most painfully. At dawn, here by the pond, it was possible to see the sun. I watched her as she rose. I was not mistaken about the sides of pines upon which moss grew.

By now my shoulder wound had become unbearably painful. The bandages and leaves I had used for dressing were stuck with coagulated blood, so fast that in order to loosen them it was necessary to dip my shoulder again and again into the pond. It was well after noon before I had properly cleaned my wound and rebandaged it.

I moved forward again, giving the greatest attention to my footing as I stepped around trees. This day came to its conclusion with me still surrounded by trees. Then another day was over, then another and then another.

I knew now that I was hopelessly lost.

Reasoning that I could not reach the Little Miami by direction of the moss, I decided my only recourse was to walk until I came upon a stream, which would surely be one of the river's tributaries. Four, possibly five days passed. I did not come upon a stream.

About this time the diet of wild berries brought on dyspepsia. Although recognizing my illness, I did not have the faintest notion of how to bring about its cure. Despite my discomfiture, I forced myself to move on, time after time dropping to my knees from sheer weakness. I shall never cease to marvel at man's instinctive ability to find a means to relieve his body's woes. Coming upon a patch of wild ginger, some inner voice told me to chew this herb. The doing of it brought on relief.

Thereafter my stomach refused to accept wild berries. I had nothing else to eat. Days and nights simply followed each other. A time came when I had no more clothing left to rebandage my shoulder wound or bind my feet. I walked on and on, stark naked, seemingly going nowhere, like a man on a treadmill.

I was aware that more and more I was talking to myself. There were periods, when still on my feet, I would suddenly return to the world of reality with a sudden start. It was as if I had been aroused from a deep sleep in the middle of a dream.

My first intimation that I might be going woods crazy came when I at last stumbled upon a stream. Probing under rocks, I sought a crawfish, which I was prepared to eat raw. Unsuccessful, I moved on, realizing hours later that the purpose of my walking was to find just such a stream. The desire *not* to retrace my steps and seek the stream welled up strong within me. Recognizing clearly what was taking place, I still needed to call upon my greatest powers of will to turn around. I was unable to find the stream.

Hungry as I was, if I placed a wild berry in my mouth, the mere taste of it nauseated me and I would spit it out. I sustained myself on the juices of chewed grass and haw. A drink of water brought momentary relief, then violent stomach pains, as my digestive organs attempted to function on nothing. Crazed by hunger, I clawed the extremities of fallen trees, fancying them to be Indian food logs. From my raw fingertips, I sucked my own blood.

One day I came upon a black duck resting in willows beside a small pond. It sat there still as a decoy. Warning myself that a rifle shot could bring on Indians, I pleaded out loud that I should not raise my rifle and press the trigger. I, nonetheless did so. There was no report, for the packing had come loose.

Creeping forward steathily, I hurled my rifle at the duck, stunning it. Pouncing upon the bird, I began ripping off its feathers while it was still alive. Under the duck was an egg, which no doubt it was hatching, otherwise it would certainly have flown off at my approach. Putting down the duck, I picked up the egg, broke it, dropped its contents into my mouth. Feeling what was like the pricking of pins, I expectorated. I vomited when I saw that I had attempted to eat a partly formed duckling.

After this experience, I lost all ability to behave as a man possessed with reason. Laughing, weeping, shouting out until I was hoarse, I raced through the woods. When exhaustion dropped me, I crawled.

VII

I do not remember any more of it. I am told that I hurled myself down a two-hundred foot embankment, to where Asa Hartshorn and his patrol was camped overnight. Seeing the fire it may be presumed that it was in this manner that I overcame my desire to run away from those who would help me. That I possessed such a desire, there is no doubt. Once I was found, Asa told me, I fought his men with the ferocity of an enraged puma.

Why didn't the moss lead me to the Miami River? My own inexperience as a woodsman is a possible explanation. Phineas Ford believes it is more likely I was actually beyond the water shed or so close to it that the river I was seeking, being only a trickle of water, was unrecognizable.

In all I was away from Cincinnati exactly seven weeks. My first ten days of recuperation, so I am told, were spent tied-up, most of the time, in Fort Washington's guardhouse. Although only skin and bones, I was constantly in a pugnacious mood, exhibiting considerable skills as both a pugilist and a leg man in making an effort to escape captivity and get back into the woods. During this period, Melissa eventually informed me, it is highly unlikely a single occupant of Fort Washington existed who did not come at least once to the guardhouse, to have a look at me, as if I were a wild animal on exhibit in a cage.

"When we tried to serve you food in a normal manner," Melissa told me, "you would not touch it. You brushed the plate off the table. Dr. Allison finally solved the problem by placing a bowl of food on the floor. Going to your all-fours, you ate without benefit of cutlery. While you never barked or caterwauled, I do believe, Tom, you thought you were an animal. Yet, oddly enough, when Dr. Allison offered you your clay, you accepted it, thanked him most graciously, and puffed away to your heart's content."

This was interesting, for with only dried willow bark available, I had given up the weed.

"When at last that phase of it was over," Melissa said, "we took you to my quarters. For days you simply lay in the bed seemingly unaware of anything. Occasionally you would open your eyes and look at me. At times I thought you were going to speak, but for day after day you did not."

I was able to remember that part of it. I could hear what was going on, yet when I attempted to speak, no words came out. It was simply that I was too weak to talk.

One afternoon while still in this extremely weak condition, I heard Dr. Allison's assistant, Albert, tell Kitty Kummerschmitt that it would be necessary to amputate both my feet. This conversation took place outside the door of Melissa's quarters. I am certain my experience in the woods had rendered my hearing more acute. Although Albert and Kitty spoke in whispers, I could hear everything said with crystal clarity. "The amputation of a human foot," Albert said with the profoundness of a sixteen-year-old boy, "is actually a relatively simple operation. Someone accomplished as Dr. Allison can have it all over and done with in less than eight minutes."

In my case, Albert went on to say, the operation, in his opinion, would be performed under most favorable conditions, for I was insensible to shock.

I was terrified by this information. Yet, in my weakened condition, I could muster no reaction except a sharpening of my breath. Although my brain had taken cognizance of what I heard and seemed to wish it could call upon my body to help it to function, nothing went on inside my head.

It was not necessary to amputate my feet. After removing some two hundred thorns, Melissa and Kitty Kummerschmitt, aided by Emil and Phineas, massaged my feet and legs throughout my waking hours. "My toes!" I recall crying out. "I can feel them." Dr. Allison called it a miracle.

During the first week of September, although still weak as a kitten, I expressed the desire to leave my bed. "Not for a while yet, Tom," Dr. Allison said.

"How long?"

"I don't know."

"A week?"

"Possibly. Tom, please don't try to pin me down."

"I heard cannon-fire this morning. What was it all about?"

"In honor of the arrival of Governor St. Clair."

"What does that mean?"

"We don't know for certain yet," Dr. Allison said wryly.

"Surely Governor St. Clair isn't going to take personal charge of the expedition?"

"We are reasonably certain he doesn't expect to go quite that far."

I understood what Dr. Allison had left unsaid. "Damn that man!" I said. "He'll be all over the fort, sticking his nose into where it doesn't belong, issuing orders in fields that are the General's." Having never so much as laid eyes upon Governor Arthur St. Clair, I am aware I had no right to make such a statement.

"He leaves for Louisville the day after tomorrow," Dr. Allison said.

"Good riddance," I said.

"But he'll be back in time to greet the arriving militiamen," the doctor said. "It's expected he'll stay at Fort Washington until the expedition is concluded."

"Dr. Allison," I said with a certain hesitancy, "the General has been kind enough to stop past here any number of times to inquire about my health. I couldn't help noticing. His breath . . ."

Dr. Allison nodded. "Yes, Tom," he said. "I know."

Approximately a quarter of an hour after Dr. Allison left, Melissa and I became man and wife. While the doctor and I talked, Melissa had gone for my lunch. Returning without it, Melissa had apparently run back, for her breath came quite sharp and her cheeks were flushed. "Shortly you may expect a caller," she said. "Lieutenant Ebenezer Denny."

"Is that so," I said. "Does that mean he arrived with Governor St. Clair?"

"It does."

"Are you upset about something?" I asked.

"I am," Melissa said. "Quite. It is possible that you may be too when I tell you that Lieutenant Denny, much to his deep regret, will soon be compelled to come here in order to inform us that we have been violating not only the Ten Commandments, but Army Regulations as well."

"What in the world are you talking about?"

"The charge against us," Melissa said, "is adultery."

"I beg your pardon!"

"Adultery," Melissa repeated and pointed to the cot upon which she had been sleeping during my period of convalescence. "According to Lieutenant Denny, we have been living in sin on government property. You are liable to a hundred lashes. I, being a woman and therefore the more guilty in such an instance, am liable to a hundred-fifty. You will lose your commission. We must both leave the fort."

"You know very well all that can't happen to us," I said.

"I am not too sure it can't," Melissa said. "I learned the penalties of the military law from Governor St. Clair himself."

"You went to Governor St. Clair!"

"Immediately after talking with Lieutenant Denny."

"St. Clair!" I said. "Why didn't you go to the General? He would have straightened it all out."

"That is where I *was* going," Melissa said. "Governor St. Clair was in headquarters at the time. He was quite acquainted with our predicament and showed little sympathy. It made no difference, he said, that I slept on a cot beside your bed. The point of issue is that I have spent many nights with you in an officer's quarters. That you were sick unto death and incapable of using me, on government property, in a manner unbecoming to an officer in the United States Army—did not alter the situation."

In the manner of someone emerging from a jack-in-the-box, Emil Kummerschmitt stuck his head into the door. "Be most careful what you say to Lieutenant Denny, Tom," he stage-whispered. "He's trying to arrest Phineas for trading rifles to the Indians."

"He knows about it!"

"No, but he knows Phineas."

"Where is Phineas?"

"In the guardhouse."

"On what charge?"

"Insubordination. Phineas told Lieutenant Denny to go to hell," Emil said and handed me a piece of paper which upon examination proved to be a wedding bans form. "If you and your intended will sign this, the army will be powerless to bring charges of having lived together in sin."

"Emil," I said, "that won't do any good."

"State that the place of posting is Bracken," Emil said.

"That won't do any good either," I said. "I know Lieutenant Denny. That wouldn't fool him for a minute. He'll send somebody to Bracken to verify everything."

"Phineas will be there first."

"Phineas is in the guardhouse!"

"He will be out shortly. Ensign Sedam, just back from patrol, has been kind enough to say the woods are full of Indians and something appears to be brewing. It is of the utmost necessity that Phineas survey the situation. Major Doughty has signed a release. Phineas will serve out his sentence at a more convenient time."

"Who'll be the witnesses?"

"Phineas and me."

"You!"

"It is well known that I have taken frequent trips to Limestone and Bracken. Actually I was close to Bracken when you were there. That part makes no difference, for it can be shown that I was not in Cincinnati when you and your intended were in Bracken."

"You're sure of that!"

"Yes, I returned to Cincinnati only a day before you and Phineas arrived."

I looked at Melissa. Simply nodding to me, she got out pen and ink. I filled the forms, we both signed. Bowing and bringing his heels together, Emil said: "I can think only to say that I wish you both a long married life, happy as mine and Kitty's has been."

For some moments after Emil had beat a hasty exit, Melissa and I looked at each other in silence. "Well," Melissa said eventually, "that certainly belies the person who said there was no such thing as a simple wedding."

"Yes," I said, "it does. Melissa, do you feel somewhat uneasy about being married—without benefit of clergy?"

"Somewhat," she admitted, "but at the moment I'm reminding myself that if Cincinnati had had a minister, we'd have been in a real pickle." She had moved to the door. "Tom, Lieutenant Denny is coming across the parade. What are we going to say to him?"

"As little as possible," I said.

Shortly Lieutenant Denny, well-powdered and immaculately attired, put in his appearance. "It is so pleasing to see you again, Mr.—or should I say, Lieutenant—Morrow," he greeted in his most engaging manner. "My I come in?"

I had decided to meet him head-on. "If you have written authorization," I said, "yes, you may."

"This whole situation is most regrettable," Lieutenant Denny said. "My sympathies are totally with you. Rest assured I am going to do my utmost to straighten things out."

"Have you written authority?"

"No, I have not."

"Come in," I said. "It is to be understood, of course, that all conversation will be of an informal nature?"

"Of course," the lieutenant said stiffly, entering our quarters and sitting down.

"My I put a question to you, sir?" I said.

"By all means."

"Please tell me precisely what you hope to gain by causing Melissa and me such humiliation?"

Although Lieutenant Denny's cheeks reddened slightly, his aplomb was not shattered. "I do not make Army Regulations, Mr. Morrow. I am, however, under oath to carry them out."

I said nothing.

"The laxity of discipline here at the fort," Lieutenant Denny said, "is causing the Governor considerable concern. It is necessary, he feels, that from now on all regulations must be scrupulously carried out. Let one lapse, the entire structure collapses. Actually that is why you dare not be allowed to be an exception. Admittedly yours is an unfortunate by-product. Both the Governor and I are sorry you should be caught in the web."

I still said nothing.

"When your case was brought to the Governor's attention," Lieutenant Denny went on to say.

"By whom?" I inquired.

"As a matter of fact, by me." Lieutenant Denny raised his arm, as if to halt the expression of my thoughts. "That is not the way it seems at first glance, Mr. Morrow. In due time your situation would have come to the Governor's attention willy-nilly. My statement to the Governor was made purely in the spirit of being helpful to you."

"Helpful to me!"

"Definitely so," Lieutenant Denny said, flashing his most winning smile.

The lieutenant came quickly to the point. While he could not prove it, he knew that Phineas had obtained rifles in Pittsburgh. What he was about to say next, he assured me, had Governor St. Clair's approval. I had merely to testify that Phineas had traded rifles with the Indians and all charges against me would be dropped. "This can be arranged, Mr. Morrow," he added, "without jeopardizing strict adherence to military regulations. It may be regarded as a reward for patriotic behavior."

"Were I to so testify," I said, "I would be guilty of perjury."

"I beg your pardon, sir."

"To the best of my knowledge," I said firmly, "your suspicions are groundless. En route from Pittsburgh to Cincinnati, Phineas Ford did *not* trade rifles with Indians."

"You state this categorically?"

"I do."

"You, of course, realize this means that my efforts to help you have come to naught?"

"Be relieved on that score, Lieutenant," I said. "You will be most happy to learn that Melissa and I were married in Bracken. The bans are posted there."

"So that is how the goose has been cooked." Lieutenant Denny stood up and started for the door.

"One more question before you leave, Lieutenant," I said. "Was it part of your scheme of things, when you made transportation arrangements for me in Pittsburgh, that I should end up testifying against Phineas Ford?"

"Yes, Mr. Morrow, it was. However, please bear in mind that I strongly urged and advised you to return to Philadelphia."

"Thank you," I said.

"You are quite welcome, Mr. Morrow," he said. "And now may I ask you a question?"

"You may."

"Do you believe it proper for Phineas Ford to trade rifles with Indians?"

"I do not."

"What an odd world we live in," Lieutenant Denny said and left.

VIII

Although fully aware that I was still too weak to carry out the duties expected of a newly married man, Melissa announced, since it was her wedding night, she was going to forsake her cot and share her husband's bed. The proximity of her presence was most comforting and provided added impetus to my natural desire to recover.

Four days later Emil Kummerschmitt, presumably at the fort to pick up Kitty's milk allotment, called at our quarters. "I just saw Melissa at the pump," Emil said. "She appears to be most happy and contented."

It was always difficult for me to ascertain whether or not there were hidden meanings behind Emil's statements. At any rate I was still not what might be called a *bona fide* husband. "Well, none of us are under indictment yet," I said. "Emil, I can't help worrying. Lieutenant Denny won't rest until he catches Phineas."

"Yes, I know," Emil said. "It is most unfortunate that we must continually connive. However, the time will come when we will be honored and respected citizens."

Emil was stating one of his favorite theses. Most poor men who eventually gained wealth, he contended, had found it necessary to pull many strings in order to reach their goals. Once having arrived, it became their duty to be generous and helpful to others.

"Phineas thinks you should move to your new home tomorrow," Emil said and told me that a battalion of Pennsylvania militiamen, five hundred strong, under command of Lieutenant Colonel Trubley and Major Paul, was at Bracken and could be expected daily.

It had already been discussed and agreed upon that Melissa should not be at the fort while the militiamen were on hand. Our cabin would be raised on the Kummerschmitt inlot. Safety and the fact that Melissa and Kitty would be good company for each other were the principal reasons for reaching this decision. Others were that I hadn't had time to select a block of lots of my own and, with Mr. Riley now a schoolmaster, the settlement had no welldigger. The arrangement had come about following Emil's suggestion. "We both gain, Tom," he'd pointed out. "The cabin won't cost you anything. The value of my inlot, since now my cabin may be looked upon as well-constructed shed, will increase."

"Where is Phineas?" I asked.

"At my place," Emil said. "He arrived yesterday morning. We spent the day putting up your chimney." He went on to say that Phineas, after making the necessary arrangements to post Melissa's and my marriage bans, had expected to do a bit of scouting on the way back. However, seeing the caliber of the Pennsylvania militiamen, he had decided to return immediately to get our cabin raised.

It was advisable, Emil added, that, for the time being, Phineas should stay out of Governor St. Clair's sight. "I thought the Governor was in Louisville," I said.

"He leaves for there tomorrow," Emil said. "He's been laid up with the gout."

"You say the Pennsylvanians are at Bracken?" I said. "What's holding them up?"

"Grievances had to be talked over," Emil told me. "For some time the situation was critical. The militiamen's enlistment periods had run out. They threatened to go home. It was necessary for General Harmar to go to Bracken to settle matters."

"Everything is settled?"

"Yes."

"Why, then, aren't the Pennsylvanians here by now?"

"Phineas tells me, it was felt wise to postpone their arrival until the Governor left. One of the militiamen's grievances was the Governor's order that, while stationed at Fort Washington, they would not be issued their daily allowance of whiskey."

"Surely the General didn't go so far as to countermand the Governor's order?"

"No, he did not," Emil said. "This particular grievance was settled by a promise that the Pennsylvanians would be moved out of the fort quickly as possible, to be engaged in what the General characterized as 'light' road construction. The daily allowance of whiskey from then on will be doubled."

"There were other grievances?"

"Yes," Emil said. "Are you by any chance acquainted with the nature of a Mrs. Mae Dwyer's work?"

"I am," I said and while I had in fact completely forgotten about Susan's letter, I now, of course, recalled having received it.

"Apparently as a means of inveigling the Pennsylvanians to join up," Emil said, "they were promised that suitable arrangements had been made with Mrs. Dwyer. This promise was not kept."

"Then there are no women?"

"No."

Although I had never anticipated any trouble from Susan, I nonetheless received this information with a mild sense of relief. "And how was that grievance settled?" I inquired.

"Apparently entirely by the General's persuasive powers," Emil said. "The matter of obtaining Indian women was discussed. The General, however, said no to that, most firmly."

Although our one-room log cabin would be only eighteen-by-twenty feet, were it a royal mansion, Melissa couldn't have been more excited by the prospect of moving into it. She was humming happily the next morning when she brought me my breakfast. I would have to remain in bed the whole day, Dr. Allison had decreed. While he realized I would not be taking part in actual manual labor, I would be moving about and over-exciting myself. I would be able, though, he said, to spend the night in my own cabin.

My breakfast finished, Melissa kissed me, took up the tray, said, "I can't wait until I see how things are going," then left. Shortly she was back with a bucket, mop, and other cleaning utensils. Working with the vigor of someone who wishes to finish a task as quickly as possible, she attacked the floor. "Please be most tidy when you get up, Tom," she said.

When she pushed over my bed and began attacking the corners of our quarters, I said, "Didn't you do that last week?"

"Yes."

"It can't get that dirty in a week," I said.

"You'd be surprised," she said.

"Believe me," I said. "Lieutenant Harrison didn't leave these quarters half so clean as they were even before you started all this cleaning and I can assure you the next occupant won't move the bed and inspect the corners."

"I know it."

"Why, then, do you go about it with such gruesome thoroughness?"

"You should never ask a woman such a question," Melissa said.

"Why not?"

"Because she can't explain it to your satisfaction."

"Can she explain it to herself?"

"Yes," Melissa said, "she most definitely can."

With Melissa away, I became extremely restless. When, around mid-morning, Dr. Allison stopped past, I was dressed and awaiting him. "I'm well enough to see how our cabin's coming along," I said.

"You are not well enough," Dr. Allison said. "However, going is the lesser of the two evils, so go, but without my professional blessings."

When I arrived at the Kummerschmitt inlot all the logs were cut, the cornerstones were laid and construction of our cabin was about to begin. Some thirty men, stripped to the waist, their shoulders wiped with spice-wood soaked in vinegar to protect them from mosquitoes and gnats, were on hand.

The men constituted about a third of the settlement's population. In a way, since my mental picture of Cincinnati proper was that it was all trees, it was difficult to envision that these men lived with their families within those trees on isolated inlots like the Kummerschmitts. Come to think of it, except for Emil Kummerschmitt, I had not until now seen a Cincinnati citizen moving about the confines of the settlement.

"Tom!" Melissa said. "Should you be here? How do you feel?"

"Fine," I said.

Melissa was so excited, I am not certain she knew I was alive. She was before the Kummerschmitt cabin where she and Kitty were stirring a turkey hash in a large iron kettle. Emil, examining the cornerstones of our cabin, waved to me.

"Is Phineas about?" I started to ask Melissa, but there was no need for her to reply for Phineas emerged from the woods with a keg of whiskey on his shoulder, which he placed beside a keg already set up.

Phineas' face was quite flushed. "Damn, Tom," he said and clicked his teeth, "these boys really like whiskey. I'm bringing them another keg for tonight. They're holding an election."

"For what?"

"Damned if I know," Phineas said. "What do you think of your chimney?"

"I haven't had a chance to look at it closely."

"It's the best God-damned chimney in Cincinnati," Phineas said, "but I'll have to show you a couple things about her. She won't draw right at first. None of them do. Tom, Melissa told me how you made a jackass out of Ebenezer Denny. That was fine."

I was aware this was Phineas' interpretation of what Melissa had said. "I'm not at all sure who made a jackass out of whom," I said. "Phineas, he'll never give up on you."

"He's been trying to catch me for a year, Tom. Has he got me yet?"

"The bans," I said. "They *are* posted in Bracken? That's definite, isn't it?"

"Sure," Phineas said. "Everything's fine."

"Emil told me you saw the Pennsylvania militiamen. What are they like?"

"Jesus!" Phineas said.

"What does that mean?"

"It means," Phineas said and took a stout swig of whiskey, "that I never saw worse. Nothing but old men and boys. Simon was telling me a good third of them can't even take off a rifle-lock to oil it or put in a flint the right way. Plenty of them hadn't even shot a gun before signing up."

"Simon?"

"Simon Kenton," Phineas said.

"The celebrated Indian fighter?"

Phineas nodded. "Simon was in Bracken when I was. He's an old friend of the General's and is going to raise him a troop of real Indian fighters."

"That's good news," I said.

"It sure is," Phineas said.

"How many men will Simon Kenton be able to raise?"

"A hundred, maybe more. All Simon has to do is put out the word. The men'll come flocking. If I was the General I'd ship all the God-damned militiamen back to where they came from and march out with the federals and Simon's boys."

"You're not serious!"

"The hell I'm not," Phineas said, "and I'll bet my last dollar the General wishes it was that way."

"You're saying a hundred of Simon Kenton's men would be more effective than twelve hundred militiamen!"

"You're damned right I am. You just wait and see what happens up in the woods when the militiamen start coming down with cannon fever."

A young, rather good-looking young man with bushy black hair moved to the whiskey keg. As he drank, he looked over his mug at Melissa and Kitty, the expression in his eyes making it apparent that, having mentally undressed both ladies, he was pleased with his imaginary picture. "Andrew, this is Tom," Phineas said. "Tom's the one you're raising the cabin for. Andrew, what the hell is it you're running for tonight?"

"Committeeman," Andrew said.

"Andrew's a lawyer," Phineas said.

"What sort of a government has Cincinnati?" I asked Andrew.

"Actually none, sir," Andrew said, smiling affably, but with his eyes still on Melissa and Kitty. "For the time being we're simply electing a committee of three who'll act as a sort of court when difficulties arise."

"Am I permitted to vote?" I asked.

Andrew glanced toward my cabin. "Are you a property owner?"

"No."

"As a matter of fact only property owners are supposed to vote. It wouldn't make much difference though, for only three of us are standing for election. The main purpose of the committee is to give a sort of legal status to a ruling that Cincinnati will form a company of Rangers."

Andrew left.

"Phineas," I said, "why don't you mention a person's last name when you introduce him?"

"I guess I should at that," Phineas said.

"Well, what was Andrew's last name?"

"Damned if I know," Phineas said.

While Phineas and I talked a man, leading Cincinnati's only team of oxen, snaked the larger logs to the cabin site. Other men carried the smaller ones. "I'd better go over and keep an eye on things," Phineas said.

"Isn't there anything I can do?"

"Sure," Phineas said. "Stand here and give out the whiskey."

Although four hours went by before the task was completed, it seemed to me that the cabin went up before my very eyes. So far as I could tell, nobody was in actual charge, yet everyone appeared to know what he was supposed to do. There were men who made the clapboards for the roof, there were puncheon men.

While in due time I would learn what was taking place, at this moment I could only look on with amazement. Four axmen "carried-up" the corners while others with skids and handspikes rolled up the logs and delivered them to the "corner men." The bearers for the roof logs were adjusted; the broad clapboards were laid, wright-poles were placed upon the successive courses and the shell of the cabin was completed. No more than six iron nails were needed for the entire undertaking.

When the clinking and daubing began, Melissa moved beside me and took hold of my hand. "Tom," she said, "have you seen our—furniture?"

"No!" I said. "I haven't."

We moved to the rear of the Kummerschmitt cabin. Here was a hutch table, four three-legged stools, a hominy block, deerskins, and sundry household necessities such as wooden dishes and bowls, tinder boxes, lug poles for tea kettles, pepper grinders, a butter bowl made of appletree knot, cherry seeders, a coffee mill, a butter paddle. Since it was next to impossible to get a lamp in Cincinnati at this time, somebody had been thoughtful enough to hollow out a turnip, filled it with bear oil and placed a wick therein.

"I've asked any number of people how this wonderful custom came about," Melissa said. "Nobody seems to know."

IX

The Pennsylvania militiamen had arrived while our cabin was being raised. With the greatest haste the General moved most of them out of Fort Washington, to an encampment five miles up the Mill Creek.

"Talk about your clowns," Phineas said, referring to the militiamen, two days later, as he accompanied me while I was en route to Fort Washington to resume my duties as the General's scribe. "It's a good thing St. Clair wasn't around or he'd be dead by now from a split gut."

Upon their arrival, Phineas told me, the General had assembled the militiamen. During the course of the General's address a flock of passenger pigeons had flown over the parade. A militiaman had shot into the flock, bringing down two birds, an act which provoked general laughter. In order that the culprit's identity could not be determined, he and some two dozen of his fellows had thrown their rifles onto the ground.

"Good Lord!" I said. "What did the General do?"

"He handled it smooth as silk, Tom. Without so much as batting an eye, he said, 'Well, gentlemen, I only hope you can shoot that accurately against the Indians.' Then he went right on with what he was talking about. He sure got a big cheer when he was finished."

"Phineas," I said, "a seemingly insignificant thing like that could change the whole morale of the militiamen."

"It could," Phineas said, "but it won't. Tom, believe me, those boys are nothing but a bunch of rotten apples."

"There's some good in everybody," I said.

"Tom," Phineas said, "sometimes you sure can say some awful dumb things."

When Phineas and I entered the fort we were in a place that could blow up at any moment. Although supplies of a sort had come through during the past month, the method of shipment was not carried out in an orderly fashion. For example, on the day before I was captured a flatboat had arrived with traveling forges, but there were no anvils.

Thus it wasn't until the arrival of the Pennsylvania militiamen that the last of the military stores were on hand and the task of making up nearly all of the ammunition for the expedition could begin. Under Major Doughty's direction, a laboratory had been prepared for making musket cartridges in the stockade. This was safe enough.

However, because loose powder couldn't with any degree of safety be left around any other place, the shells for the artillery and howitzer cartridges had to be filled in the northwest blockhouse, which was half full of stored material which could not be moved. As anyone acquainted with the fixing of ammunition knows, shell filling is a tedious business and must be carried out with the greatest care. Unless there is ample working room and the workers are provided with the recognized conveniences, accidents are likely to happen. All the shell powder we had was stored in this one blockhouse and because no time dared be lost, so many men had to be assigned to the task that there was hardly space for them to move about. Not to mention the danger of accidents caused by the carelessness of overworked men, with all those feet shuffling on the floor, the threat of an explosion from body sparks was always present.

As I approached headquarters, a staff meeting had just been concluded. By now the various members of the General's family, who'd been away on recruiting and other assignments, were back at the fort. These included: Majors Wyllys, Ray, Fontaine, Ziegler. Captains Doyle, Strong, Ashton, Ferguson. Lieutenants Kersey and Denny. Ensigns Morgan, Armstrong, Shamburgh, and Gaines, who was now Captain of the Horse, Asa Hartshorn having been named a lieutenant.

Greeting me warmly, Major Doughty introduced me around. Apparently my run through the woods had become common knowledge, for nearly all the officers mentioned it. Major Wyllys told me he had had the pleasure of hearing my father speak. I was being treated as one of the family. Why I should even mention this, I am not quite certain. What I am saying, I suppose, is that I was never able to completely convince myself that, despite a uniform and rank, I was a soldier.

I was somewhat uneasy when I faced Lieutenant Denny. He, however, greeted me quite cordially. "You look so much better than when I saw you last, Lieutenant," he said.

"I feel so," I replied. There was no time for further talk, but as I moved into headquarters I wondered if Lieutenant Denny was willing to let by-gones be by-gones or whether he deemed it prudent to give such an impression.

General Harmar was in his inner office. He looked very tired as well he might for he was getting little sleep these days. A whiskey bottle and glass stood on his desk, for everybody to see. There is no doubt the General was drinking a great deal at this time, but I say it categorically—he was never drunk. And with all his trials and tribulations, General Harmar never ceased to behave as the gentleman he was.

"You look quite well, Tom," the General said. "We're glad to have you back."

"Thank you, sir," I said. "I am glad to be back. Melissa has asked me to tell you that she, so much as I, greatly appreciated the bottle of brandy you sent us."

"I hope you enjoyed it."

"We're saving it, sir," I said. "I want to be fully recovered and enjoy it to its fullest."

"You *are* well enough to put in a full day's work?"

"Yes, sir."

"Use your own discretion, Tom," the General said. "If you become overly tired, go home and rest."

"Thank you, sir."

I was wearing my buckskins. "You'd better see about getting a uniform," the General said.

"Yes, sir."

"Since the other one wasn't destroyed in the line of duty," the General said, "it might be wise to charge the new one against your salary. Regulations, you know."

"I understand, sir," I said.

Sometime during that afternoon it might be said that I made a constructive contribution to the Harmar Expedition. Quartermaster's-Assistant O'Malley entered headquarters. "I'm glad to see you, Horatius," I said. "The General says I ought to have a uniform."

"Just keep your pants on, Tom," Horatius surprised me by saying brusquely, "you'll get a uniform. Right now I want to see the General."

Horatius, I could now see, was quite stirred up. A chunky fellow, with no neck and a square head, he had noticeably large ears which at the moment were very red. "I'll find out if the General's free," I said.

When the General told me he'd see Horatius he tapped his desk twice with his forefinger, an indication that I should remain on the scene for the purpose of doing my best to help get the caller out, quickly but gracefully as possible.

"General," Horatius fumed, "those damned Pennsylvania militiamen! You've got to hear my side of it before Major Paul gets here."

"I'm listening, Horatius," the General said patiently.

"It happened the day before yesterday, sir. You know what kind of rifles those fellows brought, that is those who didn't trade theirs in for whiskey?"

"Yes, Horatius, I know all about that."

"Well, these two Pennsylvanians came up to me with their rifles. One rifle didn't have a lock, the other didn't have a stock. They said they wanted their rifles repaired. 'Now how in the hell do you think I can repair something that isn't there?' I asked them. Then what do you think they said? They said that's how the rifles were issued in Pittsburgh and they were told all repairs would be made at Fort Washington. 'Well, the artificers can't repair these rifles,' I said. 'I'll have to issue you new ones. You'll have to sign up for them and there'll be an estoppage against your wages.'

"The one fellow," Horatius went on to say, "took it all right and left. The other got nasty. There was a whiskey bottle—"

"A whiskey bottle! You mean to say you had a whiskey bottle—practically on display?"

"Well, yes, sir."

"Horatius," the General chided mildly, "didn't you hear me at assembly when I said that while it's agreed that all militiamen and generals haven't got any common sense, everybody else in the army is supposed to have some and is expected to use it?"

"Yes, sir," Horatius said, "I heard you say that. There wasn't any whiskey in the bottle. It was full of gun oil."

"Please continue, Horatius," the General said.

"Well, when the Pennsylvanian went for the whiskey bottle, I tapped him on the head with my mallet. Just enough to knock him out, sir. He wasn't hurt and when he came to he went away real peaceful."

"Just what is it you're attempting to establish, Horatius?"

"You know about the grievance committee the Pennsylvanians have?"

"Yes."

"Well, I just heard that the fellow I tapped on the head reported me in and said I assaulted him from behind and beat the holy hell out of him. The committee took it up with Major Paul and you're going to hear about it."

"Thank you for telling me all this, Horatius," the General said somewhat wearily. "I wouldn't worry too much though, Major Paul and I pretty well understand situations of this nature."

"Thank you, sir," Horatius said, visibly relieved. "And there's one more thing, sir. Some Pennsylvanians just came in and wanted five more boxes of flints."

"Well?"

"You know what's happening to our flints, don't you, sir?"

"I had presumed I could assume what our flints were being used for."

"The Pennsylvanians are acting like babies with toy guns over their flints, sir. They're going around snapping the locks of their rifles and wearing out their flints."

A flint was usable for only about sixty operations. "What!" the General exclaimed.

"If they keep it up," Horatius said, "we won't have any flints left and they cost six cents apiece besides."

"Six cents!" the General said and turned to me for verification.

Since the flints had been shipped through before my capture, I was familiar with what was what. "That is correct, sir," I said.

"The price in Louisville is two cents," the General said.

"Our flints came from South Carolina," I explained. "They were shipped to New York Town, then sent on here via Fort Pitt."

The General turned to Horatius. "Did you issue the flints?"

"No, sir," Horatius said. "I said they had to be inspected first and entered in the records. That made the Pennsylvanians mad and they wanted to know how in the hell they were expected to fight without flints."

"You handled that very well, Horatius," the General said. "Don't issue any flints until you hear further from me."

"Yes, sir," Horatius said and when he'd left the General said: "Those God-damned bastards!" It was one of the few times I heard him swear.

Possibly an hour or so later Major Paul arrived, to make his daily statement about how things were coming along at the militiamen's encampment.

Although I saw Major Paul only on these visits and only saw Colonel
Trubley from a distance, I am able to say that General Harmar held both
commanders of the Pennsylvania militiamen in high regard. Major Paul
was a tall, lanky man with extremely deep-set eyes, whose manner of speaking
indicated that he was well educated. When he arrived at headquarters he
handed me a list of the militiamen's grievances and told me it was to be
turned over to what was called the Federal Officers' Board of Review. Glancing quickly at the list, I saw the charges against Quartermaster's-Assistant
Horatius O'Malley had been duly noted.

"Yes, sir," I said and we both smiled slightly for there was no Federal
Officers' Board of Review.

When ushered into the inner office, Major Paul told the General that
twenty-three militiamen had deserted during the past night. A sentry had
reported seeing two Indians, which had brought on a near panic, and there
were many complaints about the flour. "The flour *is* sour," Major Paul said.

"It is here at the fort too," the General said.

"Our boys are getting awfully restless," Major Paul said. "If we don't
get under way soon, there'll be more desertion."

"You'll simply have to do your best, John."

"Josiah," Major Paul inquired anxiously, "when can we expect the Virginians?"

"Not for another week at best," the General said, shaking his head sadly,
and told Major Paul news which had arrived only within the past two hours.
The Virginians *were* assembled at Louisville. However, they were not permitted to leave the state's boundaries without the written consent of its
governor. Such consent had been granted and the proper documents had
come through. Unfortunately all the documents had to be sent back to the
state capitol, for the Governor had neglected to sign them.

The General then brought up the matter of flint-snapping. "Yes, I know,"
Major Paul said gravely. "Colonel Trubley and I have both pleaded and
reasoned until we are hoarse."

"That has to stop, John," the General said.

"We daren't whip anybody," Major Paul said. "The colonel and I have
discussed this and we are both agreed it shouldn't be done." Somewhat
wearily he added: "You know what happened in Marietta?" He meant that
in Marietta a militiaman had been whipped for desertion. The result was
the militiamen rioted in a body and threatened to return home.

It is now that I made my constructive contribution. "If you'll permit me,
sir," I said to the General, "possibly I can suggest a solution?"

"By all means, Tom," the General said. "Please speak up."

"We have on hand twelve boxes of wooden snaps," I said. "These are useless to us. We could issue them temporarily to Major Paul's men."

Both General Harmar and Major Paul agreed this was the solution to the problem and thanked me for having made the suggestion. "Why in the world would we have twelve boxes of wooden snaps?" the General asked me.

"I don't think we should have received them, sir," I said and explained that the wooden snaps had come down from Fort Pitt where, due to a shortage of supplies, they were being used. Since the wooden snaps had arrived in boxes marked as South Carolina flints, it was not too difficult to guess what must have happened.

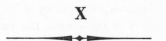

X

My records showed that General Harmar's army, not including the Simon Kentonians, once it was fully assembled, would be 1453 strong:

The battalion of Pennsylvania militiamen.

Three-hundred-twenty federals, forming two small battalions under Majors John Doughty and Pleasgrave Wyllys, together with Captain William Ferguson's company of artillery and three pieces of ordnance.

Three battalions of Virginians, including a battalion of light troops mounted militia, headed by Majors Hall, McMullen, and Ray. On the surface, at least, the rivalry between Colonels John Hardin and Robert Trotter had been resolved. After lengthy discussions, which took place in Louisville, the General had finally placated the two men by naming Hardin commander of all the militia, while Trotter became commander of the three Virginia battalions.

Two days before the arrival of the Virginians, Governor Arthur St. Clair returned from Louisville, having been carried on a litter from Northbend to Fort Washington, for he was suffering from the gout. After repairing to his quarters for an hour of rest, he appeared at headquarters. Although only fifty-seven years old, the Governor walked with the faltering steps of someone who is senile. His stern, smallpox pitted face had turned to the clay color of death. He was, however, freshly powdered and queued. Despite his obvious discomfort, the man comported himself in soldierly fashion, his spirit of determination being greater than the weakness of his body.

I, of course, had come to attention upon the Governor's arrival. We two were the only ones present in the outer office. "I am Arthur St. Clair," the Governor announced in his rasping voice. "I wish to speak with Brevet Brigadier General Josiah Harmar."

"Yes, sir," I said. "I will tell General Harmar that you are here."

"Young man," the Governor said. "You will do nothing of the sort. Since I do not have an appointment, you will request of the federal officer in command of this fort if it is convenient for him to see me. If it is not, you will find out when it is."

The Governor, I was aware, while reprimanding me, was also making evident his disapproval of General Harmar's policy of granting as many audiences as possible. The two men had passed sharp words over this. Contending that in an army of this size and nature, a general must not remain aloof of his men, in fact must make every effort to know them personally, General Harmar had stood his ground.

"Yes, sir," I said.

"You are Lieutenant Morrow, are you not?"

"Yes, sir."

"I was quite well acquainted with your father, sir, and recall with pleasure the letter you wrote me relative to being willing to teach here during your sabbatical."

"Thank you, sir."

"That was a damned lie you told Lieutenant Denny in defense of Phineas Ford, was it not?"

"No, sir," I said, "it was not."

"Young man, would you be prepared to say that with your right hand on the Holy Bible?"

"Yes, sir, I would."

"Yes, I think you would," the Governor said, straightened his shoulders and glared at me. In this pose he reminded me of certain of my Philadelphia fellow schoolmasters who, with rods in their hands, used their privileged positions to intimidate students.

Looking the Governor squarely in the eyes, I said: "I will find out, sir, if it is convenient for General Harmar to see you at this time." I am under the impression that my statement startled Governor St. Clair somewhat.

While admitted at once, of course, by General Harmar, it might be interesting to conjecture upon what the Governor's reaction is likely to have been, had he been asked to wait. Almost immediately after entering the inner office, I heard the Governor's voice ring out. "Damn it, sir, such wanton disrespect of authority cannot be tolerated in this army."

A heated discussion, clearly audible to me, followed. Its upshot meant our army would lose the services of Simon Kenton's men. Expert Indian fighters or no, Governor St. Clair contended that in order to take part in the expedition, the Kentonians must follow Army Regulations, shear off their long hair, and wear queue ties. This they would not do, General Harmar said, and pleaded with the Governor to look upon these volunteers as scouts. "A hundred scouts for an army of this size!" Governor St. Clair roared. "General Harmar, you must be stark mad." After making his point of view an official order, Governor St. Clair stalked out of headquarters and took to his bed.

"We want our whiskey!" Upon reaching Fort Washington's main gate, this is what the some seven hundred Virginia militiamen began shouting, in protest of the Governor's no-whiskey-within-the-confines-of-the-fort order.

Once they were inside the fort, bedlam reigned. Most of the militiamen were quite drunk. Refusing to be assigned to their barracks, they mulled about the parade, shouting out that their enlistment periods were up. If their request was not honored, they were going home.

Colonels John Hardin and Robert Trotter had arrived at Fort Washington somewhat in advance of their men. The truce effected between these two officers in Louisville was over. Such was their open animosity that, as they glared at each other in General Harmar's inner office, it was possible to evision an enraged tiger meeting a hungry boa constrictor in a jungle.

Hardin, a small, plump man, considerably past middle-age, spoke with the injured air of a martyr. The situation now ensuing on the parade, he contended, was the direct result of Colonel Trotter's conniving. Yes, he— Hardin—was in command of all the militiamen. Colonel Trotter, however, being in command of the three battalions, had the closer contact with the men. Trotter had used this advantage to undermine his immediate superior. By surreptitious methods he had won over Majors Hall, McMullen, and Ray, who in the beginning had been most cooperative, but were now behaving with insufferable disrespect. By permitting gross laxity in disciplinary measures and turning the march from Louisville into a drunken orgy, Trotter had ingratiated himself with the volunteers. It was Trotter who had told the militiamen about the Governor's no-whiskey order, information which he —Hardin—had asked Trotter to keep secret. In a fiery speech that bordered upon treason, Trotter had told the men their enlistment agreements stated they would receive daily whiskey allowances and that daily meant daily. Four miles off from Fort Washington, Trotter had permitted the militiamen to drink their fill. It was then that Trotter suggested that the men should gain their objective by resorting to unified clamor. "His object, of course," Colonel Hardin concluded, "was to ingratiate himself with his men. As you know, sir, Colonel Trotter is a lawyer who aspires to public office. Having no war record of his own, worth mentioning, he wishes to acquire one here— at my expense and with no regard for the welfare of the Army of the United States of America."

Colonel Trotter had listened to Colonel Hardin with his eyes half-closed, a benign, amused expression playing across his florid face. A tall, fleshy middle-aged man, he arose and moved toward General Harmar's desk with the slow, deliberate steps of a trial lawyer. "Colonel Hardin's accusations," he said in a deep, self-assured voice, "are, of course, ridiculous. He is, I am most sorry to say, an embittered man.

"True, I do not possess Colonel Hardin's illustrious war record. I was not a private during Lord Dunmore's War and named honorary ensign at its conclusion. True, I was not a noncommissioned officer of General Morgan's riflemen corps and, like Colonel Hardin, I have never been wounded in battle.

"True, I felt it advisable to be liked and respected by my fellow Kentuckians. True, I am a lawyer, aspiring to public office. But at heart I am a soldier to the core, sir, as my militia activities will prove.

"And never, never was I disloyal to Colonel Hardin, sir, albeit our disagreements as to how militiamen should be disciplined were many and varied. True, I did permit my men to drink whiskey, as Colonel Hardin stated, four miles from here. Untrue, manifestly untrue that I did so without good reason. The rumor of the Governor's no-whiskey ruling had been circulating about even while we were still in Louisville. When asked, I admitted to the fact. Sir, I will never lie to my men! Sir, by the time we were four miles away dissatisfaction of the Governor's order had reached such proportions that my men were on the verge of riot. Colonel Hardin, not being close to his men, was unaware of how serious the situation was. I got the matter settled by allowing drinks all around and assuring my Kentuckians that you, being a man of good reason and understanding, sir, would listen with sympathy to their pleas."

Concluding his statement, Colonel Trotter sat down, apparently quite pleased with his presentation. At this moment Governor St. Clair, now in a somewhat better state of health, stormed into headquarters. His face livid with rage, such was the Governor's indignation that his false teeth had come loose and his words, addressed to Colonel Hardin, came out as a wooden chatter. "This is insufferable, sir," he said. "You will see to it that order is immediately restored."

There was between Colonel Hardin and the Governor considerable coolness, for Hardin considered himself as having been betrayed. In Louisville the Governor had at first named Hardin sole commander of the Virginia militiamen. Such, however, was the strength of Trotter's opposition that St. Clair had been compelled to agree to the Harmar-suggested compromise.

"That is Colonel Trotter's duty and obligation, sir," Colonel Hardin replied quite testily. "I have already reminded him of his responsibility."

Wheeling about, the Governor glared at Colonel Trotter. The antagonism between these two men, as was generally known, bordered on hatred and had begun before their recent clash at Louisville. Although a sturdy believer that governors and generals should never openly admit to the committing of an error, St. Clair freely acknowledged he had made one in assuring the British at Niagara that the Harmar Expedition was not being directed against them. The British had lost no time passing this information on to the Indians.

While most people were content to look upon the Governor's action as being a diplomatic maneuver which might well have been successful, Colonel Robert Trotter, however, had not allowed it to rest. In the very beginning the Governor had wanted a federal officer in command of the militiamen. In opposing this, Colonel Trotter had been most scathing in his remarks before the Virginia Assembly. Citing the Niagara parleys as an indication of the Governor's inability to render prudent judgments, referring to him as the General who had surrendered Fort Ticonderoga without a struggle, he'd charged St. Clair with having failed in every major undertaking in which he was involved. Neglecting to mention that St. Clair had performed well at Trenton and Princeton, Trotter had cried out, "You are asked to accept the judgment of such a man, a man whose very presence presages failure. Was he not a Colonel of the 2nd Regiment Pennsylvania, serving under John Sullivan during the disastrous raid of Canada in 1775? I ask you what happened when he became president of our Continental Congress? Did it not, under him, come to its inglorious end?"

Colonel Trotter had not risen at St. Clair's arrival. "And your explanation, sir?" the Governor said to Colonel Trotter.

With studied insolence, his pudgy hands resting on his protruding stomach, Colonel Trotter said, "Governor, in Louisville it became apparent that our methods of disciplining militiamen do not have a common meeting of minds. Therefore, let us simply say amen to that." His expression narrowed and his face became quite red. "There is no explanation required. I am warning you, sir, in the presence of responsible witnesses. If you do not rescind your order, my Kentuckians will return to their homes."

Without replying to Colonel Trotter, the Governor turned to General Harmar. "I am aware, sir, that you cannot be held responsible for the state of drunkenness in which the Virginia volunteers arrived at this fort. You are, however, accountable for their behavior from now on. I hereby advise you that no order of any nature issued by me, has been rescinded."

The Governor left. As he did, firing began on the parade. "Lieutenant Morrow," the General said, "please find out what the firing is about. When you return, be so kind as to bring with you paper and pen."

"Yes, sir," I said.

I obtained the required information from one of the General's waiters, standing outside the headquarters' door. "The firing is of little consequence, sir," I said upon my return. "The federals are herding in some two dozen of the volunteers' galloping-about horses that had been given whiskied-water."

"Thank you, Lieutenant," General Harmar said and turned to Colonel Hardin. "In your judgment, sir, is Colonel Trotter's statement of the mind of your militiamen an accurate and well-founded appraisal?"

"Colonel Trotter is responsible for it and could have prevented what is now happening," Colonel Hardin said and it occurred to me that General Harmar had never voiced confidence in Hardin, he had merely said he was to be preferred to Colonel Trotter.

Colonel Trotter had laughed outright at Colonel Hardin's reply. "I was about to add," Colonel Hardin said quickly, "if you and I, sir, addressed the men together, they might listen to reason."

"Thank you, Colonel Hardin," General Harmar said and gave his attention to Colonel Trotter. "You are quite certain, sir, that you have not overstated the seriousness of the situation?"

"I am, sir."

"Let us suppose, sir, that I were to tell you that my federal officers would close their eyes to drinking in the barracks, at the end of the day. Herein, would there be room for compromise?"

Trotter smiled blandly. "I am afraid not, sir. My Kentuckians like their nips when the mood strikes them."

"So it's to be all or nothing, Colonel?"

"It would appear so, General."

"Well, that is that then," the General said and turned to me. "Lieutenant Morrow, we may as well get to the business of drawing up a draft for the record of the day. Make a second copy, please, to be sent immediately to New York Town." He began dictating slowly enough for me to write: "On this day Colonel Robert Trotter arrived at Fort Washington with seven hundred Virginia militiamen, most of whom were drunk. In reporting to me that he had lost control over his men, Colonel Trotter said—"

"Just a minute, General!" Colonel Trotter said, jumping up.

"Shall I tell Lieutenant Morrow to tear up that paper, Colonel?" the General inquired.

Colonel Trotter's reply was in the affirmative. Considerable discussion followed, the result being that, while the St. Clair order stood, the federals would close their eyes to drinking within the barracks at the close of day. This arrangement worked out quite well. While pleased to be pulling the wool over St. Clair's eyes, the volunteers, nonetheless feared the man's wrath if caught. Thus there was no drunkenness.

St. Clair's subsequent behavior deserves praise too. Although taking no official cognizance of the arrangement, he varied his nightly practice of entering a barrack, without warning, and conducting an inspection tour. Now, before making an entrance, he invariably stopped to chat a while with the sentinel. As he walked stern-faced up and down the aisles, he saw no signs of whiskey. I have it, also, on the best of authorities, that Governor Arthur St. Clair later called upon Brevet Brigadier General Josiah Harmar for the express purpose of complimenting him most highly for having eradicated the United States Army from a ticklish situation.

XI

Of the Virginians, Lieutenant Denny wrote: "General Harmar was much disheartened at the kind of people from Kentucky. One-half certainly served no other purpose than to swell their number. If the leading *patriots* of Kentucky don't turn out rascals, then some of the men that I know are greatly mistaken."

Like the Pennsylvanians, the Virginians were mostly old men and inexperienced young boys. Although supposed to be adequately armed and supplied, they had arrived at Fort Washington almost destitute of camp kettles and axes. The fort did not have enough of these essential articles to make up the deficit.

More than half the Virginians had come without arms of any sort, many carried early French muskets with gooseneck cocks, few indeed had rifles which did not need to be repaired.

It became absolutely necessary to hold over the Virginians at Fort Washington for ten days. This length of time was needed not only to render their arms and supplies reasonably adequate, but also to teach them the rudiments of Indian warfare. In carrying out their tasks our federal officers and artificers had very little sleep and became extremely tired men. Such was the pressure of work for the General's scribe, I could not leave the fort to be with Melissa. During these ten days she stayed at the Kummerschmitt's, sleeping in their loft.

Since the Virginians were "permitted" to remain at the fort, the Pennsylvanians felt themselves discriminated against. In a formal pronouncement of protest, their grievance committee noted that, among other instances of gross partiality, the Virginians were able to have bread baked in the fort's ovens, while theirs had to be baked on hot stones or shovels. When Major Paul brought in this particular grievance, he mentioned that I should turn it over to the Federal Officers' Board of Review.

Phineas Ford had taken to the woods, to scout, on the day I resumed my duties as General Harmar's scribe. He returned to Fort Washington on October 3rd, around noon, looking disgustingly hale and hearty. "Christ, Tom," he said upon arriving at headquarters, "what's wrong with you?"

He meant that, because of fatigue, I could scarcely keep my eyes open. "I haven't slept for twenty-three hours and I don't know when I'll be able to," I said and was too tired to explain that I'd been up the whole night trying to get the messed-up accounts with the horse-masters settled. Still far from being in order, the army stood to lose heavily in this arena. Horse-masters were paid not only a dollar a day for their charges, but were to be reimbursed in full for all animals lost during the expedition. Since more than half of the horses had arrived only the day previously, we did not know how many there were, nor to whom they belonged. Had we had on hand as many animals as the horse-masters' invoices indicated, as Ensign Gaines had said, we'd be able to field a rattling, good, spanking company of hussars.

"I hear the army's all set to march out?" Phineas said.

"Yes, tomorrow morning," I said.

"Melissa says 'hello,'" Phineas said, "and told me to tell you she'd like to be remembered to her husband."

"How is she?" I asked.

"Blooming like a rose!" Phineas said and clicked his teeth. "Tom, I've got to take my hat off to you. I didn't figure you to be that good."

Albeit generally irked by remarks of this nature, no matter how kindly their intent, in this case I could not help smiling. Although married now approximately for two weeks, I was still a husband only by proxy. In the beginning I was too weak to be otherwise, then the time became un-propitious for Melissa to be a wife, then it was necessary for me to devote all my time and energies in forestalling the horse-masters' efforts to rob the army.

Phineas misconstrued the reason for my smile. "Nice to think about it anyway, eh!" he said and gave me a playful nudge in the ribs.

"Phineas," I said, "for the past two days the General has been wondering where you've been keeping yourself."

"Well, here I am," Phineas said. "Let's go in and see him."

"He's at the Pennsylvanians' encampment," I said, "making final marching arrangements."

"I passed through there this morning," Phineas said. "What the hell are they doing with wooden snaps?"

"It's a long and dreary story," I said. "I'll tell you all about it when I'm not so tired."

"It's one hell of an army, isn't it?" Phineas said.

"Yes," I said, "it is."

"When will the General get back here?" Phineas asked.

I glanced at the headquarters' timepiece. "Not for three hours. That would be the General's estimate. He may well be held up longer."

"Well, I'll go back to Emil," Phineas said. "God damn it, Tom, I'm worried about Emil. The baby."

"It was born!"

"Hell, no, it wasn't born. How long does it take to have a baby?" Phineas had, of course, put this question rhetorically.

"Nine months," I said.

"Well, it's nine months," Phineas said, "and there's no baby. Does it ever take longer than nine months?"

"I'm quite sure it doesn't," I said. "Sometimes babies are born prematurely, but it never takes more than nine months."

"Well, then something's wrong," Phineas said.

"Frequently a woman makes a mistake about when her baby was con-ceived," I said.

"I know all about that," Phineas said.

"Phineas, what are you driving at?" In spite of my sleepiness, I became wide awake.

"I don't know," Phineas said. "All I know is that there's no baby and Emil's worried to hell and back about something. He started to tell me about it, but that's when Melissa saw me. She came over and Emil had to clam up."

Shortly after Phineas left, Ensign Gaines, looking tired as all other of the fort's officers, came into headquarters. As he opened the door, a gust of wind blew all my papers on to the floor. "I'm sorry, Tom," Ensign Gaines said and helped me gather up the papers.

The papers had been spread all over my desk. The horse-master's records were so mixed up, the task of bringing order out of chaos was like trying to solve a Chinese puzzle. "It was my fault," I said. "I should have had them weighted down."

"What do the invoices show?" Ensign Gaines asked.

"According to my records," I said, "the horse-masters should have delivered three-hundred-thirteen horses."

"We've just finished the count," Ensign Gaines said. "There are exactly a hundred-nineteen horses. Look up how many horses Mr. Wells says he brought."

I fumbled through the invoices. "Twenty-four."

"That's what he's got," Ensign Gaines said, "so Wells is honest. I thought so. The rest of them are crooks."

"What are we going to do, George?" I asked. "They'll say the horses were lost between Louisville and here. There are no Louisville invoices or records of any kind. It's their word against ours."

"Yes, I know, Tom," Ensign Gaines said, then muttered more to himself than to me, "and with those crooks around, it'll knock the hell out of our line of march." At this time I did not understand what Ensign Gaines meant, but, since apparently it had to do with military matters, there seemed no point in asking for an explanation.

"I'm afraid the army's stuck with the price of the 'lost' horses," I said.

"Well, not for all of them," Ensign Gaines said grimly. "We'll call the horse-masters together and talk this thing out. When will the records be straightened out?"

"Not before midnight at best, George."

"Well, midnight or dawn," Ensign Gaines said, "we'll have a talk with them." After a moment of hesitation, he said bravely, "Is there any way I can help you, Tom?"

"No, but thank you," I said. "Only I understand the intricacies of how this bookkeeping problem is being approached."

While Ensign Gaines couldn't completely disguise his feeling of relief, his effort to do so was admirable and I am certain, if asked, he would have made an effort to help. He was honest enough not to pretend he planned upon doing otherwise. "In that case," he said, "I might as well lie down for a while."

XII

When, during late afternoon, General Harmar returned to headquarters the rings around his eyes were as black as gunpowder. "It's incredible, Tom," he said, "simply unbelievable." Those Pennsylvanians who that morning had been issued flints, the General told me, had immediately begun snapping them. To forestall wholesale participation in this pastime, the Pennsylvanians were not going to be issued orthodox flints until the army was well on the march.

"Phineas Ford returned while you were away, sir," I said.

"Where is he?" the General inquired.

"Somewhere about, sir," I said. "He said he'd be back shortly."

"How very sporting of him," the General said and went into the innner office.

In due time, Phineas arrived. "Things are worse than I thought, Tom," he said.

"I would say that by this time the General is accustomed to bad news," I said.

"I'm talking about Emil and Kitty," Phineas said. "I'll tell you about it later."

When Phineas and I entered the inner office, the General had not yet quite pushed himself up into an erect sitting position. The heaviness of his eyelids indicated that he had been sleeping at his desk. "Come to the point quickly, please, Phineas," the General said. "We'll discuss the details tomorrow while on the march."

"Little Turtle's in command of everything," Phineas said. "Only Miamis, Shawnees and maybe a few Delawares will be fighting us."

The General winced, for this was most unhappy news. If we had any hope of prevailing, it lay in having the Indian chiefs start quarreling amongst themselves over tactics.

"You're certain of this, Phineas?"

Phineas nodded. "I was talking to Little Turtle."

"Where?"

"At his main village."

Personally acquainted with Little Turtle, General Harmar accounted him to be a most reasonable man and a brilliant military strategist and always referred to the Miami chief by his Indian name. "Did you give Michikinikwa my personal regards?" the General inquired.

"Sure," Phineas said. "Little Turtle says 'hello' to you too and told me to say he feels sorry for you."

The General smiled dryly. "You're sure that no Wyandots and Mingos were around?"

"They're all back at their villages and, like I told you before, there haven't been any Ottawas this far west in over a year."

"What do you make of it?"

"Little Turtle doesn't need the Wyandots and Mingos. Nothing's changed, Josiah. Little Turtle'll draw you into the woods, far north as you'll go."

"He won't defend his villages?"

"The Indians were already starting to gather their corn and were carting it away. I could see it all over, Josiah, they're all set for a fast pull-out."

"Michikinikwa allowed you to witness this?"

Phineas shrugged his shoulders. "He knows I know what he's going to do and he knows you've got orders to engage him. With the kind of militiamen you were handed! He's laughing about those boys, Josiah, and knows every day they're in the woods things'll get worse for us. If he can make you chase him to the North Pole, it'll suit him fine."

"Were you able to estimate the Indians' equipment?"

"Enough to be able to say they're in a hell of a lot better shape than we are."

"Anything else?"

"Nothing that you don't already know, Josiah. You'll get the hell knocked out of you if you move your army past the main villages."

"Thank you, Phineas," the General said, indicated the interview was over, and as Phineas and I took our leave he asked me to send for Majors Doughty and Wyllys.

When we were alone, Phineas pulled me to a far end of the outer office where we could talk without being overheard. "God damn it, Tom," he said, "Emil's dead sure he's not the baby's father."

"What!"

"You know those trading trips Emil takes?"

"Yes."

"Well, Emil went on one right after Christmas and was gone for six weeks. It was when he got back that Kitty told him she was going to have a baby. You remember that young fellow, Andrew, the one I had you say 'hello' to the day your cabin was raised?"

"Yes."

"While Emil was away, Kitty lived with Andrew and his folks. Emil figures it had to be Andrew."

"That's hard to believe," I said. "I don't necessarily mean because of Andrew. I mean because of Kitty."

"I know," Phineas said, "but Kitty didn't want Emil to go off and cried about it. Emil thinks she got lonely and let Andrew make her. He's trying so hard to find an excuse for her that he's got himself to thinking that while Andrew was giving it to her, Kitty was pretending to herself that it was *him*."

I shook my head.

"That doesn't figure with me either," Phineas said and glanced at his knuckles which I could see were quite raw. "Besides, Andrew and I just had a little talk. Andrew admits he tried to get somewhere with Kitty, but swears to God Kitty was thinking so much about Emil that she didn't even know what he was playing for."

"That I believe," I said.

"So do I, God damn it," Phineas said.

"Could there be anybody else?"

"No," Phineas said, "there couldn't."

"Then Emil's having a brainstorm," I said. "Kitty just thought she was pregnant at Christmastime. She became pregnant after Emil's return. Mistakes of such a nature certainly aren't uncommon. It could be especially quite possible in the case of a highly strung woman like Kitty Kummerschmitt."

"Didn't you hear me right!" Phineas said. "I said that it was when Emil came back from his trip that Kitty told him she was in a family way."

"Well?"

"Well!" Phineas said. "That means Emil hasn't been to bed with Kitty since he's back."

"Why not?"

"Why not! Tom, have you lost your mind? Did you want Emil to kill what he thought was his own baby?"

"Phineas," I said, "Emil wouldn't have killed anybody. You can have sexual intercourse for months after a woman becomes pregnant."

"Are you telling me the truth!"

"Of course, I am."

"Well, I'll be damned!" Phineas said and deviated from the main subject long enough to explain that any number of times this lack of knowledge on his part had thwarted a night of pleasure.

"Emil doesn't know that either," Phineas said grimly and getting back to the subject. "Nor does Kitty. So it's for sure if Kitty got in a family way when she told Emil she did, she wouldn't have let Andrew take her to bed."

I was mentally counting off the months. There was no doubt about it, the baby should be born by now. Yet it was remotely possible if you added actual days, rather than going by months, everything might be all right. "When is the baby expected?" I asked.

"Mrs. Robinson says not for about six weeks."

"Good Lord!" I said.

"Just suppose you were Emil," Phineas said. "Six weeks! Wouldn't you have to figure that Andrew kept pushing and finally got into Kitty?"

While I would not have phrased it quite like that, this is what I could not help thinking.

"And to make things still worse," Phineas said, "there won't be a midwife around when the baby *is* born."

"What happened to Mrs.—"

"Robinson," Phineas said. "You know what a big jackass that old hag is?"

"I recall you said that she was one."

"Emil paid a visit to Mrs. Robinson, pretended he was just sort of talking, and asked her if babies sometimes took more than nine months to be born. He didn't fool the old bitch though. She laughed and told Emil that it's a wise baby who knows his own father. For that, Emil smacked Mrs. Robinson's mouth. She got sore and told Emil the only way she'd bring Kitty's baby into the world was if its *real* father asked her."

XIII

Around midnight Ensign Gaines came into headquarters. At this moment there was considerable shouting on the parade. "How's it coming, Tom?" Ensign Gaines asked.

"Five more minutes."

"Good," Ensign Gaines said. "I'll round up the horse-masters."

"Where?"

"There's no other place but in the latrine," Ensign Gaines said and apologized for being so sleepy he hadn't thought to tell me where.

"What's all the shouting about?" I asked.

"Some militiamen needed light to play dice," Ensign Gaines said, "so they built a fire right under the northwest blockhouse."

The last of the shells, Ensign Gaines told me, had been filled just before it became too dark to continue work. A great deal of loose powder was still lying about. "Don't those fellows believe in sleep?" I said.

"They're troublemakers. They're going back to Louisville tomorrow," Ensign Gaines said and left.

When I stepped out of headquarters I could see men beating out the fire with boards. Sparks rose high into the air. It might be just as well, I told myself while moving across the parade, not to dwell on the thought of what would happen if a spark was blown through one of the blockhouse's gun slots.

Fort Washington was still far from being asleep. The quartermaster's building was lit up, for the task of outfitting wasn't anywhere near complete. The forges in the armories were going full blast and men were carting supplies to the center of the parade. As I passed through this group, everybody seemed to be arguing about something. Ensign Sedam was in charge. He told me there'd been a big argument in the barracks that evening. During drills men of equal sizes had been placed side by side and nobody had objected. Now that the army was about to march out, the militiamen had suddenly decided they wanted to march beside friends.

"How was it settled, Cornelius?" I asked.

"They'll at least march out of the fort as they were," Cornelius told me.

As I already knew, our outstandingly fine latrine master had simply given up upon the arrival of the militiamen. This conscientious man's pride and joy now smelled to high heaven and his neatly whitewashed walls were written over with obscenities. Upon my entrance, "Gentlemen," Ensign Gaines said to a dozen surly looking horse-masters, "this is Lieutenant Morrow."

Then the arguments began. Three hours later we had the number of horses as reported leaving Louisville down by over a hundred and had gained the animosity of all the horse-masters except Mr. Wells. Another half hour went by before I had signatures on the new forms. Ensign Gaines, who was still young enough to think everything in this world is either jet black or snow white, was far from satisfied. "But I've got to hand it to you, Tom," he said. "When it comes to arguing over figures, you really can give them hell."

His statement, I believe, may be considered to be correct. Those horse-masters, Mr. Wells excepted, were out-and-out thieves. I had fought them hammer-and-tongs, all the way, with all the self-righteous vehemence of someone willing to sell the army flour at the rate of twenty-five dollars a barrel.

"Well, at any rate, Tom," Ensign Gaines said, "I can at last say 'good night,' or rather 'good morning' to you."

"Unhappily," I said, "I've still some paperwork to do. If I don't see you before you leave, George, best of luck and happy hunting."

"Happy hunting" had been voiced frequently by our officers during the past few days. While the expression never had sat too well with me, and I hadn't used it before, now it came out quite naturally.

"Thank you, Tom," Ensign Gaines said and gave me his hand.

Although considerable activity was still in effect about the fort, headquarters, when I returned, was empty. My task now was to draw up ten officers' wills and last testaments, the necessary information having been brought to me at the last minute. While the fort had a form book for wills, there weren't any sheets printed with the necessary introductory material. Thus, in each case, I had to write the whole thing out.

Dawn was fast approaching before I was finished. Soon officers began coming into headquarters to read over my efforts and to affix their signatures in the presence of witnesses. While this was going on day broke and our drummers started beating the reveille.

It was most difficult to comprehend that our army was at last going to march out. At the beating of assembly, all the officers left. As the last one did, Phineas entered headquarters. "You still up, Tom?" he inquired.

"No," I said, "I'm sound asleep in a luxurious feather bed, lying on silk sheets under exquisitely designed damask coverlets."

"Don't get sore," Phineas said. "Tom, Emil's in a real bad way. It's damned important that you and Melissa talk some sense into him."

"What in the world can we do?"

"Emil likes and respects you, Tom," Phineas said. "Just tell him 'what the hell' if Kitty did go to bed with somebody else. She loves him, even he knows that. It's not like she cheated while he was around."

"It doesn't strike me as being quite that simple," I said, "but I'll do what I can."

The drummers began beating the march. Phineas started to leave. In theory he was the commander of some thirty Pennsylvanians, designated on the rolls as being "spies and guides." While it is reasonable to assume that Phineas would not see too much of these gentlemen while on the march, it was considered to be good form for him to be with them when they left the fort.

"Take care of yourself, Phineas," I said.

"Don't worry about me," Phineas said and clicked his teeth.

When I went to the headquarters' door, the army was just starting to move. The spies and guides brought up the van. By running fast, Phineas just managed to get into place. He would be the first man to go through the main gate.

While running, Phineas had let down his hair. I don't know why. Was it a gesture of defiance to Governor St. Clair, who stood on the wall walk, just off the main gate? Wearing his beaver, St. Clair was attired in the full dress uniform of a general in the United States Army and, of course, everyone was supposed to salute him as they passed through the main gate. Phineas' salute was more like a wave of greeting.

After Phineas' contingent came an advance company of thirty federals, then the cavalry. McMullen's battalion of two hundred Virginia militiamen were next. Apparently the situation had changed since I'd spoken to Cornelius Sedam. The militiamen were not lined up according to size. Their general comportment and manner of marching, I should say, was not in the accepted manner as described in Baron von Steuben's Manual.

By contrast the federals looked quite smart and they did march beautifully. Four-abreast, they flanked the General and staff, music and colors. The General rode superbly and so did his officers, although I am prepared to say all were next to sound asleep on their horses. The General would ride to the Pennsylvanians' encampment, to be on hand for the formal joining of the Pennsylvania militiamen with the army. Thereafter he'd return to Fort Washington for one day of sleep and rest.

The artillery, ammunition, officers' baggage, and the packhorses and cattle were flanked on the right by Major Ray's battalion of Virginians. Ray's were the Virginians' elite. These men marched with considerable dispatch and were lined up according to size. The men of this battalion tended to favor Hardin, although Ray was an out-and-out Trotter man. Due to a shortage of men, two hundred Pennsylvanians had been brought to the fort that morning. Under Major Paul, they were on the opposite flank. I could not see them.

With almost no room between them and the cattle, came Major Hall's battalion of Virginians, followed by a rear guard of thirty federals. Hall's men were acknowledged to be the worst specimens of the entire army although Hall, now showing signs of becoming a Hardin man, was considered to be a better officer than either McMullen or Ray. Once on the march, Pennyslvanians would take over the position now assumed by Hall's. Thus, as may be seen at a glance, the flower of our militiamen were assigned the task of preventing volunteers from stealing the officers' baggage and making certain our horse-masters would not let their charges stray.

BOOK FOUR

CINCINNATI, 1790–91

I

When the rear guard had marched through Fort Washington's main gate, I moved to my quarters to change into buckskins. It might be said that I now considered my career in the United States Army as being over. Although I had not tendered a formal resignation, my understanding with the General was that once the army marched out, I would go on furlough. When the General returned, I would help him assemble the material to be presented in his defense at the Court of Inquiry which would surely be convened.

I am certain I am correct in stating that not a single federal officer believed the expedition would be a success. Many predicted out-and-out debacle. The General, I would say, actually relished appearing before a Court of Inquiry. Entertaining no doubts that he would be exonerated, he welcomed the opportunity to present a case strong enough to convince Congress that the act passed during the previous April, increasing the entire United States Army from 840 to 1250 men, was inadequate. The expected failure, deep in the Ohio woods, the General hoped, would prove conclusively that the Indians could be defeated only by enlisting a strong, well-trained army and erecting a string of forts from Cincinnati to the Great Lakes.

Without saying it in so many words, the General had suggested that life might be simpler for me if St. Clair were permitted to labor under the impression that I had marched out with the army. "The Governor will no doubt have considerable spare time on his hands and will use it to go over the records," is the way the General had put it. "I am reasonably certain, if he thinks you are here, he may be inclined to make full use of your services."

Thus, in order that the Governor would not per chance see me, once I was in buckskins, I slipped out of Fort Washington through one of the side gates.

No one was awake yet when I reached the Kummerschmitt inlot, which was just as well, for by now I was so weary and sleepy, I doubt if the strength remained in me to even say "good morning" to Melissa. Entering our cabin presented no difficulty, for our door, whose hinges were buffalo thongs, could not be locked from the outside.

Within were two of the accepted kind of Cincinnati beds—deerskins, tied to the corners of the cabin and supported by saplings. While for propriety's sake, Melissa and I had permitted these uncomfortable and confined means of resting to remain, we raised the puncheons and slept on the skins of the two bears Emil Kummerschmitt had eventually slaughtered, only to discover that their alimentary canals did not produce more than the usual amount of oil. Throwing myself onto the bearskins, which made a far more comfortable mattress than might at first thought be imagined, I went immediately to sleep.

Eighteen hours later, when I finally opened my eyes, sunlight coming through the bear-oil wrapping paper which served as our window panes, cast a golden glow about the cabin, rendering it most cheerful. Soon Melissa appeared in the doorway. "You have no idea how glad I am to see you," I said.

After closing the door and board-bolting it, Melissa moved over to me and sat down. "And may I presume," she said, "that at last I have a husband?"

"You may," I said and drew her to me.

There is little to say about the first uninterrupted two weeks of Melissa's and my married life—other than that we were deliriously happy.

All we did, actually, was bask in each other's company. October is a beautiful month in Cincinnati. The trees are beginning to turn color and the goldenrod is still at its best. Both Melissa and I enjoyed walking for the sheer pleasure of it. I don't think there was a girdled lane in Cincinnati which we didn't traverse. Discovering the paths which led to inlots, we paid our respects to those who had raised our cabin. Since the corn was already laid by, there was ample time to chat.

I would estimate there were no more than ninety people living in the settlement. This is another way of saying a third of the population, alarmed by the Indian threat, had returned to Louisville or Lexington which is from where most Cincinnatians came, in contrast to the people inhabiting Columbia and Northbend, who were mostly from Pennsylvania and New Jersey.

Among those who had left was Andrew and his family. More or less by request, at least so I gathered. After being slapped by Emil, Mrs. Robinson had lost no time circulating a rumor that Andrew was the father of Kitty Kummerschmitt's unborn child. As a result Andrew had been forced to resign from the local committee. The rumor, I gathered, was actually a straw that broke the camel's back. Andrew, a ladies' man, had been in plenty of hot water before. His antics in this arena, I was told, had been tolerated only because a lawyer's services were badly needed to straighten out the deeds to people's lots, which had been so haphazardly surveyed that no one was certain where the boundaries of his property were.

From time to time Melissa and I talked about Kitty and Emil. Actually that is all we could do. I saw virtually nothing of Emil. In the morning, as he left his cabin, he'd acknowledge my presence with a grim nod, then take to his outlot. As I understood it, he'd just sit there and stare.

Kitty remained in seclusion. I don't believe I saw her even once during the period of which I am speaking. "Emil has said nothing to her about the child," Melissa told me. "He scarcely talks to her. If he happens to brush against her, he jerks abruptly away, as if he had touched something which is vile."

"What about Kitty?"

"She's bearing up nobly, Tom. She's clinging to the hope that Emil will relent after the baby is born. They were so happy before all this."

"Have you had a real heart-to-heart talk with Kitty?" I asked.

"Not the way you mean," Melissa said. "Kitty is so loyal to Emil, she simply will not admit that it's possible he can think she was untrue to him."

"Not untrue to him!"

"I don't know what I think, Tom. You know how religious Kitty is? One day, while I was in the loft, I couldn't help overhearing Kitty while she was praying. She begged the Lord to give Emil the faith to believe in her. 'There has been no man but my husband, dear Lord!' she cried out. 'Make my husband understand this.'"

"What's she's actually saying," I said, "is that—well, while she gave in to someone else, it was circumstances rather than deep affection which prompted what she did."

Melissa shook her head. "Her prayer was quite lengthy. Later on I heard her say, in most definite terms, that no man except Emil had touched her and that he was the father of her unborn child."

"The only possible explanation then," I said, "is that Kitty is suffering from a form of temporary insanity, brought on by extreme remorse. You see that happen time after time in the cases of people about to be hanged. They will not admit, even to themselves, that they are guilty."

"Reasonable as your explanation would seem to be," Melissa said, "I am unable to convince myself that it holds in Kitty Kummerschmitt's case."

II

Beginning on October 15th or thereabouts, Melissa and I were compelled to return to the world of realities. During the late midmorning Quartermaster's-Assistant Horatius O'Malley came to our cabin. "The Governor wants to see you, Tom," Horatius said.

"Oh, good Lord!" I said.

At the moment Melissa was in our cabin, straightening things up. In a flash she was at the doorway, regarding me anxiously. "What does the Governor want to see me about?" I asked Horatius.

"I don't know," Horatius said.

Turning to Melissa, I made a futile gesture with my hands. "I'll have to go," I said.

"By all means," Melissa said quite frigidly. "And please be so kind as to give His Excellency my warmest personal regards."

Stepping over to Melissa, I kissed her cheek. "He can't do too much," I said. "I can end my furlough any time I wish, by resigning."

"That sounds much too uncomplicated to me," Melissa said. "Be careful, Tom. If need be, that man can also be a wily fox."

Once under way, I asked Horatius how the Governor had discovered I was still in Cincinnati. "Remember those sixty cows we were billed for, but didn't get?" Horatius said.

"Yes."

"Well, they came in yesterday," Horatius said, "that is, forty did. Some town folks wanted to buy the cows on credit. I guess they mentioned you were still around."

"What did the Governor say to the town folks?"

"He said, no, they couldn't have the cows."

When we went through the main gate, I could see the cows. They were grazing at the far end of the parade. Mooing loudly, they appeared to be restless. "They look well-enough fed," I said. "What kind are they?"

"Holsteins."

"Holsteins are good milking cows, aren't they?"

"They sure are."

"Who's taking care of them?"

"Nobody, the tenders went on down to Louisville with the flotilla."

"Aren't cows supposed to be milked daily?"

"Twice daily," Horatius said, "otherwise they go dry. That's why I'd never be a dairy farmer. Twice a day. Seven days a week. If a dairy farmer gets sick, he's got to milk his cows anyway."

There were only eighty-five federals left at the fort and a sizable portion of these were needed for patrol. "Have we got the men to milk all those cows twice a day?" I asked.

"The Governor's going to have them slaughtered and salted down."

"All our butchers are on the march," I said.

"The Governor says a good soldier should know how to butcher a cow or any other kind of an animal. *He* can! So he's going to show us how."

Governor St. Clair, I learned, was in headquarters. Upon my arrival there, he sat at General Harmar's desk, eating lunch. There was roast beef, wild asparagus, a bottle of wine, bread, but none of the fruit tarts of which St. Clair was so fond. The Governor was drinking wine because Dr. Allison had told him if he expected to get over his gout, he must give up brandy and rich foods. "And no butter on your bread," Dr. Allison had said. There was no butter on the Governor's bread, but there was a huge chunk on the asparagus.

"It was most kind of you to come, *Lieutenant* Morrow," Governor St. Clair said, accentuating the word lieutenant, "please be seated."

"Thank you, sir," I said. "May I inquire if there is news of the army?"

"You may, sir. It has been moving ahead at the rate of about six miles a day. This is not good, yet it is not so bad either. We have not yet engaged the enemy. We are, I would estimate, by now within thirty miles of the main villages. Will you join me in a glass of wine?"

"Thank you, sir."

"I have read over your enlistment arrangement with General Harmar. It is a somewhat unusual one, is it not?"

"The circumstances were somewhat unusual, sir."

"Yes, they were and may I take this opportunity, sir, to compliment you upon the excellent manner in which our records have been kept. I have gone over them most carefully. You have rendered the United States Army a considerable service."

"Thank you, sir."

"And now you are in a position to render her further service," the Governor said.

I said nothing.

"Another month's pay is shortly due the militiamen," the Governor said. "An express from General Harmar states that if the militiamen are not paid on site, they will go home. While the General can, of course, hold them on by force, it is understandable that this might undermine their morale. That is General Harmar's way of looking at it. Not mine. He feels that rather than asserting his authority, it might be just as well to humor the militiamen in this instance. Do you understand now, how you may render a great service to the United States Army?"

The Governor had not smiled, even ever so slightly, in putting his question. "Yes, sir," I said. "Since we have no money, you want me to prepare promissory notes for some eleven hundred militiamen?"

"That is correct, Lieutenant."

"We haven't enough paper on hand for such a task," I said.

"I noticed that during your final days as the United States Army's scribe, you were using wrapping paper," the Governor said. "There is plenty of it around. Quartermaster's-Assistant O'Malley will gather it up for you."

"It has to be pressed with an iron, sir, or it's too rumpled."

"I didn't realize that," the Governor said. "I will speak to Corporal O'Malley and see to it this is done."

Again I must note the absence of even a trace of a smile on the Governor's face, as he announced the sudden advancement of Quartermaster's-Assistant Horatius O'Malley, who up to this moment had been a private. "What about the estoppages?" I inquired.

"They must be assessed in full. Those accrued before leaving as well as those lost in the course of the expedition."

"That will make for rather complicated promissory notes," I said.

"Yes, it will," the Governor said. "You will have to make up notes with many blank spaces, to be filled in later."

Since their pay was three dollars a month with ninety cents deducted for food, soap and articles of such nature, it was not hard to guess the militiamen's desire for reimbursement on site rather than waiting until they were mustered out. "May I point out, sir," I said, "that few militiamen indeed will be receiving any pay at all when the estoppages have been assessed?"

"You may, sir," the Governor replied sharply, "and my answer is that this is their problem." Rather smugly, he added: "And, of course, also General Harmar's."

Although viewing the task with the greatest displeasure, I saw no way, in good conscience, to refuse doing it. Melissa, when I told her what had transpired, became quite incensed. "To put those promissory notes into proper order," she said, "means you'll have to be on the scene to get the estoppages settled?"

"Most probably," I said.

"Eleven hundred notes! How can you possibly prepare that many?"

"It'll just have to be done."

"I'll help you," Melissa said. "That is, if His Excellency will not think it is contrary to Regulations to permit someone without a queue tie to render such a service to the United States Army."

His Excellency did grant Melissa such permission and, since she was my wife, he also granted us permission to take up quarters at the fort. Since Melissa was performing her services without pay, she had reserved for herself the right to visit Kitty Kummerschmitt daily. Although there were no Indians roaming about Cincinnati at the moment, I was unwilling for Melissa to walk to the Kummerschmitts' inlot without a corporal's guard. While Melissa scoffed at this and wished no favors from Governor St. Clair, I was adamant. When I placed this term before the Governor, he was not pleased. He did, however, acquiesce.

III

Four, possibly five days later, as Melissa and I wrote away furiously in the outer office, Ensign Gaines, accompanied by a sizable escort, arrived at Fort Washington. It was around midmorning.

Ensign Gaines, when he reported at headquarters, was spattered from head to foot with mud. As unual, since Governor St. Clair apparently felt it necessary to keep an eye on Melissa and me, the door to the inner office was open. Noting this, Ensign Gaines dared only make me a futile gesture with his hands, to indicate that he brought unhappy news. In a voice loud enough for Governor St. Clair to hear, he asked me to request an immediate audience, despite his disheveled appearance, for which he apologized.

"You may admit the ensign as he is," Governor St. Clair called out.

Ensign Gaines entered the inner office without closing the door, but quickly turned and did so, no doubt upon the Governor's order. He was closeted with the Governor for possibly a quarter of an hour, before I was called. As I entered the inner office, Ensign Gaines took his leave.

"Please write a dispatch, to be sent off without delay to Secretary of War Henry Knox," Governor St. Clair said and began dictating the moment I had procured a dispatch sheet: *Dear sir, I have the pleasure to inform you of the entire success of General Harmar at the Indian towns on the Miami and St. Joseph rivers, of which he has destroyed five in number and a very great quantity of corn and other vegetable provisions.*

I had trouble convincing myself that I was not dreaming. The Governor was not the sort of person with whom a scribe remarked upon official matters. "I take it, sir," I said, "you wish this sent east through Pittsburgh?"

"I do."

"Shall I send a secondary dispatch through Louisville?"

"You will, and I wish to see you immediately after you have attended to the matter."

With the door between the inner and outer office still open, when I went to Melissa, I addressed her in the official manner required in headquarters. However, with my back to St. Clair, I was able to smile. "Mrs. Morrow," I said, "you will please make a second copy of this dispatch, immediately." In order to be able to stay a moment or so longer, I added: "Are you able to read my writing?"

"Yes, sir," Melissa said and read rapidly. Her eyes opened wide with surprise. "Ensign Gaines," she whispered, "shook his head when he passed me. With his lips he said, 'Militia are revolting.'"

After telling a waiter to call two dispatch bearers, I went into the inner office. "You will prepare to accompany Ensign Gaines when he returns to his command," Governor St. Clair said.

"May I point out, sir, that the promissory notes are only three-quarters compiled?"

"You may, sir," Governor St. Clair said. "It is knowledge of which I am well acquainted." He handed me a sheet of paper upon which the lost-horse records were noted. "Do you know a Mr. Wells?"

"I know he is a horse-master, sir."

"An honest horse-master?"

"That is Ensign Gaines' impression, sir."

"But not yours!"

"It is mine too, sir. Ensign Gaines, being the more familiar with Mr. Wells' *modus operandi* and thus better able to render a judgment, is my reason for answering as I did."

As I spoke, I had been reading the record sheet. Mr. Wells had lost only one horse. The others! One could almost imagine that the horses reported lost en route from Louisville to Fort Washington had been recovered and lost over again.

"Beyond a doubt," the Governor said, "these records indicate considerable falsification."

"I would say so, sir."

"The army stands to lose thousands of dollars here, Lieutenant Morrow," the Governor said. "You will take up what promissory notes you have already prepared and do the best you can with that situation. You will get this horse matter placed upon an honest footing. You will discover if intervals have been left between the battalions and bring back a complete report to me."

While I had only a hazy notion of what intervals between battalions meant, I was certain Ensign Gaines could enlighten me. "When is Ensign Gaines leaving, sir?" I inquired.

"He is presently eating lunch. He will be leaving almost immediately thereafter."

There was scarcely time to say good-bye to Melissa. While preparing to mount and be off, I told Ensign Gaines about Governor St. Clair's dispatch. "My holy Jesus Christ!" he exclaimed. Later, while resting our horses, he was able to expand upon this statement. "Those damned militiamen!" he said.

The army, he told me, marching over solid ground, had reached Loramie's Store, on the portage between the Great Miami and Maumee rivers. The Indian villages were now some thirty or thirty-five miles off. "Up to this time," Ensign Gaines said, "we hadn't seen a single Indian. The militiamen were braver than hell at this point, because they knew Little Turtle was on the run and wouldn't attack. Well, Phineas Ford came back to the army and told the General that while the Indians were all set to pull out of their villages, plenty of them were still around. They could be surprised, Phineas said.

"So the General ordered Colonel Hardin to move ahead with six hundred militiamen and fifty federals to make a lightning thrust on the villages. Believe me, Tom, what I'm about to tell you is the gospel and literal truth. Now that it looked like there might be some fighting, the militiamen ordered to go cried like babies and demanded that selection should be made by drawing lots.

"God, Tom, but it was a pitiful sight! Hardin had to spend practically the whole first day stopping wholesale desertion. I wouldn't venture to say how many of his men ducked into the woods and headed for home, but it was aplenty. Hardin made four miles that first day, Tom. Four miles! This was supposed to be a lightning thrust. It wasn't until late afternoon of the third day that Hardin finally reached the villages. Hell, by noon of the next day, the whole God-damned army was there."

Hardin, Ensign Gaines went on to say, had come upon some eighty deserted lodges and wigwams, but with all indications showing that the Indians had left their villages in confusion. "Even with the slow way Hardin moved," Ensign Gaines said, "the Indians were *almost* surprised. Tom, I'm serious—they *must* have thought at first that Hardin was the vanguard, looking for an encampment site. Then Hardin kept on coming! Christ, oh mighty, can you blame Indians for thinking white soldiers haven't any sense?

"God only knows what the Indians must have thought after that, Tom. Even a boy in military school would have had sense enough to know the Indians couldn't be too far off. There Hardin was. Out in the open. A river ahead of him. He's surrounded by trees! Not an Indian's in sight. Wouldn't that have been enough to put anybody on the alert?

"Hardin, of course, knew what danger he was in, but he couldn't do anything. The militiamen went out of control. They were so damned glad they'd won the villages without a fight that they started running around like mad men. They plundered and burned the corn fields. They set the lodges and wigwams on fire. They were drunker than hell and there wasn't even a semblance of order. An attack by a hundred-fifty Indians could have wiped them out.

"But God protects fools and drunkards, Tom. They'd moved ahead so slow that the main army was too close on their heels. The Indians knew where the main army was, even if Hardin and the militiamen *didn't*."

A certain amount of order, Ensign Gaines said, was restored when General Harmar and the main army arrived, but already the militiamen were hailing what had happened as a "victory" and were talking about going home.

"The Indians' cows and dogs started wandering back to the villages," Ensign Gaines went on to say, "so it figured the Indian families couldn't be too far off. Phineas verified this. The families were moving north fast, but plenty of Indians were behind them. These weren't assembled, Phineas said, and there was a good chance that some of them could be hit.

"So the General sent out Colonel Trotter and three hundred militiamen to reconnoiter. That pompous ass Trotter! He really loved that assignment, Tom. A rumor had gotten around that the Indians knew their goose was cooked and were hot-footing it to Canada. Trotter believed it and marched out of camp, big as life.

"He had a small detachment of cavalry with him, some of Fontaine's horse. The woods are thicker than hell up there, so the cavalry went along the river and the infantry up on the bank. After about a mile or so the cavalry saw one Indian, chased after him, caught him, shot him, and skinned his hide to be divided up by the boys for razor strops.

"Well, they had their Indian but now the cavalry was separated from the infantry. Meanwhile the infantry also bumped into an Indian. This poor bugger was old as Methuselah, didn't have a tooth in his head. When he loomed into view four field officers left their commands and chased after him. So there the infantry was, for a good half hour, without any directions.

"Yes, they got that Indian too. The field officers cut off his head, brought it back, and there was a big argument about who would get the scalp fee.

"About this time the cavalry, on their own, decided they'd had enough and headed back to camp. One of the boys got lost and saw some Indians on top of a hill. Panicking, he gave his horse the spur and tried to ride through the trees. Pretty soon he fell off his horse and started to run. First thing he knew, he'd run into our infantry. Excuse the joke, Tom, but this was the first contact our infantry and cavalry had made since they marched out together.

"The cavalryman said he was being chased by fifty Indians and told this to Trotter. McMullen was there and heard the whole thing, Tom! McMullen said he'd never in his life seen a man stricken with cannon fever worse than Colonel Trotter was. The man turned white as a ghost, McMullen said. These are Trotter's very words:

" 'Young man, where is our horse now?'

" 'They've gone back to camp, sir.'

" 'Is that so! Why?'

" 'I don't know, sir. They just decided to go back.'

" 'They must have had a good reason . . . Yes, of course, they must have. Since they were closer to the scene of possible combat, they surely must have known what they were doing. It therefore behooves us to do likewise.'

"Tom, those were Trotter's very words. Then he turned his detachment around and marched them back to our encampment.

"When Trotter reported to headquarters, the General was so mad he almost went after Trotter with two fists. Trotter sulked and said he'd made a judgment that seemed militarily wise. And he didn't neglect to get in that the militiamen didn't have to stay unless they were paid. And that at a word from him, they'd go home. Tom, there wasn't anything the General could do except send me after the pay. There was talk just before I left of Hardin going out to retrieve the militiamen's honor. I don't know if it was finally decided that he should."

"I've only got about three-quarters of the militiamen's pay," I said. "And, George, I'm supposed to report on whether there were intervals between the battalions. What exactly does that mean?"

"That damned St. Clair!" Ensign Gaines fumed. "He's talking about while on the march. He's dying to blame the General for something. Tom, the horses weren't lost while on the march. It happens at night, when we're encamped. Our encampments have been ringed with sentinels, with orders to keep a sharp lookout for straying horses. Believe me, the lost horses weren't strays."

IV

After three days of what I called hard riding, we reached the army, still encamped at the Indian villages, which were located along where the St. Joseph's and St. Mary's rivers meet to form the Maumee.

Entering the rear of the encampment, we rode through Hall's battalion. Hall, who had appeared to be the best of the Virginia majors, hadn't turned out so well when bullets started flying, Ensign Gaines told me. "McMullen," he said, "finally found out what a big wind bag Trotter is. I'd say when it comes to fighting, McMullen's the best of the lot. He's no good for anything else, but he does love to fight."

From my horse I had a good view of where the Indian villages had been. Everywhere I looked, the ground was black as if covered with tar. The vast corn fields, twenty thousand bushels in ears, and the gardens and the orchards had been burned down—utterly. Not a house, of which there had been a hundred-eighty-five, was left. In all that area of blackness the only sign of activity was some dozen militiamen digging on the northern bank of the St. Joseph's, the site of the principal Miami and Shawnee towns. "Are they digging graves?" I asked Ensign Gaines. "They're digging for treasures," he replied drolly and told me the present surge of activity had come about because somebody had discovered a buried brass kettle containing thirty-two silver dollars.

Most of Hall's militiamen were simply lolling about, drinking and playing cards. A few were building biers for the wounded and similar activity was in progress at various other places about the encampment. Noting this, Ensign Gaines said, "It certainly looks as if the General decided to send out Hardin."

Reaching headquarters, located at the rear right flank amid Major

Doughty's battalion of federals, Ensign Gaines and I dismounted. We were admitted immediately. The General and Majors Doughty and Wyllys sat at a makeshift desk, drawing up, I would learn, a line of march. The tent reeked of the smoke from their clays. A whiskey bottle stood before each of the officers.

"Lieutenant Morrow and Ensign Gaines reporting, sir," I said. Ensign Gaines had suggested that I, holding the higher rank, should make the announcement. The General wouldn't have cared one way or the other, Ensign Gaines had said, but since it was possible that somebody like Trotter or Hardin might be about, the niceties of good military manners should be observed.

"Good morning, gentlemen," the General said in an extremely tired-sounding voice. His face was drawn, its expression being that of someone at the funeral of a person he cared about. "I see you have brought the payments, Tom," he added after noting the two mail pouches in which I had the promissory notes.

"Only about three-quarters of them, sir."

"Place them anywhere, Tom," the General said. "Did you affix my signature?"

"No, sir."

"I should say the pressing need for them is past," the General said and managed a wry smile. "We're returning to Fort Washington in the morning. I labor under the impression the militiamen will require no persuasion or special inducements to carry out that order."

There was a weariness in the General's voice which was pitiful to hear. "May I assume, sir," I said, "that payments will be made at Fort Washington, when the men are mustered out?"

"Yes, Tom, you may," the General said. "And please accept my apologies for having brought you up here on a fruitless journey."

Requesting Ensign Gaines to remain, the General indicated that I should leave. Outside the tent I asked Arthur Wainwright, one of the General's waiters, if Colonel Hardin had marched out. "That he did," Arthur said bitterly, "and he got the holy hell beat out of him."

"Is Phineas Ford about?"

"I think I saw him over to Wyllys'," Arthur said and told me Major Wyllys' battalion was directly across from us.

This information proved incorrect, but Phineas, who had wandered over to Ray's battalion on the right flank, spotted me as I moved toward Trubley's. "Tom!" he called out and came running through the military stores and cannon.

"I heard you'd be up here," Phineas said. "How's Emil?"

"I really don't know," I said and told Phineas what little I could.

"Walking every day to his outlot and just sitting there . . ." Phineas said and shook his head.

"Phineas, there was no chance to talk to him."

"It probably wouldn't have done any good anyway," Phineas said. "Tom, I'm worried as hell. I sure wish I didn't have to hang around here."

"We're leaving tomorrow."

"I know," Phineas said, "but I'll have to stay around a day or so."

"What happened when Hardin marched out?" I asked.

"Oh, Christ, Tom, I don't even want to talk about it. It makes me sick."

"I'd appreciate it if you would," I said.

"I guess you would at that," Phineas said. "Did Gaines tell you about Trotter?"

"Yes, he did."

"Jesus, that damned Trotter!" Phineas said. "Well, the next morning the General sent out Hardin with two hundred militiamen and thirty federals. They were supposed to retrieve the militiamen's honor! The General told me to go along, to show Hardin the route Trotter had covered.

"I'd say we weren't in the woods fifteen minutes before a good third of the militiamen deserted. Those rats didn't come back to the encampment, so I guess they're halfway to Louisville by now. Anyway, pretty soon we located a morass where Indians had camped. Some of the fires were still smoldering.

"Of course, Hardin called for a halt. We looked around, didn't see anyone and started out again. Maybe three miles later Armstrong came up to Hardin and said there wasn't any sign of Captain Faulkner's detachment. Hardin's face turned white as a ghost and he had to admit he'd forgotten to order Faulkner to move ahead. So Major Fontaine and I had to go back with the cavalry and tell Faulkner it was all right to start moving again.

"Just about the time everybody got together, the Indians attacked. They couldn't have been more than a hundred strong, because it was a frontal attack. It had to be a hit-and-run because they didn't try to surround us and I'll bet anything they caught hell from Little Turtle for doing what they did.

"Tom, did you ever see cattle stampede? That's what happened to us. The militiamen threw down their rifles and ran. The minute they heard the Indian fire, they broke. Christ, if we'd been surrounded, they'd have been easy to hit as a flock of passenger pigeons. Do you know how many men Hardin had left? He had his thirty federals and ten militiamen. You heard me right, Tom, *ten* militiamen.

"I was standing right next to Hardin. 'For Christ's sake, Colonel,' I said, 'pipe an orderly retreat. It's your only chance. The boys you've got left won't panic.' Hardin's teeth were chattering so loud I thought they'd break in his mouth, but he said, 'No, we're going to fight it out.'

"When the Indians saw what was what, they stayed behind the trees and peppered the hell out of us from a hundred-fifty yards. When we were down to Hardin and six men, Hardin started crying and said I was right, he should have piped a retreat.

"We took off and Hardin cried all the way back, about how he'd lost so many federals and about what bastard cowards the militiamen were. When we got back to the encampment, the retreaters were massed in front of headquarters, shouting that their enlistments were up and they wanted to go home.

"Trotter was there too, looking pleased as punch that Hardin was beat. Tom, let me tell you something. Those were young, wild bucks that hit us. They followed right on our heels. They were flushed with victory and just itching for more fighting. We could have gone back and beaten the holy hell out of them. But don't let anybody tell you different. If the General had given such an order, the militiamen would have refused to go.

"Hardin was still crying when he entered headquarters. Trotter made a slurring remark and Hardin hauled off and hit him in the eye. The two tangled. The rest of us just stood there and let them go at each other. It wasn't until Trotter tried to bite off Hardin's ear, that Doughty and Sedam pulled them apart.

"The next day both Trotter and Hardin said their boys had enough and refused to march any farther north. And that's about the whole story, Tom. On the day after that we burned the Indian villages down to nothing. Our militiamen were brave enough to do that."

V

The army started its march back to Fort Washington shortly after dawn. Word had it that Trotter and a sizable detachment of "his Kentuckians" had left the previous afternoon. This may or may not be the fact. I am able, however, to say that when I looked up and down our lines I saw all of our officers except Colonel Robert Trotter.

At the General's request, I rode a while by his side. He would be leaving almost immediately for Philadelphia, he told me, as would most of his staff. Major David Ziegler would stay on as commander of the fort. The major would assist me in assembling the data on the expedition. "I have a feeling," the General said, "that the problem of mustering out pay will be greatly simplified." Waving his arm in the direction of the militiamen, he added: "Most of them won't even stop off at the fort." Since considerable of the material amassed while on the march might need explanation, the General suggested that I go over it during the next two or three evenings at headquarters.

Although we had suffered only thirty-four casualties, such had been the desertions that our army now stood less than eight hundred strong. We were able to move fairly rapidly. By midafternoon we'd progressed some eight miles to a previous encampment site. Here the General halted us for the night.

Sometime during the early evening Phineas arrived at headquarters to report that about a hundred-twenty Indians had returned to their burned-out villages. "They're right out in the open, Josiah," Phineas said. "Surprise them and they can be wiped out."

At the moment only Phineas, the General, Colonel Hardin, and I were in headquarters. "I beg of you, sir," Colonel Hardin pleaded of the General so feverently that he seemed to have gone down to his knees, "give me the right to lead out a detachment."

When Phineas had rendered his report, a certain brightening of the General's expression had indicated he thought a surprise attack might be feasible. "Heavens only knows, Colonel," the General said, "I wish to return with more accomplished than the burning of villages. Will you be so kind as to excuse yourself, while I consider your request?"

When Colonel Hardin left, the General sent waiters for Majors Doughty and Wyllys. Upon arrival both officers stated that an attack should be successful and voiced their approval of the General's decision to make it. Hardin could go along, it was agreed, but a federal officer must be in command.

Colonel Hardin was called in. "I agree, sir," he said when advised of the decision. "I am afraid, however, the militiamen will refuse to serve under federal officers."

Hardin, it was most apparent to see, was stating facts, not thinking of himself. "We are aware of that, Colonel," the General said. "We will send along a detachment of federals under command of Major Wyllys. The major will make the decisions. You will issue the orders. Would such an arrangement be agreeable to you, sir?"

"It would be, sir," Colonel Hardin said. His voice on the verge of breaking, he added: "Reduce me to the rank of private if you wish, sir, but do not order me to remain behind."

"Thank you most kindly, Colonel," the General said. "We will march out at midnight, attack at sunrise. Three-hundred-forty militiamen will be required."

"You shall have them, sir," Colonel Hardin said and left.

With their state of mind being what it was, it was a feat in itself for Colonel Hardin to be able to convince three-hundred-forty militiamen to fight. Yet, by midnight, he had them assembled. A sullen, dispirited group of men on the whole, but they were going to march out.

Accompanied by sixty federals, the detachment left at midnight, marching in three columns, with Major Wyllys and Colonel Hardin at the front, followed by Major Fontaine and some two dozen militia horsemen. Captain Ashton and Lieutenant Farthington were the federal officers, I noticed while watching the leave-taking. Majors Hall and McMullen, who were now not on speaking terms, were in command of two separate contingents of militiamen, most of whom were Virginians.

The plan of attack called for Hall's men to take a circuitous route around a bend of the Maumee, which would bring them directly in the rear of the Indians. Fontaine's horse, McMullen's militiamen, and Wyllys' federals would cross the Maumee and open up the attack.

When the detachment was gone, the General suggested that I sleep on one of the headquarters' cots. He would go, he said, to his own quarters. However, shortly after I'd lain down, the General came into headquarters, paced up and down, and drank whiskey in great quantities. Finishing a bottle, he called for another. "This is brandy," I heard him say to his waiter.

"That is all we have left, sir," the waiter replied.

"Very well then, it will have to do," the General said. "Thank you."

Eventually Major Doughty came into headquarters. "Those militiamen, John," the General said, slurring his words, "they'll crack. I feel it in my bones."

"They are the best we have, Josiah," Major Doughty said gently.

"And I didn't like giving that assignment to Hall."

"McMullen's too headstrong," Major Doughty soothed. "Ray's not good for much of anything. You had no other choice."

"I know it, John, I know it . . ." the General said. "God, but I'm drunk!"

The General was sound asleep at nine o'clock the following morning when an express from Major Wyllys brought news that because of delays caused by the militiamen, who insisted upon periods of rest, it was well after sunrise before the detachment reached the Maumee River. Although the element of surprise was lost, the attack would nonetheless be made.

At ten o'clock the General awakened, ate a hearty breakfast. He had received the express news quite calmly, from all outward appearances at least. If he suffered in the least from his drinking bout, he gave no such indication.

The unhappy news came shortly before noon. Pennsylvania Militiaman Ensign Wilbur Barton brought it. Major Wyllys was dead. The detachment was defeated, utterly. It was returning to the encampment in a state of complete rout. Only by threatening to shoot his own men had Hardin been able to gain obedience to an order for the fleeing men to bring back the wounded.

Lieutenant Farthington was also dead, Ensign Barton went on to say. Of the federals only Captain Ashton and six enlisted men had come out of it alive. At least half the militiamen had been killed. Major Fontaine was dead. So were Captains Thorp, McMurty, Scott. Lieutenants Clark and Rogers. Ensigns Bridges, Sweet, Higgins, Thielkeld . . .

Despite late arrival, Ensign Barton said, the detachment was strong enough to carry out the original plan of attack. Hall had gained his ground undiscovered, but had wantonly disobeyed orders and fired at a single Indian who was merely roaming about the woods. This had warned other Indians not too far away. They had fled in all directions with Hall's men chasing after them. Bit by bit, Hall's contingent had been shot to pieces.

Thus the main detachment had been left unsupported. Fontaine had been killed almost instantly and his men had dispersed. At least forty Indians had fallen at the first federal volley, Wyllys had got in considerable gallant fighting, but when he was killed all semblance of leadership was gone. As the federals began falling, one after another, the militiamen had panicked. Hardin and McMullen, in an effort to hold them together, had threatened with their swords. It was useless. The militiamen went into head-long panic. Rushing both Hardin and McMullen, they had knocked down their commanding officers, picked them up by the arms and legs, and carried them off.

Even as Ensign Barton spoke, what was left of Fontaine's horse came galloping into the encampment, shouting out the bad news. Immediately the encampment was in a state of riot. Beating on their camp kettles with knives and forks, the militiamen demanded of the General that departure be made at once. Sizable groups began taking their leave. To prevent wholesale desertion, our artillerists blocked the road with cannons and threatened to mow the men down.

With federal rifles pointed at them, the General ordered Major Ray's battalion to the support of the retreating detachment. Within an hour the two groups met and returned together. During Ray's absence the General had restored order by having our drummers beat out to arms. Word was circulated that our encampment, surrounded, was in danger of being attacked. While there was no truth in this, later in the day, a presence of a few Indian snipers gave credence to the rumor. Thus the army was held intact.

We spent the next day caring for our wounded, thirty-seven in number. We had one-hundred-eighty-three known dead. On October 24th we marched out. Snipers kept us together until we reached the water shed. Thereafter, with no more Indians about, our militiamen began deserting in droves.

We were, however, far enough along now to have saved our cannons and equipment. On November 3rd, what was left of us limped into Fort Washington. Governor St. Clair wrote to Secretary of War Henry Knox:

On the 20th of last month, I had the honor to inform you, generally of the success that attended General Harmar. I could not then give you the particulars, as the General's letters had not reached me; it is not necessary now, because he writes himself. One thing, however, is certain, that the savages have got a terrible stroke, of which nothing can be greater proof than that they have not attempted to harass the army on its return. They arrived at this place on the third instant in good health and spirits.

VI

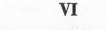

Phineas, at General Harmar's request, had stayed on in the woods to discover what the Indians had in mind. The information would be turned over to Major Ziegler, of course, and also to me. I would send it on to the General along with the other material I was assembling. Most assuredly there would be a Court of Inquiry, the General had told me, but usually a year or more passed before one was called. He no doubt would be soon retiring from the army, he said, but before doing so he was going to New York Town. As his final contribution to the welfare of the United States Army, he expected to plead before Congress for a well-trained army and the erection of forts.

Phineas came into headquarters five or six days after the army's return to Fort Washington. "Good morning, Tom," he said gloomily, "the fort looks like a big empty barn."

Phineas' statement was apt. The Governor, the General and most of his staff, many of the federals and all the militiamen were gone. The exodus had reminded me of the way it was at the William Penn Charter School just prior to the Christmas holidays. First there was confusion, then emptiness and unnatural silence.

My work had moved along more smoothly than I had anticipated. No complications had arisen while assessing estoppages against the militiamen's wages. Those gentlemen who'd come to Fort Washington had been prudent enough to replenish their lost equipment from general supplies and were mustered out with full pay. Since those who did not return to the fort were deserters and would receive nothing, in dollars and cents the army had come out ahead.

In fact, the officers had caused more bookkeeping problems than the militiamen. Of the opinion that real estate in the Ohio Country would not be a good investment for some time to come, the officers wished to sell the lots they had purchased in Cincinnati against their unpaid wages. This brought on many complications. While credited in a ledger book with owning property in Cincinnati, there had been no surveys, so nobody knew where the officers' lot sites were. As word of the officers' action got around, the price of all lots dropped to three dollars a block and even at that price there were no buyers. The directors of the Miami Purchase gave the officers land title certificates which couldn't be turned into money. I gave them long statements of the credits and debits, the latter, in most cases, having eaten up the former.

"Yes, it does seem like a big empty barn," I told Phineas.

The door to the inner office was open. "Where's Ziegler?" Phineas inquired.

"In Louisville," I said.

"Who in the hell's in command then? You?"

"Come to think of it," I said. "I do happen to be the ranking officer of the moment. Ensign Sedam is still here."

"Why in the hell didn't Cornelius leave?"

"He likes it here," I said. "He and his family are going to make Cincinnati their permanent residence."

"Well, tell them to stay in the fort this winter," Phineas said, "or they'll be here forever, six feet under the ground."

"What is the news from the north?" I asked after going for wrapping paper on which to make notes.

"The Indians are rebuilding their lodges almost as fast as we burned them down," Phineas said. "They hid away enough corn to last them through the winter and if they need any more they'll get it from the Wyandots and Mingos. That was all agreed to in advance."

The Ohio Country, from Pittsburgh to the Falls, Phineas went on to say, could look forward to a lively winter. The result of the Harmar Expedition was to encourage all Indians of northwestern Ohio. War whoops were resounding throughout all the tribes. Even those who, up to this time, had been friendly disposed toward the whites, were now about to be won over by the powerful influence of savage enthusiasm. Little Turtle, Blue Jacket of the Shawnees and Buckongehelas of the Delawares were at the moment conferring with Joseph Brant of the Mohawks. A great confederacy, in which the renegades Girty, Elliott, and McKee would participate, was in the making, its purpose being to drive all whites beyond the Ohio River. Headed by such leaders, Phineas said, there would come into being a band of warriors whose discipline had never been equaled in the annals of Ohio Country Indian warfare.

Momentous as this news was, Phineas' gloomy mood was not brought on by concern over the survival of the Territory Northwest of the River Ohio. Before coming to headquarters, he had stopped off at the Kummerschmitts'. "Emil's worse," Phineas said. "I can't pound any sense into his stubborn Dutch head. I think he's losing his mind."

"I have only seen him to say 'hello' to," I said.

"Melissa says Mrs. Robinson won't help out."

"I've gathered as much," I said. "From what Melissa says, Mrs. Robinson may have moved back to Louisville."

"I know," Phineas said, "Melissa told me that's what she'd heard."

"Luckily Dr. Allison is still here with the wounded," I said. "Phineas, whether Kitty likes it or not, she's going to have to make use of a man doctor."

"Kitty won't stand for that," Phineas said. "God damn it, Tom, this thing sure is turning into a real mess."

Phineas left. Shortly thereafter, Lieutenant Denny came into headquarters. He had just arrived from Pittsburgh, he told me. "I thought you were in Louisville," I said.

"I was subsequently sent to straighten out a few matters at Fort Pitt," Lieutenant Denny said, his sharp manner of speaking making it clear we were dealing with a touchy subject.

At the moment the lieutenant's race to be a general before reaching the age of thirty was not moving ahead at full speed. His efforts to ingratiate himself with Governor St. Clair had been quickly noted by General Harmar. Shortly after the Virginia militiamen had arrived at Fort Washington, word had come through that Louisville was threatened by Indian attack. The General had sent Lieutenant Denny to survey the situation, then apparently ordered him on to Fort Pitt. That he was being given an "ambassadorship to Bengal," as the army saying goes, had not escaped Lieutenant Denny's notice. If the word of one of Governor St. Clair's eavesdropping waiters may be considered trustworthy evidence, Lieutenant Denny had gone to the Governor and pleaded that the Louisville order be rescinded. The Governor, expressing surprise that an officer of Lieutenant Denny's convictions should question the wisdom of a superior officer's judgment, had refused the request. Thus Lieutenant Denny, who had expected to return from the expedition as a captain was not only still a lieutenant but did not have any combat experience on his military record.

"Oh," Lieutenant Denny said, "before I forget it. In Pittsburgh I met a friend of yours."

While he spoke casually, it was with the studied casualness of a beginning actor who has committed his words to memory with proper diligence, but has not yet had the stage experience to get them out convincingly. He is up to something, I thought, so the less said by me, the better. "Is that so?" I said.

"Yes, it is so," the lieutenant said. "An extremely comely young lady named Susan. She sends you her kindest regards."

"How thoughtful of her," I said.

"I was most discrete," he said. "I did not mention that you were married."

"I wish you had done so," I said.

"Well, one never knows just what to do in such circumstances," Lieutenant Denny said. "Susan, you will be pleased to learn, is doing well, quite well in fact. It is not necessary for her to spend much time on her back these days. She has become one of Mae Dwyer's most trusted assistants, the mistress of Mae's Pittsburgh establishment. You may recall Mae's experiment with the mulattoes?"

"I recall you told me she was making one."

"It failed miserably in the East, but has scored a triumph in Pittsburgh. One of the reasons for Mae's success is her generosity toward her associates. Susan, I would say, is reaping a pretty penny. But I seem to be gathering, Mr. Morrow, that you are not overly interested?"

"I am not overly interested," I said, "but I do wish Susan well."

"Then let us change the subject," Lieutenant Denny said and smiled in the self-satisfied manner of someone withholding esoteric information. "Didn't I see Phineas Ford leaving through the main gate?"

While pleased with myself for not appearing to be overly curious, I *was* wondering what information, concerning Susan, Lieutenant Denny had at least pretended to be withholding. And surely he was leading up to something. Certainly he had more in mind than to merely acquaint me with the fact that he knew I had at one time had a mistress. "You may well have seen Phineas," I said. "He was just here."

"I am wondering," Lieutenant Denny said, "if Phineas has served out his forty-eight hours in the guardhouse?"

"I have no idea."

"I would imagine he hasn't. The sentence will have to be carried out, of course."

"If so," I said, "I imagine it will have to be upon a direct order from you."

"No doubt you are right," Lieutenant Denny said with a sigh. "Frankly, I am weary of Phineas and his beavers. I would forget the whole matter if I dared. However, Governor St. Clair insists I must continue the task of catching Phineas and an order is an order."

I said nothing.

"The noose around Phineas' neck is tightening a bit," Lieutenant Denny said. "He wasn't fool enough to have brought the beavers to Cincinnati, of that we are certain. We are, however, reasonably assured that he did have them aboard his flatboat while at Limestone."

I still said nothing.

"In Limestone," the lieutenant said, "do you recall a midwife named Mrs. Andreson?"

"I remember her very well."

"Mrs. Andreson has told me that she sold a dozen excellently made sheep's gut English riding coats to Phineas. For these, he paid her three prime beaver skins."

While I had not seen Phineas give beaver skins to Mrs. Andreson, there was no reason to doubt the veracity of Lieutenant Denny's statement. Time and time again I had heard Phineas bemoan the fact that if he didn't somehow manage to procure some assurance caps, a certain young lady, residing in Columbia, would not consent to become his bed partner.

Phineas, it occurred to me, had not voiced his lament after we had left Limestone. "We have the local captain of the Rangers' word that Phineas did not store his beavers in Limestone," the lieutenant went on to say. "Therefore, one may conclude that he has stored them in Bracken."

But, I thought, Lieutenant Denny does not know where, in Bracken, the beavers are stored.

As a matter of fact, I did not know either. The cabin of the friend with whom Phineas had stored his beavers, and where he'd said Melissa's and my bans were posted, stood quite deep in the woods. Unless its whereabouts were known, it would be difficult to find.

"It may take some doing, but it will only be a matter of time before we locate where the beavers are stored," Lieutenant Denny said and moved to the door. "There is something else you should know, Mr. Morrow, yet I hesitate to bring it up."

"Please speak out."

"You may be offended."

"Each day I live my skin becomes thicker, Lieutenant."

"While I assure you it is no longer a concern of the United States Army, it is quite possible that you are still living with a woman in sin."

"You are prepared to explain that statement, of course?"

"Of course," Lieutenant Denny said. "You are aware that I consider myself as having been outmaneuvered in my previous effort to apprehend Phineas Ford?"

"Since you voiced it all over the fort that Phineas rushed to Bracken with Melissa's and my wedding bans—yes, I am only too well aware of your version."

How odd a human mind, mine at least, can behave! I was actually able to believe that I, an injured party, was being slandered by a vile and malicious accusation which was not true.

"I notice that you did not sue me for libel," Lieutenant Denny said easily, "but let us not become involved in whose version is right. Let us assume, for the moment, that mine is. I am saying that Phineas Ford went to Bracken in keeping with your plans of maneuver. However, being by nature a person not overly concerned with minor details, he neglected to actually post the bans. Yesterday I was in Bracken, sir. Your wedding bans are not posted within the settlement limits and the settlement crier has no knowledge of their existence."

So that was his approach! Having surmised that the beavers were stored at the cabin where the bans were posted, he wanted to goad me into blurting out the location.

I did not nibble at this bait and Lieutenant Denny did not appear to be overly disappointed. "For your sake, Mr. Morrow," he said as he took his leave, "I do hope your version is correct. Shortly we will be questioning Phineas again, rather thoroughly. The matter of your bans will most certainly be brought up during the cross-examination."

Being certain that Lieutenant Denny had not laid all his cards upon the table, I pondered for some time over what he had and had not said. Since my time was now my own, shortly I made for the Kummerschmitt inlot. Melissa and Phineas, engaged in serious conversation, sat on a split-log bench beside the well. "Phineas," I said, "you *did* post Melissa's and my wedding bans, didn't you?"

"Of course," Phineas said. "What's eating you?"

"Lieutenant Denny just got back to Fort Washington," I said. "Yesterday he was in Bracken. He told me the settlement crier never heard of our bans."

"Because the crier's a friend of mine," Phineas said. "I told him to play dumb if Ebenezer or any federals started snooping around."

"That isn't good enough," I said and related my conversation with Denny. "The whole area around Bracken will be scoured for the cabin where our bans are posted. I'd say Lieutenant Denny will be watching your movements like a hawk. He's assuming I'll warn you. In fact, that was his unplayed trump card. If you go to Bracken to move the beavers, you'll be playing right into his hands."

"I already have moved the beavers," Phineas said. "When I went to Bracken, my friend and I took them to a cave."

"It is most kind of you to enlighten me of the fact—at long last," I said.

"You worry too much, Tom," Phineas said.

"Well, here's something for *you* to worry about," I said. "Lieutenant Denny's going to see to it you'll spend forty-eight hours in the guardhouse."

"Oh, hell!" Phineas said and looked apologetically at Melissa for having used such language. "I forgot all about that."

Phineas stood up and started across the clearing. "Where are you going?" I asked.

"To the guardhouse," Phineas said, "to get it over with. I've got three hours credit coming to me. Maybe Cornelius Sedam and I can work out something."

"Phineas!" Melissa said, quite alarmed.

"Don't worry your little head about anything, Melissa," Phineas said, "everything will be all right."

When Phineas was gone I asked Melissa what was going to be all right. "Bringing Kitty's baby into the world," Melissa said. "Mrs. Robinson *has* gone to Louisville. Kitty still refuses to have Dr. Allison. I will have to be the attending midwife."

"Good Lord!" I said.

"Phineas will be back before the baby is born, I am sure," Melissa said, adding that while she had never seen a baby born nor talked at length with a woman who had had one, she was certain Kitty's baby was not going to be born during the next forty-eight hours.

"Melissa," I said, "to deliver a child—you have to know what to do."

"Phineas has explained it to me in full detail," Melissa said and told me Phineas had delivered all his children except the first one.

"If anything goes wrong," I said, "you'll blame yourself."

"If the baby isn't born within the next forty-eight hours, Phineas will be on hand to give advice."

"Isn't Phineas a man!"

"Of many parts," Melissa said quite wearily. "There will be a rag around Phineas' eyes. Kitty will think he is blindfolded. That is how things stand at the moment, at least." It was still hoped, she added, that Kitty might agree to call upon Dr. Allison.

VII

The following morning, as I approached Fort Washington, Phineas, moving with jaunty strides, came through the main gate. "Are you out of the guardhouse or haven't you started your sentence?" I asked.

"I'm out," Phineas said and clicked his teeth. "Cornelius fixed things up for me."

"Where are you going?"

"To see Emil. The baby wasn't born last night, was it?"

"No," I said, "it wasn't."

"That sure is a funny baby," Phineas said. "It's giving Kitty pains all right, but they don't look like labor pains to me. Do you think it's because Kitty's so big and plump?"

"I haven't the faintest idea," I said. "I haven't seen Kitty since I'm back and I don't know anything about labor pains except that women have them."

"All I know is that Kitty's aren't like Ayomah's were," Phineas said. "Of course Ayomah wasn't big and plump and she didn't lie around all day, just waiting for her babies to arrive."

"Well, neither of us is sufficiently versed on the subject to render a judgment on labor pains," I said. "Melissa told me last night that you're planning to leave for New Orleans with a cargo of your water, right after the baby is born."

Phineas nodded. "And I'm hoping Emil'll be over his peeve by then and come along, with Kitty and the baby."

"Phineas," I said, "I haven't seen Emil enough to know what is actually the fact, but from what Melissa tells me, Emil's much more than merely peeved."

"I know that," Phineas said irritably, "but he still loves Kitty, so he's a big jackass if he stays sore forever."

"Do you think it's that simple?"

"Sure, it's that simple," Phineas said, "but I'm not saying that Emil's got sense enough to know it."

"Melissa," I said, "told me last night that you told her if we decided to go back to Philadelphia, she and I are more than welcome to ride as far as Cairo with you."

"You sure are," Phineas said. "You can come all the way to New Orleans, if you want."

"That's most kind of you," I said, "however, if you'll recall our understanding in Pittsburgh, the flatboat is mine."

"Damn if it isn't!"

"Not that it matters a great deal, but I think you should ask me if you may use the flatboat."

"What good is it?" Phineas said. "Nobody's going to buy it for planks the way things are around here now. All the boat's doing is standing still and rotting."

"I'm simply saying," I said, "that there are some things you can do and some you can't. No matter how friendly people are, certain rights may not be presumed."

"Do you want the flatboat?"

"No," I said, "I do not want the flatboat. All you have to do is ask me for it and you may have it."

Phineas looked at me in blank amazement.

"That's all there is to it, Phineas," I said. "Just say, 'Tom, may I have the flatboat?' "

"Tom, may I have the flatboat?" Phineas said.

"Yes," I said, "you may."

"So now it's mine?"

"Of course," I said, "and now we understand each other. You're pleased to have the boat and I'm pleased to have given it to you."

"Well, I'll be damned," Phineas said. "So now she's mine and, if I want, I can tell you and Melissa to go to hell if you want me to take you to Cairo?"

"Yes, if you wish."

"Jesus!" Phineas said. "What's the name of that school where you teach back in Philadelphia?"

"The William Penn Charter School."

"I sure am damned glad," Phineas said, "I didn't go there."

Phineas went his way, I went mine. Ensign Sedam was awaiting me when I arrived at headquarters. "Good morning, Tom," Cornelius said and asked if he might have the expedition log book, which was actually a batch of wrapping paper cut to book size.

"Of course," I said.

Thumbing through the papers, Cornelius located blank spaces between the dates of October 15th and 20th. Herein he entered that Phineas had served out his sentence in four-hour tricks in the encampment guardhouse. Late entries, I should add, were not only permissible, but were invited, for the log book was far from having been kept up-to-date.

Looking over his shoulder, to make certain no one was in the outer office, Cornelius said, "I don't like doing this, but I owed Phineas a number of favors and it was a ridiculous sentence in the first place. Denny, as you can imagine, is boiling mad."

"Yes, I can imagine," I said.

"Damn it, Tom," Cornelius said. "I wish you'd talk to Phineas. The man showed no judgment at all. When he got out of the guardhouse, he gave Denny what was just about as close to a thumb-to-the-nose salute as you can get. There's no point in doing things like that."

"I'll talk to Phineas," I said.

Cornelius was scarcely gone, before Lieutenant Denny entered headquarters. "Good morning, Tom," he said much too pleasantly for someone I knew was boiling inwardly, "may I look at the log book?"

"It is right in front of you," I said.

"This is the official log book, is it not?" Lieutenant Denny said after locating the pages which interested him.

"Yes."

"Thank you," he said in the manner of someone who is quite pleased with himself and left.

Although I was certain Lieutenant Denny was up to something, I did not dwell upon what it might be, nor was my mind on my work. On this morning most of my mental energies were concerned with whether or not Melissa and I should leave Cincinnati when Phineas did. We had talked over the matter at length on the previous evening, without arriving at a conclusion. Which means, I suppose, that while Melissa and I had sense enough to know that no prudent person would stay in Cincinnati unless he had to, we actually wished to stay on.

It is difficult for me to say exactly why Melissa and I apparently wished to stay on in Cincinnati as it was for me to say why I wished to leave Philadelphia. For there was no single all-compelling reason. What comes to my mind is that while walking about the settlement, during my furlough, Melissa had time after time pointed to the surrounding hills and mentioned how nice it would be to have a home up there. "The view of the river must be magnificent," she'd said.

One night Melissa had brought up the subject again while we were in bed and somehow this got us to talking about whether I wished to continue being a schoolmaster. I'd said that I wasn't sure. We'd also talked about the book I suppose I still wished to write. The book had come up again in our previous night's conversation while we were talking about the two dispatches St. Clair had sent out. "People in the East will think we've won a victory here, that is at first," I'd said. "As the facts gradually emerge, I think a book, written by someone on the scene, would sell very well," and it is interesting to note that I spoke of the book selling well, rather than its contribution to the knowledge of the Ohio Country.

"Then, by all means, we must stay on, so you can write it," Melissa had said.

"I'm sure Major Ziegler will be glad to keep me on as his scribe," I'd said, "so we could live at the fort where we'd be safe."

It had been one of those rambling, probing conversations which, while understood by Melissa and me, would have baffled an eavesdropper. We'd also discussed the possibility of Melissa's becoming pregnant. "This is no place to have a baby," I'd said. "I shouldn't mind in the least," Melissa'd said, adding that she wanted us to have a child very much, the sooner the better.

I also wanted a child, the sooner the better, yet the very thought of Melissa having one here, especially if Dr. Allison should be transferred, caused me to actually shudder. I would say that the processes of my reasoning were leading me to a reluctant conclusion that Melissa and I must return to Philadelphia.

Shortly before noon, Phineas burst into headquarters. "Phineas," I said, "you've got to learn to treat Lieutenant Denny with more respect. This business of—"

"To hell with Ebenezer Denny!" Phineas said. "Emil's gone."

"Gone?"

"He took to the woods and hasn't come back."

"Can't you find him?"

"Now why in the hell would I tell you he's gone, if I could find him," Phineas said. "Emil went to Eastern Row and took to the woods from there. He did that so I couldn't locate where he went in and track him down. He's gone and he won't come back. I can't find Jeremiah Allison, Tom. You find him and tell him to hot-foot it to Kitty fast as he can."

"Is the baby—"

"Hell, no, there's no baby yet. Kitty's hysterical. Melissa says she's so bad it might bring on the baby before it's due."

"Where are you going?"

"To chase after the patrol," Phineas said. "They can be on the lookout for Emil, but if he doesn't want them to find him, they can't."

The reason Phineas could not find Dr. Allison was because Albert would not tell him that the doctor, weary from caring for our wounded, had gone to the cove at the foot of Eastern Row, to fish, and did not wish to be disturbed. Albert would not tell me Dr. Allison's whereabouts either, but did agree to seek him out and learn if Kitty's predicament was serious enough to warrant Dr. Allison's attention.

Within a half hour Albert, quite out of breath, came into headquarters with Dr. Allison's medical kit. Dr. Allison, Albert told me, was already walking up Eastern Row. I should take the medical kit and meet him.

As I went through the main gate, Dr. Allison was approaching it. "Albert was able to give me only a sketchy notion of what is what," Dr. Allison said and mentioned that while he had seen Kitty occasionally while she nursed Melissa, he knew very little about her. "Precisely what has happened?" he asked.

Dr. Allison listened most attentively as I described the circumstances. "When is the baby expected to be born?" he inquired.

"We don't know," I said, "it is expected almost daily, but it just doesn't seem to want to be born."

"Have there been recent labor pains?"

"Melissa tells me there have been pains."

"But she does not think they are labor pains?"

"Melissa has never seen a woman having labor pains," I said. "All she knows about them is what she heard in school when young girls talked. Phineas said only this morning that Kitty's labor pains aren't like those of his Indian wife."

"Did Melissa or Phineas describe what Mrs. Kummerschmitt's labor pains were like?"

"I do recall Melissa saying," I said, "that if she hadn't known that Kitty were pregnant, she would have presumed she was suffering from acute indigestion or that—there was gas on her stomach."

By now we were at Hill Street and it had become most apparent that Dr. Allison was in an extremely grave mood. It would not be necessary, he told me, to accompany him to the Kummerschmitt cabin. I did not learn the unhappy news until I returned home after my day's work. Melissa, awaiting me, came running across the clearing. "Have you talked to Dr. Allison?" she asked me, meaning since I had asked him to call upon Kitty.

"No," I said, "I haven't."

"Kitty is not pregnant," Melissa told me. "She has an ovarian tumor."

VIII

━━━━━━━◀◆▶━━━━━━━

What followed may be told better by Melissa than by me:

I remember [Melissa has written] the day Emil Kummerschmitt disappeared clearly as if it had happened yesterday. Up to now the weather,
unseasonably warm, suddenly became quite nippy and the day before we
had used our fireplace for the first time.

That was the day Phineas Ford began serving his forty-eight hours in
the guardhouse, or rather its equivalent. Tom has stated that immediately
upon hearing what Lieutenant Denny was up to, Phineas started for Fort
Washington. Tom has forgotten, possibly conveniently! Before leaving,
Phineas delivered a lecture on how to build a fire which would burn all
night and explained the vagaries of our chimney.

"You should have been burning a few logs now and then," I can still
hear Phineas saying, "to get the dampness out of the chimney."

"Thank you for telling me—now," Tom replied.

Tom was determined that the fire would burn all night and that there
would be no smoke. He had written down all of Phineas' instructions.
Wood of all kinds, we had aplenty. Hickory for a very hot fire. Maples,
which we called sugar trees, for a hot, steady fire. Oak, for one that burned
hot but slowly. Pine knots for kindling. Red cedar, which leaves almost
no ash.

Tom had it all down on wrapping paper! A half hour before we went to
bed, with me reading off the instructions, Tom meticulously threw chunks
of oak against the back log. When these were reduced to live coals, with
the utmost care he scraped them together well up against the back log.
These he covered with ashes to the depth of two or three inches, precisely
as Phineas had said. "This will insure a good bed of coals for tomorrow
morning," Tom explained to me while viewing his accomplishment with
satisfaction.

An hour later the fire was out and Tom was furious. To this day my
husband is incapable of making a first-rate fire, he simply hasn't the touch.
That night, amid shivers, Tom and I discussed whether or not we would
spend the winter in Cincinnati. We had talked about this before. Now,

however, confronted with Phineas' announcement that he was going to New Orleans immediately after the birth of Kitty's baby, it was necessary for us to make a definite decision.

I do believe my husband is the most transparent man alive. While he has said that by the next morning we had not come to a conclusion, he had already, possibly without realizing it himself, decided to return to Philadelphia. This was on my account. That he wished to stay on oozed out of every pore of his body. Yet I was unable to convince him that I was not made of fragile china and wished to stay on also.

I was deliriously happy as things were. And why shouldn't I have been? For the first time in my life I was free of a domineering father. I had a loving husband whom I loved dearly. I was almost certain that Tom did not wish to continue being a schoolmaster. Why shouldn't he stay out his sabbatical? Why shouldn't he take this opportunity to discover, if possible, what kind of a life he wished to lead? Goodness only knows, we had no financial worries. Money! Nobody had any in Cincinnati. It wasn't needed.

And, of course, I was capable of knowing that Tom and I could not be content forever in a one-room log cabin. I become so impatient with young girls today who look at me aghast and ask how Tom and I stood it, especially being married without a minister and with no wedding ring. We didn't have to "stand" anything. The future was ahead of us.

No doubt I was tidying up our home when Emil Kummerschmitt left for his outlot on the morning of which I am writing. I did not see him on that day. In due time, I called on Kitty. Although Tom was fond of Kitty, he scarcely knew her. Between Kitty and me there was the deepest affection. If Tom has given the impression that Kitty was not well-read, this should be corrected. The Pennsylvania Dutch believe in educating their daughters. Kitty's knowledge of arithmetic, grammar, and the classics was far more thorough than mine, for my education was gained in what Tom calls "one of those Frenchman's schools."

On this morning Kitty's hopes ran high. There was a sign of color in her beautifully rosy cheeks which had been bleak for so many days. "Melissa!" she said. "Emil kissed me good-bye this morning."

This being Emil's first display of affection since the unhappy situation had come into being, Kitty and I analyzed its implications with all the excitement of two young school girls. Kitty was convinced that at last Emil was relenting. "He will come back to me when I have his baby, Melissa," she said happily. "But why isn't it born?" she asked pitifully. "Could it be shriveling up inside of me because of what Emil thinks?" Kitty could believe that this might be possible, for the Pennsylvania Dutch are superstitious people, strong believers in old wives' tales.

Some time later Phineas arrived at the inlot. "Come out here, Melissa," he called out. "I want to show you something." He was awaiting me halfway between the cabins. "Emil's gone," he told me. "I tracked him to Eastern Row, but there's no way to know where he went in. He'll go woods crazy and I'll never be able to find him."

Phineas, I am certain, thought he had lowered his voice. Behind us, we heard a shriek. Kitty stood in her cabin doorway, shrieking, shrieking, shrieking.

Fearing, as Tom has related, that Kitty's hysteria would bring on an unnatural birth of her baby, I sent Phineas after Dr. Allison. During the period while Dr. Allison was examining Kitty, Phineas returned to the clearing. We sat on the log bench beside the well. Emil, Phineas told me, might come back on his own free will, but that it was most doubtful that he would. It would be impossible to track him down, Phineas said, and pointed his brawny arm in the direction of the trees, all around us. At this moment those trees looked endless and unconquerable. It was the first time, I believe, that I could actually comprehend why so many people hoping to make their homes in the Ohio Country, hated those trees and thought of them as mortal enemies.

Eventually Dr. Allison came out of the cabin and told us of Kitty's affliction. I knew no more of what ovarian tumors were like then, than my husband does now. "This means Kitty will die, does it not?" I asked Dr. Allison. "Yes, it does, Melissa," Dr. Allison replied and told Phineas and me that it would be a lingering and most painful death. Kitty, he said, might live on in agony for as long as two years.

Phineas' reaction was to become enraged. One vile invective after another, directed against Mrs. Robinson, came out of his mouth. He calmed down, however, when Dr. Allison explained why Mrs. Robinson should not be censured. The symptoms of pregnancy and ovarian tumors, especially if the afflicted were large and fleshy, were so similar that it was frequently, in fact usually, next to impossible for anyone—doctors as well as midwives —to tell one from the other.

"Has Kitty been told?" I inquired.

"I felt it best to do so," Dr. Allison said. As he spoke Phineas indicated with his eyes that I should look toward the Kummerschmitt cabin. Kitty came toward us. She walked erect and all the natural rosiness had returned to her cheeks. She was as beautiful as an angel. "Phineas," she said, "now Emil will know. Find him, Phineas, please find him and bring him back."

Phineas assured Kitty that he would and took to the woods. I suggested that Kitty should go into her cabin and lie down. "There is no need for that," Dr. Allison said in that kindly way of his, "it would be much better if she walked about, got some sunlight."

Kitty and I walked about the clearing, eventually seating ourselves on the sunny side of Kitty's cabin, where we engaged in woman talk. It was impossible for me to comprehend that I was in the company of someone who must shortly die.

I spent that night with Kitty. Returning to the inlot under cover of darkness, Phineas told Tom that for the next two days he'd wait at the spring where what he called his "magic" water was. There was hope that Emil might wander there, but it was a most forlorn one.

As Phineas had expected, nothing came of this. There was nothing he could do, he told Tom, nothing. In order to make Kitty think he was still in the woods, seeking Emil, he was going to load his flatboat with kegs of his magic water, take them to Cairo, sell the water, and thus raise the money to get Kitty back to Pennsylvania. It was going to be my task to convince Kitty this was the proper thing to do. "She will not leave here, so long as there is a chance that Emil may return," I said. That would have to be that then, Phineas said. There was nothing he could do in the woods. Since Kitty must think he was at least trying, he might as well go to Cairo.

Phineas' departure, while unknown to Kitty, was of course noted by the ubiquitous Lieutenant Denny. Convinced that the departure was a decoy maneuver designed to eventually get the beavers, Lieutenant Denny rushed two squads of federals to Bracken. Once again that ambitious young man's efforts to catch his culprit came to naught.

Within two weeks or thereabouts Phineas was back from Cairo, his pockets bulging with money and also bringing a wedding ring he had purchased at Tom's request for me. The magic water would reap a fortune, he said. It hadn't even been necessary to buy bottles. Cairo storekeepers were selling the water on tap. At two dollars a cup.

All was not a bed of roses, however, Phineas explained. Somewhere up in the Indiana Country was an underground stream whose waters produced results similar to his. Already a group of Cairo scoundrels, stealers of his idea, were going for this water. They, too, expected to sell it in New Orleans.

There were, Phineas said, a dozen or more army flatboats which might be purchased for five dollars each. Phineas proposed to buy them all. Plenty of empty powder kegs were still lying about and barrels could be found in one way or another. If necessary he would buy up barrels of Monongahela rye and dump out the contents! He was taking a flotilla of his water to New Orleans.

"Tom," Phineas said. "You and Melissa come to New Orleans with me. You'll be my partner. You get a third and Kitty gets a third."

Tom was jubilant. If there was any doubt in my mind that he preferred the world of trade to that of schoolmasters', it was now completely dispelled. Turning to me, he pleaded for understanding. "What do you say, Melissa?" he said. "The allure of it! Fail or win. What a venture it would be!"

There was no need for him to plead for my understanding. I was caught up in it too. I could think of nothing I wished more than to get to New Orleans before those "scoundrels" from Cairo did. "Of course I want to do it," I said. Tom took me in his arms and actually danced me about the clearing in a display of enthusiasm, which might be expected from a Phineas Ford but not from Thomas A. Morrow, Esquire, of Philadelphia as he was in the year 1790.

Phineas was presupposing that Kitty would leave Cincinnati, if we all did. Although I do not think she would have, this matter did not have to be settled. Later during the day, while Tom and Phineas were making arrangements to buy the army flatboats, Dr. Allison paid Kitty one of his daily visits. At this time, since Kitty's cabin had no chimney, Kitty was living with Tom and me. His visit concluded, Dr. Allison motioned for me to come outside with him. "I understand that Phineas has returned?" Dr. Allison said.

"Yes," I said, "he has."

"I would like to talk with you and Tom and Phineas in my quarters this evening," Dr. Allison said. "I will send Albert to look out for Mrs. Kummerschmitt."

At the meeting, Dr. Allison came quickly to the point. "I am convinced," he said, "that Mrs. Kummerschmitt's life may be saved by means of an operation."

The proposal left us momentarily dumfounded. Like most people, we believed—for all doctors said it—that were a part of the inner body exposed to air, nothing could protect it from infection. We knew too, at least Tom and I did, that such was the medical opposition to the invasion of the great cavities of the human body, that all people involved in such operations were accounted to be murderers if the operations were unsuccessful, potential murderers even if the results were not fatal.

Our bewilderment was, of course, recognized by Dr. Allison. "Doctors say what they do in public," he told us, "because they fear the wrath of the church and also that of the more conservative members of our profession." He spoke with quiet conviction. "But believe me, for years our more enlightened physicians have believed, deep in their hearts, that barring complications the extirpation of an infected ovary should bring a permanent cure. As an operation, it is scarcely different from the spaying of an animal."

There was no doubt that Dr. Allison had chosen his words carefully. His use of "barring complications" was most frightening to hear. It was Tom who spoke up. "I have not read of such an operation ever having been performed," he said.

"I don't believe any such accounts have been published," Dr. Allison replied, "that is by doctors of the Christian world. Any number of physicians have dared to write treatises contending that the operation should be successful. For these efforts, they have been criticized most severely. In some instances they have been ostracized."

"I have read a number of these treatises," Tom said. "Have any such operations actually been performed?"

"In secret, yes," Dr. Allison said. "I know of one successful operation performed in Edinburgh more than a half century ago in which a young medical student was an assisting physician. Subsequently all those involved were thrown into jail. The young medical student escaped and eventually came to America. He is still alive, has done considerable reading and experimentation on the subject, and will stake his soul that the operation will save the lives of many women who will otherwise die."

It was not necessary for Dr. Allison to say that he was that young medical student. "You spoke of complications?" Tom said.

"Infection," Dr. Allison said. "Not from exposure to air, but there is always the danger of infection. Since I will be able to give Mrs. Kummerschmitt only a few opium pills, it is possible that she will not be able to stand the shock of the pain."

"Will Kitty agree to such an operation?" Tom inquired.

"I have a strong feeling that she will," Dr. Allison said and his judgment would prove to be correct. "Mrs. Kummerschmitt believes with a childlike faith that Emil will come back. She will do anything to be here when he does."

"Are we to presume," Tom asked, "that if such an operation were to be performed, you will require our help?"

"You are, Tom. I will need the help of the three of you and that of two more strong men as well." The men, Dr. Allison said, would have to hold Kitty down, for such was the nature of the operation that she had to be turned on her side and could not be tied. My task would be that of principal assistant.

Tom turned to me. My nod meant that if he said yes, so would I. And I knew that Tom was going to say yes. Aside from giving Kitty her chance to live, Tom is an iconoclast. I know no better way to describe my husband's feeling that it is a mistake to accept blindly what is generally regarded as the absolute, than to say that nothing he has read has excited him more than the account of Galileo confronting the church hierarchy with proof that the Copernican theory was in error.

"The operation would have to be performed with the greatest secrecy, would it not?" Tom inquired.

"Yes, Tom, it would."

"How would this be accomplished?"

"The impression must be given," Dr. Allison said, "that Mrs. Kummer-schmitt has given birth to a stillborn child This means we will have to hold what appears to be a properly conducted funeral . . . Phineas, immediately after the operation, you will have to make us a small coffin."

Our answer was yes. Since the utmost secrecy was required, the problem of getting two men who could be trusted arose. Phineas got them in Bracken. They were slaves, belonging to one of Phineas' friends. Their names were Abraham and Wallace. They were quite old. As I understand it, Phineas offered to buy them their freedom, but they did not wish it, saying that they were content where they were.

When Phineas left for Bracken, Lieutenant Denny thought that at last he had him. Foiled again, the day after Phineas returned, the lieutenant came to me at a time when Tom was at the fort. "This may interest you and your husband, Mrs. Morrow," Lieutenant Denny said and handed me a copy of the *Pittsburg Gazette,* dated August 30th. The principal items were announcements of Benjamin Franklin's death, which had occurred in April, and a lengthy article, with a Paris dateline of March 2nd, dealing with the doings of the Corsican, Bonaparte.

"I thank you, Lieutenant," I said, "my husband is always glad to see a newsprint." I spoke coldly. How I despised that man!

"Will you please take notice of this," Lieutenant Denny said and pointed to a brief statement at the bottom of the sheet, concerned with the possibilities of England and Spain going to war. "I would imagine," Lieutenant Denny said when I was finished reading, "that the item holds a peculiar interest for you?"

"Should it?"

"You read, did you not, that General James Wilkinson is in New Orelans?"

"Yes," I said, "I read that."

"Then surely you must know that with the imminence of war, New Orleans has become a hotbed of intrigue? General Wilkinson has conferred with the Spanish Governor and has taken an oath of allegiance to the Spanish Crown. He has promised to encourage western territories to

separate from our Union and plans to establish an empire of his own
on this continent. He is, of course, a traitor."

"I was not aware of any of this, Lieutenant," I said, "but I am gathering
that most assuredly you are leading up to something."

"I am, Mrs. Morrow," Lieutenant Denny said. "We have known for some
time that General Wilkinson bribed a number of citizens from the general
Philadelphia area to come to New Orleans and become his associates. 'Associates' is a most kind way to put it, Mrs. Morrow, a more accurate word
is 'spies' or, if you prefer, espionage agents. I have a list of these agents,
Mrs. Morrow, and your late father's name is included as being one of them."

"I do not believe that," I said.

Yet, I did. My father, I am ashamed to admit, was a weak man. My
mother, whose name was also Melissa, was the only child of Morris Williamson, a well-established Trenton bookbinder. My father was employed by my
grandfather and it is understandable why my mother became attracted to
him, for in his younger days my father was quite handsome and even to the
very end could talk of his schemes for reaping a fortune in a most convincing manner.

When my grandfather died, my father sold the bookbindery, using the
capital thus obtained to make investments. Prior to the War of the Rebellion,
when almost anyone with ready money could turn over a dollar advantageously, my father's fortunes flourished. Afterward, like so many others,
he failed and was not strong enough to fight back. My mother had died
two years previously, which is also when my father's financial position approached a critical stage. After the Holland Company plunge, he was hopelessly in debt and he became desperate.

"You will have no trouble verifying the truth of my statement, Mrs.
Morrow," Lieutenant Denny said. "Simply ask your husband and he will
tell you it is so."

"You have spoken to my husband?"

"Within the past hour, Mrs. Morrow," Lieutenant Denny said. "When I
suggested that the whole matter might well be forgotten if your husband
reconsidered on testifying against Phineas Ford, he became quite incensed.
In fact, so strong was his conviction that you should not be mortified, he
threatened to challenge me to a duel, should I speak up. Therefore, I must
appeal to you."

"A duel!"

"Wasn't that silly of him, Mrs. Morrow? The man cannot even wear his
sword in proper military manner. My abilities with a pistol are well known.
Please do not be shocked, Mrs. Morrow, it is most unlikely that there will
be a duel. The rules of gentlemanly behavior do not permit me to engage

someone who is clearly my inferior in the art of dueling. Unless, of course, he should provoke me beyond bounds which no man of honor may be expected to endure. What I am hoping is that you will be able to convince your husband that his career and possibly your married happiness is at stake. When Phineas Ford is brought to trial your father's activities can be brought out. News has a way of traveling fast, Mrs. Morrow. It will reach Philadelphia. The ears of many ladies, most anxious to learn the background of the young bride Thomas A. Morrow has brought home with him, will be cocked wide open."

"Are you finished, Lieutenant?" I asked, with a calmness which I most certainly did not feel.

"I am, Mrs. Morrow," Lieutenant Denny said. "I believe you understand the implications far better than your husband. And, now, may I wish you a good day."

The remainder of that day, as I awaited my husband's return, was a most trying one. When he arrived, I rushed across the clearing, threw myself into his arms, and told him what had happened. The beast permitted me to plead, beg, and cajole that under no circumstances must he provoke Lieutenant Denny into having grounds for accepting a challenge to a duel. "Are you quite finished?" Tom in due time inquired.

"No," I said, "I am not. We will talk about the rest of it at your will, but I will continue to stand here until I drop from exhaustion or starvation and then I will lie here until you promise there will be no duel."

"A most noble expression of determination," Tom said, "but its execution will not be required. There will be no duel." My husband, who in fact accounts dueling to be a most ridiculous pastime, then told me that having momentarily lost his senses, he later decided to use them. Calling in Lieutenant Denny, he showed him an entry in the expedition log book which read: *"On this day, learning that Fort Knox was in danger of an Indian attack, General Harmar dispatched Lieutenant Ebenezer Denny to Louisville in order to survey the situation and take command of the fort, should an emergency arise."*

"I would say," my husband said to Lieutenant Denny, "the entry, which is in my handwriting, reads in a rather complimentary fashion?"

"Yes," the lieutenant replied warily, "I should say it does."

"You will notice," my husband said, "there is considerable blank space left on the page. Would you advise me to explain why the General, aware the news was in all probability an unfounded rumor, nonetheless gave the assignment to his aide-de-camp?"

"No," Lieutenant Denny said, "I would not."

"Then, I take it, Lieutenant, that we understand each other?"

"Yes, Mr. Morrow," he replied, "we do."

Once over my feeling of relief, I complimented my husband upon his handling of the situation, but explained that his manner of holding me in suspense was a kind of humor which most mature women do not appreciate. His reply that I looked my best when righteously aroused was, I said, quite beside the point, albeit I was pleased to hear this. "What is the point then?" Tom inquired and I spent the greater part of that night trying to explain it.

Dr. Allison had announced that Kitty's operation would take place one week hence. During the period intervening, I spent considerable time being Dr. Allison's pupil. I read and reread one of his most prized possessions: a treatise he had written, but never dared to have published, on how the Edinburgh operation had been performed. To acquaint myself still further with my duties, I watched Dr. Allison spay a mare and two bitches. I learned what knives to hand over, what I should do to stop excessive bleeding. By week's end words such as musculus rectus abdominis, contusions, Fallopian tube, and the like became a part of my vocabulary.

On the day before the operation when Tom left our cabin for the fort, he said, "Melissa, I think it's become somewhat colder."

"Yes," I said, "it has. Look—you can see your breath."

Glancing across the clearing, I noted the pair of mallards that regularly slept in a swampy section which Emil had not been able to drain. The birds were still as if made of stone. "I've never seen them that motionless," I said.

"Neither have I," Tom said and threw a boulder which landed quite close to the birds. They did not move.

"Something's odd," I said.

Walking over to the mallards, Tom discovered that their feet were frozen in the mud. Getting an ax, he chopped them free. That is how fast the temperature had dropped and what became known as the "hard winter" began. By evening all Cincinnati, the whole Ohio Valley we would learn, became blanketed with snow.

Despite the snow, Dr. Allison said the operation would be performed. Actually the turn in the weather was to our advantage, he pointed out, for it lessened the chances of someone coming to the inlot.

The temperature continued to drop. On the day of the operation it was bitterly cold, but there was no wind. There were no clouds and I have never seen the sky so blue. The boughs of the trees, heavy with snow, bent down gracefully. Everything was so white and the air was so clear. It was such a beautiful day.

Abraham and Wallace, who were quartered at the fort, came to the inlot and made preparations to build a roaring fire outside of Kitty's cabin, such as is needed when a child is born. Since our cabin was too smoky, the operation would be performed in Kitty's. Phineas had raised the floor, so there would be some heat, provided by hot stones. We would need all the heat we could get for, in order that there be sufficient light, the door would have to be kept open.

As was prearranged, Tom went to the fort to announce to Dr. Allison that Kitty's baby was about to be born. I gave Kitty two opium pills. Kitty, huddled beside our fireplace, appeared quite composed. I do not recall that either of us spoke. Dr. Allison had told Kitty that even more important than the opium pills, would be her ability to concentrate upon why she wished to live. "Emil," I saw form on Kitty's lips any number of times, but she did not speak the word out loud.

By the time Dr. Allison arrived, Kitty was slightly drowsy. I gave her two more opium pills. Phineas carried her to her cabin. I walked beside them. "Emil," Kitty muttered. She was quite drowsy by now, speaking out loud.

Everyone had been schooled what to do. Phineas laid Kitty on a table he had built especially for this purpose. Wallace would hold down Kitty's shoulders, Tom her midsection, Phineas and Abraham her legs.

I gave Kitty sponges to hold in her hands and placed others between her toes. "Grip them, Kitty," I said and her toes clutched the sponges with the dexterity of fingers.

Despite the cold, Dr. Allison stripped to his woolen undershirt. Kitty was dressed warmly. She had on three pairs of woolen stockings. Raising her skirt and petticoats, Dr. Allison said: "We are not quite ready to begin, Mrs. Kummerschmitt. You know what I am doing now?" With a pen, Dr. Allison marked the course of the incision on Kitty's swollen abdomen.

Kitty had been drowsing. Now her eyes opened wide and I could see the pupils darting about as if Kitty were looking at all the corners of the ceiling.

On a small table were four butcher knives of various sizes, forceps, a small sponge, various bandages, scissors, and threaded needles. The knives had been designated by number. Over and over again Dr. Allison and I had practiced. "One," he would call to me, "three." I was not afraid of becoming panicky. I knew that I could have given him the proper instrument with my eyes closed.

Dr. Allison nodded to me and I placed the sponge in Kitty's mouth. "Remember, Mrs. Kummerschmitt," Dr. Allison said. "Bite, bite, bite on it. If you open your mouth, you may be gagged."

Turning to me, Dr. Allison raised a single finger. I handed him the proper knife. Dr. Allison made an incision about three inches from the musculus rectus abdominis, on the left side. When the knife cut into Kitty's flesh, her whole being trembled, then it was as if she were stretching her legs, trying with all her might to wrench them loose from her body.

Such was the spurting of blood that I could see nothing else. I knew though that Dr. Allison was cutting parallel with the fibers of the musculus rectus abdominis, into the cavity of Kitty's abdomen.

When I wiped the blood, Dr. Allison saw that the walls of Kitty's abdomen were quite contused. The tumor was now in full view. It was so large— a dirty, gelantinous-looking substance, weighing fifteen pounds—that Dr. Allison could not take it away in entirety.

Putting a strong ligature around the Fallopian tube, near the uterus, Dr. Allison, still using the same knife, cut open the tumor, which was the ovarium and fimbrious part of the Fallopian tube, very much enlarged. Cutting through the Fallopian tube, he cut out the sac, which weighed seven-and-a-half pounds.

Once the external opening was made, Kitty's intestines rushed out upon the table, so completely that they could not be replaced during the operation. Turning Kitty on her left side, so as to permit the blood to escape, Dr. Allison closed the external opening with a series of stitches, leaving out, at the lower end of the incision, the ligature which surrounded the Fallopian tube. Between every two stitches, he put a strip of adhesive paste, which, by keeping the parts intact, would hasten the healing of the incision. He then applied the usual dressings. The entire operation was completed within twenty-five minutes. By now Kitty had sunk into a coma. After searching her body for signs of approaching death, Dr. Allison said, "She will live. I am certain of it."

We took Kitty to our cabin. By morning, although so weak she could do no more than smile at us, it was most reasonable to conclude that her recovery might be expected. The irony of it! Emil gone. Dr. Allison, as had other courageous physicians, had proved such operations could save women's lives. A world of hope for the dying lay on the horizon. Yet, what had been accomplished must be kept a secret.

Two days later, amid a howling blizzard, proper funeral services were conducted, with a sizable group of citizens in attendance. As the group stood with bowed heads at the far corner of the inlot, the removed tumor and sac, preserved in the snow, were not a stone's throw away. Dr. Allison had not yet taken them to his quarters for examination and study.

One week later Kitty, now strong enough, was moved to Fort Washington, for the snows continued and the drifts became too deep for Dr. Allison to plod through. In due time, smoked out of our cabin by winds that blew down our chimney, Tom and I took up quarters there also. Phineas was already there. All plans for going to New Orleans had been abandoned. The stream in which the magic water ran, was frozen solid.

The winter became colder and colder. For Tom and me, however, there was no discomfort. Our quarters were most satisfactory, the fort was well-stocked with food. Within a month, Kitty was as good as new. She provided me with excellent company and time, that great healer of all ills, began coming to her aid. She clung, nonetheless, steadfastly to the belief that Emil would come back to her. I am certain she was not aware that a number of young officers and at least two of the few remaining eligible townsmen would have been delighted to pay her court.

Elsewhere, however, people of the Ohio Valley were far less fortunate. With the temperatures remaining down, the river froze solidly, forming into masses of ice that piled up high in weird shapes. Looking from Fort Washington's wall walk, with the white Kentucky hills in the background, one needed little imagination to fancy himself lost in the wilds of the Arctic. The crust of all that snow broke with every step hunters took, warning deer of their approach, leaving them nothing but the forlorn hope of finding bear holes. We heard of people reduced to living on roots and the grains of wheat found in their straw beds. We heard of them gathering up fox and wildcat bones which ravens and turkey buzzards had already picked over. They boiled these bones until the sinew that remained stripped off and from these they made relishes.

And despite the weather, the Indians went about their task of killing, from Pittsburgh to the Falls, with grim efficiency. The horrible massacre at Big Bottom on the Muskingum River was the worst, but they were all over. On any number of mornings, we saw the prints of their fancily designed snowshoes within a few feet of Fort Washington's main gate.

BOOK FIVE

---◆---

CAMPAIGN

I

During mid-January, fairly early in the morning, a sentinel came into head-quarters. "Tom," he said, "there's a man across the river, waving what looks like a mail pouch. I think he wants us to come and get him."

On this day the wind was blowing strong and the river, which didn't freeze until February, was running quite fast. The only way we could get to the Kentucky side was by canoe.

"I can't imagine a canoe bucking this wind," I said, "but I'll see what Major Ziegler says."

Major Ziegler was at his desk, smoking his favorite clay, which was black as tar, had a most malodorous aroma, and gurgled with each puff. Twelve beautiful matched clays, in a handsome mahogany case, unused, were behind him atop a file cabinet. These were a present from the major's wife, who had pleaded with her husband to smoke them in rotation.

Big-boned and broad-shouldered Major Ziegler was a slow-moving man who pondered his decisions with Teutonic deliberation, then stuck to them. While none of us called him by his first name, which was David, this does not mean the major was not liked and respected. One of those people who are hard to know, Major Ziegler seemed to keep everything inside of him. He very seldom used the words "thank you" and when he did, they did not come out naturally. Yet, I am certain, he thought them to himself. I recall his reaction to one of my reports. "It will do," he'd said, frowning deeply after having read it. His voice had carried no enthusiasm and I gathered that he was generally displeased. Later, after a staff meeting, which

I did not attend, a number of officers mentioned that the major had referred three times to "Lieutenant Morrow's excellent and thorough report."

Major Ziegler nodded when I acquainted him with the news. "Expecting him, I am," he said. "Over here, we must bring him."

Some four hours later a tall, middle-aged man came into headquarters. He was so bundled up that, in the gap between his coonskin cap and his fur collar, nothing was visible but tiny brilliant brown eyes and a huge nose blue with cold.

"Yesterday, already I was expecting you," Major Ziegler said and handed the man a bottle of brandy.

While an unlimited supply of Monongahela rye was furnished commanding officers, the brandy was bought and paid for by the major. "I was walking through snow drifts three and four feet deep, sir," the man said.

"That I know," Major Ziegler said. "Hungry you are?"

"As a bear."

"Something to eat, you must get," Major Ziegler said. "The bottle, you will take with you."

By the time the carrier was gone, I had opened up the pouch and had begun sorting out the mail, which had come via Louisville. "This, I believe, is what you're waiting for, Major," I said and handed over a dispatch from Fort Knox.

Major Ziegler read quickly. "To Louisville I must go right away," he said and handed me the dispatch, to be filed. "In command, while I am gone, will be Lieutenant Denny."

Although the dispatch merely stated that Brigadier General Charles Scott, head of the Kentucky Militia, requested the major's presence at Fort Knox, I was aware its arrival meant that some word had come through concerning Congress' plans for a new expedition against the Indians. At this moment Fort Washington knew only that there was almost certainly going to be one. As to how the expedition would be conducted, we had no information. In April, Congress had voted to increase the army by adding a second regiment. My reports indicated that so far not fifty men had been enlisted. Once sworn in, after reporting to Fort Pitt, they had been sent down the river to bolster the garrisons at Forts Steuben, Harmar, and Knox.

"Good luck, sir," I said to the major as he left headquarters.

"Talk!" the major snorted. "The meeting, that is all it will be. Talk. *Smuck*. So much *smuck*."

Almost immediately after Major Ziegler left Fort Washington, Lieutenant Denny came into headquarters. I stood up and saluted. "Now look here, Lieutenant Morrow," Denny said irritably, "there's no need for such histrionics. There are no militiamen around to impress."

"I'll keep that in mind, sir," I said.

"And you don't have to say 'sir' when nobody's around," he said. "Let's get this straight. We have personal misunderstandings, yes. But you're a schoolmaster and know plane geometry. Parallel planes never meet no matter how far they are extended. Our personal misunderstandings are on one parallel plane, what we do here is on another. That's certainly logical reasoning, isn't it?"

"Are you asking me," I inquired, "or simply expounding?"

"I'm asking you, God damn it."

"Then my answer is no. Parallel planes are inanimate objects. You and I are personal equations."

Lieutenant Denny regarded me oddly, then laughed. "And I thought I had you on that one," he said. "Come into the inner office, won't you? The major wants me to go through the rest of the mail."

Seating himself at Major Ziegler's desk, Lieutenant Denny thumbed through the mail with the rapidity of someone shuffling a deck of cards. "I see there's no news from New York Town," he said.

"No," I said, "there isn't."

"What's the difference," he replied. "The army that *will shortly be raised,*" he added with withering sarcasm, "that's all the dispatches say anyway."

Although familiar enough with the words, which were Secretary of War Henry Knox's, I had not had an occasion to even so much as read them for quite a while. Since the army's return to Fort Washington, we had not received any official mail from New York Town. Lieutenant Denny began reading the letters. "They're all alike," he said, as he handed me the letters for filing. "Everybody wants food and more protection."

"That's all the mail we've been getting lately," I said.

After taking a swig of Major Ziegler's brandy, Lieutenant Denny moved to the fireplace and began fiddling with the logs, although the fire was actually burning beautifully. "Is there anything else to do?" he asked.

"I don't know about you," I said, "but I have to answer these requests."

"What do you reply?"

"What is there to reply?" I said. "I tell them we've only got eighty-five federals here and if we give food to one, we'll have to give it to all. There's not enough for that."

"I'll bet that pleases them," Lieutenant Denny grumbled. Moving back to the desk, he took another swig of brandy. "I haven't got a damned thing to do," he said. "Being snowbound's driving me batty. You're lucky to have a wife who still likes you. What did you put down?"

Lieutenant Denny was referring to our officers' pool, in which everyone ventured his guess as to the size and makeup of the new expeditionary force.

"I put down," I said, "that Congress, after hearing General Harmar's report, will give us at least two more regiments of federals and will order a string of forts built."

"Are you crazy?"

"That all depends upon the point of view," I said. "I've only won two bets in my whole life. Both times I bet on what I didn't think could possibly happen."

Lieutenant Denny laughed dryly. "Well, you won't win this time," he said. "I put down that we won't even get a full second regiment and that we'll end up with a batch of volunteers again, numbskulls every bit as bad as those Harmar got. I said we wouldn't march out on time, would be short of supplies, and with the Indians flushed with victory and better organized, we'll take another licking."

"Do you actually think it'll be that bad?"

"I do."

"You certainly can't think the second regiment won't be filled?"

"Unlike you," Lieutenant Denny said, "I bet what I think will happen, not what I hope."

"Then we'd be fools to march out," I said.

"We were fools to march out last fall," he said. "It's Congress, not the army. Judge Symmes was in Pittsburgh when I was and I had a long talk with him. By the way Polly Symmes is going to marry Bill Harrison over the old man's objections! All it is in Congress, is a big squabble. President Washington wants to treat with the peaceful Indians, so we won't alienate them. Jefferson says to hell with friendship, wipe them all out."

"I read that was Jefferson's stand," I said. "I was surprised."

"Nothing a congressman does surprises me," Lieutenant Denny said. "That jackass from Massachusetts says get the British out of Niagara and everything will take care of itself. Did you know that a lot of congressmen think we should give up the Ohio Country? We've got enough trees between the Atlantic Ocean and the Alleghenies, they're saying, so why in the hell should we take on some more."

"It's only a few congressmen who are saying that," I said.

"It's more than a few," the lieutenant said. "Believe me, there's enough of them to make more than just a lot of noise. But it's not how many that really matters. They've joined up with those who don't think we should increase our army. Together the two blocs have got the votes.

It's because they combined forces that all the President could get was one more regiment.

"They won't be swayed by General Harmar's report?"

"Hell, no, they won't," Lieutenant Denny said. "The word's already going around that the General was a blundering ass. If he'd been any good, it's being claimed, he'd have trained the volunteers right and there'd been plenty of time to build and man forts."

"That's ridiculous."

"Of course it is," he replied, "but that's the talk. And mark my word and Judge Symmes' too, the General won't get any backing from St. Clair."

"No, I don't suppose he will," I conceded.

"And that reminds me," Lieutenant Denny said, "who do you think I put down will command the new expedition?"

"No!" I said. "You couldn't have."

"Oh, yes, I could have and I did," Lieutenant Denny said. "I put down the name, bold as John Hancock's: Arthur St. Clair."

"You're joking, of course?"

"The devil I am," he replied. "Look at it realistically. And I admit I'm basing what I'm about to say on what Judge Symmes told me. St. Clair's dying to show he can do what Harmar couldn't. He *wants* the command. I know St. Clair's generally hated, but he does have one friend who counts in New York Town—his old Revolutionary comrade-in-arms."

"You mean—the President?"

"I mean the President," Lieutenant Denny said.

The next morning, shortly after I arrived at headquarters, somebody came from Columbia to announce that Indians had broken into the stockade, scalped two citizens, and made off with seventeen horses. It was now snowing quite hard. The patrol had lost track of the marauders. It was, of course, unthinkable that Fort Washington would be attacked. The strength of the Indians, however, was unknown. And what else they might be up to, was anyone's guess.

Lieutenant Denny's role as Fort Washington's commanding officer was not a happy one. Somebody had to find out where the Indians were and what they had in mind. The only man capable of carrying out such a task was Phineas Ford.

Saying he needed a few moments for solitary meditation, Lieutenant Denny went into the inner office, closing the door behind him. I could hear him pacing the floor. One of the oddities of military thinking was that while commanding officers were expected to compel civilian scouts to follow Army Regulations, they were also expected to be able to keep these men in cooperative frames of mind. Thus if Phineas refused to go out and look for the Indians, a black mark would go on Lieutenant Denny's record.

In due time Lieutenant Denny opened the door. In his best military manner, he said, "Lieutenant Morrow, you will please send for Mr. Ford."

Phineas did not respond to Lieutenant Denny's request on the double. A good half hour passed before he sauntered into headquarters. As I ushered him into the inner office, he gave me an all-knowing wink.

Lieutenant Denny sat erect at his desk. One got the impression he had been sitting thus since issuing his call for Phineas Ford. "Morning, Ebenezer," Phineas said heartily. "Damned cold day, isn't it?"

"Yes, Phineas, it is," Lieutenant Denny said and appeared to be somewhat flustered by the convivial greeting. I am prepared to wager my bottom dollar that in mapping out his approach tactics, Denny had planned upon putting on his best military front and addressing Phineas as Mr. Ford. "Whiskey?"

"Don't mind if I do," Phineas said and brought out a bottle from under his buckskins.

"I am assuming," Lieutenant Denny said, "that you have some idea why I have summoned you?"

"I sure have," Phineas said easily. "You haven't got anybody else who can find out where the Indians are, so you want me to do it."

"That is substantially correct," Lieutenant Denny said.

"I'm not in the army any more," Phineas said with a shrug of his shoulders. "I don't have to go anywhere."

"I am aware of that," Lieutenant Denny said. Picking up a pencil, he drew two straight lines on a piece of paper. "Do you see those two lines?" he asked Phineas.

"Sure," Phineas said. "I see them."

"They are the same distance apart," the lieutenant went on. "We call them parallel lines. Since they are the same distance apart, you can see, can't you, that no matter how far they are extended, they will never meet?"

"I'll be damned if you're not right!" Phineas said.

"Now I want you to think of the lines as boards, Phineas," Lieutenant Denny said. "Wide, flat boards, big enough for two men to stand on."

"Planks, you mean?" Phineas said.

"All right, planks," Lieutenant Denny agreed. "If the lines were planks and they were on top of each other, the same distance apart, they, like the lines, would never touch each other no matter how far they were extended."

"No," Phineas agreed, "they sure wouldn't."

"Now then," the lieutenant said, so absorbed in himself that he did not notice the surreptitious wink Phineas cast in my direction, "I'm going to label one of the lines 'A' and the other 'B.' But I don't want you to think of them as lines. I want you to think of them as being planks. If you and I are standing on plank 'A,' we're on one plank. If we're standing on plank 'B,' that's being on another plank."

"Why are we standing on them?" Phineas wanted to know.

"That's my point," Lieutenant Denny said. "You and I have had some differences, but going out to locate the Indians is something else again. When we are having our differences, we are standing on plank 'B,' let us say. When you go out to locate the whereabouts of the Indians, we are standing on plank 'A.'"

"I didn't say I'd go out," Phineas said.

"I know you didn't. But I, as the commanding officer of Fort Washington, am going to ask you to. And in giving me your reply, I want you to think that at this moment you and I are standing on plank 'A.'"

"I don't quite get that, Ebenezer," Phineas said. "We're still the same people."

Lieutenant Denny shook his head. "We're the same people, yes. But we're different people also because now we are standing on plank 'A.'"

"All right," Phineas said. "I understand it. We're on plank 'A.' So what's the commanding officer of Fort Washington think I should be paid for going out?"

"Double the regular rate of a dollar a day because the weather is so cold."

"Army paper?"

"Of course."

"It's no good."

"It's equivalent then?"

"What?"

"Whiskey."

"Don't need any, Ebenezer. I've got seven barrels of Monongahela rye stored in Emil Kummerschmitt's loft."

"Well, what do you want then?"

"Can't think of a damned thing except how hard it's snowing."

"All right, God damn it, Phineas," Lieutenant Denny said. "You've got me at the end of a plank. In the records it'll say you went out for a dollar a day. Privately I give you six sheepsgut English riding coats?"

Phineas blinked. His surprise was genuine. There was no doubt of this. "Well, now, Ebenezer," he said, "that's something else again. Who's used them?"

"Nobody!"

"It's a deal," Phineas said. "I get to look them over before I go out?"

"Of course," Lieutenant Denny said and stood up. "I'll get them."

"Well, I'll be damned," Phineas said when the officer was gone. "Funny, isn't it, how things come out sometimes." He began conjecturing out loud. "He got those riding coats from Mrs. Andreson in Limestone. I've been wondering who else has been jumping my lady friend in Columbia. So it was Ebenezer!"

"Just what did you want from Lieutenant Denny?" I asked.

"Nothing," Phineas said. "You don't think I wouldn't go out, do you? I just wanted to watch the bastard crawl."

Twenty-four hours later, looking like a snowman, Phineas was back in headquarters. "Simon Girty's out there," he announced, moved to the fireplace and brought out his whiskey bottle. "He's close to a hundred strong."

"They can't be that strong," Lieutenant Denny said, stood up and began pacing the floor, with short impatient strides. It required no mind reader to envision his thoughts. If he could bag Simon Girty, his reputation was made.

"Yes, they can," Phineas said. "I couldn't believe it myself when I caught up with their tracks, so I followed them."

"You saw them and made an actual count?"

Phineas nodded. By now melted snow was running off his buckskins in streams. "I saw Girty and his brother, George. I'm pretty sure Blue Jacket's with them."

"Where are they headed?"

"Dunlap's Station."

Some sixty people lived at Dunlap's Station which was a thousand-acre settlement located on the east side of the Great Miami River, seventeen miles northwest of the fort. Since the stockade was so poorly constructed, General Harmar had strongly urged the Station's inhabitants to move to Northbend. This they not only had refused to do, but had demanded the military protection due them. Thus, under the formula in effect before our army marched out, they had been allowed eighteen federals under Lieutenant Jacob Kingsbury. They still had this contingent, although we now had only eighty-five federals at Fort Washington. Two days previously a dispatch from Lieutenant Kingsbury stated that ten of his men were ill with pneumonia. He was sending the sick men to the fort, he informed us, with a request that they be replaced. "That I cannot replace those men, Jacob very well knows," Major Ziegler had remarked to me upon receiving the dispatch. "To satisfy the inhabitants, is why he writes that."

"I hot-footed it to Dunlap's," Phineas said, "and told Jacob what to expect. He says he can hold out two days. Coming through Cincinnati, I alerted the Rangers. They ought to be here soon. And I sent word to Columbia that their boys should come fast as they can."

I, of course, was taking notes. Looking in my direction, Lieutenant Denny's expression clouded. Although Major Ziegler, like General Harmar, had allowed Phineas what might be regarded as extraordinary authority in emergencies, it was clear that Lieutenant Denny would have preferred to have been the one who had issued these orders.

The sound of shuffling feet could be heard in the outer office. "What's that?" Lieutenant Denny asked me.

I moved to the outer office. The fort's seven officers were assembled there. They knew the news and their eager young faces made it evident that they wanted to go after Simon Girty. Not one of those men was twenty-five years old. Lieutenant Denny was only twenty-three. "May I inquire, gentlemen, the purpose of this visit?" I said and they told me, all speaking at once, how anxious they were to catch Simon Girty.

When I returned to the inner office, Lieutenant Denny had a map of the Miami Purchase spread out on his desk. "Well, what was it?" he asked me.

"Your officers request that I should inform you that they are most anxious to catch Simon Girty," I said.

"It can't be done, Ebenezer," Phineas said. "Girty'll fade when the relief gets to two hours from the Station."

Lieutenant Denny glared at the map. "It's not possible that Girty's going after Northbend?"

"He'd be a God-damned fool, Ebenezer. I just told you. He wants food. They ate those horses they stole at Columbia. Girty'll take the Station's grain and cattle. Sure, he'll hit the Station, but before we get there, he'll fade."

Lieutenant Denny was still glaring at the map.

"Christ, Ebenezer," Phineas said. "Girty's smart as they come. If he goes to Northbend, he's got the Ohio River on one side, the Great Miami on the other. We'd have him hemmed in. Don't you think he knows that?"

"Yes, I know he knows that!" Lieutenant Denny retorted angrily. "And I know it too."

"Then what's eating you? I know how bad you want Girty, but you can't get him. There's nothing to do but send out the relief fast as you can."

Lieutenant Denny stood up and moved to the window facing the parade. "Girty's at the Station by now?"

"For eight, maybe ten hours I'd figure."

"The stockade," Lieutenant Denny said. "I've never seen it. It's supposed to be in woeful shape."

"If you tried your best, you couldn't build one worse," Phineas said. "What it is, is eight or ten one-room log cabins connected by a picket fence." The picket fence, eight feet high, had been an afterthought. The cabins, Phineas explained, for the sake of convenience, were built with the roofs sloping outward, the reverse of what they should have been for defense. The outer eaves, Phineas said, were so low that it was not uncommon for dogs, when shut out of the stockade to spring from adjacent stumps upon the roofs of the cabins and thence into the enclosure.

Lieutenant Denny moved back to the map. "How big is the enclosure?"

"An acre."

"The river?"

"Deep enough to protect one side," Phineas said. "She's not frozen solid yet."

"The clearing?"

"Plenty of it, but it's full of big tree stumps that go right up to the stockade."

"Who in the hell allowed something like that?"

"Jacob begged them to clear out those stumps," Phineas said. "They just never got around to it." He added that Lieutenant Kingsbury had also begged the inhabitants to replace the windows of their cabins with portholes, but they had not done so. Only the cabin which Lieutenant Kingsbury used as his headquarters had portholes.

Lieutenant Denny looked up from the map. "Kingsbury, you say, claims he can hold out two days?"

"Yes."

"I've never met Kingsbury."

"Jacob's one of the best, Ebenezer."

"Exactly what did he say about his situation?"

"He's short of lead. He's got next to no water because his wells are frozen. What's going to help him is that everything's covered with a sheet of ice. Girty can't get far throwing in torches."

On a piece of paper, Lieutenant Denny drew three sides of a square, indicative of the stockade, the absent line representing the side of the stockade facing the Great Miami River. He then wrote down the number "*eight*," which is how many able-bodied federals Lieutenant Kingsbury had. "How many of the inhabitants can fight?" he asked Phineas.

"Maybe thirty men, if you count the young boys. Jacob's got the women trained fairly well. He claims a dozen can fill in. Damned near all can load."

Lieutenant Denny put a *"three"* before the *"eight."* "They can hold off a hundred Indians," he said, "even with all those stumps in the clearing."

"Just what are you trying to hatch up, Ebenezer?"

Lieutenant Denny spoke eagerly. "The siege of the stockade will be actually incidental? What Girty wants is the grain and cattle?"

"Yes."

"He'll run soon as the relief approaches?"

"Yes."

"There'll be fifty Cincinnati Rangers. I'll add fifteen federals, let us say. That's enough to lift the siege?"

"Yes."

"I send them out under Truman. They won't hurry. When Gano and the boys from Columbia get here, they and forty federals will follow under your command. You will take off as if after Truman, but you will break north. Girty can't cross the Great Miami. If you can get your boys above Girty and Truman times it right, you've got Girty."

"Not a chance, Ebenezer," Phineas said. "Girty's left a ring of scouts behind that's thicker than a swarm of mosquitoes."

"I know that! You can get through them?"

"Never. You'd never fool Girty that way, Ebenezer. Even if we did, we'd never get Girty. All we'd be doing is trading dead federals for dead Indians."

"Oh, Christ!" Lieutenant Denny said. "Certainly there's some way to devise a workable plan along the ideas I've suggested?"

"There isn't, Ebenezer," Phineas said. "If it makes you feel any better, I'll lay you fifty to one that nobody but old Father Time'll ever catch Simon Girty. And I'll tell you why. The Indians think he's a tin god. They never let him fight it out. The minute things get hot, they send him packing."

Lieutenant Denny sighed so deeply, it was almost as if he were groaning. "That's that then," he said. "You'll command the relief, Phineas. Will fifteen federals be enough?"

"Yes."

"I'll tell Truman he's taking his orders from you. Happy hunting."

"Thanks."

"You're welcome and I'll take that damned fifty to one bet."

"Deal," Phineas said.

"Deal," Lieutenant Denny said.

Lieutenant Denny moved to the outer office. "Gentlemen," I heard him saying before closing the door, "it is with the deepest regret that I must inform you that we cannot go after Simon Girty . . ."

"Phineas," I said, "that was a crazy bet. Think it through. You didn't set a time limit. Denny can't lose."

"I won't either," Phineas said. "If I do, I'll be glad."

"And walking to Dunlap's Station," I said. "You haven't slept in over thirty hours."

"I'll be all right," Phineas said. "I'll catch some sleep at the stockade, then I'm heading for Detroit."

"Detroit!"

"Yes, God damn it, I've got to go there. Don't tell Kitty, but I bumped into one of Girty's rear scouts I know from years back. He told me about a woods crazy fellow they caught last week. It sure sounds like he was Emil. They took him to Detroit."

"I thought they weren't taking prisoners these days?"

"He's woods crazy. Didn't you hear me say that?"

"I heard you say it," I said, "but what's that got to do with it?"

"Indians won't lay a hand on somebody's who's woods crazy. They think he's possessed of the devil. They'll give Emil to the British who'll throw him in jail like you were. When he gets better, they'll trade him off. Let's figure he gets better in a month or so. If I'm not up there to tell Emil what a big jackass he was about Kitty, he'll be gone and I'll never find him."

"Can you make it to Detroit in a month?"

"Just about," Phineas said, "if I hurry."

II

————◀◆▶————

Two hours before Phineas' contingent reached Dunlap's Station, Simon Girty raised the siege and took to the woods. Within eighteen hours after taking its leave, the contingency, accompanied by the Station's sick federals, was back at Fort Washington. They brought the news that all of the Station's inhabitants had signed a petition stating:

We, the inhabitants at the settlement called Dunlap's Station have considered under what great disadvantages we are to labor for the great part of this year, after the reduction of our live stock, grain and all

other necessities of life, by an attack lately made upon us by a party
of savages—and therefore have concluded to leave this place as soon
as we can possibly build craft to remove ourselves down the Great
Miami River.

A young man, named Michael Lutz, a citizen of Dunlap's Station, who
had helped bring in the sick, came into headquarters. "You Lieutenant
Morrow?" he asked.

"Yes."

"Lieutenant Denny wants me to tell you what happened, so you can
write it into the records."

"Sit down and help yourself to whiskey," I said.

"Thank you, sir," Lutz said. "This whiskey sure does taste good. I've
been trying to think what to say. Can't think of a thing except that Girty
and three hundred Indians attacked us. We just did manage to hold them
off."

Michael Lutz's estimate that there were three hundred Indians should
not be regarded as accurate. Our returning federals had said there was no
way of knowing the Indians' strength. Any number of the Station's inhabitants had been convinced that Girty's contingency numbered at least
five hundred. "It may help," I said, "if you'll recall what happened and
tell it to me, step by step."

"You know about Abner Hunt?"

"I've heard what happened to him," I said, "but since this is going
into the records as your account, you had better give me your version."

"Hunt and three other men from Cincinnati were in our neck of the
woods, surveying. Girty—"

"Pardon me," I said. "We should enter the names of the other three
men. I've been told they were Colonel John S. Wallace, John Sloan, and a
Mr. Cunningham?"

"That's right."

"Do you know Mr. Cunningham's first name?"

"No."

"Please go on. I'm sorry to have interrupted you."

"That's all right," Lutz said. "Girty ambushed them while they were
finishing breakfast. Cunningham was killed. Hunt fell off his horse while
trying to get away and was captured. Wallace wasn't hit. Sloan was wounded
bad in the chest. What saved Wallace was that while he was running
away one of his leggings came loose and he tripped. The Indians thought
they'd hit him. First Wallace and Sloan tried to go to Fort Washington, but
Sloan was too weak, so they came to us."

"Lieutenant Kingsbury had already been alerted by Phineas Ford, hadn't he?"

"So I'm told," Michael Lutz said. "I was at my cabin when Phineas Ford showed up. Lieutenant Kingsbury had everybody come to the stockade and bring what he could of his belongings. But what could I bring! Only what my wife and me and my young ones could carry. We couldn't bring our livestock or food. Just some clothes and some pots and pans. Those with babes in arms, couldn't even bring that.

"When we got to the stockade, there was no sign of Indians and everybody wanted to go back to his cabin and get some more of his belongings. But Lieutenant Kingsbury said he smelled a rat and wouldn't let us. He sent out a patrol. They found Cunningham's body, scalped and tomahawked, and they buried him. When they got back, they said it looked like the Indians had headed north.

"Of course they wouldn't have without first going after the outlying cabins, so Lieutenant Kingsbury made us stay in the stockade and had us go through what we should do when we were attacked.

"All the stations were manned that night. How the Indians ever managed to sneak up on us, I'll never know because we sure were watching for them. But just before sunrise, there they were, damned near at our garrison gate. They scared a dog, who jumped into the enclosure and that's what warned us. If it hadn't been for that dog, they'd have made it to the gate and that would have been the end of us.

"Lieutenant Kingsbury sounded the alarm. At first those sleeping thought the lieutenant was just putting us to proof with another drill, so hardly anybody got out of bed. Then the shooting began and they came out of the cabins in their underwear. A federal named McVickers was wounded when the Indians started shooting, not bad though, and nobody else was hit.

"With sunrise we could see that the clearing was full of Indians. They were painted and all dolled up with fancy feathers and they had deer hoofs and horns tied around their knees. The clank of those things sure made a weird sound.

"The Indians were behind tree stumps, shooting at us like mad. God damned, but we should have cleared out those stumps! Lieutenant Kingsbury must have told us to do it a dozen times. One Sunday it was agreed we'd do it, but only three of us showed up. 'The hell with it!' we said and it just never got done.

"Pretty soon Girty stood up Hunt. Hunt was tied up and Girty, who was behind a stump, had him by a rope. Hunt yelled out that if the garrison gave up his own life would be spared and so would everybody else's.

"Lieutenant Kingsbury, of course, didn't bite at that bait. 'Shoot Hunt,' he ordered, but nobody would. 'Six of you fire at him,' the lieutenant then said, 'that way nobody'll know who hit him for sure.' But nobody wanted to do that either. 'Then I'll do it!' Lieutenant Kingsbury said and grabbed my musket. But when it came down to it, he couldn't do it either. I guess now, all of us wish we had.

"Lieutenant Kingsbury told Hunt he couldn't accept Girty's promise. Girty yelled out that he wanted a parley. He said he was five hundred strong, with a ring of scouts behind him and three hundred Miamis weren't a day off.

"Lieutenant Kingsbury said he didn't give a damn because he'd sent word to Judge Symmes and relief was coming up from Northbend.

"Girty laughed at that and said he knew damned well Judge Symmes was in New Jersey which, of course, was the truth.

"Lieutenant Kingsbury's boys started taking pot shots at any Indian who showed himself and I'm pretty sure they winged a few.

"Girty said that wasn't fair while a parley was going on.

"Lieutenant Kingsbury pretended he was mad at his boys for doing this and, in a voice loud enough for Girty to hear, he told them that they should stop it. Then he whispered for them to keep it up.

"That made Girty sore and the bastard told his boys to shoot at us. They really let fly. Bullets knocked the white plumage off the lieutenant's hat and he had to jump down from his position, but he wasn't hurt.

"Around noon, Girty yelled out that he was going to quit shooting until the moon went down. He told Lieutenant Kingsbury he had that long to think over giving up.

"Lieutenant Kingsbury told Girty to go to hell.

"Girty reminded him that he was five hundred strong and said that if we didn't give up, he'd burn down the stockade and massacre us all.

"Lieutenant Kingsbury told Girty to come ahead. 'I don't care if you have five hundred devils at your command,' he told Girty, 'you'll never get inside this enclosure.'

"We didn't have anything but parched corn to eat. The women came around and fed us. There was next to no water. Our lead was going down fast. Lieutenant Kingsbury joked with everybody though, so nobody was close to panicking even when we saw our cabins going up in smoke and the Indians were taking our grain and leading off our cattle.

"Lieutenant Kingsbury was counting on Phineas Ford getting back to

Fort Washington and bringing us relief. In case Phineas Ford didn't make it, he offered two joes to anyone who'd slip out of the enclosure and go to Fort Washington. William Wiseman agreed to try it and he slipped out just after dark. He went down the Miami on a raft.

"The moon went down shortly after sunset and Girty sure kept his promise. Flaming arrows and firebrands started coming at us, so many of them, it was like it was daytime. The only thing that saved us was that everything was covered with ice. It was our women, mostly, who put out the fires.

"Around midnight, Girty brought out Abner Hunt again, but had him in the dark where we couldn't see him. Hunt pleaded with us to give up and said if we didn't, he'd be burned to death. There was nothing we could do for him.

"Girty tied Hunt to a log and kindled a slow fire on his belly. Hunt's shrieks were terrible to hear. All night long and into the morning we could hear them.

"By morning our lead was almost gone. We brought out pewter plates and spoons and ran them into bullets. We couldn't exchange fire for fire, so Girty was sure to suspect what was what. Mrs. Morgan got panicky, got a pair of shears, and started to cut off her hair so she couldn't be scalped. That started some of the other women to shrieking. Lieutenant Kingsbury managed to quiet them down.

"Around half-after eight o'clock, Girty stepped up his shooting. It sure looked like this was a prelude to an attack. If he made it, we couldn't stop him. A lot of people went to their knees and prayed, but everybody was calm. Even Mrs. Morgan. Lieutenant Kingsbury kept telling us not to despair. It was a miracle, he said, that so far nobody had been killed. 'You must believe in miracles,' he kept saying. 'Our relief will come.'

"All this while we could still hear Hunt's moaning. At maybe nine o'clock, it suddenly stopped. Then after a fierce volley of musketry, the Indian shooting stopped. Then we saw them fading into the woods and pretty soon everything was quiet. While the shooting was going on, everybody had to yell to be heard. People was still yelling at each other, out of force of habit. That's how sudden the shooting stopped and Girty faded.

"Two hours later Phineas Ford and his boys showed up. Wiseman had run into them and they'd sent him on to Fort Washington because he was damned near frozen to death. He slipped through the Indians all right, but he wouldn't have gotten to the fort in time. It was the relief that saved us and I say God bless Lieutenant Ebenezer Denny for sending them out so fast. Girty left two dead Indians behind. We skinned them. We buried Abner Hunt. His brains were beat out and his body was mangled. When we found him, he was lying on top of a still smoldering fire. Two war clubs were laid across his chest."

III

Major Ziegler had gone to Louisville by flatboat. When a commanding officer, if he was a federal, arrived at his destination by flatboat it was customary for him to stand at the bow in dress uniform while the boat was putting to. The people at the fort would shoot cannon balls into a mound of earth, so they could be retrieved, as a salute.

While Major Ziegler was being so honored, his flatboat rammed into a mudbar and the major was jolted overboard. When fished out of the water, it was discovered that his left leg has broken, no doubt the result of having struck against the gunnel. The carrier who brought us this news, approximately a week after the major's departure, said the bone was protruding. This meant the major's leg would have to be amputated.

Six weeks passed before we had news of Major Ziegler's state of health, in fact news of any kind. The cold weather held, keeping us snowbound. Our patrols reported no signs of Indians. As a result of the enforced inactivity, most of the fort's inhabitants were bored stiff and in the evenings had nothing better to do than to become drunk.

For Melissa and me the time passed rapidly and pleasantly. We had each other's company and that of Kitty's, Cornelius Sedam's and his wife's, and Dr. Allison's. Since Dr. Allison's quarters contained a Franklin stove, it was here that our get-togethers were held. They were always most enjoyable occasions.

While in the larger sense nothing of a stupendous nature transpired during this period, it is next to impossible for human beings to coexist without something happening. For example there were two anxious days when Melissa was certain she was pregnant. But she was not. I probably should mention also that with considerable spare time on my hands, I made an effort to begin my book. To my great annoyance, I got nowhere.

I am able to see now that, being so close to what was taking place, I was unable to view my material with objective perspective.

Then there was the night when a young ensign, whose name need not be mentioned, forced open the door of Kitty Kummerschmitt's cabin. He was quite drunk and Kitty had no trouble pushing him out into the snow.

Kitty, Melissa, and Dolly Sedam were the only women living at the fort and all the officers were trying to seduce Kitty. From a man's point of view, this is understandable. Since her operation, Kitty had lost all her excess poundage, but none of her physical attributes. Kitty's body, it must be agreed, was voluptuous. Her sparkling blue eyes entered into it too. They opened wide whenever anyone talked to her, giving the impression she was hanging on every word.

Thus Kitty, who thought only of Emil, simply by being alive, was in constant danger. When a second attempt to storm her threshold was made, we all realized that protective measures were necessary. After discussing the matter with Melissa and Dolly, Kitty asked Dr. Allison if she might move into his quarters. "Of course you may," Dr. Allison told her. This shocked me. "Kitty and you under the same roof!" I said to Dr. Allison. "Thank you, Tom," Dr. Allison replied. "I cannot recall ever having received so flattering a compliment."

One day before Major Ziegler returned, we received, via Pittsburgh, our first news of the new year from the East. The mail pouch had lain over in Bracken for almost a month. Arriving at Bracken, the carrier had announced that he would not take another step until the snow melted. A citizen of Bracken, on his way to Northbend, made the delivery.

Limestone, this man informed us, had beat off an Indian attack in late December, but Bracken had seen no sign of Indians. He had walked considerable of the way, he said, on the frozen Ohio River. "That was most foolish," Lieutenant Denny told him.

"There are no Indians around," the man said.

"It was still most foolish," Lieutenant Denny said.

"All right," the man said, "it was most foolish."

"Do you expect to do any more walking on the Ohio River?" Lieutenant Denny asked.

"Yes."

"I want it in the records," Lieutenant Denny said to me, "that I have warned Mr. Isaac Gibson not to walk on the frozen Ohio River."

"Yes, sir," I said.

The mail carrier had said that, once the snow started, no new candidates for the second regiment had arrived at Fort Pitt. Other than that, the man said, neither Bracken nor Limestone had received any word concerning the state of the new expeditionary force. The only news was that a group of French émigrés had founded the settlement of Gallipolis, "The City of the Gauls," on the Ohio side of the river, some three miles below the Kanawha. Apparently these people had believed what they read in the newsprints about the wonders of the Ohio Country. They had come totally unprepared, knew nothing of coping with life in the wilderness. Many did not have warm clothes. After attempting to live out the winter in lean-tos, they had given up and left.

While the man talked, I opened the mail pouch. Except for a single official dispatch, it contained only personal mail, addressed to many enlisted men already transferred to other forts. One letter was addressed to me. Recognizing the childish handwriting as being Susan's, I quickly slipped this letter into my jacket.

"There's just this one dispatch," I told Lieutenant Denny after the man left. "Who is Samuel Hodgdon?"

After reading the dispatch, Lieutenant Denny said, "Hodgdon's the new Quartermaster General, so it at least looks as if something is being done. Hodgdon's sent through some tents. I suppose they're still in Pittsburgh. They were bought in Philadelphia."

"That's all the news?"

"That's all," Lieutenant Denny said. "Didn't I see you stick a letter into your jacket?"

"You did."

Lieutenant Denny laughed dryly. "I'm supposed to see all the envelopes, you know."

"I hadn't thought of that," I said. "Do you want to examine the envelope? It's a personal letter, I assure you."

"Never mind," he said. "The guilty look on your face tells me it's purely personal and I can guess who it's from. If I see Susan again in Pittsburgh, shall I tell her you're a happily married man?"

"By all means," I said, "if that's who you think the letter is from."

Appearing to be quite pleased with his powers of deduction, Lieutenant Denny handed me the Hodgdon dispatch, which contained only an invoice. "Are you familiar with this Philadelphia canvas firm?" he asked me.

"No," I said, "I am not."

"I am," he replied. "Shysters. Read the invoice. It's the Harmar Expedition all over again. The army's not only being overcharged, but we're being sent junk as well."

"The invoice says the tents are made of first class Russian sheeting," I said.

"Sure they are," he said. "That's the flanks. Look at the ends. Osnaburg.

Inferior stuff. And they're not big enough. They won't keep out the rain."

Putting on his campaign coat, Lieutenant Denny moved to the door. "I guess I'll see what's going on at the armory," he said in the manner of someone who has nothing better to do with his time.

"Enjoy yourself," I said.

"I don't consider that a particularly funny remark," he said and slammed the door as he left.

For a moment or so I wondered if Lieutenant Denny would ever discover that, as a result of what was going on in the armory, our cooks, at the request of the enlisted men, were spitting and sometimes even urinating in Lieutenant Denny's soup. We had 675 stands of arms at the fort, totally out of repair, actually worthy of the junk pile. To put them in order, if indeed it were possible, required a great number of fatigue men and artificers, but we had no artificers nor any tools save files and hammers. Infuriated at being snowbound while in command of the fort, Lieutenant Denny, in order that there be some show of progress on his record, had ordered the enlisted men to repair the arms. He had done this over the unanimous objections of his staff. Grumbling, cursing Lieutenant Denny, the enlisted men were putting in a full day of filing and hammering away, accomplishing nothing.

Opening Susan's letter, I read that she expected to be at Fort Washington in July and was looking forward to resuming our Philadelphia relationship. "Fat Dicky," Susan wrote, had seen Mae Dwyer and an arrangement had been made to supply the new expeditionary force with women. This was all settled, Susan stated, so there was no doubt about it, she was coming. As in her previous letter, she concluded with a string of x-x-x-x's.

"Fat Dicky" meant Major General Richard Butler, to whom I had been introduced any number of times, at various social functions in Philadelphia, without being remembered upon any of the occasions. While Susan's letter was quite disjointed and assumed I knew things which I didn't, she had referred to the "new army." Thus it is quite possible that I was the first person at Fort Washington to receive word that there was actually a new expeditionary force.

Properly, I believe, I had made no mention to Melissa of Susan's previous letter nor her greetings sent via Lieutenant Denny. Now Susan was no longer someone who could be forgotten and something told me that Lieutenant Denny was merely awaiting an opportune moment to let his information slip out in Melissa's presence.

After giving the matter considerable thought, I decided to wait at least a few days before reaching a decision upon what to do about Susan's letter. When I went to our quarters Melissa and Dolly and Kitty were chatting away while awaiting a cake to bake. This was Dr. Allison's birthday, Melissa told me. A surprise party was being contemplated.

"To be given here?" I asked.

"At Dr. Allison's quarters," Melissa said and we went over the details about how we would lure Dr. Allison to the hospital, slip into his quarters and have everything in readiness when he returned.

We did surprise Dr. Allison, completely, and the affair was a success. "Tom," Melissa said when we were back in our own quarters and preparing to retire, "were you worrying about something this evening?"

"Not especially," I said.

"At times your mind seemed miles away."

My response was impulsive. "It's possible that it may have been," I said and handed Melissa Susan's letter. "I think that you should read this."

After reading the letter, Melissa handed it back. "How interesting," she said.

I threw the letter into the fireplace.

"That is that," I said.

"Yes," Melissa said, "it is."

Melissa did not appear to be angry or hurt. It is difficult to say how she was except that she was not her natural self. We undressed in silence and went to bed. When I kissed her, Melissa's body was quite stiff. After wondering if I should pretend not to notice this, I said, "I do hope this hasn't made you feel badly?"

"And why should it?" Melissa said and sat up.

There was still enough blaze in the fire for me to be able to see Melissa's face. Her expression made it abundantly clear that her reply had been rhetorical. "It shouldn't," I said, "I never quite understood what it was with Susan and me. It was something that merely happened. I think, now that the matter has come up, I should tell you all about it."

"I do not wish to hear it," Melissa said, which wasn't so, and was proven by the avid attention she gave as I told her how the Susan affair had come about. "That is all there ever was to it," I said, by way of conclusion.

"It was not necessary for you to have told me all this," Melissa said. "I am certainly sophisticated enough, I believe, to be aware that I am not the only woman whose body you have possessed."

"Possessing anybody's body, that is as such," I said, "hasn't got anything to do with it."

"There is no need to philosophize," Melissa said. "I listened most attentively to your explanation and was able to comprehend the point you are attempting to establish. And now, it might be well if we dropped the subject and went to sleep."

"Before doing so," I said, "I should like you to tell me that I am—forgiven, I was about to say, but that is not the proper word. I should like to hear you say that you understand."

"I do," Melissa said, "and now may I say good night?"

"If you wish," I said.

"I do so wish," Melissa said, lay down, and pulled the blanket up to her chin.

I kissed her hair, for her face was turned the other way. "Good night, Melissa," I said.

"Good night," she said.

"This will be the first time since we are married," I said, "that you will not have kissed me good night. Do you think that is wise?"

"No, I don't," she said, turned and gave me a kiss.

"Thank you," I said.

"You are welcome," she said.

I pulled her to me. "I love you," I said. "Actually there has never been anybody else."

"Please, Tom," she said, "not tonight."

At this moment the sentry on the wall walk called out that it was twelve o'clock and that all was well.

"It is no longer tonight," I said.

"No, it is not," Melissa said and responded to my embrace.

IV

The following day, around noon, is when Major Ziegler returned to Fort Washington. He came on horse, with a militiamen escort, and to our surprise and relief the assumption that he'd lost a leg proved erroneous. "Off, I would not let them saw it," he told the group of us who'd greeted him at the main gate. "'Die you surely will then, Major,' they told me. 'Die, I surely will not,' to them, I said. 'Impossible it is,' they are now saying. Dead I should already be, from gangrene. But alive I must be, for here I am."

After repairing to his quarters for two hours of rest, Major Ziegler came into headquarters to discuss, with Lieutenant Denny, what had taken place during the past seven weeks. "Correct you were, Lieutenant," he said when the Dunlap Station matter came up. "Simon Girty, you could never have caught."

"The temptation to go after him was great, sir," Lieutenant Denny said. "I was primarily influenced by advice given me by Phineas Ford."

Lieutenant Denny said this with most becoming modesty. It was, however, also prudent behavior. I had written into the records that Lieutenant Denny, after exhausting all possible means of devising a successful method of catching Simon Girty, had based his decision on Phineas Ford's appraisal of the situation.

Saluting, Lieutenant Denny turned over command of the fort to Major Ziegler and prepared to leave. "A staff meeting I am calling tonight at eight o'clock," Major Ziegler told him.

"Yes, sir," Lieutenant Denny said, somewhat crestfallen, for the major's announcement meant that instead of being given advance information of the news relative to the new expeditionary force, he would be receiving it no sooner than anyone else. It was a fine point, to be sure, but Lieutenant Denny had caught it.

When the lieutenant left, Major Ziegler examined his brandy stock. Although he said nothing, he knew very well that it was not me who had been doing the sampling.

"Do you need me for anything, sir?" I inquired.

"An order for me to sign, you will write out, to stop work in the armory," Major Ziegler said.

"Yes, sir."

"In two days you will post it. The knack you have, Lieutenant Morrow, of making words sound better than they are."

I understood that this meant the major did not wish to humiliate a fellow officer by an out-and-out countermanded order. "May I suggest, sir," I said, "that the order be worded to the effect that since as much has been accomplished in the armory as might be expected, you are relieving the men of this duty?"

"An excellent way to say it, that is," Major Ziegler told me.

"Thank you, sir," I said and started for the door.

"From General Harmar, I have a letter," Major Ziegler said. "His kindest regards, he sends to you. Your report, he says, was excellent."

It was most kind of the General to have done this and I was quite touched. "Thank you for telling me, sir," I said. "May I inquire if you are aware of the General's state of health?"

"Good enough, it is. Back home he has gone. Adjutant General of Pennsylvania he has become. You wish to know, no doubt, what of his report, Congress thought?"

"Yes, sir, I do."

Major Ziegler shook his head sadly. "On deaf ears, it fell. Blamed, our fine General is being, for our defeat."

That night's staff meeting was held in the outer room of headquarters. Shortly before Major Ziegler's arrival, two of his waiters brought each officer a bottle of brandy, saying this was the major's homecoming present.

We, of course, all came to attention upon Major Ziegler's entrance. "Seated you please will be, gentlemen," he said brusquely. His mood, it was plain to see, was most dour.

Lieutenant Denny, as was expected of him, remained standing. "Is it something you wish to say, Lieutenant?" Major Ziegler inquired.

"Yes, sir," Lieutenant Denny said. "Speaking for your staff, I wish to express our extreme gratification that you are back at Fort Washington and in the best of health."

"Happy to be back, I am," Major Ziegler said. "Now to business, down we will quickly get. Questions you may ask, when finished I am. The news you all wish to hear is that if by negotiation, peace cannot be had, an army will be raised. In command will be Major General Arthur St. Clair. Second-in-command will be Major General Richard Butler. Gentlemen, to your feet you will please rise. A toast, I propose, to the new Commander-in-Chief of the United States Army."

"A toast to the Commander-in-Chief of the United States Army," everyone recited dutifully and sat down.

By looking about sternly, Major Ziegler quieted the murmur of disappointment which the announcement of the St. Clair appointment had brought on. Putting on his spectacles and bringing out a piece of paper, Major Ziegler spoke from notes. Congress, he said, had appropriated $312,-686.20 to finance the new expedition.

Before writing down the figure, I looked up. "Yes, Lieutenant Morrow," Major Ziegler said gruffly and pointed to his notes, "the twenty cents, it belongs there."

If the money could not be raised by taxes, Major Ziegler went on to say, a loan would be secured.

"Three thousand strong, the new army will be," Major Ziegler said and explained this meant six hundred federals when the second and depleted first regiments were filled, plus some four hundred federals now stationed at Forts Steuben, Harmar, Washington, Knox, and at various stations. The remaining two thousand would be made up of fourteen hundred six-month levies recruited by quota from the Eastern states and six hundred Kentucky militiamen.

Recruiting of the federals, he pointed out, was presently in effect. Raising the levies, would have to await the results of the peace talks.

These may well have already begun, Major Ziegler said. "On Cornplanter, Colonel Thomas Procter will first call," he told us. "If happy this talk turns out, to the chiefs of the Ohio tribes, Colonel Procter will go. A treaty, it is hoped, will here in Fort Washington be signed."

No matter what, Major Ziegler said, Colonel Procter should be back in New York Town by early May. If his mission were unsuccessful, recruiting of the levies would begin and shortly General Charles Scott would march out of Fort Knox with five-hundred-twenty-five Kentucky militiamen, to harass and keep the Indiana and Illinois tribes occupied.

On July 10th, General St. Clair's army would set out from Fort Washington, under instructions to destroy forever the power of the Ohio Country Indians.

"Over the meeting now is," Major Ziegler said and brought out his clay. "Lieutenant Morrow, your record book you will please close. Questions you may now ask, gentlemen."

Lieutenant Denny put the first one. "Sir, can Congress possibly believe that the Procter Mission has even the slightest hope of success?"

"A congressman, I am not, Lieutenant Denny," Major Ziegler said sternly. "Gentlemen, no questions will I answer about what Congress thinks."

"I did not hear you make any mention of the erection of forts, sir?"

"Build some, General St. Clair expects to do."

"How many, sir?"

"That, I do not know."

"Have you any idea, sir, when erection will begin?"

"That, I have not."

"Sir, I hope my next question will not be considered a political one. May I assume, sir, that in order not to anger the British, the forts will not be strung all the way to Niagara?"

"Greatly will I be surprised if the forts are built beyond the water shed. Why, is not for me to say."

"Thank you, sir. May I ask another question?"

"Later, Lieutenant. Ensign Sedam, I see, has stood up."

"May I inquire, sir, who is in charge of the recruiting?"

"Major General Richard Butler."

"The federals and also the levies?"

"So far as I know."

"Is there news as to our arms and supplies, sir?"

"From the East, they will come. Quartermaster General will be Samuel Hodgdon. Contractor will be William Duer . . . Lieutenant Denny?"

"I should like to get back, sir, to Ensign Sedam's question about recruiting. Is there word on what progress has been made to fill the first and second regiments?"

"I have none."

"Is the present method of recruiting federals still in effect and, if so, do you know if General Butler plans to improve upon it?"

The present method was for captains, coming from Philadelphia to Fort Pitt, to enlist men for the United States Army while en route. For this they received two dollars for each enlisted man, no matter what the state of his health or abilities. Most of the enlistees were jail sweepings, drunkards, or men scheduled for the debtors' prison. Many were accompanied by whores.

"Of how he will recruit our new army," Major Ziegler said, "General Butler has not acquainted me . . . Ensign Marks?"

"When will General St. Clair be arriving here, sir?"

"Expected he is, when the snow melts."

Ensign Marks was nineteen years old, a rosy-cheeked lad, who looked much younger. A gullible chap, he was the victim of considerable officers' horseplay. "May I ask, sir, if General St. Clair is still the Governor of the Northwest Territory?"

"He is."

"The reason I ask, sir," Ensign Marks said with deadly earnestness, and his question produced the only laughter of the evening, "is that I wish to know whether he should be addressed as 'Governor' or 'General'?"

"Your own judgment you must use, Ensign," Major Ziegler said.

From the rear of the room someone, without rising, pointed out in a voice loud enough for everyone to hear, that now St. Clair would be receiving two thousand dollars yearly for being Governor and four dollars a day for being a major general. "But I still don't understand," this officer remarked, "where the twenty cents comes in."

Major Ziegler stood up. "The brandy, I can see, you are beginning to feel. Wise it is, that I should leave. My permission to enjoy yourselves here, you have."

"Please, sir," Ensign Marks pleaded. "I have one more question which concerns me greatly."

"Ask it you may," Major Ziegler, who was now at the door, replied.

"Those six hundred Kentucky militiamen, sir? Will they again be under command of Colonels Trotter and Hardin?"

"Under command of Major Hamtranck, they will be, *Gott sei dank*," Major Ziegler said and left.

Cornelius Sedam and I left shortly thereafter. The drinking bout which followed was, I learned, rather boisterous. During the course of the night's general activity someone, as an indication of his opinion that our army was in a state of dire distress, raised the fort's flag—upside down.

V

The cold weather held until late March. When the snow melted the Ohio River became a roaring stream, flooding her banks, rising up to Fort Washington's outer wall, reaching heights our engineers had said could not possibly be attained. On the Kentucky side it was as if here was an inland sea. The slate-gray, glacier-like water had lapped its way to the very base of the hills.

Then beating a hasty retreat, the river became serene and beautiful again. As you watched this, you could not help thinking of other streams, starting out as trickles of water in the mountains, fighting their way downward to the sea. The Ohio had none of this because she was born great. But she had achieved her greatness by stealing what the efforts of the Allegheny and Monongahela rivers produced. And I sense this, every time I look at her.

It was a superb spring. Forsythia and redbuds gave the surrounding hills gorgeous coloration. The woods abounded with violets and wild plum blossoms. Melissa, I discovered, was most adept at making floral arrangements. Some of her redbud and wild plum blossom creations were truly remarkable.

It was also, outwardly, a peaceful spring. Our patrols reported no signs of Indians during April and May. The citizens of Cincinnati went about their planting, many disregarding a local ordinance which required them to carry firearms at all times. It would be a good year for farming, everyone was predicting. In the bottom lands, where the Ohio River had left her rich deposits, green peas planted in mid-April were being eaten during the third week of May.

One, however, could never feel quite at ease. During April and May there was no news from New York Town, or even from Fort Pitt. Officially,

Fort Washington never was notified that Colonel Procter's peace mission had failed. We learned of this fully expected result, indirectly, via a dispatch which arrived from Louisville on May 30th. A week prior, the dispatch stated, General Scott and his Kentuckians had marched out of Fort Knox.

In the mail pouch were also orders for Major Ziegler to go to Marietta. In command at Fort Harmar, he was to whip the second regiment into shape and bring it to Fort Washington to take part in the coming campaign.

"A *campaign*, they are now calling it!" Major Ziegler snorted when he read his removal order. This and his *"Gott sei dank"* remark issued at the staff meeting were the only verbal statements I heard him make which might be offered as definite testimony to his private thoughts.

"In command here, will be Lieutenant Denny," Major Ziegler said. "Lieutenant Morrow, appreciate it I will if my last nine bottles of brandy you will take to your quarters to keep safe for me."

Major Ziegler left before the day was over. Lieutenant Denny's first request as acting commander of Fort Washington was to ask to see the dispatches. "Nothing's said about when St. Clair will arrive," he said.

"That was very noticeable," I said.

". . . Procter's mission didn't get past Cornplanter," Lieutenant Denny muttered as he read on. "I could have told them that. These damned dispatches! They tell you everything except what you want to know. It's May the 30th! We're supposed to march out on July 10th. And what in the hell do they mean by *campaign?* Did you notice that that's what it's now being called?"

"Yes," I said, "I did notice that."

"St. Clair's got to be showing up soon," Lieutenant Denny said. "Campaign! An expedition, that's what it'll be. The Harmar Expedition all over again. Just like I said! And if Ziegler was sent to Fort Harmar that means they need a professional to train troops who are supposed to be trained and ready for action before leaving Fort Pitt. Wasn't there any word at all on supplies?"

"No," I said, "there wasn't."

"William Duer is not averse to picking up a stray dollar on the side," Lieutenant Denny grumbled. "Samuel Hodgdon's honest, but Duer is a thief."

Although I had heard this said by others, I offered no comment.

"And I can't think of anyone worse to be in charge of recruiting than Dicky Butler," Lieutenant Denny said. "He's a nice enough fellow and was a damned good general during the Rebellion, but now he weighs over three hundred pounds. You think I'm exaggerating, don't you? I mean it literally, he weighs over three hundred pounds."

"Yes, I know," I said.

"You do!" Lieutenant Denny said, listened most attentively to my reply, and seemed impressed that I had been invited to social gatherings at which General Butler was in attendance.

"Then you know," Lieutenant Denny said, "that since the Rebellion Butler's been living the life of a royal debauchee. Going from one party to another. His name's always in the newsprints. From Philadelphia to Boston! Do you know if he has private means?"

"No," I said, "I don't."

Lieutenant Denny paused a moment, apparently wondering about General Butler's financial situation. "St. Clair hates Butler worse than poison," he then said. "I take it, you know that?"

"I don't know it," I said. I could, however, well imagine that between the easygoing, loud-laughing General Richard Butler and the austere General Arthur St. Clair, there could well be a clash of personalities.

"The fur will really fly when those two meet head-on," Lieutenant Denny said and laughed dryly. "Butler's headstrong as hell and hasn't got Harmar's tact."

"One thing in Butler's favor," I said. "He's a former Indian Commissioner. He's been to the Ohio Country."

"One trip down the Ohio River!" Lieutenant Denny said. "That's something else that sickens me. A man gets on a flatboat, rides down the river, and New York Town now thinks he's become an expert on the Ohio Country."

"Amen, to that," I said, which was an indication of agreement to Lieutenant Denny's generalization. In all fairness to General Butler, it should be stated that his earlier trip to the Ohio Country had been a bit more than merely a ride down the river. He had visited various stations and held the role of observer when the Treaty of Fort Finney was signed.

Despite his righteous indignation, Lieutenant Denny had his wits about him. He wished to be named St. Clair's aide-de-camp. "I suppose," he said, "we'll have to hold some sort of an affair to honor St. Clair's arrival?"

"I suppose so," I said.

"Your wife and Dolly Sedam and that Kitty what-ever-in-the-hell her last name is? I take it they'll be willing to act as hostesses?"

"I'm sure they will," I said, "but I do think they should be asked."

"Of course that would be done!" Lieutenant Denny said. "You—and I will appreciate it—will ask them, as a special representative of the commander of the fort. We'll want a nice dinner and that sort of thing. St. Clair likes clay-baked catfish. Twenty-pounders, he fancies, are the most tender. I think it would be a nice gesture if we had one ready for him along with everything else. He can just take a bit, if he wants. It's the thought mainly. The women won't have to do any actual work. The cooks, anybody else they need, will be at their disposal."

Despite Melissa's and Dolly's and Kitty's dislike for Lieutenant Denny and General St. Clair, the prospect of being given a free hand in preparing for a festive occasion, and with all needed help provided for, was too good to resist. Their answer was yes. "May I presume," Dolly Sedam asked me with her face innocent-looking as a cherub's, "that our cooks will season the General's soup in a manner similar to that served to Lieutenant Denny?"

Two days later, shortly before noon, word reached us that a flotilla of twenty or more flatboats was a mile above Columbia. St. Clair and the army!

Immediately the prevailing atmosphere at Fort Washington became as if our drummers were beating to arms. Melissa, Dolly, and Kitty turned into spinning tops. Cooks scurried about. On the walls, cannons were being polished. About the parade, men policed up. Squad after squad was called out for inspection, by Lieutenant Denny himself.

Actually there was no panic, for Lieutenant Denny had laid his plans carefully. Everybody knew what to do. A dozen federals had been assigned to go to the river and catch a catfish. "It must be a twenty-pounder," I heard Lieutenant Denny admonishing the group as it prepared to leave. "Keep on until you get one."

When the tables were set up in the outer room of headquarters, where the dinner would be held, and most of the other arrangements were more or less in order, Lieutenant Denny suddenly decided that, since this was a beautiful day, it might be a pleasant change to hold a buffet style dinner on the parade. This suggestion infuriated Melissa, Dolly, and Kitty. Nothing came of it.

After searching his soul, Lieutenant Denny had decided that rather than await St. Clair on the wall walk, it would be more proper that he should canoe out to the flotilla and personally escort the Commander-in-Chief of the United States Army to Fort Washington. Two aides, he said, would be required. To Cornelius Sedam's and my surprise, he selected us. Melissa and Dolly, however, were not surprised. "What an obtuse man you are, Cornie," Dolly said. "Can't you see why Tom and you were selected?"

"I am quite capable of comprehending what you are intimating," Cornelius replied. "Should we be flattered?"

"If you are naïve enough, yes," Dolly said, "but you *could* look upon this as an excellent opportunity to accidentally dump Ebenezer Denny into the river."

Well before the flotilla rounded the upstream bend, everything was in readiness. As Lieutenant Denny, Cornelius and I, accompanied by music, colors, and honor guard, moved to the riverbank we saw that the Cincinnati Rangers and most of the settlement's citizens were assembled on Eastern Row. Cheering us lustily, they brought up our rear. Although St. Clair was generally disliked by the local citizenry, his name carried considerable weight with them. Highly regarded as a general it was believed, not only in Cincinnati, but elsewhere along the Ohio, I would learn, that under the command of General Arthur St. Clair, our army would vanquish the enemy.

Lieutenant Denny had instructed our artillerists to begin firing the moment the flotilla came into view and to keep it up until the Commander-in-Chief put foot upon Ohio soil. When both Cornelius and I pointed out that this meant more salutes then the President of the United States received, after consideration, Lieutenant Denny said it would make no difference. St. Clair, he felt, since the cannon balls would not be wasted, would be highly pleased.

Paddled by eight federals, we left shore when the cannons began booming. "God only knows how many salvos St. Clair'll get," Cornelius whispered to me. "But Denny's right. In this case St. Clair won't think regulations have been violated."

The river was running quite calmly. We headed for Kentucky, planned upon making an arclike approach and boarding St. Clair's flatboat on the leeward side. Lieutenant Denny had instructed his men to paddle with the utmost care. Not a drop of water must be allowed to touch our uniforms. We were, of course, dressed, powdered and polished up to the hilt.

Somebody at the bow of the flotilla's lead boat began waving his arms violently. "What's he trying to say?" Lieutenant Denny said. "And where's St. Clair? You'd think he'd be on that boat."

"Maybe he was riding a middle one, for safety's sake," Cornelius suggested.

"Not today, he wouldn't be," Lieutenant Denny said and ordered our paddlers to make directly for the flotilla.

When we were within hailing distance of the lead boat, Lieutenant Denny asked where General St. Clair was. "How in the hell do I know?" the boatman replied and inquired if Fort Washington were under attack.

"No, it's not under attack!" Lieutenant Denny shouted. "Who are you?"

"Alex Martinburg," the man said. "I'm taking grain to Fort Knox. On the last three boats are a hundred horses, for Fort Washington."

"Oh, Christ!" Lieutenant Denny said. "Oh, Jesus Christ! How can we shut up those damned cannons?"

There was no way to do that until we went ashore. And on the riverbank the citizens of Cincinnati had ignited a number of bonfires as part of their celebration, honoring St. Clair's arrival.

"A hundred horses!" Cornelius said. "We've no place to quarter them at the fort."

"I know that!" Lieutenant Denny said and pointed to the upper side of the Licking River. "That's good pasture, isn't it?"

"Yes," Cornelius said.

"Can you think of a better place?"

"I can't think of any other place," Cornelius said.

"Oh, Christ!" Lieutenant Denny said. "And how many men will be needed to guard them?"

"Thirty at least."

"I suppose so," Lieutenant Denny said. "God damn it! Thirty men. Almost half our garrison. I'll put Ensign Marks in charge of the guard. Ensign Sedam, will you please inform Ensign Marks of his new command?"

"Yes, sir," Cornelius said.

"Land the horses," Lieutenant Denny shouted out to Mr. Martinburg, "on the upper side of the Licking."

"It's too late," Mr. Martinburg replied. "The boats are already tailing off. They've been told to land at the fort."

"Well, tell them to tail around!" Lieutenant Denny said.

"How?" Mr. Martinburg inquired and remarked that he did not have a carrier pigeon.

"Relay the news!" Lieutenant Denny said.

That was most impractical, Mr. Martinburg pointed out. The message would be garbled beyond recognition by the time it reached the tenth boat. "If you want the horses on the Kentucky side," he said, "you'll have to tell them yourself."

By "them" Mr. Martinburg meant, of course, the boatmen, not the horses and we had no alternative but to carry out his suggestion. As we paddled to the flotilla's stern boats our cannons continued to boom and along the riverbank more and more bonfires were being ignited. Nothing is gained by reciting the derisive remarks made by the citizens of Cincinnati when we came ashore and acquainted them with what was what. Nor what was said at the fort.

Possibly an hour or so after Lieutenant Denny and I were back in headquarters, a waiter brought in the information that something definitely appeared to be amiss on the upper side of the Licking. When Lieutenant Denny and I went to the wall walk, which was already crowded with a considerable portion of the fort's population, we could see the horses running about in a state of stampede. No one knew what was happening, but Ensign Marks, who had crossed the river with thirty federals, was being canoed back.

Eventually Ensign Marks reported to Lieutenant Denny in headquarters.

"The situation is rather grave, sir," he said and explained that the horses had been sent from Fort Pitt in care of rivermen. There was no conductor and no forage-master. There were no hopples or bells. The rivermen, unacquainted with the behavior of horses, had simply landed them on the shore. Crowded in the boats, the beasts, most happy to find themselves on the loose, began running about and taking to the woods. Before the federals arrived, Ensign Marks went on to say, the rivermen, rather than making troughs of tree barks, had strewn the forage along the riverbank for the animals to pick out of the mud as best they could. "Not only has a great deal of forage been wasted, sir," Ensign Marks said, "but the horses started fighting about the food and before we could quiet them down many were injured by kicking and biting."

By now, I should say, Lieutenant Denny didn't care what became of the horses. "May I inquire, sir," he asked, "what you have done other than report to me what happened?"

"I have instructed my men to convert halters into hopples, sir," Ensign Marks said. "We have no bells at the fort, nor the material with which to make any."

Lieutenant Denny nodded wearily. "You have done what you could under the circumstances, Ensign."

"Thank you, sir," Ensign Marks said.

It was necessary to send over more federals to recover the some seventy horses that had taken to the woods. Henceforth the animals were confined within a chain of sentries during the daytime and tied up at night.

VI

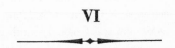

The following morning Lieutenant Ebenezer Denny, determined to "get to the bottom" of how the false rumor had started, went to Columbia. Some two hours after Lieutenant Denny's departure, Commander-in-Chief of the United States Army Major General Arthur St. Clair arrived at Fort Washington. He had come up from Louisville. Unannounced, the General, accompanied by his escort, rode through the fort's main gate like any ordinary mortal would have and came to headquarters. Had St. Clair appeared a half hour earlier, he would have found the outer office of headquarters in a state of considerable disarray. Since the food for the General's welcoming was already practically prepared, we had consumed it at an officers' party which lasted too long into the morning to clean up afterward. But by now, everything was in good order.

Only I was in headquarters when General St. Clair entered. Being unaware of his presence at the fort, I was quite surprised to see him. "Good morning, Lieutenant Morrow," General St. Clair said. As such, this was not a greeting. From the General's manner of speaking one might have supposed that we had been seeing each other daily. "Will you be so kind as to inform Major Ziegler that I request an audience?"

"Major Ziegler is now in command of Fort Harmar, sir," I said. "Lieutenant Denny is our acting commander."

"Then you will please make my request to Lieutenant Denny?"

"Lieutenant Denny is in Columbia at the moment, sir."

General St. Clair pointed to the inner office. "Is the ranking officer in there?"

"No, sir," I said, "he is not."

"Under these circumstances, possibly *you* are able to inform me which quarters have been placed at my disposal?"

"I don't know anything about it, sir," I said. "Your arrival was unexpected. It comes as a complete surprise."

"You have not been so informed?"

"No, sir, we have not."

"You will then please call a waiter to make me arrangements immediately for temporary quarters. I am quite tired and should like to lie down."

To me, the General appeared to be ill. His face was drawn, its skin had a pasty color, and his eyes were noticeably glassy. "Yes, sir," I said.

A middle-aged man and a young fellow of about twenty-five years had accompanied General St. Clair into headquarters. We were introduced. The older man was Colonel Winthrop Sargent, who was going to be the General's adjutant general. The younger was Viscount Malartie, a Frenchman who after traveling extensively about America had sought his fortunes at the short-lived Gallipolis settlement. His official title was "volunteer-aid" to General St. Clair. I am not certain that anyone ever learned what the Viscount's duties were, that is precisely.

Colonel Sargent left with General St. Clair. Viscount Malartie stayed. "Would it be too much of an imposition," Viscount Malartie asked in a travel-weary but quite friendly tone of voice, "if I were to borrow a pinch of your snuff? My nostrils are pleading for a bit."

"There is not only no snuff, but no smoking tobacco at Fort Washington," I said.

"What a pity," Viscount Malartie said, sighed, and moved his right hand before his nostrils, as if waving away a foul odor with a handkerchief. He had violet-colored eyes, with long lashes. Quite slender, his body and its movements were effeminate. So was his manner of speaking. "There was, unhappily, no snuff at Fort Knox either," he added mournfully.

"I am," I said, "in a position to offer you a poor grade of grape wine or excellent Monongahela rye."

"I should very much enjoy the whiskey, if you please," Viscount Malartie said. "I have already sampled Ohio Country wine."

He spoke without a trace of an accent.

"I can well understand your reaction to our Ohio Country wine," I said.

"A most ghastly concoction, is it not?" Viscount Malartie said and smiled brightly. "Yet as I looked at your beautiful hills here, with their many natural terraces, I found myself thinking how admirable they were adapted to be vineyards."

My first impression that Viscount Malartie was a fop, was changing. He was, I was now quite certain, a French intellectualist. "Thank you so very much," he said as I poured a glass of whiskey. "Monongahela rye! Once one becomes accustomed to it, one realizes it has a matchless quality all of its own."

"I am somewhat surprised that you should have come up from Fort Knox," I said. "We had supposed that the General was in the East and would be coming here from Fort Pitt."

"We had fully expected to travel that route," the Viscount said. "At the last moment, in Philadelphia, there came this opportunity to go by fast boat to Charlestown."

"The General came over the Wilderness Trail!"

"And a most arduous journey it was," Viscount Malartie said. "Our general was ill during the last week and had to be carried on a litter."

The reason his general had decided to travel thus, Viscount Malartie explained, was that time would be gained for him to discuss personally with General Scott details of the expedition against the Indiana-Illinois tribes. "As it was," Viscount Malartie went on to say, "we arrived at Fort Knox less than a day after General Scott had marched out. Isn't that the way it always goes? Nobody had informed General Scott that since the recruiting of the levies is so far behind schedule, his expected endeavor must be postponed."

"The recruiting of the levies is that far behind schedule?"

"Frankly, I do not believe it has even begun."

"There is no news from General Butler?"

"Secretary of War Knox," Viscount Malartie said wryly, "has assured our general that General Butler is making progress."

"What does General Butler say?"

"Who knows? Neither our general nor General Butler has met since his appointment. Only the other day our general remarked that come August it will be three full years since he has so much as seen his second-in-command. General Butler has not replied to any of our general's many inquiries and admonitions to move ahead with all possible haste. While recently in your bustling New York Town, we learned that General Butler was in Philadelphia. When we hastened to that city, we discovered that General Butler had gone to Boston, to attend the wedding of one of his daughters."

"General St. Clair's army," I said, "is supposed to march from here on July 10th."

"There will be, beyond a doubt, a considerable delay."

That is all Viscount Malartie knew of the progress being made in behalf of the campaign. He had heard, however, about the arrangement Susan had told me General Butler had entered into with Mae Dwyer. "Our general is rather displeased with this transaction and plans to negate it," Viscount Malartie said. "A great mistake, I feel. Possibly it is my European background, but whoever heard of an army going to war unaccompanied by women?"

He said this quite seriously and I could not help smiling. "Any number of our battles during the War of the Rebellion," I said, "were won without the help of women."

"So I have been told," Viscount Malartie said, "and a number of the more important ones at that." His amazement, I was prepared to swear, was genuine. "Exactly what is this ruling you Americans have about a regiment's washerwomen? I heard talk of it at Fort Knox."

"According to Army Regulations," I said, "there shall be four washerwomen for each regiment."

"It is not enough," Viscount Malartie said.

After stating that he hadn't the faintest idea what to do with himself, Viscount Malartie asked me if he would be in the way if he remained where he was. "Not at all," I said, "this is not one of my busy days."

We got to talking about Philadelphia. "Of course, having been there only for two months," Viscount Malartie said, "I am unable, as my fellow countryman de Warville was, to give what might be considered an authoritative impression. I do get the feeling that in Philadelphia so many people, when they quote the Bible, interpret its passages to suit their own interests."

"Couldn't that also be said of the people of Paris?"

"Of course it could," Viscount Malartie said, "but my countrymen know they are doing it."

Viscount Malartie belonged to that segment of French Intellectuals who we, back in Philadelphia, sometimes called "jelly fish." The jelly fish, or some creature of that ilk, they believed, was the highest form of life on this earth. It was ridiculous, they contended, that a human being, made up of an intricate conglomeration of viscera which are in a constant state of disorder, should be considered the best an omnipotent God could produce. The jelly fish, on the other hand, had got his body down to essentials. And who could say, for certain, that jelly fish were unable to communicate with one another? It was indicative of man's inborn stupidity to assume that communication could be attained only in the manner he did. You believers in God, these French Intellectuals were wont to say, are constantly talking about holy spirits. Is it beyond the realms of reason to presume that jelly fish, as organisms certainty far superior to man, are able to communicate spiritually?

Viscount Malartie's philosophy entered our conversation also. "You, of course," he said, "do not agree with me."

"I find what you say rather interesting, thought-provoking in fact. I fear, however, I am a trifle too civilized to be able to subscribe to it."

"A trifle too civilized!" Viscount Malartie said and his face beamed with pleasure. "What a clever reply! It can be used in so many instances. I must remember it."

Shortly before the noon break, Colonel Sargent stalked into headquarters. He had been inspecting the fort, he said, at General St. Clair's request. "Your commanding officer should be informed," he said, "that your supply of arms is extremely inadequate and you have next to no tools."

Colonel Sargent's pointed face was so stern that it seemed to have been cast of plaster. His high-pitched voice was most irritating. "Your discovery," I said, "will not come under the heading of news to our commanding officer, sir."

"You will please get me the fort's records," Colonel Sargent said.

"I am sorry, sir," I said. "For that, permission of the fort's commanding officer is required."

"I, sir," Colonel Sargent said, "am General St. Clair's adjutant general."

"So I was informed, sir," I said, "when we were introduced."

"You are refusing me access to the records?"

"I am carrying out the regulations of this fort, sir."

"The permission will be forthcoming, sir. That I assure you," Colonel Sargent said, glared at me, then wheeled about and left.

"Bravo!" Viscount Malartie said when the door was closed.

With his back against the wall, his feet on a desk, Viscount Malartie had watched all this with amusement. "I am surprised," I said, "that he didn't pull rank on me."

"He can't," Viscount Malartie said and chuckled. "The 'Colonel' goes back to your War of the Rebellion. Winthrop is not presently enrolled in the United States Army."

"Who is he?"

Viscount Malartie shrugged his shoulders. "A devoted servant of our General, his second pair of eyes and ears. The man, you will soon discover, hasn't a single redeeming defect. Nothing pleases him more than to discover some minor infraction which may be called to our general's attention."

"While he is at Fort Washington," I said, "I should say, he will be rather busy."

"As a bee," Viscount Malartie said. "In time, so I am told, one can learn to like him. I have known him only slightly over six months."

Lieutenant Denny returned to headquarters possibly a half hour before the workday's end. "Did you find out how the rumor started?" I asked him.

"It simply started," Lieutenant Denny said. He appeared to be in high spirits. "By the way, if a Colonel Sargent wants to look at the records, let him."

"I take it you've seen General St. Clair?"

Lieutenant Denny nodded. His good mood led me to guess, correctly it so turned out, that he'd been named General St. Clair's aide-de-camp. "I, of course, mentioned yesterday's fiasco," Lieutenant Denny said. "The General was quite amused, especially by all the salvos fired in his honor."

"That's interesting," I said. "I've frequently wondered if the man possessed any kind of a sense of humor."

"Come to think of it," Lieutenant Denny said, "so have I."

"Did you meet Colonel Sargent?"

"The answer is, yes, but 'confronted' him is the more accurate way of putting it," Lieutenant Denny said. "He came, I saw, and I conquered. He's due here momentarily. Watch how I handle him."

Within moments Colonel Sargent entered headquarters. "I am most pleased to find you here, Lieutenant Denny," he said. "Will you be kind enough to inform Lieutenant Morrow that I have been granted permission to examine the fort's records?"

"I have already so informed Lieutenant Morrow," Lieutenant Denny said. "And I am most pleased that you are here, for it gives me the opportunity to ask if you wish our officers to address you as 'Colonel' or 'Mister'?"

"I am accustomed to being addressed as 'Colonel,' sir," Colonel Sargent said stiffly.

"As you wish, sir," Lieutenant Denny said.

"May I request a word with you in private, sir?" Colonel Sargent said.

"Of course, you may," Lieutenant Denny said. "You will forgive me, I trust, if I ask you to wait a few minutes. There is a letter I simply must read immediately, before affixing my signature."

There was no letter to be signed. "That ass!" Lieutenant Denny said when we were in the inner office. "That unmitigated ass. You certainly see what he's up to, don't you? He thinks he can become commander of this fort."

"The first skirmish was definitely yours," I said.

"And so will the others be," Lieutenant Denny said. "I know what he wants to talk to me about. He wants to start building a fort twenty miles north of here."

"Impossible," I said. "We have neither the tools nor the carpenters."

"As if I hadn't already explored the matter thoroughly and reached that conclusion! I explained it all to St. Clair. Sargent, the bastard, would simply love to show he can get it done anyway."

"Did General St. Clair give you an idea when his army will be marching out?"

"God, no!" Lieutenant Denny said. "He's putting on a bold front though. He's acting as if he expects to move out on schedule." He reached into his coat. "He got this dispatch from Secretary of War Knox when he was in Louisville. You're to copy it into our records. He wants the original back though."

The dispatch began: *"The President is greatly anxious that the campaign be distinguished by decisive measures . . ."*

"Even the President's calling it a campaign," Lieutenant Denny remarked while I read.

"So I notice," I said.

"What do you make of the General wanting the original back?" Lieutenant Denny asked.

"I hadn't given it any thought."

"This is how I see it," Lieutenant Denny said. "St. Clair knows this campaign is bound to fail. He's already assembling material for his defense. That's why he's got that Frenchman here. To write it all up for him."

Lieutenant Denny and Colonel Sargent were still closeted in the inner office when my workday came to a close. Upon my arrival at our quarters, Melissa informed me that many inhabitants of Fort Washington thought there was another possible explanation for the Frenchman's presence. Waiters, she said, had lost no time letting it be known that they had been ordered to place Viscount Malartie's bed next to General St. Clair's.

VII

Colonel Sargent did not get his fort built. That June turned into one of those months which simply runs the required number of days and is torn off the calendar. We received no communications from New York Town or Philadelphia. No supplies or troops, federals or levies, came through. Our only indication that somebody back East labored under the impression that the campaign was going to begin on schedule came during the month's third week. A flotilla of five flatboats brought us a shipment of cattle from Fort Pitt. The animals soon ate out the country around Fort Washington and had to be taken to Ludlow's Station, six miles off, where they required a guard of twenty. Since thirty of our federals were still guarding the horses on the upper side of the Licking, this meant that more than half of the fort's eighty-five federals were animal tenders.

For the first two weeks of this month General St. Clair was confined to his quarters. He was suffering from a mild touch of the gout, Colonel Sargent announced. Without consulting Lieutenant Denny, who had not yet been relieved of his command, Colonel Sargent then posted an adjutant general's statement saying that General St. Clair would not be receiving any callers until further notice.

Yes, Colonel Sargent said, this included Lieutenant Denny.

Lieutenant Denny, of course, was furious.

Henceforth Colonel Sargent behaved as if he were the commander of Fort Washington. Each morning he announced the Orders of the Day, presumably speaking for General St. Clair. Then he moved about the premises, issuing his own orders. From his manner of speaking, one might have gathered that the lack of supplies was our fault. Nothing was being done to his liking. Yet for all the changes he made in routine, he brought about no improvements.

In due time the real state of affairs was wormed out of attending waiters. The General was a very sick man. Along with his rheumatism, he was suffering from a recurrence of his liver ailment and had contracted pneumonia. Frequently delirious, he was crying out that he was at the mercy of General Butler and Quartermaster General Hodgdon. If these gentlemen failed him, he was lost.

About half-after nine o'clock on the morning of June 16th, Colonel Sargent came into headquarters. "The General has fully recovered from his gout," he told me. "You may expect him within the hour. You will tell Lieutenant Denny to begin clearing out his desk."

"Very well," I said. I did not add the "sir." None of our officers paid Colonel Sargent such a show of respect. This was not something agreed upon by tacit consent. It was simply a natural reaction, shared by everyone.

Colonel Sargent handed me a report of some ten or twelve pages. "The General wants you to copy this into your records," he said. "The original is to be returned to Viscount Malartie." After glaring about the outer office, in the pernicious manner of a head valet on the lookout for dust, he took his leave.

Before speaking to Lieutenant Denny I called in the headquarters' custodian. "Robert," I said. "General St. Clair is expected within the hour. Everything looks clean to me, but I'm no judge. Do as you please, but my free advice is for you to be in here with a broom in your hand when the General shows up."

"Thanks, Tom," Robert said.

Lieutenant Denny, when I informed him that he was about to be officially relieved of his command, merely shrugged his shoulders. "It's about time," he said grimly. "Now that bastard Sargent won't have things all his own way any more."

The report Colonel Sargent had given me was from General Scott, an account of his now completed expedition against the Indiana-Illinois tribes. With the loss of only one man killed and five wounded, General Scott stated that his army had destroyed a number of Indian villages along the Wabash River. More than fifty Indians, mostly warriors, had been killed. He'd brought back forty-one prisoners, women and men, who had been sent on to Fort Steuben. In citing those who had behaved with valor General Scott highly praised Colonel John Hardin, who had served as a noncomissioned officer without pay. Also a *Colonel* James Wilkinson.

I had just about finished copying the report when Robert, broom in hand and standing at the door, said, "St. Clair's coming."

Robert was sweeping away diligently when General St. Clair arrived. Appearing to be in excellent health, the General's steps were spry, the color of his cheeks was robust. It struck me that General St. Clair's ability to recover from his various ailments bordered upon the miraculous. I am convinced that his dogged determination not to be sick had a great deal to do with it.

Noting Robert's presence, General St. Clair's quick, all-seeing glance took in all corners of the outer office and the walls and ceilings. He seemed to be satisfied with what he saw. Robert gave me an appreciative nod. "Good morning, Lieutenant Morrow," General St. Clair said.

"Good morning, sir," I said and only this. No matter how solicitous my intent, any reference to his recent illness would have annoyed the General.

"I take it Lieutenant Denny is in there," General St. Clair said, gesturing toward the inner office.

"Yes, sir," I said, "he is."

"You will please inform him that I wish to see him."

A half hour later Lieutenant Denny came out, his arms loaded with his personal belongings. "Jesus Christ!" he whispered before moving over to the aide-de-camp's desk, "St. Clair's taking the stand we're going to march out on July 10th." He added that he'd been told to read the General Scott report and that General St. Clair wished to see me.

I knocked on the inner office door. "Is it convenient for you to see me now, sir?" I called out.

"It is."

General St. Clair had on his spectacles. Scarcely looking up from the batch of papers which had his attention, he handed me a bill for the Scott expedition. It totaled an even twenty thousand dollars. "You will enter that in the record, Lieutenant Morrow," General St. Clair said. "The original you will give to Viscount Malartie. From now on, after being entered in your records, all original communications and copies of my General Orders will be turned over to Viscount Malartie."

"Yes, sir," I said.

General St. Clair peered at me over his spectacles. "Am I correct in assuming that you are somewhat surprised by that Scott invoice?" he inquired.

Aside from the fact that it was next to impossible to believe that the expedition could have cost an even twenty thousand dollars, nothing was itemized. There were no accompanying receipts. No effort had been made to substantiate the figure. "Yes, sir," I said, "you are. May I inquire, sir, if you plan to honor this bill?"

"The figure, I should say," General St. Clair said, "is approximately correct. You will write General Scott that while his bill, as such, cannot be approved, he is granted permission to credit his account with twenty thousand dollars, to meet the expenses of his expedition."

"Yes, sir," I said, and another interesting aspect of this conversation is that at the moment there was no money in the coffers at either Fort Washington or Fort Knox.

"You will also compose letters to General Butler and Quartermaster General Hodgdon," General St. Clair said, "urging both these gentlemen to get on with their assignments, with all possible haste. You will say that I will appreciate greatly a reply informing me of the progress they have made."

"I am not familiar, sir," I said, "with the whereabouts of either of the gentlemen."

"Both gentlemen," General St. Clair said sternly, "are under order of Secretary of War Knox to be at Fort Pitt no later than July first."

"Yes, sir," I said.

"To Secretary of War Knox," General St. Clair said, "you will write that I am prepared to march out of here on the date set by him and the President of the United States of America."

Could he possibly believe this!

"Yes, sir," I said.

"To the officers in command of Forts Steuben, Harmar, and Knox . . . You are familiar with whom they are, are you not?"

"I believe so, sir. Captain Ashton commands at Fort Steuben. Major Ziegler is at Fort Harmar and Major Hamtranck is at Fort Knox."

"That is correct. To them you will write that all previous orders are still in effect. They will rendezvous at Fort Washington on their assigned dates."

"Yes, sir."

Removing his spectacles, General St. Clair stood up. "I believe, sir," he said, "that once before I informed you of my pleasure with the caliber of your reports and letters. They are legible and distinctive in so much as the reader is able to comprehend what is being said. May I take this opportunity to repeat my earlier assertion."

"Thank you, sir," I said.

The General left and I went to work. Beside each entry I noted that by order of the General all original communications had been turned over to Viscount Malartie.

Finished, I placed the material on the General's desk, for his reading and signature. When I went to the outer office, Lieutenant Denny stood at the door. "St. Clair's going over every inch of the fort," he said, without turning about. "Sargent's at his heels like some damned groveling puppy hound."

I said nothing.

"What did you think of the Scott report?" Lieutenant Denny said. "It was nothing but a damned goose chase, if you ask me."

"I noticed," I said, "that a Colonel James Wilkinson was cited for valorous behavior."

"Yes . . ." Lieutenant Denny said, still looking toward the parade. "Say what you want about Wilkinson, he's a hell of a brilliant soldier."

"Would he be related to General James Wilkinson?" I asked.

"He *is* General Wilkinson," Lieutenant Denny said. "To serve under Scott, he accepted a colonelship."

"I labored under the distinct impression," I said, "that General James Wilkinson was in New Orleans, engaged in activities which made him a traitor to his country."

Lieutenant Denny turned and faced me. "So that's what you're leading up to," he said. "I thought there was something odd about your voice. You think I was lying about Wilkinson?"

"That thought *was* crossing my mind."

"Well, let it cross out again," Lieutenant Denny said. "Wilkinson is once more an American citizen of good repute. That man can talk his way out of anything."

"St. Clair certainly knows of Wilkinson's traitorous involvements?"

"Of course, he does. But don't forget that Wilkinson's an old friend of St. Clair's from Fort Ticonderoga days. If you read the proceedings of the Court of Inquiry, you'll see how strongly Wilkinson stood up for St. Clair."

"You can't possibly have deducted all this merely from a reading of the Court of Inquiry proceedings?"

"I think I was quite capable of doing so," Lieutenant Denny said, "but I didn't have to. The other day when I was in Northbend, Judge Symmes told me the whole story. But keep your eyes on Wilkinson. He's slippery as a perch."

My thinking had moved from General James Wilkinson to Judge John Cleves Symmes. There was talk about the fort that, in coming up from Louisville, General St. Clair had stopped off at Northbend where he and Judge Symmes had engaged in quite a heated squabble over land grants and the conduct of the coming campaign.

"Did you find out for certain," I asked, "if Symmes actually offered to raise a company for the coming campaign and St. Clair said, no, point-blank?"

"The rumor going about the fort is true," Lieutenant Denny said, "and at the moment Judge Symmes is one hell of a bitter man. But to give St. Clair his due, the Judge wanted to command the company personally. You knew Symmes led a company of militiamen at Trenton, didn't you?"

"I should say everybody in the Miami Purchase by now knows that," I said.

"Well, Symmes, as he told me in his own self-righteous way, wanted St. Clair to fight the Battle of Trenton all over again in the Ohio woods.

Symmes has been up north, you know, and fancies himself to be an expert on military terrain. He could show St. Clair a half-dozen areas, he says, where we could force the Indians to engage us and bring about what should have been done at Trenton."

"Is it a fact," I asked and I was wondering where Judge Symmes could have gotten enough men to fill out a company, "that a lot of people are quitting Northbend and leaving for home?"

"It certainly is," Lieutenant Denny said. "They're leaving in droves." His expression livened. "And you can include Judge Symmes' wife in this number."

"What!"

"She's going to divorce him and I'd say she's got the friends back home to get it through the New Jersey Legislature. You knew she was his third wife, didn't you?"

I nodded and we both smiled esoterically. It is frequently said that women enjoy gossip more than men. If for the sake of argument, this is so —at this moment, I can well imagine, Lieutenant Denny and I were behaving in a manner well-calculated to be cited as excellent examples of exceptions which prove the rule.

"What did you think of Mrs. Symmes?" Lieutenant Denny asked.

He was asking me for an impresssion gained from a short visit which Mrs. Symmes paid to Fort Washington a few days after Major Ziegler had left for Fort Harmar. Lieutenant Denny had asked Melissa and Dolly Sedam to pour tea for Mrs. Symmes. "Well, I must confess," I said, "that Mrs. Symmes lost no time letting me know that she was the daughter of the wartime Governor of New Jersey and also generally acknowledged to be the 'Pretty Susan' of André's *Cow Chase*."

"And a ghastly bit of writing the *Cow Chase* was," Lieutenant Denny said. "Do you think she's such an outstanding beauty?"

Apparently I was not in one of my more generous moods. "In her younger days," I said, "it is conceivable that this may have been remotely possible."

"With that long nose!"

Mrs. Symmes did have a long nose.

"I have wondered," I said, "why a woman of her so-called social standing should be interested in coming to Ohio. To be quite honest, though, I thought it was rather fine that she was willing to accompany her husband here and give up the luxuries she said she was accustomed to."

"I've given up wondering why anybody does anything," Lieutenant Denny said and became thoughtful. "She's definitely got money of her own," he said. "I don't see her as being noble, by any stretch of the imagination. I picture her as being a woman with both feet on the ground, one who'd look hard and long at a man's bank account before setting her cap for him. It strikes me that she's beating a strategic retreat. The Judge is in bad financial straits. This Miami Purchase venture of his, has cost him his shirt. These days you can't give away a lot in Northbend."

Lieutenant Denny was now talking as much to himself as to me. "No," he said, "I can't see it any other way. Mrs. Symmes is getting the divorce to protect herself as well as wanting to be rid of the Judge and getting out of Symmes' Hole."

"Symmes' Hole" is what many people called Northbend.

"The Judge is really out on the end of the plank financially," Lieutenant Denny went on to say. "That's why he's had to make his latest land sale offer."

"I know nothing about that," I said.

"That choice land of his up the Great Miami," Lieutenant Denny said. "It's up for sale. You can buy in for next to nothing down."

"What would you pay eventually?"

"Whatever the prevailing price is. You've got a whole year to take up your option."

"If St. Clair loses," I said, "the prevailing price won't be anything."

"That's right."

"Symmes needs money that badly!"

"Why else would he let that choice land go? From what I hear the Judge has stalled off Congress long as he can. He's got to come up with some kind of a payment. So far as Congress is concerned, these will be *bona fide* sales. Symmes' credit can be extended. To Congress the prevailing price is what the lots were originally offered at."

"That's something I'll never be able to understand," I said. "Congress knows the price of lots dropped after the Harmar Expedition."

"Why try to understand it," Lieutenant Denny said. "That's the way buying on credit goes."

"I give Symmes one more year and he's sunk," I said.

"Not necessarily," Lieutenant Denny said, "by then he'll have thought up something else."

Lieutenant Denny looked out the door. "My God!" he said. "St. Clair and Sargent are even inspecting the latrine."

"It's just possible," I said, "that they're going in there for a more natural reason."

"In the enlisted men's latrine!" Lieutenant Denny said. "St. Clair would piss in his pants before he'd do a thing like that."

When I went to our quarters for lunch, I was prepared to tell Melissa that Mrs. Symmes had left her husband. Before I could, Melissa told *me* that this bit of gossip was the day's principal topic of conversation at Fort Washington.

I then told Melissa about the sale of land at Northbend and we discussed this at considerable length. On the following Sunday, we rode to Northbend. For twelve-and-a-half dollars down we bought six-hundred-forty acres. It was beautiful, flat, fertile land, with good streams and with a considerable area where there were no trees. Here was acre after acre of wild rice.

VIII

Within twenty-four hours after General St. Clair took over the active command of Fort Washington, all of our officers had read the records and knew that the commanders of the Ohio River forts had been ordered to adhere to their original instructions.

Surely, all of our officers thought, the General would call a staff meeting. He did not. Only Colonel Sargent and Viscount Malartie enjoyed the General's confidence. Sargent gloried in this. Malartie, if my impression is correct, appeared to be a lonely and bewildered young man. He did make an effort to be affable. He had, however, it was clear to see, been ordered to keep his lips sealed.

Speculation, as might be expected, was rife. Was it possible that enlistments and preparations for the campaign were up to schedule? No officer at Fort Washington thought this could be so.

We received no replies from General Butler or Quartermaster General Hodgdon. The Ohio River fort commanders, of course, obeyed their instructions and began arriving at Fort Washington between July 5th and 7th. Captain Ashton came first. From Fort Steuben he brought a hundred-fifty dregs of humanity, officially designated as enlistees of the first regiment, and the forty-one Indian prisoners which General Scott had sent him.

Captain Ashton brought no supplies. His troops were not properly armed or clothed. Not one had a haversack! Few indeed had been trained. Next to none had any previous military experience. Recently recruited, they had been sent to Fort Steuben immediately after their arrival at Fort Pitt. It was absolutely necessary, Captain Ashton said, to get them downstream.

Had these fellows been allowed to stay in Pittsburgh, they would have deserted.

General St. Clair had turned livid with rage at the sight of the forty-one Indian prisoners. Why, in the name of holy God in Heaven, the General wished to know, had they not been left at Fort Steuben? He had no choice, Captain Ashton explained, but to bring them. With his fort now under control of local militiamen, the Indians would have been tortured as reprisals for recent scalpings. He was under strict orders from Secretary of War Knox to see to it that no harm should come to Indian prisoners while Colonel Procter was on his peace mission.

"You were not advised that the Procter mission was over with?" General St. Clair said. "And that it ended in failure?"

"No, sir, I was not," Captain Ashton said. "I am certain Fort Pitt does not know this either."

Captain Ashton was about twenty-five, a rather handsome chap with an excellent complexion. He was generally regarded as being a capable officer.

"It would seem to me, sir," General St. Clair said, "that, when the Scott prisoners were brought in, you should have surmised the failure of Procter's mission."

"It is only now, sir," Captain Ashton said, "that I am learning the facts. I had no idea that General Scott's expedition was minor to the coming campaign."

"You did not question those who brought in the prisoners?"

"I did, sir, most thoroughly. They were woodsmen, sir. These fellows had no knowledge of the general over-all strategy involved. They thought they had been off on what they described as 'another Indian chase.'"

The forty-one Indian prisoners included an odd assortment of Kickapoo princesses, half-starved children, and a number of ill-smelling, flea-bitten squaws. Having no suitable place to confine these prisoners, we quartered them in the barracks. After considerable skirmishing about, we managed to get them cots. Such hospitality they refused to accept from white men and insisted upon sleeping on the floor. Eventually we built a pavilion onto the barracks and quartered them there.

Captain Ashton brought the latest news from Fort Pitt. Neither General Butler nor Quartermaster General Hodgdon was in Pittsburgh. No communications had been received from General Butler, although it was believed he was in Boston. Quartermaster General Hodgdon was still in Philadelphia. No word had been received as to when the Quartermaster General might be expected at Fort Pitt. So far he'd sent through next to no supplies, no ammunition or arms.

Levies? There weren't two dozen at Fort Pitt, Captain Ashton said. Mail carriers, coming through from Philadelphia, were all reporting that they saw no enlistees marching through or any signs of recruiting activities.

The following day Major Ziegler brought down two hundred federals from Fort Harmar. Half of these troops were seasoned veterans, the others were of the caliber of Captain Ashton's men. Their arms were inadequate and their uniforms were threadbare. Such was the shortage of shoes that Major Ziegler had been compelled to order his men to carry out many of their routine assignments in bare feet.

Supplies? "Thirty axes, I bring you, sir," Major Ziegler said and General St. Clair ordered the statement entered into the records. "Soft as dumplings they are. Also a shipment of packsaddles, I received. Big enough for elephants they were! Of paper, they could have been made. Useless they were, so back I have sent them to Fort Pitt."

We now had a total of forty-three axes at Fort Washington.

During midmorning of the next day a Captain Mountfort arrived with seventy North Carolina levies. Mountfort and his men were tired to a point of exhaustion. To get here on time, Captain Mountfort said with understandable chagrin, he and his men, for the past three days, had walked a mile, then jogged one. Captain Mountfort labored under the impression that Fort Washington would fully equip his men. He did not know that General Butler was in charge of enlistments. His orders had come from the Governor of North Carolina, who had received them from the Secretary of War.

During the afternoon of that day Major John Hamtranck brought up two hundred federals from Fort Knox. His men had rifles, but no ammunition. They wore buckskins. They were so attired, General St. Clair had presumed, to spare their uniforms while on the march. When he called out these men for inspection and to receive his official words of greeting, he discovered they had no other clothes.

The six hundred Kentucky militiamen, Major Hamtranck said, were in Louisville, practically assembled. "I can't say when they'll get here, sir," Major Hamtranck said. Lieutenant Colonel Darke, he stated, had won the election and was the militiamen's commander. "Darke named his son first captain, sir. Everybody's boiling mad about that, sir. They're holding another election."

John Hamtranck was a lanky fellow, who spoke with a drawl, and accepted things for what they were. If it was at all possible, John saw the humorous side of life.

"I labored under the impression," General St. Clair said, "that General Scott was going to ease out Darke."

"There was nothing General Scott could do, sir," John said, "Darke had the votes."

The election of Darke was bad news. The man, as was generally known, was a headstrong commander, consumed by a burning desire to slaughter Indians with his own hands. His ability to lead a large body of men, however, was conceded to be most questionable.

To Colonel Darke, General St. Clair sent off an immediate dispatch, ordering him to remain in Louisville until further notice.

It was presumed that Major Hamtranck would bring with him money to pay the federals. Twenty thousand dollars in hard cash was supposed to have been delivered to Fort Knox. "It came about a week ago," Major Hamtranck told General St. Clair.

"And many I inquire, sir, why you did not bring this money with you?"

"There's none of it left, sir," Major Hamtranck said and explained that General Scott had used this money to pay the expenses for the Indiana-Illinois expedition.

On the side John told me that this was the most real money seen in Louisville in quite some time. "Things are really hopping down there these days, Tom," he said. "Every night when they go to bed, the merchants pray for another Indian chase."

To quote my friend, Cornelius Sedam, the presence of so many men at Fort Washington, "at least solved the problem of what to do with that drove of cattle at Ludlow's Station." It was necessary to slaughter them, to provide food. They would, though, have to be replaced, for they were campaign cattle.

One may well wonder why, without news from General Butler and Quartermaster General Hodgdon, General St. Clair called in the Ohio River fort contingencies? Is it possible that he was guilty of wishful thinking, as a few of our officers contended? Orders to General St. Clair were sacred. Is this why he did it? Was it out of spite for General Butler, as many of our officers believed? Was it a mixture of all this?

Whatever the reason for that premature order, it is possible to sympathize with General St. Clair's predicament and recognize that he was under considerable strain. On the tenth of July when he arrived at headquarters his face showed that clay color of death, such as it took on when his liver ailment was recurring. "I do not wish to be disturbed nor will I see anyone this morning, Lieutenant Morrow," he said brusquely and went into the inner office.

I could hear him pacing the floor. Off and on, all morning long, this went on.

At noon a waiter brought the General's lunch. There was a twenty-pound catfish, gutted of course, but clay-baked in whole otherwise, which is the way General St. Clair always had his fish prepared. Almost immediately thereafter, Colonel Sargent entered the outer office. "You will give this dispatch to the General," Colonel Sargent said.

The dispatch, I could see, had been opened. Colonel Sargent was permitted to read all of the General's mail and had been given the task of deciding what might or might not require his commander's attention. "The General," I said, "is eating lunch. He gave me specific orders, that he should not be disturbed."

"This dispatch," Colonel Sargent said in his superior tone of voice, "will, I am certain, be of considerable interest to the General."

To protect myself, I said, "You are telling me, despite what I have told you, that the dispatch is of sufficient moment to be given to the General?"

"I am," Colonel Sargent said.

I knocked on the inner office door. "General St. Clair," I said, "Colonel Sargent has brought a dispatch which he insists is worthy of your immediate attention."

"You may bring it in," General St. Clair growled.

As I opened the door, the General put down his glass of claret. He had not yet, I could see, begun picking at the catfish.

"Are you familiar with the contents of the dispatch?" General St. Clair inquired.

"No, sir," I said, "I am not."

"Then read it over and acquaint me with the gist of it."

I read it, then reread it.

"Well?" General St. Clair finally said.

"It is a communication from Secretary of War Knox, sir," I said. "The Secretary wishes to know why General Scott has not yet marched out and exhorts you to see to it that this expedition shall be set into operation with a minimum of delay."

General St. Clair stood up with the rapidity of someone who has sat on a pin. His lips moved, but no words came out. Picking up the catfish, he slammed it with all the power he possessed against the wall. As anyone who has seen a catfish knows, this fish has barbed spines that are sharp as daggers. The General's right hand began bleeding profusely. Looking at his bleeding hand, General St. Clair said in a completely controlled voice: "Lieutenant Morrow, you will please prepare, for my signature, a reply to the Secretary of War, stating that his order was executed during the month of May."

General St. Clair then made directly for his own quarters, where he was confined for the next three days.

IX

All of July went by with still no word from General Butler. He was not in Pittsburgh. That is all we knew of Dicky Butler's whereabouts. During this month we received no official news from anyone concerning progress being made in recruiting. Our only source of information came from boatmen. Next to no levies, they told us, had arrived at Fort Pitt.

Quartermaster General Hodgdon, the boatmen told us, was at Fort Pitt. I should say that during this month, at General St. Clair's request, I wrote at least a half-dozen letters to Mr. Hodgdon. He sent us no replies. As the month moved toward its conclusion, a smathering of supplies began coming through.

"Mark my word," Lieutenant Denny said on August the first when he came into headquarters, "we won't see Butler and the levies before September."

While this surely, I thought, *had* to be an overstatement, I had stopped challenging Lieutenant Denny's predictions. So far, they had all been right.

For me this was a harried time. With no money to pay the federals, my staff and I were up to our necks in work, writing out promissory notes. My staff was Melissa and Dolly Sedam, who filled out blank forms in their own quarters. Kitty Kummerschmitt helped us as much as she could. Kitty, however, was needed by Dr. Allison, whose life these days was far more hectic than mine.

Lieutenant Denny sat at his desk and began fumbling with a batch of papers. This was a trying time for him also. Colonel Sargent had succeeded in wedging him out completely. In effect Aide-de-camp Lieutenant Ebenezer Denny was scarcely more than General St. Clair's waiter.

Shortly Colonel Sargent, carefully powdered and queued, entered the outer office. Neither Lieutenant Denny nor I arose. "Lieutenant Morrow," Colonel Sargent said, "you will please write a letter for the General, addressed to the Quartermaster General, stating that General St. Clair is dissatisfied with the recent shipment of shoes. You are familiar, are you not, with what is what in the case of the shoes?"

"Yes," I said, "I am familiar with what is what in the case of the shoes."

Everyone at Fort Washington was by now familiar with what was what in the case of the shoes. The shoes had arrived during the previous week. They were made of such inferior stuff that our federals had worn them out within four days.

"Shall I mention also," I said, "that the axes which came along with that shipment are so soft that they bend like dumplings?"

Colonel Sargent frowned deeply. He always looked pained while considering a suggestion which was not his own. "It might be just as well to do so," he said, "but you will, of course, refrain from using the word 'dumplings.'"

The shipment had been of twenty-three axes. Like those brought by Major Ziegler, they were so poorly tempered that, to keep them serviceable, our men were constantly at the forge and grindstone. We needed those axes most urgently for general construction about the fort and at Ludlow's Station. Had competent axmen and carpenters been on hand, we would also have needed the axes to get the military road started and for the construction of Forts Hamilton and Jefferson. It was by now known that General St. Clair planned upon building two forts in the Ohio woods. Fort Hamilton would be constructed on the Great Miami River, some twenty miles north of Fort Washington. Fort Jefferson would be built somewhere in the vicinity of the water shed. Plans for these forts were already drawn up. They were to be permanent structures, manned the year around.

"While you're at it," Lieutenant Denny called over, "you might as well add that Hodgdon's tents won't keep out the rain."

"Very well, Lieutenant Morrow," Colonel Sargent said, without looking at Lieutenant Denny, "you may also mention the inadequacy of the tents."

The tents which came in that shipment were those of which Lieutenant Denny had spoken to me about during the month of March. As he had then pointed out, while looking at the original invoice, the tents' ends were of inferior osnaburg and too small to keep out rain.

"You will prepare the letter for the General's signature immediately, Lieutenant Morrow," Colonel Sargent said. "As you know, the General and I plan to leave for Louisville before noon."

When Colonel Sargent left us, Lieutenant Denny said, quite bitterly, "The General and I plan to . . . You'd think I wasn't going along."

"I didn't realize you were," I said.

General St. Clair was going to Louisville to be on hand when some five-hundred-fifty Kentucky volunteers marched out of Fort Knox on an expedition similar to that of General Scott's. This time, however, General James Wilkinson was in command. While I had not seen any official statements authorizing this second minor expedition, John Hamtranck had told me that General St. Clair's orders permitted him the right to order one out.

"Oh, yes, I'm going along too," Lieutenant Denny said. "It wouldn't look right, would it, for the commander of the Army of the United States of America to arrive anywhere without an aide-de-camp?"

I felt rather sorry for Lieutenant Denny at this moment. As if drawn together by a common bond of discouragement over the general state of affairs, there had come about a certain *rapprochement* between us. During his present period of adversity, I found Lieutenant Denny quite likable. When I mentioned this to Melissa and Dolly and Cornelius, they all said I was being too softhearted. Let him so much as smell success, they predicted, and, phoenix-like, the real Lieutenant Ebenezer Denny would rise from the dust. No doubt they were right.

From on the parade, we could hear the sound of tramping feet. Lieutenant Denny went to the door. "Another detachment's going to Ludlow's Station," he said.

To prevent desertion, more and more federals were being sent to Ludlow's Station. It was the boatmen who were the real culprits. Shorthanded, they were inducing our discontented to desert by promising them passage to New Orleans. As a matter of fact, few boatmen went farther downstream than Fort Knox. Nonetheless, such were the desertions that General St. Clair had placed a statement in the *Kentucky Gazette*, offering a ten dollar reward for a deserter's apprehension.

"This expedition of Wilkinson's," Lieutenant Denny grumbled, still standing at the door. "St. Clair was a fool to let Wilkinson talk him into it. All it'll do is infuriate more Indians."

Lieutenant Denny did not expect me to reply and I didn't. He was simply stating what was general talk about Fort Washington. That Wilkinson was a scoundrel, I should say, was by now generally known and the man is a story all of his own, to be told elsewhere. What is important of the moment is that Wilkinson had been able to fawn his way into the good graces of General St. Clair. That St. Clair had as his pets Wilkinson and Sargent and, in my opinion, the unfairly maligned Malartie, did not sit at all well with our officers and had a most adverse effect upon their morale.

"Christ, oh, Mighty," Lieutenant Denny said, sighed deeply, and waved his arm in a listless gesture which took in all of Fort Washington. "It looks more like a big manufactory than a fort."

Lieutenant Denny's statement was apt. Almost all drilling and military training was being carried out at Ludlow's Station, under direction of John Hamtranck, who had been named commander of our first regiment.

Fort Washington was presently, actually, an armory. During the middle of July Major William Ferguson had arrived from Fort Pitt, bringing a quantity of military stores. This had been another black day in General St.

Clair's life. Major Ferguson had brought the news that, contrary to Secretary of War Knox's instructions, Quartermaster General Hodgdon had decreed that ammunition for the campaign must be made up at Fort Washington. Hearing this General St. Clair turned pale, as if stricken. "You have this information from Quartermaster General Hodgdon himself, sir?" he inquired of Major Ferguson.

"Yes, sir, I have," Major Ferguson said.

"Place that in the records, Lieutenant Morrow," General St. Clair told me. "Prepare a letter immediately, calling this new state of affairs to the Secretary of War's attention."

"Yes, sir," I said.

"And to Quartermaster General Hodgdon, you will write a letter expressing my extreme disapproval. Mince no words with him, Lieutenant. You have my permission, no, I am ordering you to say that his behavior, in my opinion, is outrageous."

"Yes, sir," I said.

General St. Clair turned to Major Ferguson. "William," he said. "I thank God you are here." This was the only time I ever heard General St. Clair address one of his officers by first name.

Under the direction of Major Ferguson, ably aided by Major Henry Gaither, who had come up from Louisville with a handful of reasonably competent artificers, Fort Washington had become—a manufactory. Despite the lack of raw materials, tools, and experienced help, these two men were overcoming one difficulty and another.

Their task was tremendous. All of the carriages for guns that came through from Philadelphia were unfit for service and these pieces had to be new-mounted. At least two thousand arms, forwarded without inspection to Fort Pitt, required repair. William Ferguson was a quiet, soft-spoken young man, who never complained. I never saw him out of sorts, in fact I never saw him even ruffled. I recall the evening he came into headquarters to report for the records that we had only enough powder, lead, paper, and thread to give three thousand men a hundred-thirty rounds each. I had heard others bemoaning the general condition of these materials. "I think," I said, "we should make note of the poor state of these materials, as we received them."

William nodded. "The casks for the powder," he said, "are slight and not properly secured. The musket cartridge paper is not of the proper sort. I doubt if we'll be able to use it. It will tear too easily and cartridges made of it will not bear much carriage."

"That presents you with quite a task, does it not?" I said.

"Yes," William said in the manner of someone who hasn't thought of this before, "it does."

William built new shops, added to our armory. His ingenuity was truly amazing. There comes to my mind a shipment of cartridge boxes that had been gathering mold for years in a damp storehouse at West Point. These, merely oiled and blackened, had been sent on to us. How William got them refurbished, I shall never know. He had our blacksmiths turning out canisters for shot, along with kettles and bells for horses and oxen. He made gunsmiths out of men who hardly knew how to shoot and had them repairing faulty springs, triggers, ramrods, and bayonets. And William was the one officer at Fort Washington whom Colonel Sargent let strictly alone. This was not the way it was during the first days of William's arrival. The clash between the two men had been quiet, yet in its own way quite dramatic. In one of his "efficiency" moods, Colonel Sargent had ordered the six-hundred-seventy-five stand of useless guns left over from the Harmar Expedition thrown away. They were taking up too much valuable space, Colonel Sargent said.

William had simply told his men to let the guns stay where they were. Sargent, infuriated, had accosted William. Quite calmly, William explained that many of the guns coming in were without stocks and all too many had been fashioned without adding a touchhole. From the Harmar guns, he said to Colonel Sargent, he expected to be able to supply many of the missing parts.

"We'll be in one hell of a fix," Lieutenant Denny said, still standing at the door, "if Ferguson or Gaither get sick."

"Yes," I said, "we will."

"The last of the detachment just went through the main gate," Lieutenant Denny said. "God, what a batch of scarecrows! Have you talked to Ashton or Hamtranck lately?"

"Only to say 'hello' to."

"John was telling me only yesterday that it'll be two more weeks before most of his bastards can tell right- from left-face."

Lieutenant Denny said that so mournfully that I couldn't help smiling. "That, of course," I said, "is a slight exaggeration."

"A slight one," Lieutenant Denny conceded. "God, what a mess we're in." He emitted one of his dry laughs. "Well, there go Major Ziegler's packsaddles that are big enough for elephants."

"What are you talking about?"

Lieutenant Denny turned. "You signed in the shipment of packsaddles that came through yesterday, didn't you?"

"I signed in that they had been received, yes," I said. "There's no report yet on proper quality or quantity."

"They've been examined all right," Lieutenant Denny said. "They're the same damned packsaddles that Ziegler shipped back from Fort Harmar to Fort Pitt."

"Good Lord!" I said.

"Sargent's ordered them recrated. We're taking them down to Fort Knox with us."

"What will be done with them at Fort Knox?"

"How in the hell do I know?" Lieutenant Denny said. "Maybe Sargent thinks they have elephants in Louisville."

Two evenings later, shortly after Melissa and I had washed and dried our supper dishes, Phineas Ford came to our quarters. The moment we opened the door to his knock, both Melissa and I could tell by the expression on Phineas' face that he was bringing back sad news from Detroit. "Emil's dead," Phineas said and sat on the three-legged stool I offered him.

"You're sure?" I said.

Phineas made a futile gesture with his hands. "While Emil was woods crazy in the Detroit jail, he babbled about how he deserted from the Hessians. When he got so he could talk a bit sensible, he confessed and they shot him."

"He was dead when you got there?"

"No, I got there while they were trying him. It wasn't much of a trial though."

"Then you *were* at least able to tell him about Kitty?"

"I told him, but I'm not sure he understood. He was thinner than a rail and didn't seem to hear what I was saying. Some people never get over being woods crazy. I figure that's what happened to Emil. So maybe it's better that he's dead."

Phineas had come straight to us. Melissa, we felt, should be the one to inform Kitty of the unhappy news. During the period while Melissa was away, Phineas said, "I came through Ludlow's Station. Christ, things are worse than they were under Harmar. Is it right that nobody knows where Butler's levies are?"

"It's not only right," I said, "but we haven't even heard from Butler."

"This will be one hell of a campaign," Phineas said.

"I would say so," I said.

Phineas appeared to be in the best of health. Tired? No, Phineas said, why should he be? Any interesting experiences? He couldn't think of any. Our conversation moved along so casually, it seemed unrealistic to bear in mind that since I had last seen him, Phineas Ford had walked to Detroit and back.

"I hear that St. Clair and Denny are in Louisville," Phineas said.

"They left two days ago," I said.

"Well, that's good news," Phineas said. "Tomorrow, I'll go to Bracken and get the beavers."

He'd sell the beavers, Phineas told me, at Cairo. "Kitty gets a third, you get a third, I get a third," he said.

"Not me," I said.

"We can talk about that when I get back," Phineas said.

"We can settle it right now," I said. "I won't accept anything even remotely connected with those beavers. I consider even knowing about them a principal tragedy of my life."

The following morning Phineas came into headquarters to bid me goodbye. John Hamtranck, who had ridden in from Ludlow's Station, had preceded him by a few minutes. John had said his men were clamoring for their whiskey allowances and I had sent off a waiter to attend to this. At the time of Phineas' arrival, John and I had simply been chatting.

"Where in the hell are you going, Phineas?" John asked.

"Nowhere," Phineas said. "I'm just going."

"You're not staying on to scout for St. Clair?"

"Hell, no," Phineas said. "Why should I put myself out for St. Clair?"

"To the hell with St. Clair!" John said. "It's the army that needs you. Now listen! I'm going to tell you something, but keep it under your hat for a while."

Phineas cocked an eyebrow. "I'm listening," he said.

"You know how St. Clair's blamed Harmar for not having good scouts?"

"You're damned right I do!"

"So St. Clair's gone ahead and hired twenty Chickasaw to be our scouts. The bastards are supposed to be here by now, but they haven't come."

"They're camped twenty-five miles up the Little Miami," Phineas said. "I spent a night with them."

"You did!" John exclaimed. "In the name of God! We didn't know they were around. What in the hell are they doing up there?"

"They chased after a herd of bison," Phineas said. "When Butler shows up, they'll be around."

"Well, I'll be damned!" John said. "What were they like?"

"They're just Chickasaw," Phineas said.

"Man-to-man, Phineas," John said. "Just between you and me and Tom. Is St. Clair a God-damned fool for having hired those Chickasaw?"

"That's hard to say, John," Phineas said. "They hate the Ohio Country

Indians, like all Chickasaw do. So I'd say St. Clair's all right there. As to the boys he's hired—well, I wouldn't know what to say."

"Well, try," John said, his voice rising. "It's damned important to know what they're like."

"They've got two chiefs with them," Phineas said. "They're fighting amongst themselves. I only talked to the one—Colbert. All he had on his mind was killing some Kickapoos. The other, Piamingo, thinks this is a big hunting trip. That's where he was when I came through—off hunting. It's my guess that once they start scouting for St. Clair, if they run into game, Piamingo'll forget he's a scout and chase after it. If they run into any Indians, Colbert'll pick a fight."

"Oh, my Lord!" John said.

I walked with Phineas to the rear gate. "Kitty, Melissa tells me," I said while en route, "is bearing up extremely well."

"Nobody can mourn forever," Phineas said. "Do you think Kitty's getting it from Jeremiah?"

"That's ridiculous!" I said.

"I wouldn't be too sure of that," Phineas said.

At the rear gate I asked Phineas when he'd be back. "I don't know," he said. "If the price isn't right in Cairo, I'll go on down to New Orleans."

However, Phineas did not get to New Orleans or even to Bracken. At Columbia he'd stopped off to visit his lady friend. The visit concluded, he was about to be on his way when Captain Ashton, sent by Major Hamtranck, caught up with him. Ashton begged Phineas to come to Ludlow's Station for just one day. Amid the mess of rifles delivered, Captain Ashton said, were a dozen Kaintucks that were usable. There were, Captain Ashton explained, among Captain Mountfort's North Carolinians a dozen alert young fellows who could be taught to use these rifles. "Just the one day, Phineas," Captain Ashton had pleaded. "It's not just teaching them to shoot. I guess we could do that. What I want you to do is to show them how to fire and reload on the run."

Captain Ashton had struck at Phineas' Achilles' heel. Phineas was, rightly, proud of his ability to fire and reload on the run and was not averse to giving exhibitions of his prowess.

"All right," Phineas had said. "Just for one day." The teaching profession, I am convinced, lost a most capable man in Phineas Ford. Taking a liking to the boys in his "class," Phineas ended up conducting a seminar in woodcraft, hunting, trapping, fighting with the use of the legs. "Those boys," Captain Ashton told me, "would go through hell and back for Phineas Ford." The "class" was still in session when General St. Clair and Lieutenant Denny returned to Fort Washington.

X

On August 18th General St. Clair received a dispatch from the Secretary of War stating:

The President is persuaded you will brace to exertion every nerve under your command . . .

By the 24th of this month General James Wilkinson was back at Fort Knox, having suffered only three casualties, two men killed, one man wounded. Wilkinson's men had burned to the ground the town of L'Anguille, some hundred miles north of Fort Washington. They destroyed four-hundred-thirty acres of corn and brought back a handful of mangy squaws, who were sent on to us to be quartered and fed. General St. Clair immediately sent off a dispatch to General Wilkinson thanking him for his "good conduct . . . of the expedition." Wilkinson's Raid, as everyone at Fort Washington knew, had been useless, worse than useless. L'Anguille was the capital and metropolis of Little Turtle's own subtribe, the Eel River Miamis. Now Little Turtle's rage would be at fever pitch.

On the 29th of this month Colonel Darke brought up his six hundred Kentucky militiamen. It was come now, Colonel Darke said, or his men would have dispersed. At least half of the Kentuckians were without rifles, three-quarters did not have uniforms. A group of a hundred announced most vociferously that if they did not receive their wages, which were due in two weeks, they were going home. In the second election, Darke had again prevailed. His son was still a first captain. The company, I now learned, had actually been raised by a Mr. Mc'Rea and a Mr. Glenn. Glenn, Darke had expelled from the company. Mc'Rea, a most discontented man, had been appointed Lieutenant of the Horse.

On September 1st General St. Clair received still another dispatch from the Secretary of War:

He (the President) enjoins you, by every principle that is sacred, to stimulate your operation to the highest degree . . .

XI

During most of the week prior to September 2nd, General St. Clair was confined to his quarters with what Colonel Sargent announced was a mild case of the gout. The announcement this time, I am prepared to say, could well have been the fact. Before taking ill, General St. Clair had been eating like a horse. By constantly nibbling, the man seemed to be able to relieve his tensions.

On September 1st, around midmorning, Colonel Sargent came into headquarters. "You will enter into the records, Lieutenant Morrow," he said, "that on this date we learned from boatmen that General Butler is at Bracken. With him is the main body of levies and what may be considered to be the major portion of our supplies and arms."

"At last!" I said.

"At last," Colonel Sargent said and for a fleeting moment I thought he was going to unbend, but he did not. "You will make note," he added with customary sternness, "that we have acquired this information on our own. You will state in precise language that as of this date General St. Clair has not received from General Butler, nor from Quartermaster General Hodgdon, any replies whatsoever to the numerous communications we have addressed to them."

The following morning while Melissa and I were eating breakfast one of Colonel Sargent's waiters came to our quarters. "General Butler is expected sometime today, sir," the waiter said, adding that General Butler would be received with full military honors and that I had been designated as a member of General St. Clair's entourage.

"Thank you," I said. "What is General St. Clair's state of health?"

"He looks awful bad to me, sir," the waiter said.

"When is General Butler expected?" I inquired.

"All I know, sir, is that he's left Bracken."

Being a member of St. Clair's entourage meant I had to polish the buttons on my dress uniform. "I'll do that," Melissa said. "You'll be late."

"I'll have a good excuse," I said.

"I won't have that Colonel Sargent making any of his snide remarks to you," Melissa said and shooed me off.

On the way to headquarters I saw Cornelius Sedam, who told me that he, too, was a member of the St. Clair entourage and that General Butler might be expected shortly after noon. "I'm told," Cornelius said, "that Butler's flotilla is more than a mile long."

"We can only hope," I said, "that something worthwhile will be on the boats."

"I should say that's all we can do—hope," Cornelius said.

Around midmorning Dr. Allison entered the outer office. I stood up. We shook hands, then we both smiled, as if realizing this was overdoing things a bit.

Yet it was understandable. Although we caught glimpses of each other daily there had been no time to actually talk and our pleasant get-togethers at Dr. Allison's quarters had for the past month been given up. Melissa and I probably could have found the time, but Dr. Allison could not. Since the arrival of the federals Dr. Allison's days were fully occupied with making splints and litters and supervising the improvisation of hospital supplies from whatever materials were on hand. John Hamtranck had brought with him a Dr. Victor Grasson, who along with Albert, would make up the army's entire medical staff. I had been introduced to Dr. Grasson, but scarcely knew him. "He's most able and likable," Jeremiah had told me. However, presently Dr. Grasson was of no help to Dr. Allison. Grasson had formerly been a tanner. Discovering this, Colonel Sargent had taken him from Dr. Allison and set him to patching sets of harness and altering packsaddles, the later shipments of which, while not big enough for elephants, were still far too large to fit small Western horses.

Jeremiah looked unusually well. Contented and happy are the descriptive words which come to my mind. These words also describe my impression of Kitty Kummerschmitt during the off-and-on occasions I'd seen her during the past month. "This is an official visit, Tom," Jeremiah said. "I must have it placed in the records that this morning, after a week of constant survey-ance and thorough examination, I have notified General St. Clair that he is physically unfit to assume the command of the coming campaign."

"He is giving up his command!"

"No, no, Tom," Dr. Allison said. "You are merely recording my professional advice. I haven't the slightest doubt that the General will ignore it."

"Is the General well enough to receive General Butler?" I asked.

"He is not," Jeremiah said.

After lunch, I changed into full dress uniform. Shortly after returning to headquarters the booming of our cannons told me that the Butler flotilla had rounded the bend and I could hear people crossing the parade, making for the wall walk. In due time General St. Clair, cleanly shaved, powdered and queued, in full dress uniform, entered the outer office. By now the booming of the cannons had stopped. Butler had been given the salvos due a major general, no more.

If General St. Clair was not running a high fever, I am greatly mistaken. His cheeks were red as if rouged. His eyes were as glassy as a mirror. He had difficulty keeping his stride. Each step he took seemed to be calculated, as if he were a tightrope walker. "Lieutenant Morrow," he said and his voice cracked in the middle of his sentence, "am I correct in assuming that this morning Dr. Allison paid you a visit?"

"You are, sir."

"You will please bring me the records and a pair of scissors."

General St. Clair cut out from the records what Dr. Allison had instructed me to enter.

"You have, I presume, made a copy for Viscount Malartie?" General St. Clair said.

"Yes, sir, I have."

"You will please give it to me."

This duplicate, General St. Clair tore into small bits.

Although I would have preferred to be on the wall walk, to watch the arrival of the Butler flotilla, it was necessary for me to remain in the outer office. Some two hours later Lieutenant Denny came in. Through the open door I could see that the General's entourage had assembled outside. "The flatboats are starting to put to?" I said.

Lieutenant Denny nodded, then whispered: "Hell's really going to break loose when St. Clair finds out. Butler's ignored orders. He's brought down a hundred or more whores."

I had scarcely admitted Lieutenant Denny into the inner office before he and General St. Clair came out. Moving with the strides of someone forcing his way through a crowd, the General made his way out of headquarters. Giving no heed to the greetings of his entourage, he stalked across the parade.

We all followed him. Present were Colonel Sargent and Viscount Malartie. Majors Ziegler, Hamtranck, Ferguson, Gaither, and Bedinger, the commander of the second regiment. Captain Ashton. Lieutenants Sedam, Denny, and me.

Teetering as he climbed up the wall walk, General St. Clair shook off Viscount Malartie's offer to give a helping hand. We went into the blockhouse. The boats of the mile-long flotilla were in their last circles of putting to. Lieutenant Denny's estimate of the number of women present seemed to be reasonably accurate. I should say there were eight or nine women along with a hundred men on each of the boats carrying levies. By way of greeting, the first two women were hoisting their skirts. The distance was such that their faces were unrecognizable. It may be presumed, however, that while wondering about General St. Clair's reaction, I was also wondering if Susan was among those present.

For what seemed to be quite a long time, General St. Clair glared at the activity on the river. "Those women," he said finally, "will not be permitted to enter Fort Washington."

They, of course, had to go somewhere, but no one seemed to be willing to offer a suggestion to the General. In due time, apparently, the General realized that his statement needed clarification. "Lieutenant Sedam," he said, "get word to someone on the riverbank. Those damned women, every last one of them, are to be sent to Ludlow's Station."

"Yes, sir," Cornelius said.

"I do not see General Butler," General St. Clair said.

I am certain that, like I, everyone present was also wondering where General Butler was. Having been officially welcomed by the fort's cannons, one might have expected to see him standing in full dress uniform at the bow of the flotilla's lead boat. General Butler was not there, nor had anyone been designated to represent him. If anybody at all was in uniform on any of the boats, I did not see him.

The flatboats, experiencing some difficulties for the river was running quite fast, were now beginning to land. "Lieutenant Sedam," General St. Clair said, "you will please find out where General Butler is."

As the General spoke, his eyes had a vacant stare. His lips were tightly compressed and his right hand was pressed against his stomach. His face had turned white as a ghost's and I am certain that had he not steadied himself by leaning against the blockhouse wall, he would have keeled over.

Cornelius must have sent a runner to the riverbank. Before any of the boats bumped against the shore, he brought in the news. "General Butler is ill-disposed, sir."

"Then he *is* aboard?"

"Yes, sir," Cornelius said. "I gather he's on one of the middle boats, either sleeping or resting."

One could guess that at least an hour would pass before the middle boats landed. One could be almost certain that General St. Clair was physically incapable of standing and waiting that long. Yet that is what, apparently, he was determined to do.

While, in my opinion, it was Colonel Sargent's duty to risk the General's wrath by suggesting that he was not well enough to remain standing for an hour or more, Colonel Sargent remained discreetly silent. It was Viscount Malartie who finally came to the rescue. "Under the circumstances, sir," Viscount Malartie said, "may I suggest that General Butler has forfeited his right to a formal greeting. Might it not be better, sir, to receive him at headquarters?"

Viscount Malartie said that beautifully. "A properly made suggestion," General St. Clair said. "Thank you, I shall follow it."

While crossing the parade Viscount Malartie, in tactfully chosen words, suggested that St. Clair should lie down and force General Butler to request an audience. This effort failed. General St. Clair, before taking to his head-quarters' office, announced firmly that he would wait there to receive General Butler or his representative.

The afternoon wore on. In due time I heard the derisive shouts of the women as they passed Fort Washington's main gate. Supplies began rolling in. Most of the levies were being shuffled off to Ludlow's Station. They were without arms and practically naked, I heard somebody saying. Somebody else said that the three hundred pound Dicky Butler was suffering from the gout and had been transported to his quarters by litter.

Sometime during the afternoon General St. Clair opened his office door and glared at Lieutenant Denny and me, who presently were the only oc-cupants of the outer office. "Lieutenant Morrow," he said, "I do not get the impression that General Butler has delivered me the contracted-for two thousand levies. In my judgment, he has brought me no more than thirteen hundred. You will please find out the exact number."

"Yes, sir," I said and started for the door.

"Not now, sir," General St. Clair said with considerable annoyance. "You will do this after General Butler has paid his respects. And from Major Ferguson I should like a preliminary report, if it is possible, as to the state of the supplies which Mr. Hodgdon has sent me. Find out also what money has been brought down. I shall be here tomorrow morning at nine o'clock and will appreciate receiving the information at that time."

"Yes, sir," I said. "Do you wish a verbal or written report?"

"A written one," General St. Clair said, then spoke to Lieutenant Denny. "You will leave, sir, immediately for Ludlow's Station. Find out the general state of affairs there and supply me with this knowledge tomorrow morning."

"Yes, sir," Lieutenant Denny said and lost no time getting off on his way.

It was almost dusk before Major Edward Butler came into headquarters to say his brother was too ill to pay his compliments personally to General

St. Clair. General Butler, Major Butler stated, would be only too pleased
to meet with General St. Clair at ten o'clock the following morning.

It was inexcusable for General Butler to have kept General St. Clair
waiting so long. And it was an out-and-out affront for General Butler to
have set a time.

XII

Immediately after his brief conversation with Major Butler, General St.
Clair made for his quarters. While crossing the parade he tottered a number
of times, like someone who is drunk, and I imagine some of the people
who saw him may have thought that he was. General St. Clair was far
sicker than he would acknowledge. Despite his dogged determination to
overcome his ailments by sheer power of will, I strongly doubted that I
would be seeing him at nine o'clock the next morning.

The information General St. Clair had requested, of course, had to be
gathered. I went about this task after supper. Fortunately Lieutenant
Colonel George Gibson of the Pennsylvania Militia, who I had been told
had the levies' enrollment list, had not yet gone to Ludlow's Station.

Colonel Gibson was reading *Romeo and Juliet,* or rather seemed to be
more or less just looking at his book, when I entered his quarters. A clean-
cut looking man of about forty-five, Colonel Gibson appeared to be happy
enough to have someone to talk to. "To be perfectly honest," he said. "I
have never actually counted the enrollment list."

"I can do that," I said.

"You count half," Colonel Gibson said, "and I'll count half."

The total came to fourteen-hundred-ninety-one. Since the first and second
regiment had not been completely filled, this meant our army would be
approximately twenty-six thousand strong. When I remarked upon this,
Colonel Gibson said, "The fourteen-hundred-ninety-one figure is gross. It
doesn't take into account our desertions."

"How many have deserted?" I asked.

"That, I would not know," Colonel Gibson said and told me that no
roll calls had been made while coming down the river.

"Are you able to hazard a guess?" I inquired.

"I would be afraid to do so," Colonel Gibson said.

"A hundred?"

"More than that, I should say. Definitely more than that."

"Two hundred?"

"Possibly. If I had to hazard a guess, I would say two hundred."

We chatted a bit. Like me, Colonel Gibson had been a schoolmaster. When I asked him why he had joined the militia, he laughed. "I've frequently wondered about that of late," he said. "I'm beginning to think I just got weary of looking at a schoolroom full of little apes."

"What delayed General Butler?" I asked.

"And may I ask you, sir," Colonel Gibson said, suddenly bristling, "what delays anyone?"

I was quite certain now that I recognized his kind. He was a most charming pedant, until you gave the slightest indication that he might not, in your opinion, be an oracle. We had a lot of them in Philadelphia. "I would presume," I said, "that you mean General Butler encountered obstacles."

"That is precisely what I mean, sir," Colonel Gibson said. "A congressman needs only to have vocal cords to pass enabling legislation. Raising an army, I assure you, is somewhat more difficult. Have you ever seen a dog standing on its hind legs?"

"I suppose I have," I said.

"I hope then, sir, rather than laughing and thinking how clumsy the dog looked, you were also generous enough to marvel that he was able to get up there in the first place."

I waited for Colonel Gibson to add that for this bit of wisdom he was indebted to Ben Jonson. He did not and I gathered from his self-satisfied chuckle that I was supposed to think it was his own brain child.

My interview with Assistant Paymaster Beatty did not consume much of his or my time. His chest, Beatty told me, was empty. He had arrived at Fort Pitt, he said, with $17,840.50 Pennsylvania, to meet sundry expenses. This amount, he explained, was approximately the sum needed to pay the levies their monthly wages, now long overdue. General Butler had used the money for this purpose.

At the armory the forges were ablaze and men were grumbling, as only enlisted men can, while they worked. Major Ferguson showed me a shipment of shovels. The shovels did not have handles. His inspection of the supplies, William said, must be regarded as preliminary, but he was prepared to say that almost everything would need repairs or alterations. Camp kettles, he stated categorically, were lacking and so few bells had been received that many guards would be required if our horses were allowed to graze. The haversacks leaked and there were only enough for the first and second regiments. All the small arms he had so far inspected, particularly those to be issued to the levies, were in need of repair. All the kegs of powder would have to be carefully inspected. Cannon and cartridge powder were frequently mixed. Most of the kegs were not marked at all. Those that were marked for cannon, invariably seemed to hold rifle powder.

I went back to headquarters and was almost finished making a second copy of my report when Lieutenant Denny returned from Ludlow's Station. After taking a healthy swig of whiskey, he said, "Since you're a good Presbyterian, I take it you're familiar enough with the Bible to have read about Sodom and Gomorrah."

"Yes," I said, "I've read of Sodom and Gomorrah."

"Well, multiply Sodom and Gomorrah by five, no, make it ten," Lieutenant Denny said, "and you've got Ludlow's Station at the present moment. Damned near everybody's drunk and raising hell in general. It's a great big orgy, that's what it is. The whole damned first regiment is lined up, waiting to get laid."

"Who's in command?"

"Darke was when things started to get out of hand. By the time Hamtranck arrived, it was too late, so John's just letting things run their course . . . What did you find out?"

I handed Lieutenant Denny the finished pages of the duplicate of my report. "H-m-m," he said, "fourteen-hundred-ninety-one levies. Oh! So ther're two hundred desertions? Say what you want about St. Clair. The old bastard doesn't miss so much at that. I've never been able to look at a crowd and come even close to guessing the number. Sick as he was, St. Clair called it practically on the nose."

I went on writing.

"I missed the woman count aplenty," Lieutenant Denny said. "They're two hundred strong."

Lieutenant Denny began commenting upon what he read. "No money for wages," he said. "That's what everybody's yelling for at Ludlow's Station—his wages. By now Mae Dwyer's got most of the wages the levies were paid in Pittsburgh. She's been tipped off there's no money here. She says she's going to St. Clair and offer to lend him this money at no interest. In return, she'll want a hands-off policy for her girls."

"St. Clair won't stand for that," I said.

"That's what I told Mae," Lieutenant Denny said. "But she's a damned persuasive female and just might get away with it. This much, I *do* know. If those wages aren't paid, St. Clair's in for a hell of a lot of trouble."

"My guess," I said, "is that tomorrow, or just as soon as he's feeling better, St. Clair will ship Mae Dwyer and her army of two hundred down the river to Louisville."

Lieutenant Denny shook his head. "Mae didn't bring down more than twenty-five of her girls."

"Who brought the rest?"

"They came down with the men. Their own men," Lieutenant Denny said.

"You mean they are wives?"

"Some of them might be, I guess," Lieutenant Denny said. "From what Mae tells me most of them are just the men's women. That's why the first regiment's lined up and waiting. It's only Mae's girls who are taking on customers. And you know Mae's rule?"

"No," I said, "I don't."

"None of her girls ever has to take on more than six a night," Lieutenant Denny said and got back to the point he had originally been making. "These other women, Mae says, aren't giving it to anybody but their own men. And they aren't going to leave them! When the army marches out, they're going along."

"St. Clair'll die before he allows—"

"I wouldn't bet on that," Lieutenant Denny broke in. "From what I saw and from what Mae tells me, this is a damned determined batch of women. They're not ordinary prostitutes, by any stretch of the imagination."

"Exactly what are they?"

"Women who weren't anything but dirt back home. They've been hearing about what a great place the Ohio Country is and how cheap it is to get land. This, they figure, is their chance to get out of the ghetto."

"Good Lord!" I said. "I'm impressed."

"Come to think of it, so am I," Lieutenant Denny said. "It was these women who got their men to join up, Mae says. The men they're with are altogether different from the rest of the jail sweepings and good-for-nothings Butler brought down. And I'll tell you something else. Butler's pleased with the way these women have been helping out. He's put every last one of them on the rolls, drawing a salary—as washerwomen."

"That can't be done," I said. "You know the regulations as well as I do— there are only four washerwomen allowed to a regiment."

"You're damned right I know about that regulation," Lieutenant Denny said, "and I can't wait to hear how Butler'll explain it to St. Clair."

Lieutenant Denny began reading again. "Christ, my Jesus Christ," he muttered, but did not enlarge upon this statement.

"I take it," I said, "that aside from the hundred-seventy-five odd men you were telling me about, Butler's brought down nothing but good-for-nothings."

"They're even worse than what Harmar got," Lieutenant Denny said. "They're stupid to begin with and have had no training. We can't possibly march out of here before October."

"October!" I said. "It'll be cold enough for blankets. We have next to no blankets."

"I wish that's all we had to worry about—blankets," Lieutenant Denny said. "But I did hear some were being sent up from Lexington."

By now I had finished my copying. "Do you want to read the last three pages?" I asked.

"It's just more of the same, isn't it?"

"Yes," I said, "that's all it is."

"Then to hell with it," Lieutenant Denny said.

It was after ten o'clock.

"I'm off," I said, "good night."

"Your friend—Susan," Lieutenant Denny said, "is at Ludlow's Station. She asked about you and I told her you were married, happily married. That was all right, wasn't it?"

"Of course it was all right," I said and left.

XIII

I was scarcely asleep before Melissa, a light sleeper and who has exceedingly acute hearing, awakened me. "Something's going on outside," she said. "I heard the drums. I can never tell when they stop and repeat or are just going on. It was either a stroke and ten-stroke roll or a number of two strokes and a flam."

Drum signals confused Melissa completely. It is difficult to understand why, for she had an excellent ear for music.

"Your first interpretation," I said, "would mean that men are being sent for wood; the second, for water. At this hour of night, I doubt if it would be either."

The "something" going on outside turned out to be a sizable contingent of the second regiment, under command of Lieutenant Denny, leaving for

Ludlow's Station. A Station patrol had spotted an advance guard of Indians, I learned. The Station was being alerted for an expected attack.

There was, of course, nothing Melissa and I could do, so we went back to bed.

The following morning, within ten minutes after I arrived at headquarters, Lieutenant Denny came in. "You're back!" I said.

"No, I'm not back," the lieutenant said. "It's my ghost you're looking at."

"I stand corrected," I said. "What happened?"

"Nothing," he said, "except that I lost a night's sleep. It was a false alarm. Hamtranck sent out Phineas Ford to see what was really what. God damned if it wasn't the Chickasaw scouts the stupid patrol spotted. Only half of them at that! And they thought that was an advance guard. It was only Colbert who came in. He doesn't know where Piamingo is. Hunting, he 'guesses'! When Colbert saw Butler's flotilla, he figured we'd be marching out soon and decided it was about time to report in for duty."

"I didn't hear your contingency come in," I said.

"I left them at the Station, under Marks, to guard the cattle. When the levies heard about the Indians, they damned near rioted. I don't suppose it's quieted down even yet. Hamtranck's got the first regiment ringed around the Station to stop wholesale desertion."

Lieutenant Denny took a swig of whiskey and ran his hand across his chin. "I'll have to shave before seeing St. Clair," he said. "God damn it, I have all the bad luck. I begged Bedinger for the command and got it over a half-dozen volunteers. Now when something good comes up, he'll owe it to somebody else."

Lieutenant Denny went to the alcove at the far end of the outer office and began lathering his face. "Who in the hell do you think Phineas Ford is shacked up with?" he asked.

"I haven't the faintest idea," I said.

"Mae Dwyer," he replied. "That's really something! I never heard of Mae working before." His voice trailed off. "No, it can't be for money. Mae's got all of that she wants. Now will you please tell me what she sees in Phineas Ford?"

"There's no accounting for tastes," I said and immediately was aware that I must have sounded pontifical.

"There certainly must not be," Lieutenant Denny said. "Mae's every day of fifty. But from what her girls tell me she's forgotten more than they'll ever know. She'd be a great lay, I'm sure, if she felt like it. I still can't see, though, why she's taking on Phineas Ford. I tried to get somewhere with her one night in Bedford and didn't even come close. Is Phineas going to scout for St. Clair?"

"I don't know," I said, "I haven't seen Phineas since he went to Ludlow's Station."

"I hope he does," Lieutenant Denny said. "I don't trust those Chickasaw. Hamtranck's worried about them too."

At exactly nine o'clock General St. Clair entered headquarters. The natural color was back in his cheeks and he appeared to be in good health. "Good morning, gentlemen," he said. "I will speak first with Lieutenant Denny."

When my turn came, General St. Clair merely asked for my written report. "That will be all, Lieutenant," he said.

It was approximately half-after nine o'clock when I returned to my desk.

"St. Clair didn't know anything about what happened at Ludlow's Station until I told him," Lieutenant Denny said. "He said he slept like a log, but I imagine Allison must have given him a morphine pill."

"He seemed to be in a good mood," I said.

"But like he was licking his chops," Lieutenant Denny said. "I'd give a lot to hear what's said when St. Clair and Butler tangle."

When General Butler did not appear at ten o'clock, Lieutenant Denny stepped over to the door. "Christ!" he said. "Butler's nowhere in sight. The fur's really going to fly."

At five minutes after ten o'clock, we could hear General St. Clair begin to pace the floor.

Lieutenant Denny remained at the door. It was almost half-after ten o'clock when he said, "Here comes Butler. Christ! He's stopped to shake hands and talk to Bedinger . . . Here come Gaither and Ashton. Butler's shaking hands and talking to them too . . . Good God! Now your friend Cornelius Sedam has come over. You can bet your boots St. Clair is watching all this.

"They're still talking," Lieutenant Denny said, "like Butler didn't have a care in the world. And here comes Ziegler! Did you know St. Clair's sending Ziegler down to Fort Knox?"

"No," I said, "I didn't."

"I heard about it while I was at Ludlow's Station. Nobody seems to know why. But I smell Sargent. You know Ziegler? That Dutchman won't take snot for anyone . . . Here comes Butler!"

Lieutenant Denny went to his desk and began looking busy. I did likewise. Soon we heard General Butler's booming laugh as he greeted the waiters outside of headquarters. I should say he chatted with them at least two full minutes.

It was now ten minutes before eleven o'clock.

Lieutenant Denny and I came to attention when General Butler entered the outer office. "A most pleasant good morning to you on this beautiful day, gentlemen," General Butler said so heartily that one could almost believe that the day, in fact overcast and with a threat of rain, was what he said.

There is no doubt that General Butler's booming laugh, deep voice, and jocular manner made him seem to be a more active man, physically, than he actually was. He was considerably heavier than when I had last seen him in Philadelphia. Such were the layers of fat on his protruding stomach that he appeared to be eight-and-a-half months pregnant. Carrying all that weight, his movements were necessarily lumbersome. Yet the athletic physique he had once possessed showed through. There was an elephantine grace about his carriage. And while the extremely fair skin of his fleshy face—on this morning quite florid—looked stretched to a point where it must soon burst, like an overinflated balloon, there were no wrinkles or signs of sagging jowls. His chin line was still detectable. It should have been a fat man's face, but it was not.

And for all General Butler's jolliness, no one could miss the shrewdness in his squinting agate-gray eyes.

"Lieutenant Ebenezer Denny, aide-de-camp to General Arthur St. Clair, sir," Lieutenant Denny said.

"Lieutenant Thomas A. Morrow, scribe to General Arthur St. Clair, sir," I said.

"I am most honored to meet you, sir," General Butler said, first to Lieutenant Denny and offered his hand.

"We have had the pleasure before, sir," Lieutenant Denny said with becoming modesty. "I had the honor of being presented to you, sir, some two years ago at Carlisle."

"Ah, yes, of course!" General Butler said. "I remember distinctly now and beg the indulgence of your forgiveness. Your shoulders, I note, have broadened considerably in the meantime."

I am certain General Butler hadn't the faintest recollection of having previously met Lieutenant Denny and I should say that Lieutenant Denny knew this too. This observation, however, is inconsequential. General Butler's perfidy was well-meant and his sincere, charming manner of delivery made it all seem believable.

Turning to me, General Butler's greeting was equally gracious as the one he had tendered Lieutenant Denny. "I, too," I said, "have had the pleasure of being presented to you, sir."

A glint in General Butler's eyes indicated that his memory had been stirred. He was, I am sure, making an honest effort to recall where we had met. It would have been cruel to say there had been four previous occasions, so I merely mentioned the last one. "At the Parkinson ball, sir," I said.

"It is so!" General Butler said and beamed at me. "And what a delightful evening that was. At such occasions a self-centered egotist such as I becomes totally lost in the excitement of his surroundings. Morrow! Would you be, is it possible, sir, that you could be the son of Robert A. Morrow?"

"Yes, sir," I said, "I am."

"Your father was a great and fine man, sir," General Butler said. "A truly great and fine man."

"Thank you, sir," I said.

I had looked up the proper words to be used when a major general called upon a fellow officer of the same rank. Knocking on the inner office door, I said, "General St. Clair, I have the honor of telling you that General Butler is here. May I inform him, sir, that you will be pleased to see him?"

"You may," General St. Clair barked.

"My dear Arthur," General Butler said, the moment I ushered him through the door, "it must be all of three years."

"Yes, Richard," General St. Clair said, "it is—"

By now I was out of the inner office.

"I bet on Butler," Lieutenant Denny said.

"I bet on St. Clair," I said. "He sat at his desk like a bald eagle in its nest. His talons looked sharp."

Lieutenant Denny stepped over to my desk and pressed his ear against the inner office wall. "Have you lost your mind!" I said.

"Even if it reduces me to ranks," Lieutenant Denny said, "I'm going to hear this. You're not involved. Just keep your eyes on the outer door."

I made no effort to protest and am fully aware that what Lieutenant Denny and I were doing was inexcusable. "Good God!" the lieutenant whispered. "Butler said we can't possibly win. He wants St. Clair to give up the campaign. The season's way too late, Butler said, and the levies he's brought down are nothing but a bunch of pandering poops."

It was necessary for me to keep my eyes glued on the headquarters' door. Lieutenant Denny would listen, then bend over and whisper into my ear. We must have made quite a spectacle.

"St. Clair," Lieutenant Denny whispered, "said, come hell or high water, the army is marching out. He sounds like he's trying hard to be calm, but he's about to explode. He read off all the dispatches he got from Knox . . .

"St. Clair's just asked Butler why he was so late," Lieutenant Denny whispered quickly and went back to his listening.

"They really had it hot and heavy over that one," Lieutenant Denny whispered after a considerable length of time. "Butler said he could have had a quarter of the levies here on time, but Knox told him to hold them because the forts and stations were unprotected. That got them off on St. Clair's order bringing the federals down. Butler said that was a damned fool order. St. Clair hit the ceiling and said he was accustomed to following orders unless otherwise advised."

Apparently by now both Generals were quite aroused and were jumping from one subject to another. Lieutenant Denny's whisperings became a series of one- or two-sentence messages.

"St. Clair brought up money for wages. He wanted to know why the levies got the money that was supposed to go to the federals . . .

"Butler said if he hadn't paid the levies off, they wouldn't have come down the river . . .

"They're arguing about what good-for-nothings the levies are . . .

"St. Clair said half the federals aren't any better . . .

"Hodgdon's come into it . . .

"Butler said Duer is more to blame than Hodgdon . . .

"How in the hell, Butler wanted to know, could he train the levies when the rifles didn't arrive at Fort Pitt until the day before he left . . .

"He couldn't have gotten here any sooner anyway, Butler said, because there weren't enough flatboats . . .

"Butler said, 'You're damned right I named my brother a major.' I don't get the connection. Do you?"

"No," I said, "I don't."

"Who's Colonel Gibson?"

I told Lieutenant Denny who Colonel Gibson was.

"St. Clair said Gibson has no military experience . . .

"Knox, Butler said, brought on Gibson's appointment, as a favor to the Governor of Pennsylvania . . .

"Butler said he knows Sargent and won't take any of his snot . . .

"They argued like hell about Sargent. Butler wanted Sargent to keep his nose out of the levies. St. Clair pulled rank for the first time. That God-damned Sargent is going to be allowed to keep on doing what he damned well pleases . . .

"Who's Oldham?"

"Lieutenant Colonel William Oldham of the Kentucky Militia," I said. "He's due here soon with a detachment of horse."

"He'll be over Darke?"

"No," I said. "Gibson's to command the first regiment of levies, Oldham the second."

"I understand," Lieutenant Denny whispered. "They were back on Gibson and St. Clair pulled rank again. Oldham will have seniority over Gibson . . .

"God damn!" Lieutenant Denny said in one of his fast whispers. "Here it comes! St. Clair said the women have to go . . .

"Butler said they should be allowed to stay. He told St. Clair what I told you. We need them for nurses, Butler said. He explained how they scrubbed the boats on the way down, mended clothes . . .

"St. Clair said, *no*. Even if they were two hundred Virgin Marys, they weren't marching out with his army . . .

"Could you hear Butler laugh just now?" Lieutenant Denny asked me.

"That laugh," I said, "was probably heard out on the parade."

"It was Butler's answer," Lieutenant Denny said, "when St. Clair told him that if he forgets for one second who's commander of this campaign, he'll break him."

The meeting between the two Generals came to its conclusion shortly after one o'clock.

XIV

There were many times during the month of September when General St. Clair appeared to be so ill that I thought surely he would collapse. However, he did not miss a single day at headquarters.

Not the least of General St. Clair's worries was how to pay the levies' wages, with no money in our coffers and no word when any might be ex- ↑ By the fifth of September practically all of our officers had re- ˡᵉˢˢ the levies were paid, we must expect the equivalent of he levies, all our officers said, knew their rights, were o find an excuse to go home, and would not accept

orning of September 6th General St. Clair did not appear

at headquarters at the usual half hour after eight o'clock, I asked a waiter if he were ill-disposed. "No, sir," the young man said, "in fact he looked a bit better than usual today. About an hour-and-a-half ago he and Colonel Sargent rode out of the fort." As if anticipating my next question, he added: "Nobody seems to know where they went or when they'll be back."

Around noon General St. Clair returned to headquarters and entered his office without mentioning where he had been. This was somewhat surprising for, since the arrival of General Butler, General St. Clair had been ordering me to record almost every move he made, as well as what was going on at the fort and at Ludlow's Station.

Shortly before the workday's end Cornelius Sedam, who had been at Ludlow's Station, stopped into headquarters to tell me that, having a free evening, he hoped Melissa's and mine was too.

"We'll see to it that it is," I said. "How were things at Ludlow's Station?"

Cornelius' answer was to make a wry face. Then he added, "At least the clamoring for wages has been stopped." The levies, he told me, had been paid their wages that afternoon.

"They accepted the promissory notes!"

"They were paid in real money," Cornelius said, "Pennsylvania."

A day or two later Lieutenant Denny came into headquarters to submit what General St. Clair called: *A Statement of the Progress Being Made by the United States Army at the Station, Called Ludlow's, Located Approximately Six Miles Above Fort Washington*. At the moment General St. Clair was closeted with Colonel Oldham. While waiting, Lieutenant Denny said: "You may expect a visit from Colonel Sargent within the hour."

"Nothing would give me more pleasure," I said.

"Just for the devil of it," Lieutenant Denny said, "find out, won't you, just how much the army is allowed to pay for a bearskin?"

"Three to five dollars a skin is the average," I said after looking it up. "For a top quality skin we're allowed to pay no more than seven dollars."

"Well, blow me down," Lieutenant Denny said. "I do have to hand it to your friend Phineas Ford."

As might be expected, I requested further enlightenment.

"You know how all of our haversacks leaked?" Lieutenant Denny said.

"I do," I said, "and know also that we received only enough haversacks for the federals and from the looks of things the levies are going to march out without any."

"You're barking up the wrong tree," Lieutenant Denny said with a show of considerable amusement. "In fact you aren't even in the right forest.

Phineas mentioned to Hamtranck that the way to waterproof the haversacks was to cover them with bearskin. Hamtranck thought it was a good idea, so Phineas scoured Cincinnati for bearskins and sold them to the Station quartermaster for seven dollars each. That made it about forty cents a haversack. Sargent's just found out about it and wants Phineas lashed for profiteering. But I'd say Phineas is safe, wouldn't you? Who in the hell can prove he didn't bring in top quality skins?"

"Yes," I said, "I should say that Phineas just about makes it."

Before an hour was gone by Colonel Sargent entered headquarters. "You will please let me know the amount the army is permitted to pay for bearskins," he said, "and you will also, please, look up the penalty for overcharging the United States Army."

"I happen to know," I said, "that the army may not pay more than seven dollars for a bearskin, no matter how good its quality."

"Thank you," Colonel Sargent said and appeared to be quite frustrated.

"You wished to see the military penal code?" I inquired.

"That will not be necessary," Colonel Sargent said and left.

Before this day was over the members of the second regiment of federals were most annoyed upon receiving a specific order from Colonel Sargent that *their* haversacks must be waterproofed by a coating of paint.

Sometime during this month Colonel Darke, his face red with indignation, burst into headquarters to protest a sentence by Major Hamtranck that Darke's nephew, Michael Larrison, be given twenty-seven lashes for causing a disturbance.

Specifically Michael Larrison was charged with perpetuating the favorite bit of militiaman horseplay—shooting at a low-flying flock of geese or passenger pigeons and inducing a number of fellow platoon members to throw down their rifles in order that the culprit could not be identified.

"There is no proof that it was my nephew who shot at the pigeons," Colonel Darke said, pointed out that as things were no one knew whose rifle belonged to whom, and added that Hamtranck had been bullying his nephew beginning back in the days when Michael first enlisted at Fort Knox.

Before rendering a final judgment, General St. Clair called in Major Hamtranck. John brought with him four sergeants as witnesses to the fact that the barrel of Michael Larrison's rifle had been smudged with stove soot and that it was this rifle which had been fired.

General St. Clair agreed that Michael Larrison should receive the twenty-seven lashes and the punishment was administered. Henceforth Colonel Darke refused to speak to Major Hamtranck other than when he was officially required to.

General St. Clair had fully expected that Major John Doughty, the builder of Forts Harmar and Washington, would be here to supervise the erection of Forts Hamilton and Jefferson. On September 16th a rather testily worded dispatch from Secretary of War Knox stated that Major Doughty, while ready and willing to come to Cincinnati during June and July, was now required to be in New York Town in order to advise President Washington of the practicality of improvements contemplated at our West Point arsenal.

Immediately upon receiving the Knox dispatch, General St. Clair ordered Major Ferguson to put everything else aside and get on with the erection of Fort Hamilton. General Butler objected to the sending off of the invaluable Major Ferguson. Fort Hamilton, General Butler contended, to be located some twenty miles up the Great Miami River, was primarily a citadel of protection for the Miami Purchase and could be built after the campaign's conclusion. During the day one officer after another came into headquarters to plead for the Butler point of view. General St. Clair, however, would not budge. Fort Hamilton was going up, he insisted, and so was Fort Jefferson.

General St. Clair had also instructed Major Ferguson to hack out a twelve mile wide military road while en route to the Fort Hamilton building site. Over this General St. Clair and General Butler, who wished this road to be at least twenty feet wide, almost came to blows. They were still engaged in violent argument over this decision when my workday came to an end.

On the way to our quarters I told myself that on this evening I would forgo discussing with Melissa the woes of getting a campaign started, which is all I had talked about since the arrival of General Butler. Melissa, while listening bravely, I was beginning to gather, was by now saturated with the subject.

Any number of topics which would be interesting to Melissa revolved through my mind as I walked across the parade. It was, however, unnecessary to bring them up. When I opened the door of our quarters Melissa announced that Kitty Kummerschmitt was pregnant.

Kitty, Melissa told me, was rather pleased by her discovery, but did not wish for Dr. Allison to know he was about to become a father, for fear he would be worried while off on the campaign.

I had mentioned Phineas Ford's observation about the possible relationship between Kitty and Jeremiah. "The mere thought is outlandish," Melissa had said. "Phineas should have his mouth washed out with soap."

After reminding Melissa of her statement, I expressed my mild surprise that she had not suspected anything. "In many ways Kitty is quite secretive," Melissa said, "besides it never occurred to me to be on the lookout. Dolly Sedam was completely surprised as I."

"Dolly knows about this too?"

"Dolly was here," Melissa said, "when Kitty came in to tell us about it."

I was able to visualize the three women, sitting in conference.

Kitty, Dolly and she, Melissa said had held a heart-to-heart talk. "If there is anyone to be blamed," Melissa told me, "Kitty is convinced it is she, for she was the aggressor."

"Kitty the aggressor!"

"You recall that young soldier, the one who died of pneumonia?"

"I recall a young soldier dying of pneumonia," I said.

It began, Melissa told me, on the night of the young boy's death. Jeremiah, expecting to pull the boy through, was most disconsolate, for he could not understand wherein he had failed. "Jeremiah looked so discouraged and sad," Melissa told me Kitty had said.

Surely what followed could not be as simple as Kitty said. Yet it was, she insisted, purely a desire to be comforting that motivated her behavior. Acting upon impulse, feeling that Jeremiah needed her, she had undressed and joined Jeremiah in his bed. What followed astounded Kitty.

"Emil expected Kitty to behave as a wife every night," Melissa told me.

"Even—"

"Even," Melissa said.

Her experience with Jeremiah, Kitty said, was a revelation. There was no feeling of having performed a wifely duty as had always been the case following an encounter with Emil. Kitty had felt, to use her own expression, as if she were "cleansed" all over.

"Pardon me," I said to Melissa, "are you saying that this is the first time Kitty—"

"The first time," Melissa said. "At age thirty-three, it was the first time."

"Thirty-three!" I said. "I thought Kitty was in her earlier twenties."

"I didn't think she was quite that old either," Melissa said. "In her early twenties Kitty still believed she could become pregnant by kissing a man."

"Good Lord!" I said and then it occurred to me that my dead wife had believed this until she was eighteen. It also occurred to me that Mary's mention of this—it had been merely an inadvertently made statement—was the closest we had come to discussing our marital relationship.

"I can understand it," Melissa said. "Kitty left a domineering family for a loving but demanding husband. Actually she had jumped out of the frying pan into the fire without realizing it. With Jeremiah—she lived in a world she didn't know existed. There was freedom. There was no feeling that she was in the company of the master of the house. Can't you understand this?"

"I can understand it," I said, "but it's a fixation rather than real love. The age difference makes it an impossible situation."

"It is not an impossible situation," Melissa said, "because Kitty's love for Jeremiah is real."

"As she sees it at the moment," I said.

"Granted," Melissa said.

Melissa and I had never discussed our marital activities. There hadn't been any reason to. "Melissa," I said that night when we went to bed, "am I—a master of the house?"

"Of course not," Melissa said and laughed. "Our conversation about Kitty has gotten you to thinking, hasn't it?"

"In a way," I said, "slightly. I suppose it has."

"I am pleased to report," Melissa said, "that I am completely contented and satisfied."

"Do you," I asked and hesitated for quite a while. "Are you, every time—"

"Of course not," Melissa said.

"Oh, good Lord!" I said. "We'll have to discuss this."

"We do not have to discuss it," Melissa said. "Believe me, give me just the slightest inkling that your performance is merely a means of passing the time—then, we will discuss it."

"I see no imminent danger of that," I said.

Although academically my views on men's and women's bedtime activities tend to be definitely catholic, considering the way our world goes, I do believe it is practical for couples who have children to be married. I took up this point of view with Melissa the following morning at breakfast. "I am sure," Melissa said, "that Jeremiah will be more than pleased to marry Kitty."

"I would say so too," I said, "bans, however, should be immediately posted. If Jeremiah does not come back from the campaign, Kitty will be an unwed mother."

"Dolly and I discussed that at length with Kitty," Melissa said. "We convinced her, I believe, to a point where she is going to give the matter considerable thought."

That part resolved itself. A few days later Melissa informed me that Kitty's appraisal of her condition was in error.

XV

By October second Major Ferguson had a twelve foot wide military road hacked out through the woods and Fort Hamilton was up. Immediately upon being advised of this information, General St. Clair ordered our army to march out on the following morning.

October 2nd was, necessarily, a busy day and at dusk General St. Clair was noticeably fatigued. There was still considerable correspondence which the General wished to dictate. All day long he had been saying that he would attend to it "shortly," but one thing after another had come up. "We will do it this evening, Lieutenant Morrow," General St. Clair said as he left headquarters for his evening meal. "I shall be back here at half-after seven o'clock."

At quarter past seven o'clock I was back at headquarters. Shortly thereafter Lieutenant Denny, who had been at Ludlow's Station, came in. "They got the cattle and some of the packhorses started on their way," he said. "Everything else looks like a lot of chickens running around with their heads chopped off. You're lucky to be staying here for a while."

Lieutenant Denny was referring to the fact that I would not be with the army until later. A few days previously a dispatch from Secretary of War Knox had ordered General Butler to preside at a Court of Inquiry on the Harmar Expedition. This could not be postponed for attending officers, coming down from Fort Pitt, were already en route. Since I was instrumental in the writing of General Harmar's report, General Butler had insisted that I should testify. He also wished me to be the Court of Inquiry's scribe.

"I won't have to be on hand for the damned boring early part of the march either," Lieutenant Denny said. "I'm going down to Fort Knox to find out where in the hell the flour is."

I looked up and Lieutenant Denny must have guessed my thoughts. "No, no," he said. "I'm not being sent off to Bengal this time. I'll be back in plenty of time for action. In plenty of time."

"When do you leave?" I asked.

"In a day or two," Lieutenant Denny said. "Nobody knows for sure how much flour was sent up to Fort Hamilton. After I find out how much is there, I'll go to Fort Knox."

"Then you'll march out with the army tomorrow?"

"I imagine so. I understand St. Clair's leaving here on parade. Nobody's told me anything yet."

"We haven't received any word at all when we can expect the flour," I said.

"Don't I know it!" Lieutenant Denny said. "And damned near all the beef and pork for the campaign has already been eaten up."

"There have been no requests from out of here for more beef and pork," I said.

"I suppose I'll have to look into that too then," Lieutenant Denny said. "Did you ever mention beef and pork to St. Clair?"

I nodded. "He told me to take it up with Sargent, which I did."

"Well, then I guess somebody's put through an order," Lieutenant Denny said. "If you told Sargent, it's no skin off your behind."

Lieutenant Denny moved to the alcove. "What did I see your wife and Dolly Sedam sewing the other day?" he asked when he returned. "It looked like they had canvas."

"It was canvas," I said. "They heard about the flaps of the tents. They're making special ones for Cornelius and me."

"Where'd they get the extra sheet?"

"They cut down a discarded tent that was ripped."

"Then you'll be sleeping single? Snug, warm, and dry."

"That's the general idea," I said.

"God damn!" Lieutenant Denny said. "Sometimes I wish I had a wife. But when I look at some of them—it's a hell of a chance a man takes."

Lieutenant Denny moved to the door. "No," he said, "you're taking too big a chance because you never know what a woman's like until you've lived with her. She'll do anything to get you and once she has, well—then she's got you."

Lieutenant Denny turned and looked at me, as if for verification. "Some people, I agree," I said, "shouldn't be married, surely not during certain phases of their lives."

"You're damned right they shouldn't," Lieutenant Denny said, "and I'm one of them. But to tell you the truth I'm getting a little tired of playing around. Only the other night I had a roll at Ludlow's Station. When it was all over, I thought to myself: Now I have to get dressed and ride back to Fort Washington. It just didn't make much sense. May I ask you a personal question?"

"What about?"

"Susan," Lieutenant Denny said. "All I want to know is—was she a good lay?"

"Go to hell," I said.

"I don't understand you," Lieutenant Denny said. "You always act like it's a crime to talk about—"

"Just call it a phobia of mine," I said.

"Don't get sore," Lieutenant Denny said. "We've been getting along fine lately and I certainly don't want to stir things up. You're through with Susan, aren't you?"

"Yes," I said, "I am."

"That's all I wanted to know, so don't get sore," Lieutenant Denny said. "That's all I wanted to know."

At exactly half-after seven o'clock Colonel Sargent came into headquarters. "Lieutenant Morrow," he said, "General St. Clair finds himself far too busy to see you this evening. Tomorrow you will ride with the army to Fort Hamilton and there you will attend to the General's correspondence. That accomplished, you will return to Fort Washington, to place yourself at General Butler's disposal."

Colonel Sargent left. The venom in his voice when he said "Butler" had been most noticeable. It was as if he had spit out the word.

"So the General's far too busy—" Lieutenant Denny said. "He's collapsed again."

"I would suppose so," I said.

"He'll never last out the campaign," Lieutenant Denny said.

"I say he will," I said, "even if he ends up on a litter."

"That's the same as not lasting it out," Lieutenant Denny said. "No, it's worse."

XVI

Since most of our troops and all of our supplies, cattle, and ten pieces of artillery were at Ludlow's Station, those of us who departed from Fort Washington, the following morning shortly after dawn, did not make a formidable-looking assemblage. General St. Clair, however, had decreed that we leave in grand style.

The Chickasaw scouts made up our van. Instructed to march out eight-abreast, this order apparently was misunderstood. Once we started off, the Indians moved ahead in single-file, strung out behind Piamingo, like so many solemn geese. Colbert was not on hand. He had lost out to Piamingo in his rivalry for leadership, I was told. At the moment Colbert was off sulking. It was most unlikely that we would be seeing him again.

Next came the colors and music. Then General St. Clair, flanked by Colonel Sargent and Viscount Malartie, followed by we officers—some ten or twelve of us—who were still at Fort Washington. I rode the left side. Cornelius was beside me. Lieutenant Denny was next to Cornelius. I believe it was Ensign Marks who rode on Lieutenant Denny's right. General Butler, it probably should be mentioned, was confined to his quarters, bedridden with the gout.

I had never before seen General St. Clair astride a horse. He was, I had been told, a superb equestrian. This is so. Shoulders erect, in campaign uniform and beaver, General St. Clair was—magnificent. The gray nag he rode was a sorry-looking beast who had long ago seen her better days. Yet such was the stylish action the General engendered from this worn-out piece of horseflesh that both Melissa and Dolly Sedam would tell me later they had thought General St. Clair was astride a cob.

Half the first regiment, under Major Hamtranck, brought up our rear. These men marched well and, being veterans, knew all the tricks of a soldier's trade. With supplies so woefully inadequate, they had known how to garner the best uniforms and equipment. It was these fellows who had the bearskin-covered haversacks and they were proud as peacocks about this.

That constituted the all of us.

We moved up Eastern Row to the military road which was flanked by gigantic beeches, walnuts and hickories. While most of September had been quite warm, during the past few days the weather had begun giving indications that autumn, while still alive, was on its last legs. The woods had turned yellow. Goldenrod was brown and dry. On this day the sky was overcast, the kind of gray which is bleak but does not usually presage rain.

The relatively untrampled condition of the military road told us we were ahead of the main army. Leaving the scouts and first regiment behind, we on horse hastened our pace. Shortly before noon we reached our destination, having seen many deer, geese, turkeys, and passenger pigeons while en route.

Fort Hamilton was surrounded by acre after acre of wild oats that stood ten feet tall. Major Ferguson had already begun the military road to the north. It, too, was twelve feet wide. It went into woods so dense, a fat man would have experienced considerable difficulty getting between the trees. The boughs of the trees flanking the road were big enough to meet and form a roof. From Fort Hamilton Major Ferguson's effort looked like the entrance to a cave.

"Lieutenant Morrow," General St. Clair said when we were in the fort and had dismounted, "after lunch I wish to rest for one hour. Then we will get down to the business of my correspondence."

Thus, Cornelius and I had ample opportunity to look about Fort Hamilton. She was square in shape, a hundred-fifty yards on each side. At the four corners bastions were built to cover the approaches, two of these being provided with platforms from which cannons could sweep the ground in front. Quarters for officers and possibly a hundred-fifty men and storehouses for equipment and supplies were within the enclosure.

At the moment Fort Hamilton was almost deserted. Major Ferguson's fatigue party of a hundred-thirty men with a militia escort of two hundred were in the woods, hacking ahead on the road. As might be expected, under Major Ferguson's direction, a stoutly built fortification had been erected. The picket logs, twenty feet in length, of uniform size, were well butted and carefully trimmed so that they fit closely together. They were black walnut, lumber that would have cost a fortune in Philadelphia! A ribband was run around near the top of the pickets to hold them securely in position and the earth at the bases of the pickets was rammed down hard and fast. On the inside wall, between every two pickets, another was snugly fitted, making Fort Hamilton impenetrable to Indian missiles.

"She's a superb fort," Cornelius said, "but was she worth two weeks' delay?"

"I don't know," I said. "I have difficulty seeing us marching out two weeks ago with our levies in the shape they were then."

"You've made a point there, I admit," Cornelius said, "but are the levies any better now than they were two weeks ago?"

"*You* have made a point there," I said.

Eventually Lieutenant Denny joined us. "Christ!" he said. "We've got nothing but sour flour here."

"All of it?" Cornelius asked.

"So I'm told," Lieutenant Denny said, "and from the samplings I've made, I can well believe it."

"Good Lord!" Cornelius said. "Half our supply is here."

"Almost two-thirds," Lieutenant Denny corrected. "I'd say none of it can be used."

"What happened?" Cornelius asked.

"Maybe you'd better ask Colonel Sargent," Lieutenant Denny said. "He sent it up here in the rain, in barrels he knew were all busted up. And before the storehouses were built."

"Would that sour it all?" Cornelius inquired.

"I'd say so," Lieutenant Denny said, "considering the shape the flour was in when it left Ludlow's Station. Add if you want, for good measure, the fact that the barrels were stacked up out in the open in what was the equivalent of a swamp. That's where they stood, for four days, baking in the sun."

General St. Clair looked rather rested when we began on the correspondence. We were in a small, unfinished room within the barracks. There was no flooring. We sat on three-legged stools. My desk was a board on two sawhorses.

As his dictation progressed General St. Clair became noticeably weary. Taking nips of brandy with increasing frequency, he did considerable walking about to stretch his back. He did not offer me a nip of brandy, nor did it ever occur to him that I, too, might have wished to stretch my back.

Most of the correspondence was routine. When we came to letters relating to the state of our army, addressed to President Washington, Secretary of War Knox, and Secretary of the Treasury Hamilton, General St. Clair became enraged while dictating and seemed to be reliving every word he uttered. This drained his strength and when we were finally finished—it was now quite late in the afternoon—he appeared to be exhausted.

After selecting the material which he wished to read over in its final form and affix his signature, General St. Clair said, "I should like to attend to this by no later than nine o'clock."

"I will do my best to have it ready by then, sir," I said.

About this time a waiter came into the room to announce that the van of the main army was within a quarter-of-a-mile of the fort. Hearing this news General St. Clair scowled and pressed his hand against his abdomen. Then he turned, I am certain, in order that the waiter and I could not see his face. The movement of his shoulders indicated that he was taking in deep breaths. "You will inform my officers," General St. Clair, still not facing us, said, "that I shall expect their presence on the wall walk as I greet my army."

"Yes, sir," the waiter said and left.

When General St. Clair finally turned, his face was quite pale, but apparently he had conquered his pain. He walked briskly across the parade. I waited until our officers began congregating and fell into step beside

Lieutenant Denny. "Here's something I just learned," "Lieutenant Denny said. "St. Clair's left his general's marquee at Fort Washington. He's going to use the same kind of tent the rest of us are."

"I think that's a rather good move," I said.

"I don't," Lieutenant Denny said. "A general's a general. He should be in a marquee."

I did not pursue the matter. "Have you examined the rest of the flour?" I asked.

"None of it is any good," Lieutenant Denny said. "The army's going into the woods with less than ten days' supply."

"Are you going to be able to make up the whole flour loss in Louisville?" I asked.

"I doubt it," Lieutenant Denny said. "We'll have to use what comes to Fort Washington from Fort Pitt."

"We haven't got the horses to transport it," I said.

Lieutenant Denny smiled wryly. "I mentioned this slight detail to Colonel Sargent."

"Where will he get the horses?"

"By following my suggestion," Lieutenant Denny said. "Tomorrow morning he'll issue three days' flour supply to all the troops. That will release two-hundred-ninety horses."

Lieutenant Denny sounded rather bitter. "At any rate," I said, "for once Colonel Sargent agreed to follow someone else's suggestion."

"And like a jackass," Lieutenant Denny said, "I made my suggestion without benefit of witnesses. By the time it gets to St. Clair, it'll be just another example of how Sargent is able to get things done."

We climbed to the wall walk. The army was going to march past Fort Hamilton. It would encamp along the military road Major Ferguson's men were presently hacking out. The Chickasaw and the complete first regiment brought up the van. They were followed by the second regiment, whose haversacks were waterproofed with a Spanish brown paint.

Thereafter, except for Faulkner's riflemen, Snowden's horse and Mountfort's North Carolinians, it was a dismal sight. The levies, attired in cast-off Harmar Expedition uniforms and what else the quartermaster could find for them, simply trudged past. No effort was made to tighten up ranks or acknowledge General St. Clair's presence. Darke did salute. Gibson and Oldham, appearing to be asleep on their horses, did not so much as look up.

The women, some riding the cannons, were present in full force. At the sight of them, General St. Clair stiffened. He was fully aware, however, that they were coming along. You will find no mention of these some two hundred women in our records. I never heard General St. Clair refer to them, even in passing, although other officers talked about them a great deal. That General St. Clair made an arrangement with Mae Dwyer, I had not the slightest doubt. The money for the levies' wages could not have been obtained from any other source. As for the other women? There they were, as we all knew they would be.

While it was possible to identify officers on horses, the distance was too great to recognize people who were walking. I could not make out Phineas or Susan or Mae Dwyer. They were, I knew, among the marchers.

The army was strung out with wide gaps between the various contingent. As it wriggled along, it looked like a huge salamander, chopped up, but whose severed portions were still alive. A contingent would enter the military road, then disappear into the woods, like water going over a falls. As dusk came on those entering the hole cut into the forest took on the appearance of slow-moving processions of ghosts.

That evening, as I worked on General St. Clair's correspondence, the campaign's first casualties were brought into Fort Hamilton: seven levies, painfully cut-up by the razor-sharp hoofs of a herd of deer which had run pell-mell through their tent.

XVII

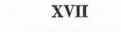

A full week went by before enough officers were present at Fort Washington to begin holding the Court of Inquiry. Although it was a foregone conclusion that General Harmar would be exonerated, the hearings dragged on and on. On the 16th of October General Butler went off to join our army. I stayed on at Fort Washington, ordered by General Butler to get all the Court of Inquiry material assembled and properly written up before going north. "I cannot afford to lose you before this is done, Tom," General Butler said, giving forth with one of his boisterous laughs. "If the Indians kill you, we'll have to hold the whole damned Inquiry all over again."

Lieutenant Denny was still in the general vicinity, having come back from Louisville and Lexington with promises but no flour. Continuing his efforts to get some, he had gone to Bracken. A shipment of sixteen hundred pounds had come through from Fort Pitt. This, loaded on a hundred pack-horses, was already on its way.

By October 22nd, I was finished with my task. Before taking my leave, however, I must wait until a contingency of some sort moved out.

On this day Ensign Marks, with an escort of ten Kentucky militiamen, arrived at Fort Washington to say that the army was on one-third flour rations and that General St. Clair wished most urgently to know when more might be expected.

Ensign Marks was the bearer of the first news Fort Washington had of what was what with our army since it had marched out of Fort Hamilton on October 4th. I don't believe that Ensign Marks had ever before made a report which was to be entered in the records. When he saw me write: *Statement Rendered By Ensign Stephen Marks,* he weighed his words carefully. "On the nineteenth day of October of the year 1791," he said, "upon taking my leave of the United States Army under command of General Arthur St. Clair, this army was engaged in the erection of Fort Jefferson which lies in latitude 40°-4'-22". Our army—"

"In heaven's name, Stephen," I said. "Exactly where is the army?"

"Forty-five miles north of Fort Hamilton," Stephen said.

"That's all the farther we've gotten!"

"There was a lot of heavy rain and lightning," Stephen said. "Trees were blown down. The tents leaked . . ."

"I'm most anxious to hear all that, Stephen," I said. "For the report, I simply have to know the purpose of your mission. You wish to know when the army will be receiving flour? That's all that goes down here. Your next step is to go to the commanding officer for your answer. If he wishes your account of the state of the army to be entered into the records, he will so order it."

"Good Lord!" Stephen said.

"I am able to appreciate your feelings, Stephen," I said. "And the commanding officer is at Ludlow's Station. He will not be back here until tomorrow. At that time he will tell you he hasn't the faintest idea when there will be any more flour."

I gave Stephen a glass of whiskey. "Now," I said, "I'd like very much to know, for my private information, what is what."

"It's awful," Stephen said. "There's no discipline and there are a lot of desertions. They'd be more, but the levies are afraid to strike out through the woods."

"We've sent up a bit of flour and some beef," I said. "You *have* gotten that?"

"Yes, but half the flour was moldy. We had to throw it away. We're running awfully short of meat. There's no green forage. Our cattle are getting sick and we're losing a lot of our horses."

"What is General St. Clair's state of health?" I asked.

"He's sicker than a dog and he and Butler had a big argument. Butler said it was ridiculous to go on. He wanted to leave St. Clair at Fort Jefferson, go ahead with a thousand picked men, give the Indians a lightning stroke, and call it a day like Scott and Wilkinson did. St. Clair said the army was still under *his* command and would stay that way and was going to march out just as soon as Fort Jefferson was completed."

"How long will that take?"

"I don't know," Stephen said. "It was high enough to lay the rafters when I left and Ferguson was working like mad." Major Ferguson, Stephen went on to say, was having his difficulties. The army had only one saw and one frow. There were only eighty axes, thirteen of which had been borrowed from the troops.

"Have you run across many Indians?"

"Until we started building Fort Jefferson," Stephen said, "we didn't see hardly any. After that, the woods became full of them."

I had expected to ride out with Stephen on the following morning. However, during the night, his entire escort deserted. On October 24th, Lieutenant Denny returned to Fort Washington. A "Captain" Benham, he said, was within a half hour of the fort with two hundred horses and twenty-seven hundred weight flour. "I'm not letting Benham in the fort," Lieutenant Denny told me. "The bastard's being paid by the day. We've got to hurry him along or he'll take forever."

"We're leaving right away!" I said.

"You're damned right we are," Lieutenant Denny said. "As soon as I can make arrangements for an escort."

"Where did you locate the flour?" I asked.

"Bracken, Limestone . . ." Lieutenant Denny said. "Christ, from all over."

For Melissa and me it was probably just as well that my leavetaking was perforce made in haste. Just before Lieutenant Denny, Ensign Marks, the escort and I rode out of the fort, Melissa went to the wall walk. That is all I remember of it—Melissa standing up there and waving until I was out of sight.

By pushing Captain Benham to the utmost, we reached Fort Jefferson on the evening of October 31st. A Captain Shay was in command, with a hundred-twenty men, mostly invalids, as a garrison.

There was almost no clearing about Fort Jefferson. In the dense woods surrounding her you could see white oaks that were six feet through. They rose high as eight feet without limbs and held their bigness. A square work of a hundred-fourteen feet sides, the fort had four small bastions. The barracks and storerooms were not quite completed. Two cannons had been left at the fort. When Lieutenant Denny wondered about this, Captain Shay said the cannons were here because our horses were too weak to pull them.

A scaffold stood in the center of the parade. Three deserters, Captain Shay told us, had been hung. The hangings, he said, had increased the troops' grumbling and resentment, but had not improved discipline. Desertions and sickness had reduced our forces to about seventeen hundred. The army had left Fort Jefferson on October 24th. The road-cutters were having many difficulties. From what scanty information he had, Captain Shady estimated our army was moving ahead at the rate of about four miles a day. His patrols, he said, reported the presence of many Indians, but so far there had been no encounters.

Leaving twelve hundred weight flour at Fort Jefferson we moved out the following morning at dawn. This was a cold enough day for ice to have formed in shallow vessels. The road ahead was now only six feet wide. There were many knee-deep meandering streams to cross. Much of this area was swampy.

The temperature continued to drop. At dawn of November 3rd there were slight snow flurries. Sometime during this morning Major Hamtranck and a large body of troops came down the road. Ordering his men to keep on moving, John reined in a horse that was all skin and bones. He was chasing, he informed us, some eighty of Darke's Kentuckians who had deserted. "You didn't see any of them, did you?" John asked.

Lieutenant Denny shook his head. "They must have skirted around us."

All the troops marching past us had bearskin-covered haversacks. "Christ!" Lieutenant Denny said. "It's the whole first regiment."

John nodded gravely. "If we'd sent levies after them, nobody'd come back."

"Good Lord, John—"

"I know how weak it makes us," John said impatiently. "We had to send out federals. St. Clair, Butler, Gibson, Oldham—everybody agreed we had no choice. It's the only thing everybody's agreed upon since we left."

"How far are you chasing them?"

"There's a convoy somewhere behind you," John said. "That's what the bastards are after—the convoy's horses. I'm supposed to get to the convoy no matter what. The deserters? If I don't catch them by the time I'm twenty-five miles past Fort Jefferson, I'm to come back."

From John's manner of speaking, I gathered he felt that the chances of apprehending the deserters was slim.

"John," Lieutenant Denny said. "It can't be true! At Fort Jefferson Captain Shay told me St. Clair hasn't got his front flanks covered."

"It's true," John said.

"Good God!" Lieutenant Denny said. "Then I guess I can believe Shay when he told me that St. Clair sent out the Chickasaw on a ten-day scouting expedition?"

"You can," John said.

"Where in the hell did they go?"

"Who knows?" John said.

"How far ahead is the army?" Lieutenant Denny asked.

"You ought to be able to catch up with it by late afternoon," John said.

XVIII

At approximately half-after three o'clock we caught up with the army's rear guard, thirty federals under Cornelius Sedam. Cornelius, who had left Fort Washington a chubby fellow concerned as well as being teased by Dolly about being overweight, must have lost thirty pounds. Had his face not been so drawn and haggard looking, Cornelius would have appeared to be in excellent physical condition.

Cornelius' eyes brightened somewhat at the sight of Lieutenant Denny and me, but he was too weary to actually smile. "Gentlemen," he said, "the General will be most pleased to see you."

"Your boys look all done in," Lieutenant Denny said.

"They are," Cornelius said. "We've been on one-eighth rations for the past three days."

We glanced toward the men. Having stepped aside, they stood along the road staring at the food which was being transported past them.

"If I give them anything, somebody's sure to talk," Lieutenant Denny said. "It'll make everybody else sore."

Cornelius nodded in agreement.

"We saw Hamtranck," Lieutenant Denny said.

"He'll never catch them," Cornelius said.

"I've been worrying all day about the whole first regiment being sent out," Lieutenant Denny said.

"What do you think we've been doing here?" Cornelius said.

"How strong are we with Hamtranck away?" Lieutenant Denny asked.

"About fourteen hundred."

"Little Turtle certainly won't wait until Hamtranck gets back," Lieutenant Denny said.

"That's what everybody thinks," Cornelius said. "We expect to be hit any time now."

"Then why are we still marching?" Lieutenant Denny said. "It'll be dark before you know it. Why aren't we encamped and setting up defenses?"

"Sargent didn't like the campsite the quartermaster selected," Cornelius said. "He and Major Butler went ahead and picked another."

"Sargent!" Lieutenant Denny said. "Is St. Clair ailing again?"

"He's back on his litter."

"About an hour ago," Lieutenant Denny said, "we passed an open space. Is that where the quartermaster wanted to encamp?"

"It could well have been."

"Then I don't blame Sargent for making a change," Lieutenant Denny grumbled.

"Except that it meant making an eight mile march," Cornelius said. "The army'll be dead on its feet."

"Did you hear what Sargent's site is like? Where is it?"

"The army ought to be there by the time you catch up with it," Cornelius said. "All I know about the site is that it's near a tributary of the St. Mary's River."

"The St. Mary's!" Lieutenant Denny said.

"That's what Sargent says it is," Cornelius said. "Phineas Ford told me it was the Wabash River."

"Cornelius, just where in the hell are we?"

"Deep in the woods," Cornelius said. "All I can tell you is that we're ninety-seven miles north of Fort Washington."

"After forty days!" Lieutenant Denny said. "Jesus Christ! Harmar made it all the way to the Indian villages in seventeen. And St. Clair claimed Harmar moved his army too slowly."

During this conversation Lieutenant Denny, from time to time, glanced toward Cornelius' men. "God damn it!" Lieutenant Denny suddenly said. "They're federals. Federals are supposed to eat." Ensign Marks rode by. "Stephen," Lieutenant Denny said, "fade back to the rear. Sneak off some beef and enough flour to make stick bread. And for Christ's sake, Stephen, tell the boys to keep their mouths shut."

Lieutenant Denny rode off to the head of our convoy. I lingered a moment. "That's the first time I ever saw Ebenezer Denny unbend," Cornelius said.

"Watching Sargent in action may have opened his eyes a bit," I said.

"How was Dolly?" Cornelius asked.

"In the very best of health," I said.

Cornelius regarded me searchingly.

"Dolly told me to tell you," I said, "that she's awfully sorry, but she was wrong. She's not pregnant."

"I wrote her last night," Cornelius said, "but I don't imagine any mail's going through."

I saw no reason to say that no mail was going out of Fort Jefferson.

"Where will I find Phineas?" I asked.

"Wherever Mae Dwyer is," Cornelius said. "Phineas is with Mountfort's. They're at the van."

"Will I be seeing you tonight?"

"I just came on," Cornelius said. "I'm here until reveille."

XIX

Within a half hour we caught up with the army. In order to forestall desertions, Bedinger's second regiment of federals brought up the rear. The van, Bedinger told us, should just about now be approaching the St. Mary's River.

Bedinger looked gaunt and weary. His greeting had been almost word for word that of Cornelius Sedam's. "Gentlemen," he had said, "the General will be very happy to see you."

Beyond Bedinger's, Gibson's levies were strung out in single file. Shivering in their wretched uniforms which by now hung on them like rags, the levies trudged along as if in a trance. A levy bent over to adjust his leggings. The man behind bumped into him, almost knocking him to the ground. The two became engaged in violent argument. It brought to my mind Herodotus' vivid description of Spartan Helots, chained, stumbling over each other as, after a day of labor in the marble mines, they were being returned to their hovels in the hills.

Next came the few cattle left, rawboned and on the point of starvation. Then the baggage horses, so weak that their heavier cargoes had been discarded and were stacked up along the side of the road. General St. Clair, being borne on a litter, was beside our artillery pieces when we reached him. Wrapped up in flannels, wearing his beaver, General St. Clair had ordered his litter-bearers to carry him up and down the length of the army. All the soldiers could see of their general were his blazing eyes, glaring at them defiantly. So long as the army marched, General St. Clair continued to do this.

"My compliments, sir," General St. Clair said to Lieutenant Denny, "I appreciate that your task was rather difficult."

General St. Clair's expression warmed up momentarily, almost in a fatherly fashion, when I presented myself. I have upon occasion wondered what he actually thought of me. "Lieutenant Morrow," General St. Clair said, "I am very far behind with my correspondence. You will please call upon me at seven o'clock."

"Yes, sir," I said.

General St. Clair glanced toward the marchers, then turned back his head with such abruptness that I at first thought he had suffered a spasm of pain. I then realized that we had come up with the women.

Among them I had no difficulty recognizing Red-headed Nan, their leader, of whom I had heard considerable talk. She was big and strong, Swedish, I had been told. Carrying an infant, she walked with sturdy strides. The child was not hers, Lieutenant Denny told me later. A tiny woman, so pregnant she seemed about to burst, walked beside Red-headed Nan.

There was an aura of determination about the way all of the women walked. What a different army we would have been, I had heard it said over and over again, if our levies had possessed half the spirit of these women. Never complaining, they nursed our sick, washed, mended. For them I heard nothing but praise. Yet General St. Clair would not acknowledge their presence. Whether on litter or on horse, when he passed them, he looked the other way.

I did not see Susan or Mae Dwyer among this group. Mae's girls, I would learn, were at the van, in the company of the Kentucky militiamen and Mountfort's North Carolinians.

The beating of drums signaled the army to an encampment halt. Colonel Sargent, coming from the front, rode up to us. "Sir," Colonel Sargent said to General St. Clair, "your tent is already raised and ready for you. All encampment orders have been issued." After making his statement, Colonel Sargent rode off without a word of greeting to Lieutenant Denny or me.

The general turmoil of preparing to encamp followed. "Where am I supposed to pitch my tent?" I asked Lieutenant Denny.

"I'd say, close as you can get to St. Clair."

"Where will you be?"

"With Sargent and Malartie," Lieutenant Denny said. "What a pair to have to tent with! But to be perfectly honest, I sometimes find Malartie rather entertaining."

I followed Lieutenant Denny as he rode to the van. When we reached the head of the army the dense woods thinned out. What we thought was a tributary of the St. Mary's but was in fact the Wabash River, ran two hundred yards ahead of us. A meandering stream, about fifteen yards wide, she was covered with a thin coat of ice. She was, I had heard some-one say, shallow enough to cross on foot.

Possibly fifty yards of swampy bottom land lay on either side of the stream. Then the ground on both sides rose rather rapidly. Heavy under-brush and considerable fallen timber was here. On the far side of the river dense forest began again approximately three hundred yards back. On our side, within two-hundred-fifty yards. One did not have to be an accom-plished military strategist to be able to recognize at a glance that Indians, advancing under good cover, would be able to fight us in the manner that suited them best.

"There's our encampment site," Lieutenant Denny said, pointing to high terrain on our left. "To be on dry ground," he added, "we're going to be crowded as hell."

Major Gaither's battalion of levies was marching toward the site. Our fatigue party was still clearing away underbrush. Two tents, St. Clair's and Sargent's, were already pitched. We had been in the midst of Darke's Kentucky militiamen. Captain Mountfort's North Carolinians now came on. "Excuse me," I said to Lieutenant Denny.

I had no difficulty in locating Phineas Ford. "Tom!" Phineas said. "I just heard you were here."

Phineas looked amply fed and so did the twelve North Carolinian rifle-men under his immediate command. While there was a strict rule against hunting in the woods, one could presume that Phineas and his boys had discovered means of circumventing it.

"Get off your horse," Phineas said. "Tom, I want to tell you something."

When I had done so, Phineas spoke in a whisper. "Do you have to stay here?" he asked.

"I'm supposed to be with St. Clair at seven o'clock," I said.

"How long will it take?"

Phineas, like many people, thought that writing letters and dispatches was like chopping down a tree. If you had so many words to get down on paper, it seemed only reasonable to Phineas that you should know in advance how long it would take to get them there.

"I don't know," I said.

"Well, get started back for home tonight," Phineas said.

"I'm sure that can't be done," I said.

"Do it anyway," Phineas said. "It's coming tomorrow, Tom." He pointed to the general area. "They'd be crazy not to hit us here. I guess you know that Hamtranck's been sent off?"

"Yes," I said, "I know that."

We were walking as we talked. By now we were up the riversbank. "Are you going over to the other side?" I asked.

"There isn't room for everybody over here," Phineas said and told me that three hundred Kentucky militiamen and Mountfort's North Carolinians would camp across the river. "Tom," Phineas said, fiercely, as we parted, "do what I told you. Get the hell on your way home."

XX

By six o'clock our army was settled. We were encamped in two lines, each approximately four hundred yards in length. The cattle and baggage were in between. Scarcely seventy yards separated the two lines. Even so, both our flanks were on wet ground, as was the greater part of the rear line.

Major Butler's battalion, four pieces of artillery, Clarke's, then Patterson's battalions composed our front line which in some places was far as a hundred yards from the river, in others close as twenty-five. In rear face Bedinger's second regiment, our remaining four pieces of artillery, Gaither's battalion, and still another battalion which was a mixture of many units under a Major Hart, whom I never met, made up the rear line. Captain Snowden's horsemen and Ensign Martz's detail were on our left flank. Captain Faulkner's riflemen and Captain Truman's horsemen were on the right. Details under Ensigns Purdy, Turner, Cobb and companies under Captains Newman and Hannah were in the outguard positions.

Headquarters was within Bedinger's. Fortunately I had been able to find an open space near General St. Clair's tent, big enough to pitch the quarter-sized one Melissa had made for me. Promptly at seven o'clock, I called upon General St. Clair. The Sargent tent was beside St. Clair's. Viscount Malartie stood before it. "Our general is resting, Lieutenant Morrow," Viscount Malartie said. "It is at eight o'clock that he now wishes to see you."

Within the tent I could hear Lieutenant Denny's and Colonel Sargent's voices, raised in argument. "They bored me," Viscount Malartie said, "so I came out here."

"What are they arguing about?" I asked.

"Who knows?" Viscount Malartie said. "When I took to the air it was over how tightly our lines have been drawn." He paused to listen. "Yes, they are still on that one. Lieutenant Denny said we should have encamped the entire army on the other side of the river. Colonel Sargent, who is only recently back from inspecting the Kentucky militiamen, astounded both Lieutenant Denny and me by admitting that he is not infallible and expressed his deep regret for not having reached such a decision."

"Then why are they still arguing about it?" I asked.

"By nature," Viscount Malartie said, "they are both very intense men."

Viscount Malartie pointed down our lines to shivering levies warming themselves beside a series of fires. With darkness the temperature had dropped considerably. I could feel the ground freezing under my feet and becoming hard.

"They think they are going to die," Viscount Malartie said, "if not tomorrow, certainly within a few days. The thought frightens them. This puzzles me."

My immediate reaction was that I had misunderstood, then Viscount Malartie's slight smile told me he was in one of his philosophical moods. "It is most interesting," he said. "Those who expect eventually to go to heaven, albeit after a possible sojourn in hell, are frightened out of their wits. I, who expect to merely disintegrate and become a part of the soil, am not in the least bit concerned about dying, that is in the larger sense."

"You may change your mind when the time comes," I said.

"A priest once told me this would happen," Viscount Malartie said. "I have given his words much thought. I have concluded that, since I am young and in good health, I shall not actually wish to die for a while yet. However, I cannot possibly think I am about to go to heaven, or even to hell."

Lieutenant Denny came out of the tent. "May I assume, Lieutenant," Viscount Malartie said, "that you and the Colonel have decided to let our encampment remain where it is?"

"What a comedian you are," Lieutenant Denny said. "The fact remains, however, that we should have encamped the entire army across the river."

"Amen," Viscount Malartie said.

I moved off with Lieutenant Denny. "What a morbid bastard that Malartie can be at times," Lieutenant Denny grumbled. "Do you know what he was telling me while we were eating? He said there's no heaven or hell. Can you imagine that! He doesn't believe in heaven and hell."

Since darkness our sentries and outguards had been doing considerable shooting. Now, off our left flank, there was quite a volley of musketry. "That was damned heavy," Lieutenant Denny said when the firing subsided. "I know everybody's jittery as hell, but I don't think those boys were shooting at shadows."

"Do you think we'll be attacked in the morning?" I asked.

"If I had to bet, I'd say yes. What did Phineas Ford say?"

"I gathered he thinks it will come tomorrow morning," I said.

"Then I'll bet it does too," Lieutenant Denny said.

"Has *anybody*," I asked, "even the slightest idea how strong the Indians are?"

"Hell, no, he hasn't," Lieutenant Denny said. "There aren't any scouts. Somebody sees a six-foot Indian and figures it has to be Blue Jacket. Somebody else sees a little runt and reports that Captain Pipe and the Delawares are here. Sargent was just telling me that Simon Girty's around. How does he know? Somebody saw a lanky fellow wearing a red silk handkerchief tight around his skull and had bright rings in his ears. So who else could it be but Girty?"

Lieutenant Denny stopped. After pondering a bit, he said, "So Phineas Ford thinks we'll be hit tomorrow morning." He was speaking as much to himself as to me. "Butler knows Phineas knows what he's talking about. Damn it, I ought to tell Butler what Phineas said."

"Would that stop the attack?"

"No, but whether the army's dead on its feet or not, we ought to set up breastworks. God damn it, the Indians know all the approaches. A dozen or more of them were still right here when the army reached the general neighborhood."

"Shouldn't that be taken up with St. Clair?"

"St. Clair's dead to the world," Lieutenant Denny said. "He was moaning his head off when he was brought to his tent. Allison, or maybe it was that other doctor, Grasson, gave him a morphine pill. 'We must set up defenses,' St. Clair muttered to Sargent just before he dropped off. I heard him say that, so did Malartie, so did Gaither."

"Well, what happened?" I asked.

"Do you see any breastworks?"

"No," I said, "I don't."

"Well, that's what happened," Lieutenant Denny said. "Sargent told Butler and Gibson what St. Clair said. They said the men were too tired and it would have to wait until morning."

After considering the matter a bit further, Lieutenant Denny said, "Yes, I'm going to tell Butler what Phineas Ford said."

XXI

I was not a witness to what I now relate:

While our army was encamping Colonel Gibson, apparently feeling that commanding officers need not obey orders, went into the woods and shot a fat raccoon. He shared it with a fellow Pennsylvanian, a Captain Slough of the levies. While the two roasted the raccoon Major Butler joined them, bringing a bottle of wine.

During the talk Butler stated that Indian horse thieves were nearby and ventured the opinion they could be easily captured. "Give me a patrol of good men," Captain Slough said, "and I'll do it."

"I'll get you the patrol," Major Butler said.

"You'll need your brother's permission," Colonel Gibson pointed out.

"That I can get too," Major Butler said.

After collecting twenty-three volunteers, mostly sergeants from various companies, Major Butler went to his brother's tent to ask for permission to send out the mission. He received it.

Taking to the woods Slough, about a mile west of the encampment, divided his patrol into two groups. Movement was along both sides of an Indian trail. Shortly six or seven Indians came along. At a range of about fifteen yards, the group on the left side of the trail opened fire, killing one Indian.

Both groups lay down among the snow-covered leaves and quietly waited. Soon a much larger party of Indians came by. After stopping and coughing and trying to discover the strength of the patrol, the Indians pushed on in the direction of the army encampment. Within a few minutes, still more Indians passed by.

Fearing he would be surrounded and taken, Slough started his men back to our encampment. So many Indians were about, Slough thought the trees were moving. There was no doubt of it, the Indians were closing in on our encampment, preparing to attack.

About midnight Slough and his men reached our encampment. Slough went to Colonel Oldham, who at the moment was on his way to General St. Clair's tent to report that he expected an attack before sunrise. Oldham, hearing Slough's report, decided not to call upon General St. Clair, delegating the task to Slough.

Slough then went to Colonel Gibson, who asked him to tell General Butler everything he had learned. Slough found General Butler standing before a fire in front of his tent. When the two men had withdrawn far enough to prevent the sentry from hearing their conversation, Slough told Butler about his reconnaissance and suggested that General St. Clair should be informed.

Butler's reply was that Captain Slough should lie down and get a bit of rest. General Butler did not take up the matter with General St. Clair.

Meanwhile Colonel Oldham returned to the Kentucky militiamen's encampment. Here he discussed with Colonel Darke the advisability of sending out a patrol. Darke stated that so unhappy was the frame of his men's minds that he strongly doubted such an order would be obeyed. Oldham did not order out a patrol.

XXII

At eight o'clock, as I expected, General St. Clair was still asleep. About now the tattoo was beat. The troops remained huddled beside the fires. One could hardly blame them for not taking to their miserable tents. It had become considerably colder. The ground was frozen solid. A frigid wind blew through the lines.

For want of something to do, I moved up and down our lines. A recent order for the men to sleep on their rifles had added to their general feeling of apprehension. The federals were calm enough, but the levies were frightened out of their wits. They were talking about dying. Many were praying. Their lack of control had its effect on some of the women. Any number were sobbing. Red-headed Nan moved about them, giving comfort. Who was Red-headed Nan? From where did she come? No one I asked knew. Yet, everyone sang her praises.

I looked about for Jeremiah Allison, but could not find him. General St. Clair slept on. At eleven o'clock, I bedded. My tent was stout. Melissa had also made me an extra heavy flannel nightgown. I had a woolen blanket. While warm enough, I could not get to sleep, for such was the constant fire of our sentries and outguard one could almost believe the opening skirmishes of battle were already begun.

"Tom?"

It was pitch dark. I could not see her, but I knew who she was. "Yes, Susan," I said.

"I'm scared, Tom," Susan said. "Everybody across the river's talking about getting killed tomorrow. They're making out their wills and shaving off their heads so they can't be scalped. Let me stay here with you."

"It would be much better," I said, "if you went to some of ladies up the line."

"Please let me stay, Tom. I wasn't coming, but I was all alone. Mae and Phineas don't want me around. I heard Lieutenant Denny was looking for me."

She was, I realized, on the verge of hysteria. "All right, Susan," I said. "Stay for a while at any rate."

"I can't stand Lieutenant Denny," Susan said. "He gives me the creeps when he touches me with his fishy hands. And he thinks he's something special in bed!" Her laugh rang with scorn. "He tried to give it to me in Pittsburgh, but I fixed him. He never got into me. I don't have to be on my back any more unless I want to. I'm Mae's assistant! I managed for her in Pittsburgh. I wouldn't have written if that damned Lieutenant Denny had told me you were married, Tom. I didn't cause any trouble, did I?"

"No, Susan," I said, "you didn't cause any trouble."

"Mae was only going to stay here until the army marched out," Susan said. "Then we were going to New Orleans. I've got money saved up! I was going to get out of the business and start a fancy hat shop. I can make beautiful hats, Tom. Ask Mae if I can't. I was going to send for Mom. She's good with a needle and could do the part that doesn't take any brains. I thought you'd be going down the river about when we did. Oh, hell, Tom, I don't know what I thought.

"Part of it's General Butler's fault. He told Mae we'd win for sure and Mae figured she could get something started here. Then Mae made that damned fool deal with General St. Clair. That's Mae's trouble! Never enough. Eighteen houses, she has. She hasn't been to some in three years. Her managers are cheating her ears off. Mae knows it, but she says a little's better than nothing.

"Honest, Tom, I've hardly been on my back for anybody since you left Philadelphia. Lieutenant Denny's been pestering the hell out of me. Acting real gallant! Bringing me food. But I know what he's after and he's not going to get it."

Susan was not only jumping suddenly from one subject to another, she was babbling, speaking so rapidly that one word tumbled over the other. It was possible, I began to suspect, that she was drunk. It did not take more than two glasses of wine to make Susan so and back in Philadelphia I had had to speak severely to her about drinking. But in all fairness it should also be said that Susan actually did not like the taste of any kind of liquor and only drank it when she was upset. When she did, after the second glass, she went wild.

"Everybody thinks we're up here because Mae's batty over Phineas Ford," Susan said. "She's batty about him, but not that batty. Or maybe she likes him better than she thinks. She keeps saying, though, that she's not batty about him. When Phineas first propositioned her, Mae laughed and told him to go button up his breeches. In all the time I've known her, Mae never once took to her back for anybody. Phineas must have gotten under her skin, I guess. 'I think I'd better show that conceited brown bear a thing or two,' Mae said. That's how it got started. Mae's fifty-seven! The way they've been banging each other, you'd think they'd both be dead. What's the name of that sour-faced colonel who's always hanging around General St. Clair?"

"Colonel Sargent," I said.

"That's him," Susan said, "and it's his fault we're up here and will get killed tomorrow. After the deal was made to get the money to pay the levies' wages, Colonel Sargent told Mae it was all right if she brought her girls up as far as Fort Jefferson. He acted like he was doing her a big favor, but he was afraid if we didn't come along a lot of the Kentucky militiamen would desert. By the time they were at Fort Jefferson, the army'd be so deep in the woods the men would be afraid to run off Colonel Sargent figured. I know Mae wanted to keep on banging away with Phineas, but the real reason she bit is because Colonel Sargent said there wouldn't be any fighting until the army was way past Fort Jefferson and we wouldn't have to go any farther and by that time we'd have all the levies' money.

"Hell, we had the levies' money long before we were at Fort Jefferson, but Mae stuck to her end of the bargain. When Mae said she wanted to go home—what do you think that bastard Colonel Sargent said? 'Go ahead,' he said. He meant we were supposed to walk back to Cincinnati by ourselves. 'You promised us protection on the way back,' Mae said. You know how Colonel Sargent smiles when he thinks he's being smart? He looks like the devil himself. 'It is with the deepest regret, Mrs. Dwyer,' he said, 'that I must inform you that we cannot spare a detail at this moment for your convenience.' Isn't he one hell of a big bastard!

"Tom, I'm so glad I can stay . . ."

Raising my blanket, Susan lay beside me. In the pitch darkness, I had not been able to see that, while she talked, she was undressing. She was stark naked. Pulling up my nightgown, she wound her arms around me and pressed her breasts against my chest. "Ram it into me, Tom," she said fiercely, "make it come out of my mouth."

She began kissing me. Although my first reaction had been one of total surprise, I was not unaware that a well-formed naked woman was in my arms. I returned Susan's kisses and did with my hands what is expected of a man under such circumstances. Yet, things were not going along overly well.

Susan must have sensed it too. "I'll get on top of you," she said. "Now! That feels good, doesn't it, honey?"

The word "honey," the way Susan said it, was most annoying to hear and dampened considerably my animal instincts which slowly but surely were beginning to assert themselves. I carried on, however, and was fully prepared to do what was expected of me. "You snobbish bastard!" Susan suddenly cried out, and jumped up.

I could hear her sobbing as she dressed. "You and every man in the whole world can go straight to hell," she said. As she left she shouted out that she was going to leave the encampment and start walking back to Cincinnati.

While I knew that, in time, she would think the better of this, I also knew that, when aroused, Susan was wont to behave irrationally. It was not unreasonable to assume that she would at least start walking to Cincinnati. All she needed to do was get into the woods and she was good as dead.

Dressing quickly, I went after her. Although most of the levies were still beside the fires, no one had seen Susan go by. I ran to the right flank. The sentries there had not seen Susan. I then ran to the left flank. The sentries here had not seen her either. I could think only that she had gone behind my tent, straight into the woods.

That I could not track her down, was a certainty. Forlorn as the hope seemed, I decided to ask Phineas Ford if there was anything anybody could do. Once beyond the lights of our encampment fires, it was so dark I could not see the many logs lying about and stumbled over any number of them. Until I stepped into water, I did not realize I had reached the river. The Kentucky militiamen's encampment fires, however, served as beacons, so I knew where I wished to go.

When I crossed the river, two shots rang out. The bullets whizzed past me, precariously close to my head. I threw myself onto the ground. "Take care," I heard someone say, "he may be faking."

"You fools!" I cried out. "I'm not an Indian."

Two Kentucky militiamen came over. Such was the blackness of the night, I could scarcely see them even when they stood beside me. "What in the hell are you doing here?" one of the militiamen wanted to know and told me Indians were moving along the river and that an order had just been issued forbidding passage from either side. "We're waiting for an escort," the militiaman explained, "then we're taking the order over."

"If you're just taking the order over now," I said, "how was I supposed to know about it?"

Since I was alive, nothing could be gained by dwelling upon this. "Did anyone come over in the past ten minutes?" I asked.

"We thought we saw somebody," the militiaman said, "but it's so damned dark, it's hard to say."

"Where is Phineas Ford's tent?" I asked.

"Somewhere up there," the militiaman said and pointed in the direction of the encampment fires behind which the tents were pitched.

I had no trouble locating Phineas for he, accompanied by his twelve North Carolinian riflemen, was just about to take to the woods. "So the drunken little fool was over to see you," Phineas said when I had explained the situation. "She wouldn't tell me where she was, but I had it figured."

"She's back here then?"

"Sure, she is," Phineas said. "Two of my men are taking care of her. It's them we're waiting for."

Phineas' statement, to my relief, did not mean what I at first thought. Certain that we would be attacked at dawn, Phineas had moved Mae and her girls into a reasonably secluded spot within the woods. It was their only hope for survival, he told me. If they were here, during the fury of battle, they would be shot down and scalped. This way, if undiscovered until later, there was a good chance they would be taken to Detroit, where Mae could buy their release. "You shouldn't have come over here, Tom," Phineas said. "If Susan wants to go batty, it's her funeral."

"In a way, I feel responsible for her," I said.

"Anybody who worries about what a whore does is a damned fool," Phineas said.

"I do think Susan is making an honest effort to better herself," I said.

"Who isn't trying to do that?" Phineas said. "But don't get yourself all worked up worrying about Susan. She's a liar. Susan's such a damned good liar that she believes her own lies."

The two riflemen returned.

"Are you going out on patrol?" I asked Phineas.

"Hell, no, we're not going out on patrol," Phineas said. "We've got no patrols over here. My boys and I are getting out while the getting's good."

"You're deserting!"

"No, no," Phineas said. "We'll fight tomorrow, but I'll be damned if I want us killed unless we have to be."

"You're just going off into the woods!" I said. "Nobody will stop you?"

"Who in the hell is there to stop us?" Phineas asked me.

"I don't know who," I said, "but something's wrong. Suppose everybody simply decided to take to the woods?"

"We might be better off at that," Phineas said. He pointed to the tents. "Tom, most of those boys never shot a gun before they came here. Tomorrow, they'll panic when the Indians hit. Oldham and Darke won't be able to do a damned thing about it. It doesn't mean those boys are more cowards than anybody else. It just means that because they've never been in a battle before, the minute the Indians start shooting, they're going to run as fast as their legs will carry them . . . Tom, you'd be a lot better off if you came along with me. I'll have you at the encampment by sunrise."

"No," I said, "I'd better go straight back to the encampment. I'll wait for the escort though."

"Then you'll wait all night," Phineas said. "They've been trying to get volunteers for the past hour. You and Susan don't know how lucky you were to get across the river. It's Captain Pipe's boys who are roaming about down there. They're mad men, Tom. They've sworn not to smile again until every white man in Ohio has been killed. One person might be lucky enough to get across the river in the dark. An escort! They'd be jumped sure as my name's Phineas Ford."

In spite of Phineas' statement, I believe I was prepared to chance going back to our encampment alone. However, before coming to a final conclusion, considerable musket fire began blazing away directly below us. This won me over to Phineas' point of view.

XXIII

We moved into the woods, crossed the river, and worked our way up to the higher ground. In the blackness of the night, this is all I am able to say about our route. I was behind Phineas. Where he went, I went. We stopped many times and waited to let Indians pass. Eventually reaching our destination—I hadn't the faintest idea where we were—we came to a halt. Some of the group lay down on the ground. This being too cold for me, I leaned against a tree and managed to sleep intermittently.

As the first traces of sun showed through the treetops—at about half-after six o'clock—Phineas, just back from surveying the area, gave me a piece of jerk and told me to follow him. No doubt Phineas had already issued orders to his twelve boys, for they were beginning to fan out into a circle-like formation.

Phineas led me to the edge of the woods. We were no more than seventy yards off the encampment's right flank. The main army was still sleeping and I noted that nothing had been done about setting up breastworks. On the far side of the river the Kentucky militiamen were beginning to stir. As many as twelve men came out of tents which had been fashioned to hold eight. Darke and Oldham were on horses. The militiamen were being called to parade. At this moment none of our sentries were firing. There was a small flight of snow, but not enough to cover the ground. A light northeast breeze prevailed. "Things seem rather quiet," I said.

"You're damned right they do," Phineas said.

Phineas pointed to what looked like a narrow path, leading toward our right flank. "I've just been over it, Tom," Phineas said. "Faulkner's riflemen are maybe fifty yards ahead. They'll be expecting you. Get on your way. The Indians'll hit while the militiamen are eating breakfast."

"Aren't you coming too?"

"I'll have to wait for the shooting to start," Phineas said. "Faulkner told me Sargent begins his inspection at the right flank. I'm not supposed to be over here. If I run into Sargent, after what I told him about what he did to Mae, I'll be in a lot of trouble. My boys and I are all right. The Indians will be closing in fast now, but they're still behind us. There aren't any of them between here and the right flank." At the encampment, the drummers began beating the reveille. By now the Kentucky militiamen were being dismissed from parade and were moving toward the breakfast kettles. "My God!" Phineas said, pointing to the militiamen lining up for food. "Those jackasses! Look at them. They've laid down their rifles."

This is when the Indian yells started. It sounded like an infinitude of horse bells suddenly opening in my ears. Then, from behind the entire length of the militiamen's encampment, Indians poured out of the woods and began shooting at our men with arrows as well as bullets.

In complete panic, the militiamen went into head-long, disorderly flight. Leaving their rifles on the ground, they ran, fast as their legs could carry them, for our main encampment. Led by a chief in a long red coat, the painted Indians followed on the militiamen's heels. It was hard to estimate the pursuers' strength. They were, though, considerably outnumbered by those whom they were chasing.

Militiamen dropped right and left. Oldham's horse was shot from under him. Unhurt, he ran with the rest. "Tom," Phineas said. "Get the hell over to Faulkner."

"I'll stay with you," I said.

At this moment I do not believe I was capable of moving. It was amazement, I am certain, rather than fear. I, who had never witnessed a battle, watched, unable to believe what I was seeing. My eyes would be trained upon a group of running militiamen. One would fall, then another, then another, then another. I thought of them as having stumbled and I expected them to get up. I was unable to comprehend that I was witnessing the slaughter of human beings.

"Well," I heard Phineas saying, "I guess you're no worse over here than over there."

Arriving at our encampment's front line, the fleeing militiamen broke through it and rushed for the rear. Their effort to reach the military road, however, was halted by a rattle of gun fire coming from behind the trees. The levies had become panicked by the militiamen's behavior. Nobody seemed to know what to do. Such was the milling about, our encampment appeared to be in a state of riot.

Somehow amid this confusion Bedinger's second regiment, drawn in tolerable order, had fixed bayonets. As the last of the militiamen plunged across the front line, Bedinger's men engaged the pursuing Indians in hand-to-hand fighting. No longer supported by their riflemen behind the trees, the Indians received the worst of it here. Retreating, but in good order, they took refuge behind the nearby fallen timber and underbrush, many being no more than twenty yards from our front line.

Now no more Indians were in sight. There was only the noise of their rifles from behind the trees. Bedlam still reigned at our encampment. Militiamen and levies, running about in complete disorder, were being dropped in droves. The Indians' heaviest fire was being directed against Bedinger's second regiment. These, our best men, stood in close order, in the open. The toll being taken was a frightful thing to see.

Our officers, exposing themselves recklessly, urged the panicked men to go into action. They received more help from the women than from the men. Most of the women had sense enough to go to their stomachs and start firing. I saw Red-headed Nan stop a group of panic-stricken Kentucky militiamen and taunt them into action by picking up the rifles of fallen men and handing them over.

General Butler, on foot, moved about encouraging his men. General St. Clair rode up and down the lines, shouting at the men, slapping them with the flat of his sword. I had seen General St. Clair come out of his tent almost immediately after the Indians attacked. Still wearing his nightgown, he had called for a horse. A waiter had thrown a coarse cappo coat over his shoulders. Someone had handed him his three-cornered hat. He had needed the help of four men to get him on his horse. Even as he mounted, the horse was shot out from under him. He had called for another and ridden up the line. While watching this Phineas had mentioned that the General's attire could well serve him in good stead. Dressed as he was, he would not become a principal target.

The fire from the trees was incessant. The Indians had targets they could see. We did not. Our officers were finally convincing at least most of the men that they should lie on their stomachs and fire. Our artillerists had our three- and six-pounders going. While the noise was deafening, with nothing but trees to shoot at, our round shot and canister, so laboriously transported for almost a hundred miles, could accomplish but little execution.

A young North Carolinian, named Amos Bradley, upon whom Phineas depended a great deal, crept up to us. "We've spotted Indians moving up, Phineas," Amos said. "They'll be coming right over us."

"How many?" Phineas asked.

"Fifty anyway."

"Nobody's behind them."

"Not for quite a ways back anyway."

"You're sure you looked careful?"

"I sure did, Phineas."

"It's all good then," Phineas said. "They haven't brought up their main strength yet."

The three of us moved back into the woods to where the rest of Phineas' contingency was gathered. Not a boy in this group was eighteen years old. They were, though, fine specimens of young manhood. "Now remember, gentlemen," Phineas said, "everything I've told you. Our main idea is to get to the encampment. The Indians are going to think they've run into an outguard and they'll want to clean us out. When they close in, hold your fire until I shoot. Then break fast, reload on the run, and get behind fallen timber. The Indians don't know you can do that. They'll think we're pulling tail and will come after us. Again, hold your fire until you hear me shoot."

We took our positions behind trees and fallen timber. I had a pistol. While I had practiced shooting it, I had never fired at a human being. We did not have to wait long before Indians began filtering through the trees. The one coming directly toward me was painted black and red. The feathers of an eagle were braided in his long scalp-locks.

This Indian was no more than ten yards from me before Phineas' rifle barked. My shot tore into the Indian's chest. I shall never forget the expression of utter surprise which came over this man's face. The force of the shot had knocked him backwards. Blood oozed through his buckskins about the chest. After making an egregious effort to stay alive and fire, he suddenly collapsed like a marionette whose strings have been cut.

Following instructions, I ran and took refuge behind fallen timber. Phineas' boys had behaved superbly. We were solidly lined up, as if behind a barricade. Only I had forgotten to reload.

As Phineas had predicted, the Indians came on in quick pursuit. Our volley tore the first rush of them into shreds. They dropped like men stricken. Their fellows took cover. As they did, we broke for the path leading to the encampment's right flank. Not a shot was fired at us. When we reached our destination, Faulkner's riflemen lay on their stomachs, waiting. They had thought our firing was presage of an Indian attack. "It'll be a good half hour before they start hitting here," Phineas told Faulkner.

"So far we've been lucky," Faulkner said. As yet, he told Phineas, almost no fire had been directed at this part of the right flank. There were no casualties.

XXIV

We moved on to Truman's horsemen, stationed no more than fifty yards beyond Faulkner's. A ravine, possibly fifteen yards wide, separated Truman from the encampment. While Faulkner's men were protected by large trees, Truman's position was more in the open. Upon our arrival, Indian fire at this area had ceased. Truman, however, had received considerable punishment.

Some two dozen moaning, wounded men lay on the ground. My guess is that of Truman's two hundred horses, more than half were dead. The dead horses had been piled up to form a breastwork.

The firing in the vicinity of the ravine was extremely heavy. "What's going on there?" Phineas asked Truman.

"Bedinger's led a countercharge," Truman said.

"We'll wait until that's over with," Phineas said.

"Christ," Truman said. "Damned near all of our outposts are wiped out." He then noted my presence. "Cornelius Sedam is lying behind the trees, Tom. No, no! He's alive. Malartie's with him."

"Malartie?"

"The Frenchman's here to get a horse for St. Clair," Truman told me.

I moved into the trees. Cornelius, in sound but labored sleep, lay on a blanket. He looked deadly pale. Viscount Malartie, who had two horses tethered nearby, stood beside Cornelius. Some ten feet off, a moaning, wounded Ensign Marks lay on the ground.

"Your friend," Viscount Malartie said, "is merely suffering from the shock of having a bullet removed from his chest. It was lodged quite deeply. Rather than permanently destroy his shoulder muscles, I cut down, then up. It was most painful."

The chest portion of Viscount Malartie's uniform was covered with blood. "Are you wounded?" I asked.

"A mere shoulder flesh wound," Viscount Malartie said. "It is actually nothing." He pointed to Ensign Marks. "I received it bringing him back here. My wound, slight as it is, may interest you, Lieutenant Morrow. As you can see, the blood is over my heart. There was this stinging sensation, accompanied by twinges of pain and the flow of considerable blood. My immediate thought was that the bullet had found my heart and that shortly I must die. Yet it never entered my thinking, as I labored under this impression, that God was about to receive me. I am still quite overwrought as I think that had the bullet been six inches lower, I would be dead. That, however, is the only emotion I am experiencing. I am sure of this. I have appraised my feelings with the completest objectivity. This, I can assure you."

"Is Marks in serious condition?" I asked.

"I am not a doctor," Viscount Malartie said. "He has been shot in the groin. My guess is that he will be all right."

Viscount Malartie spoke with most noticeable bitterness. "Just what has happened here?" I asked.

"Because I do not agree with him," Viscount Malartie said, "Ensign Marks sees fit to consider me a coward."

"You can't get the bullet out of Marks?" I asked.

"That is beyond my capabilities and beyond the capabilities of everyone else here," Viscount Malartie said. "Ensign Marks will need a doctor's attention."

"You were saying—" I said.

"Our general," Viscount Malartie said, "has been riding up and down our lines exhorting our men to behave with valor. His fourth horse was shot from under him. All the other horses at the encampment had been shot dead. 'Francis, you will please get me another horse,' our general said to me. 'Yes, sir,' I, of course, replied.

"Almost immediately upon my arrival here, Ensign Marks put in his appearance. Colonel Sargent, unaware of our general's order to me, had sent off Ensign Marks to fetch a horse. This was approximately when Bedinger began his countercharge.

"Ensign Marks wished to take a horse through all that fire. 'You will never make it,' I said. 'The General is a sick man and cannot get about on foot,' Ensign Marks said. 'I know our general is a sick man,' I said, 'however, I have been ordered to bring him a horse, not to become a magnificent failure.

"'The General has already had many bullets pierce his clothing,' Ensign Marks then remarked in a most insulting manner. 'You, Frenchman, should have some of his courage.' Thereupon Ensign Marks went off with a horse, which now lies dead in the ravine. I was obliged to go out and bring Ensign Marks back."

Phineas, who had gone forward to observe the action, returned. "Bedinger's coming back," he said. "I figure it'll be easing off a bit here now."

"What does Bedinger's being back mean?" I asked Phineas.

"That a lot more of the second regiment got killed," Phineas said. "Bedinger's still alive, but I don't think two of his officers are left."

In an effort to rout out the Indians from their cover, Phineas explained, Bedinger's men had gone after the enemy with bayonets and gunbutts, all the while being exposed to Indian fire from the woods. The Indians under cover had given ground, but now that Bedinger was back in the encampment, they were returning to the positions they had vacated.

The firing in the ravine area, to me, did not seem to be easing. Phineas, however, said I was hearing shooting that was elsewhere and called his boys forward. While we assembled Viscount Malartie led off the two horses, walking between them.

Phineas sent us across the ravine singly. We simply ran, fast as we could, from one side to another. Phineas went first, I went second. There were some trees here and considerable underbrush, which offered us a certain amount of protection. We did not lose a man. In fact, very little fire had been directed toward us. This could mean, Phineas said, that either the Indians had been forced to lay down their rifles in order to allow them to cool off or that they were busy assembling in preparation for an attack.

XXV

Most of the Indian fire, as we entered the encampment, was being directed against the left flank. We were now in the midst of what was left of the Kentucky militiamen and Hart's battalion. Major Hart, I believe, was already dead.

General St. Clair had ridden up to Colonel Oldham. "Colonel," I heard General St. Clair shouting out. "Get your men into line. Don't you understand that soon the Indians will begin their assault?"

Lieutenant Denny may have taken over for Hart, at least he seemed to be in command. "Ebenezer," Phineas called out, "where's Mountfort's?"

"Front line, beyond the artillery," Lieutenant Denny called back.

Since I was without assignment, I stayed with Phineas. "Bend over far as you can," Phineas said and behind me Phineas' boys repeated this order to each other.

Walking the way gorillas do, we followed Phineas, being somewhat protected by breastworks that had been hastily constructed by piling up dead men and dead cows. As we moved along between the two lines so many dead men and women lay sprawled on the ground, it was necessary for me to watch my footing in order not to step upon them. All about the wounded lay moaning and pleading for help. While en route I saw General Butler bandaging his hand. Beside him a levy, shot in the knee, was weeping and carrying on badly. I have no idea what General Butler had in mind. As he talked to this lad, he constantly laughed so loudly that his fat sides shook.

Mountfort was not where Lieutenant Denny had said he would be. "Take positions here," Phineas called out. We went to our stomachs amid levies and a handful of women. Here the breastworks were made up almost entirely of dead cows. I was on Phineas' right. I had picked up a fallen man's rifle. At this moment, no one was shooting at us. One could almost believe no one was hidden within the underbush which lay directly ahead.

To our right, however, the Indian fire being directed at our artillery, under command of Major Ferguson, was extremely heavy. An Ensign Spear, whom I knew slightly, lay on Phineas' other side. "They'll have Ferguson knocked out in no time," I heard Ensign Spear say to Phineas. "When in the hell is St. Clair going to pipe a retreat?"

"Who knows?" Phineas said. "Our rear line cannons are dead."

It struck me that as we passed the rear line artillery, I had noticed that the guns there were silent. I had seen this, yet I hadn't seen it.

A woman lay on my right, sobbing and babbling intermittently. Eventually I was able to make out what she was talking about. During the Bedinger countercharge she had seen a man's head shot off. Decapitated, he had kept on running until he plunged into the river. "Slap her in the face, Tom," Phineas said. "For Christ's sake, shut her up."

I did slap her face, but she did not shut up.

The Indians began an assault against our right flank. While I could not see the beginning of this action, I could surmise the deadly accuracy of the enemy fire, for I could hear the clatter of weapons striking the frozen ground as our militiamen fell. I could not see what followed immediately either. This, I would learn, is what took place. Goaded on by General St. Clair, Colonel Oldham formed his line. Colonel Darke was with him, so was Major Butler, his thigh broken by a bullet, but still able to ride his horse. With the three officers urging them on, our militiamen charged the oncoming Indians with bayonet and forced them to retreat.

Was it an Indian ruse or was this, as some were to say, the militiamen's moment of glory? I could see it all now. With the militiamen at their heels, the fleeing Indians made for our vacated encampment. They crossed the river and our militiamen chased after them. "In God's name!" I heard Phineas cry out. "Come back!"

Our men were now beyond the rifle support of our encampment. A wave of Indians suddenly burst out from the trees. Oldham, shot dead, toppled off his horse. Shrieking Indians surrounded the militiamen. That is all I could see now, a circle of Indians, shooting.

Only Butler, Darke and twelve militiamen were able to break out. Methodically the Indians went about the task of scalping the dead and wounded, holding up their trophies and waving them at those of us in the encampment. A small ravine, leading to the river, ran red with human blood. When the Indians finally returned to the woods, the ground was covered with our militiamen's bodies. The scalped heads. "My God!" I heard Ensign Spear say, "it looks like a December corn field of pumpkins."

Ensign Spear had not overstated what we all saw.

XXVI

From then on, for us, the battle became a holocaust. The vise which the brilliant Little Turtle had prepared began to tighten. Moving out of the woods, the Indians struck at our right flank, the left, the center. These were lightning-like thrusts, simultaneously delivered. When we managed to form a solid line, the enemy returned to its ally—the trees.

As more and more of us were killed, the Indians became bolder, but always cautious. Under cover of the smoke of our heavy fire, they came closer and closer to our first and second lines. Yet, we never knew where they were. Watching their chance, they charged again and again with tomahawks, gliding into close quarters while we were still firing into the smoke-shrouded woods and underbrush. Time after time as our men stood in the ranks to load and shoot, there was no sign of the enemy. Then, in a moment, dark faces showed through the haze, war-axes gleaned, and all around us we heard the clatter of weapons falling on the frozen ground. By the time we replaced those who had been killed, the Indians were vanished.

Bits of news of what was going on elsewhere along the lines came to Phineas and me through word of mouth: General Butler and a badly

wounded Colonel Gibson had pleaded with General St. Clair to pipe a retreat. General St. Clair had refused . . . Colonel Sargent was wounded . . .
Gaither's battalion was all but wiped out . . . The wounded Colonel Darke
had gone mad upon learning that his son was dead. Wishing to charge the
Indians singlehanded, it had taken six men to hold him in check . . . General Butler was dead! No, he was only wounded. The bullet spent itself in
the layers of fat about Dicky's belly! But he must think he's dying. He has
just given his watch to Lieutenant Denny, to be delivered to his wife . . .

"Good God!" I heard Phineas say to Ensign Spear. "I can only hear one of
Ferguson's cannons."

Red-headed Nan went by behind us, staggering under the weight of a
small keg, marked cannon powder, which she carried on her shoulders.
"Down, Nan!" Phineas shouted to her. "Get down, girl! Roll that thing."

Then we saw that the back of Red-headed Nan's gray dress was soaked
with blood.

Phineas went after her, crawling on all fours. He was gone for some time.
"Nan's dead," he said when he returned. "So is Ferguson." All thirty of
Ferguson's artillerists, Phineas told me, were either dead or shot through the
body. All our cannons were out of commission. The keg, marked cannon
powder, which Red-headed Nan had been taking to Ferguson, upon being
opened, had contained flints.

The Indians directed a spirited attack which forced Bedinger's depleted
second regiment to retreat into our front line. As more and more Indians
swarmed into our encampment, the front line levies panicked. In disorderly
flight, Patterson's and Clarke's battalions made for the left flank. Those in the
rear dropped their rifles and made no effort to fight back. Their sole concern
was to move into the mass of humanity ahead of them and put other bodies
behind them, for the Indians to shoot at.

Such was the influx of retreaters that we at the left center of the front
line were in danger of being shoved off the encampment site into the open.
"Let's get out of here!" Phineas called out. As I stood up, the woman beside
me wrapped her arms around my ankles so tightly that I could not get free of
her frenzied hold. Petrified with fear, her eyes looked as if they were going
to pop out of her head. Phineas kicked her in the face three times before
she finally let go. Phineas picked her up, slapped her face. It did no good.
She would not budge.

Leaving her, Phineas and I joined those making for the left flank.
We passed General Butler. Although the General sat up, with his back leaning against a crate, his eyes were closed. There was about his face that
peaceful expression of someone who has no more worries to contend with
in this world. However, Dr. Grasson was still working on General Butler's

stomach wound. Grasson himself was bleeding profusely, having been shot between the shoulder blades.

"I think General Butler's dead," I said to Phineas.

Phineas did not answer me. Taking two more steps forward, he pitched forward to the ground. The back of his head was bloody. When I turned him over, I saw that the bullet had come out through his eyes.

Retreaters, thinking of me as an obstacle, shoved me off. At the left flank we were halted by Indian fire coming from no more than thirty yards which meant Snowden's horsemen and Martz's detail must surely had been wiped out. There was enough space here for Patterson and Clarke to re-form their lines. They ordered a countercharge. It was this, or be mowed down from the left.

Suddenly the shrieks and shots of the Indians in control of the center of our encampment stopped. Surrounded as I was by others, I could not see what had taken place. "The Indians have gone off!" men began shouting.

Led by Patterson and Clarke, we moved cautiously toward the encampment's center. From our right flank, where the rest of our army had been driven under circumstances similar to ours, General St. Clair was also bringing his men out.

Why this sudden Indian withdrawal? Was it, because knowing they would have us in the end, they had done as much as they could during this particular encounter? Or was, as so many of us believe, the real purpose of this charge to strike terror into our hearts?

If the latter belief is correct, the Indians had carried out their task well. Scarcely a body lay on the ground whose reeking head was not scalped. General Butler still sat up, leaning against the crate. Scalped, his heart was cut out. This meant the Indians accounted General Butler to be an extraordinarily brave man. His heart would be cut up into as many pieces as there were tribes in the battle. By eating bits of General Butler's heart, the Indians believed they would absorb his courage.

A scalped Dr. Grasson lay at General Butler's feet.

I found Phineas. His heart, too, was cut out. He was not scalped.

The scalped dead women were stripped naked. Their breasts were cut off. Many were hacked in two. The tiny pregnant woman I had seen trudging along beside Red-headed Nan had been further mutilated. Her unborn child was ripped from her womb. The infant lay on its mother's breast, impaled by an arrow. It, too, was scalped.

As we looked at these dead bodies, no shots came from the woods. It was as if the Indians wished to give us ample time to ponder over what we saw.

Suddenly we heard shrieking. A dozen or more of our levies, scalped, their heads smoking like chimneys, broke out of the woods, and came into our

encampment, imploring us to shoot them. Then from the nearby underbrush and from behind the trees, all around us, we heard the Indian cries of
victory.

All too soon the Indians resumed their shooting and more of us fell.
Those of us still alive scurried to whatever cover was available. I lay beside
a cannon carriage. Had I reached out my hand, I could have touched the
naked Red-headed Nan's scalped head.

Any number of rifles lay about on the ground. I did not pick up one. I
could hear next to no shooting from our encampment. The stomach for
fighting was gone from General St. Clair's army.

General St. Clair, astride a weary-looking horse, its mouth dropping great
curds of foam, rode down the lines to look us over. With him were Colonel
Sargent and Viscount Malartie. Colonel Sargent, his head bandaged, seemed
about to reel off his horse. Viscount Malartie, so help me, appeared amused by
what he saw. General St. Clair sat erect on his horse. His face was expression-
less as if it were made of stone.

The trio returned to the right flank. In due time word was passed along
that General St. Clair had piped a retreat. The seriously wounded, what was
left of our food, our cannons, baggage, tools, tents, traveling forges—all must
be left behind.

It was now only half-after nine o'clock.

XXVII

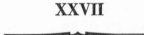

Before issuing his order General St. Clair had called for volunteers to clear
the way to the military road. Under Darke, a ferocious charge drove back
the Indians, allowing these nearest the right flank safe access to the military
road. The startled Indians, however, quickly reassembled their defenses and
the rest of us had to go over the six foot wide road exposed to enemy fire.

I was among the last to reach the right flank. General St. Clair, Colonel
Sargent and Viscount Malartie were still here. So were Lieutenant Denny
and Major Patterson, who were attempting to form a rear guard.

It was necessary for every man to look out for himself. What was left of
Truman's horsemen rode up from their station. I saw Cornelius Sedam,
his arms wrapped around the neck of a barebacked horse. "Cornelius!" I called

out. He did not answer. As I ran to him, I saw that he was about to faint. I got on his horse. "Hold tight to me, Cornelius," I said. His arms went around me, but he did not reply.

As we rode into those fleeing along the road, I saw Major Clarke take a bullet in the temple and topple off his horse. The fire of the jeering Indians shooting at us from behind the trees was incessant. We, who were fleeing, raced along like stampeded cattle. In an effort to save themselves, men frequently tried to knock me off my horse. I saw wounded men shoot themselves, rather than be scalped alive. I saw a woman hurl her infant into the woods, hoist her skirts up to her thighs and keep on running. I saw a man fall down under the weight of a wounded fellow he carried on his shoulders. Realizing he was to be abandoned, the wounded man clung on so tightly, to free himself, the carrier brought out his hunting knife and cut off the man's fingers. That Cornelius was delirious, was most obvious. From time to time, he'd ask me where the horses were. He meant the four hundred packhorses still tethered somewhere in the vicinity of the encampment. "We'll be catching up with them shortly," I would say to Cornelius. This would satisfy him for a while, then he would again ask the same question.

The Indians shot at us only during the first five or six miles of our flight. The reason, I am told, is that they went to our encampment to plunder. Fort Jefferson was twenty-seven miles off. Cornelius and I reached it around eight o'clock. Riot prevailed here, as famished men fought with each other for the little food on hand.

Captain Shay gave me food and allowed me to take Cornelius to his quarters. Throwing myself on the floor beside Cornelius' bed, I slept soundly while Dr. Allison cared for Cornelius' wound. Cornelius, Dr. Allison pronounced, would recover but could not be moved for at least a week.

Around midnight, Captain Shay awakened me. "General St. Clair wishes to see you at headquarters."

On the parade men were shouting out defiantly, milling about, stepping on the wounded lying on the ground. They were surrounded by troops whose relatively clean uniforms and bearskin-covered haversacks told me were of our first regiment.

"Hamtranck just got back with the food convoy," Captain Shay told me. "They want that food."

A rumor had apparently become started that General St. Clair expected to re-form the army and go back after the Indians. The shouts of the men made it abundantly clear that they were not going to. Hamtranck had taken to the wall walk. There would be no more fighting the Indians, he shouted out, and there was no danger of Fort Jefferson being attacked.

When I went into headquarters, General St. Clair sat at the commanding officer's desk. He still wore his nightgown, covered by his coat. Present also were Colonel Gibson, Colonel Sargent, Major Patterson, Viscount Malartie, and Lieutenant Denny. All lay on the floor, sound asleep.

General St. Clair's blood-shot eyes were half closed. "Good evening, Lieutenant Morrow," General St. Clair said. "I am pleased to find you in good health."

"Thank you, sir," I said, "and may I add, sir, that I am most pleased to be able to say that the state of your health appears to be good also."

"You may, sir," General St. Clair said and pointed to a nearby desk upon which was writing material. "I wish to send off a dispatch to President Washington. Today—" General St. Clair began, then realizing it was after midnight, he corrected himself. *"Yesterday,"* he dictated, *"the remains of the army under my command got back to this place, and I have now the painful task to give you an account of as warm and as unfortunate an action as almost any that has been fought . . ."*

General St. Clair did not spare any of the details or himself.

XXVIII

Lieutenant Denny was ordered to deliver this dispatch. The following morning, in the company of Lieutenant Denny and a hundred levies, I left Fort Jefferson for Fort Washington. On November 9th, Melissa was back in my arms.

We had lost thirty-seven officers, five-hundred-ninety-three men. Our wounded numbered thirty-one officers, two-hundred-fifty-three men. When I arrived at Fort Washington snow was falling, the river was beginning to freeze, and another hard winter lay ahead. Held up by this inclement weather, Lieutenant Denny was six weeks in getting to the East. I am told President Washington received the news of our defeat in the very room he had warned General St. Clair against surprise. *"To be cut to pieces, hacked, butchered, tomahawked, by surprise, the very thing I guarded him against,"* our incensed President cried out. *"Oh, God! Oh, God! He is worse than a murderer."* And then the President of the United States calmed down.

"General St. Clair shall have justice—I will hear him without prejudice. He shall have full justice."

As is generally known, three years later General Anthony Wayne and his well-trained Legions smashed the power of our enemy in a twenty minute engagement at Fallen Timbers. Melissa and I were a part of this. It is, however, a story of a march to victory, so different that I shall relate it in a separate account.

This much more: Almost from the day of our army's return to Fort Washington, the citizens of Cincinnati talked about burying St. Clair's dead. Nothing came of this until in December General James Wilkinson assumed command of our fort. This clever man goaded our citizens into action by floating a rumor that ten thousand dollars was still at the encampment site.

During mid-January a group of us trudged north through two feet of snow. Beginning five miles from the scene of disaster we found bodies along the military road, so blackened by frost and exposure they could not be identified. As we attempted to remove them from the frozen ground, many broke into pieces.

As we approached the encampment site, the effect of the Indian fire became readily manifest. Scarcely a tree stood which was not marked with a profusion of shot. We were greeted by the sight of General Butler's campaign cap, tied to a sapling. The General still sat where I had last seen him, black and frozen rigid, his eyes wide open and gaping, like a statue that was once alive.

We collected the frozen bodies, burying them in a great pit. When this grave was covered up, the mound rose twice my height. There was, of course, no ten thousand dollars. Some three tons of iron was salvaged from the gun carriages, wagons, and a six-pounder, the only piece of artillery the Indians had left.

Since Phineas Ford was not scalped, I had hoped to be able to identify his body. It was not where it had last lain and I could not find it anywhere, although I searched most thoroughly. I should like to believe that Phineas' friend, Little Turtle, took him away.